BEATRICE
The mother who wants
to feel love—
just one more time...

S0-BEA-448

NORA
The daughter who's learned that
sex is safer than love...

SUSANNAH
The "good" daughter who found love
in the wrong place...

"YES, THIS IS A WOMAN'S NOVEL AND ONE GOOD
ENOUGH TO BRING WOMEN BACK INTO THE
BOOKSTORES ... AN INTELLIGENT NOVEL
WHICH GOES TO THE TROUBLE OF ACCURATELY
DELINEATING WHAT THE LAST THIRTY YEARS
HAVE DONE FOR, AND TO, WOMEN. ... WHAT
DISTINGUISHES *LOOKING FOR LOVE* IS ITS EMO-
TIONAL DEPTH ... THE TRUTH OF ITS CHARAC-
TERS AS WELL AS THE AUTHOR'S WIT. THIS IS A
BOOK OF DEFT PORTRAYALS THAT DEALS WITH
THE COMMONPLACE UNCOMMONLY WELL."
—*Daily News* (New York)

LOOKING FOR LOVE
by Ellen Feldman

"A WITTY, WRY, AND TENDER TALE."
—Gloria Goldreich, author of *Mothers* and *Leah's Journey*

"YOU'LL LAUGH, YOU'LL CRY, YOU'LL EMPATHIZE
—BUT MOSTLY, YOU'LL BE DAMNED GLAD YOU
PICKED IT UP."
—Linda Gray Sexton, author of *Points of Light*

"IN HER SPLENDID NOVEL *LOOKING FOR LOVE*,
ELLEN FELDMAN HAS ACCOMPLISHED SOME-
THING FEW WRITERS HAVE: SHE HAS ENTERED
THE COUNTRY OF J. D. SALINGER AND MADE THE
VISIT MEMORABLE AND SATISFYING."
—Anne Rivers Siddons, author of *Peachtree Road*

BOOKS BY ELLEN FELDMAN

a.k.a. Katherine Walden

Conjugal Rites

Looking for Love

Looking for Love

ELLEN
FELDMAN

A DELL BOOK

Published by
Dell Publishing
a division of
Bantam Doubleday Dell Publishing Group, Inc.
666 Fifth Avenue
New York, New York 10103

ISBN: 0-440-20817-3

Reprinted by arrangement with Little, Brown and Company

Printed in the United States of America

Published simultaneously in Canada

January 1991

10 9 8 7 6 5 4 3 2 1

RAD

for Stephen

Many women inspired this book. Three made it possible. I am especially grateful to my editor, Fredrica Friedman, for her unerring eye; my agent, Binky Urban, for her unfailing humor and support; and Jane Trichter, the reader every writer dreams of.

1

Nora never did figure out how she ended up in the bedroom of that moribund Amtrak sleeping car with Max Miller. It had something to do with her mother—Nora was going to Florida to visit Beatrice—and that ear infection that kept her from flying, and the fact that Max was a train buff as well as a dutiful son who took the Silver Star or Silver Meteor to visit his own mother in Florida at regular intervals. Those were the bare facts.

Max had knocked on the door of her compartment, introduced himself, and said his mother had suggested he give her a lift from the station in West Palm Beach to Palmetto Estates. Nora knew how the conversation between mothers had gone. Max was renting a car. Why should Nora rent another or Beatrice be bothered driving to West Palm Beach to pick up her daughter when Addie's son Max was there to do it for her? Besides, the children—and Nora knew they'd been called children—had so much in common. They were both divorced.

That explained how she'd met Max Miller but not how she'd ended up going to bed, or to be more precise, berth with him. It couldn't all be Beatrice's fault.

Nora had liked his face, which was handsome in a reassuringly ordinary way. Living with Max Miller, she thought over scotch he produced from a silver flask, but which they had to drink from plastic cups with little Amtrak decals, would be like coming home to one of those upscale suburban developments every night. You could spend a perfectly pleasant evening before you realized you were in the wrong house. He also had a long, raw-boned body that was to her taste. And she was fairly sure that the son of Addie Miller, whom Beatrice had known long before they or anyone else had thought of retirement communities, wasn't harboring any lethal diseases. Nora knew her reasoning was specious—you couldn't judge a man's sexual book by his mother's cover story—but it was somehow convincing. Or maybe the fact that Max had the most beautiful hands she'd ever seen on a man convinced her. They were big with long arching fingers that ended in blunt, dully milky nails. Nora liked the nails. She would have hated it if he'd ruined the raw grace of those hands with the glossy polish of a professional manicure.

Maybe it was the hands after all, because, to be perfectly honest about it, which Nora tried to be afterward, she hadn't really intended to go to bed with Max, despite the face and the body and the probable clean bill of health. As it happened, things got out of control in the dusty compartment of that faded Amtrak train, what with his astonishing hands and all, and Nora believed that after a certain point in both age and sex, technical distinctions didn't apply. To put it more bluntly, after she'd come one way, it seemed bad form not to allow him to another.

So she'd gone to bed with Max Miller, and afterward he'd said it was the first time he'd got lucky because he was Addie Miller's son.

Nora turned the phrase around in her head for a moment until it made sense. Got lucky. As in got laid, scored, and other idioms of the same era and attitude. She poured herself more scotch from his silver flask and wondered what she was doing here. Or, more to the point, since it was her compartment, what he was.

There was a monogram on the side of the flask. MGM. "At least, you didn't promise to get me into the movies."

He smiled, or maybe it was a wince.

"I guess people are always making dumb jokes about your initials."

"Not always. Anyway, that wasn't dumb. It was cute."

Cute. Jesus! She was forty-one years old.

"What does the G stand for?"

"Geoffrey. My father insisted on Max after his father, but my mother had other ideas. Maxwell Geoffrey Miller. She thought it'd look good in the history books."

A little later he asked her if she wanted him to go back to his own bedroom. By that time she did, but she thought it would be rude to say so. She was Beatrice's daughter, all right.

"Of course not," she said.

It was just as well, because he awakened her in the middle of the night with those astonishing hands. That time Max didn't say anything about getting lucky. He didn't say anything at all, though he made some fairly eloquent sounds, which was okay with Nora. She liked good talk, but not in bed. Years ago she'd had a brief affair with a laconic economics professor whose tongue had been loosened, metaphorically if not literally, by sex. He'd shouted and thundered like some scatological Elmer Gantry. Unfortunately, he'd never converted Nora.

Max Miller had been blissfully quiet. In fact, taking into consideration the fact that it was the first time—the first three times, to be precise—Max Miller had been pretty blissful. Nora was surprised. She believed that sex, like most things done in tandem, required practice.

Sitting on the rumpled Amtrak linens the next morning, inhaling the strong smell of industrial-strength laundry detergent and the faint aroma of sex, she wasn't sorry for the night. When it came to sex, Nora tended to regret the things she hadn't done more than the things she had. Some of the regrets went all the way back to college and a boy named Michael Simon, but that was another story. Still, she wasn't quite sure how she'd ended up in that berth with Max in the first place. Again she came back to her mother, not the fact of Beatrice's living in Florida and waiting for an overdue visit from her daughter, but the influence of

Beatrice, as pervasive and lingering as the perfume her mother had worn for as long as Nora could remember.

At one period in her life, Beatrice had had four fraternity pins. Not *during* one period in her life, Nora was always careful to explain when she told the anecdote, but *at* one period in her life. As the story went—and Nora and her older sister, Susannah, had grown up on it the way some children do on fairy tales—Beatrice had managed to collect three at once. Of course, in those days fraternity pins didn't mean what they did when Beatrice was recounting the incident. They didn't mean, she instructed her daughters, you were engaged to be engaged. Then Beatrice snatched the fourth pin hot off the breast of a girl who, for some reason Beatrice pretended not to fathom, had called her a bitch. A week later Beatrice returned the pin and its owner undamaged to the chastened girl.

By the time Susannah, the beautiful one, was seventeen, she was giving Beatrice's legend a run for its money. As the saying went, Susannah could have had anyone she wanted. She wanted Nick Demopoulis, but that came later.

Nora, who was not plain, merely plainer than Susannah, was the bookish one. Beatrice worried that her second daughter would be unpopular. She didn't worry about it as much as she worried about polio and crazed drunks speeding their cars down Byron Road, but she was concerned. She pleaded with Nora to pay less attention to her books and more to her clothes and hair and makeup. Actually, Nora was obsessed with her appearance. It would have been hard not to be in that household. She spent hours brooding over curly reddish blond hair that no amount of torture could straighten, a long face that consisted entirely of angles, and pale skin that burned and peeled and blotched with every passing emotion but never tanned.

As it turned out, Beatrice needn't have worried. Nora didn't do badly as far as men were concerned. There was usually someone around, which pleased Beatrice and, though she never said so, surprised her, especially in view of what happened to Susannah, but that, like Nick Demopoulis, came later.

There was, however, no one around that February when

Nora ended up on the misnamed Silver Meteor with a handful of polyester-covered retirees and Addie Miller's son, who probably harbored no communicable diseases but had an unnatural affection for trains and an uncanny knack for the things you could do aboard them.

"I've discovered the redeeming power of sex," Nora told Lucy when she called her office that morning.

Lucy's laughter crackled like rumpled paper over the Amtrak phone. Nora pictured her long, handsome, vaguely horsy face growing longer as she opened her mouth wide to let the sound escape. "Hell, Nora, you've always known that. It's the redeeming power of love you have trouble with."

"I resent that. I was married." Nora brought out the fact like the threadbare corner of the baby blanket Cornelia had slept with through adolescence. Like Cornelia herself, it set Nora apart from the hordes of hungry women, a few years younger, whose biological clocks were making such an ungodly racket everywhere she went these days.

"You also wore a circle pin and turned your papers in on time. You were a good girl."

They talked about the magazine then. Lucy said everything was under control. The fit printout for the April issue was ready.

"So soon?"

"Did you think we couldn't do it without you?"

"I knew you could," Nora answered. That was the problem.

Nora was the publisher and editor-in-chief of a women's magazine. At some books the titles, and jobs, were separate. Nora combined them.

The magazine wasn't one of those mindless fashion books filled with eighteen-year-old anorexics wearing eighteen-hundred-dollar dresses and sullen pouts, but a handsomely designed monthly for today's woman, who, she was repeatedly reassured, had more style, taste, and intelligence than time. That meant the articles were brief and mildly informative.

Nora had gone to work at the magazine almost seventeen years earlier. It was called *American Homemaker* then and devoted to sound children, satisfied husbands, nourishing food, and continuous redecoration. At that time the publisher had been a man and the editor-in-chief a woman named Monica Storch. Monica had never married, though there were rumors of an affair with the captain of a Cunard liner. She had no children. Her diet consisted almost entirely of black coffee, cigarettes, and, it was further rumored, entirely too many Manhattans. Finally, Monica had never so much as reupholstered the mediocre family heirlooms she'd brought with her from the Midwest when she'd come to conquer the city. Yet Monica ran a tight and successful operation.

Even in those days Nora hadn't been stupid about the magazine. She knew there were only so many things you could do with a pound of ground beef. She knew that if you spent $49.95 on a living room makeover, you ended up with a couple of new pillows and not material for MoMA's design archives. She knew that the magazine's two regular features—"Is This Divorce Necessary?" and "The Heartbreak of Motherhood"—were not psychologically instructive or even morally uplifting case histories but slices of tawdry exhibitionism that netted their subjects between fifty and a hundred in cold cash and their readers twenty minutes of ghoulish titillation. Nonetheless, Nora, unlike many of her higher-minded, English-major peers at the magazine, knew that editorial content was not the issue. Advertising rate bases and circulation figures were.

As Nora worked her way from editor to senior editor to executive editor, word filtered upstairs to the corporate offices that Nora Heller understood demos, though she occasionally slipped and called them demographics. She was said to have a young nose. In fact, Nora's nose and every other part of her body were more than twenty years younger than Monica's.

When, four years ago, those same corporate powers decided to turn *American Homemaker* into *AH!*, the magazine for today's woman, and Nora into the editor-in-chief, Nora had felt a twinge of guilt. She couldn't call Monica a mentor, but that undernourished, husbandless, childless woman who lived among threadbare heirlooms had taught her a lot about magazines. Nora had always wanted to thank Monica, but Monica's departure hadn't left much time for niceties. Then, as the years had passed, Monica's imprint had grown fainter. Dozens of people who worked for Nora today had never heard of Monica Storch. Everyone thought of the magazine as Nora's book.

Nora had a fantasy about her job. On the last day of her life, she'd manage to snare first serial rights to a best-seller with actual literary merit, frame an article on women and health care, and woo three new advertisers. Then, blue pencil and p-and-l statement in hand, she'd slump gracefully forward over her desk.

The fantasy ended with her collapse. Nora had never wondered what would happen to *AH!* afterward. Lucy had just given her a pretty good idea.

"And Wheeler rescheduled the meeting again," Lucy went on. "For Tuesday."

Will Wheeler ran the publishing group's magazine division.

"Did you tell him I won't be in the office?"

"He said he wants the meeting now. You'd think we were bankrupt instead of down a few measly percentage points in advertising pages."

Lucy could afford to be cavalier. She was only the executive editor. Nora knew where the buck stopped.

"Don't worry about the meeting," Lucy said. "We can wing it without you."

Nora shuddered. You didn't wing a meeting with Will Wheeler.

She went back to her compartment. The berth was still unmade. Two plastic glasses, one with a lipstick smudge, the other with a fraction of an inch of muddy-looking water in the bottom, stood on the windowsill. Still life, the morning after. Nora had known it wasn't a good time to leave the office.

"As far as I can tell, there's never a good time to leave the magazine," Beatrice had said over the phone two weeks earlier.

Nora and her mother exchanged recriminations rarely,

harsh words never. There was no need for them. Each
woman registered the other's shifts on a more subtle Rich-
ter scale. Nora had just picked up Beatrice's tremors. They
pointed out her fault. She pictured her mother sitting
alone and increasingly frail on the fifth floor of that stark
white box called a luxury condominium. In the event of
upheaval, Beatrice had no desk to hang on to, no husband
to cling to, no abiding interest in art or antiques or the
underprivileged to steady her. She had her daughter,
Nora, and her granddaughter, Cornelia.

Nora didn't even bother hanging up the receiver. She
simply pressed the button to get another line, dialed an
airline, and made a round trip reservation. La Guardia–
West Palm Beach–La Guardia.

Then she'd got that damn ear infection, which would
only be aggravated, the doctor warned, by flight. He said it
was probably from the pool at the health club, and Bea
hinted it was divine retribution for swimming in a steamy
indoor sewer rather than her palm-shaded oasis, and Nora
ended up on a disheveled Amtrak berth trying to figure out
how she—and Max Miller—had got there.

Nora and Max almost missed the West Palm Beach stop.
She was still sitting in her bedroom worrying about
Wheeler when Max came to get her. He stepped into the
compartment and closed the door behind him. She hadn't
realized how late it was and stood to zip up the travel bag
hanging on the bathroom door.

"Ready?"

"Ready."

He'd been asking if she had her stuff together, and she'd
been saying she did, but then something funny happened.
The words took on another meaning. Max smiled. It was a
conspiratorial grin. She started to laugh.

He lifted one hand. She thought he was reaching for her
bag. He reached for her.

If they'd been in a colder climate and she'd been wearing pantyhose, they'd never have carried it off, not in the
amount of time they had. As it was, her skirt was so narrow
it took two pairs of hands to tug it up.

Max turned out to be as agile on his feet as he was in other positions. The roadbed got rough for a stretch, but all those years of riding the rails had given him a sense of balance. She was less steady on her feet, but then she wasn't on her feet for part of the time.

The train lurched into the station just as they lurched apart. The timing was lucky, since neither of them had stopped to pull down the window shade.

The encounter had been brief but effective. Nora felt rattled. Max looked the same way. The train was slowing and he was tugging at his zipper and she was trying to get that damn narrow skirt down over her hips again. So much for high fashion in the heat of passion, or even the heat.

She grabbed her traveling bag. The two ends weren't fastened together, and it kept catching on things. Max raced down to the other end of the car for his. They were still panting when they hit the platform.

The rental car was a compact model. Nora watched Max fling their two bags and her briefcase into the small trunk and slam it shut. He was wearing a faded green polo shirt with a small Golden Fleece over his heart. There were dark half-moon stains under his arms and a long dark streak down the small of his back. She wondered if the shadows were the results of those last minutes on the train or of carrying both bags.

She got in on the passenger side. He slid behind the wheel. She noticed a smudge of lipstick on his right ear. She reached over and rubbed it away. He was too busy studying the dashboard to notice.

Max Miller drove the way he screwed, with panache and without conversation. Nora made a mental note. It was less awkward going to bed with a stranger than driving I-95 with him. She wondered what he was thinking. Was he still crowing about having got lucky because he was Addie Miller's son, or was he deciding in the hot glare of the open road that he hadn't got so lucky after all? She sneaked a glance in her compact mirror. Thanks to the tropical humidity, her hair had that Little Orphan Annie look. So, come to think of it, did her eyes. That was his fault. She hadn't got much sleep. Her skirt was wrinkled and there was probably a stain on the back by now. That was his fault too.

She got angry at him, then furious at herself for backsliding. What he thought didn't matter. She knew the facts. All over the country women were plunking down millions of dollars to perm their hair into a facsimile of hers. As for the skirt, the label read, "100% linen, guaranteed to wrinkle." Besides, he probably hadn't noticed her hair or her skirt. He wasn't Beatrice, only Beatrice's friend's son.

Beyond the closed windows of the air-conditioned car, the highway heaved and shimmered in the steamy tropical sun. Shopping centers rose like brutal mirages from the flat, scrubby land. Every few miles a sign pointed the way to another oasis of gracious living. Sunset Condominiums. Everglades Estates. Palmtree Lakes. The slogans were even better than the names. One promised a return to carefree summers of childhood. "Vacation living three hundred and sixty-five days a year." Another offered athletic prowess by association. "Golf with the champions. Play tennis with the pros." Nora's favorite was an unabashed hymn to malicious one-upmanship. "If your friends could see you now."

Palmetto Estates made no billboard promises. A discreet sign simply pointed the way to a private road. Max Miller turned the car onto the small bridge that crossed the moat surrounding the development. The moat harbored an occasional alligator, or at least rumors of one. The rumors were as good as the real thing. They served to keep out the local have-nots. Lush green lawns and man-made ponds appeared without warning. Someone had dropped a movie set on the scruffy terrain.

A guard stopped them at the gatehouse, checked Max's name against a list, then passed them through. Pineapple Lane twisted into Bougainvillea Boulevard, which wound into Oleander Drive.

Nora shivered in the air-conditioned car. "This place always strikes me as so unreal."

"It's real, all right. It just isn't very connected."

He was driving slowly now. Maybe he was reluctant to

drop her off. Maybe he simply didn't want to frighten the few ambulatory natives.

"The thing I like about coming down here is it always makes me feel like a kid. My daughter doesn't believe I'm younger than Robert Redford. In this place I'm a baby."

Nora didn't answer. Palmetto Estates didn't make her feel like a kid. It made her feel like a grown woman who was shirking her responsibilities. The Eskimos put them out on the ice. She and her contemporaries sent them to palmier climates.

Except she hadn't sent Beatrice anywhere. The apartment on the movie lot had been Nora's stepfather Sam's idea. Determined to make retribution for a life spent turning trees into paper which in turn had translated into hard cash, Sam had resolved to retire to nature. But the habits, not to mention the comforts, of a life-time are not so easily shed. Sam had been no Gauguin. He liked his nature tamed. He wanted his natives white, English-speaking, and conversant with the current health of the stock market. And he wasn't about to leave his wife, who believed the natural habitat of an alligator was slung over her shoulder or wrapped around her size six-and-a-half feet. So he'd decided on an apartment in Florida overlooking a golf course where the median age of the players was sixty-seven-point-six and the only thing that had ever run wild was a cart that had gone out of control on the ninth hole.

But Sam hadn't been disappointed. In his last years he'd been able to turn off the air-conditioning and slide open the glass doors to admit earth-scented breezes. During those final evenings of his life, he'd sat on the terrace with his gin and tonic, listening to birds he was trying to learn to identify, inhaling aromas of exotic trees and flowers, and contemplating the meaning of life. Then, nineteen months after he'd sat with his first gin and tonic on his just-bought terrace watching the tropical night overtake the golf course, Sam had died, leaving his widow with a financially secure future; memories of a generally happy past, despite everything; and a three-bedroom condominium in a development that wasn't exactly a retirement community. It just had a preponderance of people who, like welfare recipients, managed to collect checks without going to work.

Max turned onto Cypress Court, and there in front of Building 1200 Addie Miller and Bea Brickner stood waiting for their children. They were both smiling broadly. Addie's ample bosom heaved with excitement. Beatrice's chest wasn't designed for such dramatic displays of emotion, but she couldn't resist stepping off the curb and walking several feet down the circular driveway to get to her daughter a few seconds sooner. Nora pushed open the door on the passenger side before Max had even turned off the ignition.

Max opened his own door and climbed out. "We got lucky," he said to both mothers.

The phrase made Nora stiffen. She was already hugging her mother and hoped Beatrice hadn't noticed.

"There was no traffic," he went on, "and we made it in less than half an hour."

"Wonderful," Addie cooed like some rare tropical bird.

Nora and Beatrice stood on the asphalt driveway that was soft from the heat and clung together in the sticky late afternoon.

"What did you think of him?" Bea asked.

Nora followed her mother into the apartment. The living room, all the bedrooms, the kitchen, and the dining room had sliding glass doors that opened onto screened terraces. Light poured in at every angle, searing the white carpet and the white upholstery and the white furniture. The apartment lay like bleached bones in the tropical sun. The glare crackled through Nora's dark glasses and made her eyes ache. Or maybe it was only the thought of her mother moving through this desert alone that made them sting like that.

"What did I think of whom?" Nora asked, though she knew perfectly well whom her mother meant.

"Addie's son."

"The man gave me a lift from the station. What am I supposed to think of him? Other than that he's a good driver."

"Addie said she told him you'd be on the train. Do you want some iced tea? She said he'd probably find you and take you to dinner or something."

Something.

"Iced tea would be fine."

Nora followed her mother into the kitchen. A single mug and one small plate stood in the white dishrack. A faint kiss of lipstick lingered on the mug. Nora averted her eyes. In earlier days of better eyesight, Beatrice never would have permitted that stain. If she saw it now, she'd be furious.

Beatrice opened a white cabinet and took out two frosted glasses.

"Let me do that," Nora said.

Beatrice turned away, hugging the glasses to her. "I'm a widow, not an invalid. And you're on vacation."

Nora sat in one of the two white wrought-iron chairs on either side of the small white wrought-iron breakfast table. As she watched her mother move around the kitchen, she thought of her own self-centered youth. Nora had grown up hearing that she had a beautiful mother, and certainly there were photographs to prove it. Leather albums full of carefully mounted and neatly labeled snapshots chronicled Beatrice's youth, marriage, and young motherhood. A wedding picture of Beatrice in a white satin gown, cut on the bias to show off her lithe figure, had stood on the piano in the house on Byron Road all through Nora's youth. She and her sister, Susannah, had each gone off to college with a framed portrait of their mother in another long, bias-cut dress, this one decorated with thousands of glistening paillettes. It had been taken to commemorate her engagement to their father. Girls who wandered into Nora's room at school always asked the same two questions. First they said, "Who's that?" When Nora told them, they always followed with "Is she an actress?" "Not professionally," Nora had taken to answering once she hit her rebellious period. But despite the reputation and the photographs, Nora had grown up seeing only a middle-aged woman who was her mother. Now that she was a middle-aged woman herself, she recognized the traces of beauty that lingered, like a carefully wrapped gift, beneath the creases of tissue-paper skin.

Beatrice moved around the kitchen with the light, sure step of the girl who'd won dance contests all over the state of New Jersey, but she let her daughter carry the full glasses to the terrace. Nora could tell by the cruel curl of her mother's fingers that her arthritis was getting worse.

They settled on the terrace off the living room. Beatrice said it was the coolest one at this time of day.

Nora kicked off her shoes and put her feet up on one of the small footstools that matched the tubular white porch chairs. Her toenails were short and jagged. Beatrice put her feet up on another footstool. Beneath the crisscross straps of her white sandals, her perfectly pedicured toes lay like coral seashells.

As a child, Nora had always admired her mother's perfectly polished finger- and toenails. They were brilliant emblems of adulthood. But by the time Nora was old enough to wear nail polish, she saw it as a sign of lack of seriousness of purpose.

Beatrice's head swiveled toward her daughter. "You're looking well. A little tired but well. I like your skirt."

"It's wrinkled."

"Wrinkled's in."

Nora wondered if she'd ever stop underestimating her mother.

"I used to argue with you about clothes," Beatrice went on.

"I remember."

"Who could blame me. A closet full of beautiful things, and all you ever wore were black sweaters. But now you have your own style."

Beatrice could give no greater praise.

"A little severe, maybe," she continued.

"We in the wonderful world of fashion writing call it understated."

"It suits you."

Nora decided to quit while she was ahead. "Tell me what you've been up to."

"What I've been up to? In the last week I went to Worth

Avenue twice, Nineteenth Street once, a funeral, and a memorial service. Life in the fast lane in Palmetto Estates." Beatrice sipped her iced tea. "Promise me one thing. Promise you won't let them give me a memorial service."

Nora uncrossed and recrossed her legs. "Actually, I was thinking of sprinkling your ashes over those four fraternities."

"I'm serious," Beatrice said.

But I'm not ready to be, Nora wanted to scream. "Was it that bad?" she asked.

"Not if you like celebrity roasts. All those women in their good jewelry delivering little speeches about what a great humanitarian Grace Worken was. Her grandson read an original poem. It made reference to her rugalach. Only he pronounced it rugahlah. To rhyme with marsala."

"I take it Grace was a good cook."

"Posthumously, everyone's a Julia Child." Beatrice sipped her tea again. "Promise you won't let them do that to me."

"Okay, I promise. Now can we change the subject?"

"You'll have to deal with it sooner or later."

"If it's all the same to you, I'd prefer later."

Beatrice reached over and patted her daughter's hand. "That makes two of us. He's very successful," Beatrice said after a moment. "A partner in a big firm."

"Who?" Nora asked, though again she knew perfectly well whom her mother was talking about.

Nora had been in Palmetto Estates less than half an hour, and she'd already regressed several decades. She sat on the terrace sipping her iced tea and feeling like that fourteen-year-old girl who'd just discovered curly reddish blond hair wasn't the worst thing in the world. It had been her first real date, and a boy named Kenny Silver had said she had nice hair, then kissed her. It was the first time she'd been kissed without benefit of a spinning bottle or a friend playing postmaster, and she was dazed with the wonder of it. She crept into the house eager to get to the dark private theater of her room, where she could stop the film and rerun that kiss again and again. But Susannah and Beatrice and Sam were all in the kitchen. Susannah must have spotted the dazed look, because she ambushed Nora. "Did he kiss you good night?" she asked right off. Nora said no, but her damnable skin told the truth, and they all laughed and teased her until Sam said it was enough. It wasn't enough. It was too much. By the time Nora got to her room she found that the film clip of that wondrous kiss she'd planned to run again and again had been smudged and torn with use.

"Addie Miller's son," Beatrice said. "Even if you discount half of what Addie says—and you always have to discount half of what Addie says—he's a good boy."

"He's a forty-four-year-old man."

"I meant he's a good son. Which can't be easy with a mother like Addie."

"I thought she was one of your closest friends down here."

"How else would I know what a hypochondriac she is? Some people get that way when they live alone. Obsessed with their own bodies. He's a good-looking boy."

This time Nora didn't bother to pretend she didn't know whom Beatrice meant or point out that Max was no kid.

"So, what went on between you two?"

Nora thought of the various stories she could invent. Coming up with story ideas was part of her job.

"Nothing. He introduced himself on the train, told me he's ridden thirty-three thousand miles of rails in his life, and offered me a lift here."

Beatrice's mouth settled into a satisfied crescent.

"What are you smiling at?"

"You. Susannah used to tell me everything, but getting information from you was always like getting blood from a stone. Until I learned."

"Learned what?"

"If I asked you anything, you'd clam up. But if I just bided my time, you'd spill everything in twenty-four hours."

"I never did have any backbone. Anyway, there's nothing to spill."

"He's tall, he's handsome, and he makes six figures a year."

Nora took her feet off the footstool and placed them firmly on the all-weather carpeting. "You're my mother, and I love you dearly, but you still have the values of an eighteen-year-old."

"I still have the heart of an eighteen-year-old. Only the body and mind are going to seed."

That night Beatrice and Nora watched the late news from opposite sides of the vast white expanse that was Beatrice's king-size bed. They hadn't done that in a long time, but the comfortable intimacy, like proficiency on a bike, came back.

During a commercial Nora went inside and poured herself another glass of wine. Beatrice watched her daughter narrowly as she put it down on the night table and got back on the bed.

Nora caught the look. "I'll be careful."

"I was thinking about your liver, not my furniture. Do you always have more wine after dinner?"

"How else do you get to sleep?"

"They say you're not supposed to drink alone."

"I live alone. Do you want me to go out and pull people in off the streets every time I want a drink?"

Nora could joke about it now, but there'd been a time, when she'd first lived alone and worked for Monica Storch, that she'd worried. Now she knew she drank more than she ought to according to the magazine's fitness column and less than was dangerous.

The news was local but familiar to Nora nonetheless. Several drug dealers had shot each other. An indicted city official swore he was innocent. A twenty-two-year-old aerobics instructor was suing her sixty-four-year-old husband for divorce and forty million dollars. Suddenly Nora had one of those flashes of vague unease that wing by like a bird. She had to stop a minute, as she always did at those times, and retrace her thoughts to find out what she was worried about. Wheeler? But Wheeler wouldn't wing by that way, just beyond consciousness. Wheeler had been on her mind all day. It was more than Wheeler.

And it was ridiculous. She was a grown woman, not some besotted kid. And she wasn't even sure she liked him. How could you like a man who talked about getting lucky as if sex were some Neanderthal conquest or the lottery? Then she remembered those extraordinary hands and the outline of his shoulders against the lights of South Carolina or Georgia or wherever the hell they'd been, and knew.

She thought she'd solved the problem years ago. She'd discussed it with her old friend Maude only a few weeks earlier. "I really like being alone," she'd told Maude. "It's easier. You don't have to wonder whether the other person is having a good time. You don't have to be places or eat meals or go to bed on anyone else's schedule. You can do whatever you damn please."

"You only say that," Maude had insisted, "because you usually have someone around. It's nice being alone if you have someone in your head."

"Did you make plans to do anything with him?" Beatrice asked.

"Who?" Nora said, though her guilty skin gave her away.

"Addie Miller's son. He's staying through Monday." Beatrice smiled. "But you already knew that."

Nora held the cold wineglass against her cheek. "I'm not eighteen, Mother."

"What's that supposed to mean?"

"It means I don't have to have a date for Saturday night. I came down here to spend some time with you."

Beatrice turned from the vividly colored image of the Dade County prosecutor to face her daughter. Her eyes were almost black. As a child, Nora had thought of them as twin camera shutters. They took in everything.

"You're a smart girl, Nora. You can walk and chew gum at the same time."

2

When Nora, as an adult, first came across the term "safe house" in a spy novel, an image flashed through her mind. It was of the Harding-Coolidge Tudor house in which she'd grown up.

Even from the outside, the house looked solid. It was guarded by towering oaks. One had been deathly ill for as long as Nora could remember, but a tree surgeon came at regular intervals to paint an ever-growing cavity with a thick black glaze, and the tree was still standing when Beatrice sold the property. In front, beds of tulips and irises and constantly manicured shrubs presented an impeccable face to the world. In the back, where things were more private, red and yellow roses ran amok over a wooden trellis. On the side next to the screened-in porch, there were beds of pansies. Nora liked the pansies best because the more you picked them, Beatrice told her, the more they grew. It was the middle-class Jewish version of the miracle of the loaves and fishes.

Built two decades before Levitt captured the lack of imagination of the American public, the house, on the outside, did not resemble its neighbors. Inside, however, the symmetry of the period prevailed. On the right of the entrance hall was the living room, on the left the dining. A screened-in porch led off one, a glassed-in porch off the other. The kitchen was as big as some of the apartments

Nora would live in later in her life, and there was always food on the white-patterned Formica counters. It wasn't junk food, though it wasn't necessarily healthy either.

Upstairs there were four bedrooms. Susannah's had a canopied bed that wore its white eyelet like a bride. Nora's had a pink linoleum floor with the word *Nora* scrolled right into it. In the master bedroom there was a big double bed. Once when Nora was little, she'd hidden under the bed to see her father get undressed, but Susannah had told on her, and she never did see a man undressed until Paul Moss came along. Off the bedroom there was a closet as big as another room, with shelves for shoes and hats and handbags. No one lived in the fourth bedroom, but sometimes Beatrice's mother or younger brother or other members of her family stayed there for weeks at a time.

It was the kind of house people came to as a refuge. Even as a child Nora sensed that, but it wasn't until much later that she realized they came not only because of the comfortable furniture and thick walls and doors that closed with resounding clicks, but because Beatrice knew how to make a refuge.

Of course, Phil helped. He made the money. He put up with—no, welcomed—the relatives. He adored Beatrice. According to the family party line, they couldn't get enough of each other.

Until Nora was in second grade, her father came home for lunch every day. After lunch it was up to Mary, who was Canadian and, to Nora's amazement, spoke French the way everyone else spoke English, to make sure that Susannah and Nora washed their faces and brushed their teeth before they went back to school. Beatrice and Phil always went to their room for a rest. Just like babies, Nora sometimes said, but she knew from the way her mother and father smiled that there was something about it that wasn't babyish. Then Susannah would tell her not to be so dumb.

Susannah was four years older than Nora. She got things and places first. On the opening day of school the teacher always asked if Nora was Susannah Heller's younger sister. When Nora finally outgrew her hated blue seersucker dress, she had to spend another two years in Susannah's.

That was the last time Beatrice bought them sister dresses. And Susannah always knew more. She knew the rules of games. Later, she knew what you were and were not allowed to let boys do. Even when they were grown, conversations could tilt like a seesaw under the weight of Susannah's seniority. Once, after Susannah's divorce, Nora pointed out that they were anomalies. As daughters of a happy marriage, they should not have become divorce statistics. Maybe Beatrice and Phil's happiness was precisely the problem. They'd given their daughters no combat training.

"I only remember one fight," Nora said.

"There were more," Susannah insisted. "You were just too young to remember."

The argument Nora did recall had occurred at dinner. Years later Nora could still see Phil's mustache working angrily as he chewed his food in the long silences that punctuated the argument and Beatrice's stricken face. The curve of contentment was gone, and her cheeks looked sunken, as if she were holding her breath.

It must have been Mary's night off, because Nora remembered Beatrice washing the dishes while she and Susannah dried. She dried carefully in the big silent kitchen. Susannah hadn't even turned on the radio. Suddenly all three of them heard Phil's voice calling from the front hall. He said he was going for a walk.

Beatrice's hands froze in the air above the soapy water. Both girls stood staring at their mother. Her eyes, wide and bright with panic, focused blindly on the night-blackened window above the sink. Phil never went for a walk after dinner. No one did. It wasn't that kind of neighborhood.

After they finished the dishes, Susannah went upstairs to her room. Nora followed her, but Susannah said she had homework and closed the door in her sister's face. That was odd too, because Susannah usually did her homework downstairs at the kitchen table.

Nora went into her own room and sat for a while staring at her name in the floor. For the first time in her life, it occurred to her that someday someone whose name wasn't Nora would live in the room. She wondered what they'd

do. Put a rug over the letters? Carpet the whole floor? She
hoped they wouldn't tear it up. She pictured workmen
peeling her name from the linoleum. It was written in
script. She wondered if she'd come up in one continuous
piece. Maybe they'd just chip her away into nothing.

Beatrice was still in the kitchen. Nora could hear the
sound of cabinets opening and closing. She went downstairs, but instead of turning right into the kitchen, she
went through the hall and turned left into the dark living
room. Nora was usually afraid of the dark, but that night
she didn't even care.

She burrowed into a corner of the sofa, pulled her legs up
to her chest, and rested her face on her knees. Her teeth
began worrying the fabric of her dungarees. By the time
Beatrice called her, the cloth was wet through and her
knee was sore, but Nora didn't answer.

She just sat there in the darkness that smelled of expensive chocolates and furniture polish. Once, several months
earlier, Nora had stolen handfuls of mints, each snuggled
into its own transparent paper envelope. She didn't know
why she thought of it as stealing—her mother seldom for-
bade her food—but after she'd eaten them all, she'd sent
the paper evidence down the gutter of Byron Road. The
wrappers had floated like a line of small life rafts in the
muddy water.

Nora wondered now if she was being punished for her
transgression. She heard her mother climb the stairs, walk
from bedroom to bedroom, and come back down. When
Beatrice finally came into the living room and turned on a
lamp, they both blinked in surprise.

"Why didn't you answer me?" Beatrice asked in a voice
Nora knew, but not well.

Nora's teeth went on worrying the fabric.

"I looked all over the house." Beatrice stood in the light
of the single lamp. Her cheeks still looked sunken, and her
lips were white. She usually put on lipstick after dinner,
but she hadn't tonight. "I was worried about you."

Nora should have believed her. Worrying about her was
something her mother did. But she wasn't convinced.

Beatrice must have seen that, because she sat beside

Nora on the sofa and put an arm around her shoulders. Beatrice's hands smelled of dish soap, but the rest of her was pure Joy, and not the dishwashing kind.

"Are you and Daddy going to get a divorce?"

Beatrice's movement released a small cloud of Joy into the air.

"Where did you get an idea like that?" she asked, though both of them knew where she'd got the idea.

"Debby Reese's parents got a divorce."

"I'm sorry for Debby, and for Mr. and Mrs. Reese, but that has nothing to do with Daddy and me. Of course, we're not going to get a divorce."

And, of course, they never did. Phil came home, though Nora was in bed by then. The next day at lunch her mother's cheeks weren't sunken anymore and her father teased Nora and Susannah, and afterward Beatrice and Phil went up to take their rest. Everything went back to normal, for six weeks.

Nora heard her mother scream. It was a high, piercing sound, all edge and no meaning. Then Beatrice screamed again. This time it was Susannah's name.

Nora got out of bed and ran into the hall. The door to her parents' bedroom was open and she could see past the double bed where Susannah was standing to the bathroom on the far side. Her mother was kneeling on the floor, crying and screaming and trying to lift the dead weight that was Nora's father. There was blood on the side of his head and blood on her mother's nightgown. As the story came down over the years, he'd hit his head on the side of the sink when he'd collapsed, but Nora didn't know that then. All she knew was that there was blood on her father's head and a dark red stain across the front of her mother's nightgown that made it look as if they were both bleeding.

Susannah came running past Nora then and kept going down the hall and across the yard while Beatrice screamed *hurry for God's sake hurry* to Susannah, and *get away get away get away* to Nora.

Nora didn't get away. She couldn't. She stood there in the door, unable to move, because she'd never seen her father lying on the floor like that, with his eyes rolled back as if he were teasing them and his mouth a slack hole, and her mother crying and screaming and clawing at him. Then Mr. Blacker from next door rushed past her and Mrs. Blacker came after him and dragged Nora from the doorway.

Next she was sitting on Susannah's canopied bed, which was usually a treat, but not that night, and an ambulance was screaming louder and louder. Suddenly the siren went dead and doors slammed and feet pounded up the stairs of Nora's house.

Susannah was crying. Nora told her not to.

"Daddy can't die." That was one thing she knew for sure.

Her mother went away in the ambulance with her father, but she came back in Mr. Blacker's car.

There were a lot of people in the house after that. Her grandmother and Uncle Lewis came right away, before it was even morning. Other relatives and more neighbors followed. A lot of them brought food. Nora had never seen so much food in the house. There was no room left on the white-patterned Formica counters. Everyone kept telling her mother she had to eat something. Once Beatrice did. She had some soup. Then she went into the bathroom and threw up. Nora knew because she heard the sounds. She wondered who was holding her mother's head.

The next day there were lots of folding chairs in the living room. They were arranged in rows on the carpeting and crowded in among the regular furniture. Someone had taken away the big Chinese coffee table that had held the silver plate of mints. In its place stood a long wooden box that was the same pale color as her mother's and Susannah's hair.

Her father was in that box. Nora knew it, though the box was closed. And she knew that meant she'd never see him again.

She started to cry. She was sitting on one of the hard wooden chairs. It was so close to the box that her knees almost touched it. Her mother was next to her, and she was crying too. Susannah was on the other side of her mother.

Nora couldn't see Susannah, but she could hear the big sloppy sound of her sobs.

Beatrice put an arm around Nora. Her other arm was around Susannah. She pulled them both to her till their heads were almost touching. They were both crying and drooling onto the front of her good black wool dress. The fabric smelled of Joy.

"Don't," her mother said. "Don't cry." But she was crying while she said it.

Nora felt her mother's face pressed into the top of her head. "If you stop crying," Beatrice cried into Nora's hair, "I will."

Nora couldn't stop crying, but it didn't matter. She knew that even if she did, her mother wouldn't.

After a while the people stopped coming, and the house was empty, except for the three of them and sometimes her grandmother or Uncle Lewis. He was her mother's favorite brother—young, everyone said, though he didn't seem young to Nora. He was handsome and a doctor, which pleased her mother and grandmother a lot, and still unmarried, which bothered them just as much.

Uncle Lewis moved a couple of suits and lots of books and magazines into the fourth bedroom. He was always carrying books, and one day he arrived with two wrapped in gift paper. He gave one, about Madame Curie, to Nora and the other, about Eleanor Roosevelt, to Susannah. Susannah unwrapped her book and said thank you, but Nora knew she never even opened it.

"If he thinks," she said later when she and Nora were sitting on the canopied bed together, "he can take Daddy's place, he's got another think coming."

Nora didn't say anything. She kept paging through her book, looking at the pictures, but she wasn't thinking about the pictures. If Uncle Lewis could pull it off, it'd be okay with her.

3

Swimming pools were scattered like loose sapphires over the emerald green of Palmetto Estates. There was one pool for every sixty-six residents. Nora wondered if the similarity between that ratio and the median age of the golfers was intentional on the part of the builders. They'd installed small pools to anchor clusters of houses and medium-sized pools to serve single apartment buildings and an Olympic-sized pool at the club where you could sign for drinks or lunch, and every morning at eleven a group of blue-rinsed women in dressmaker bathing suits gathered at the shallow end for an aquatic aerobics class. Like Cheever's swimmer, the residents of Palmetto Estates could easily swim home from anywhere, only precious little swimming went on in those shimmering pools. Grandchildren splashed and women dunked and men stood with arms folded across softening chests discussing the theory of finance now that they'd left the practice.

The pools of Palmetto Estates were its town squares. That was where the residents traded gossip, reported illnesses, and announced coming visits of children. That was where, Beatrice warned after she and Nora had vied to clean up the few breakfast things, Addie Miller's son would be.

"Put on a nice bathing suit," Beatrice said.

So much for Nora's recently vaunted style.

It wasn't even eleven o'clock, but half the lounge chairs around the pool were taken. Some were pulled together in little cliques, others dragged or banished to a solitary hinterland. Most were draped with towels; many had books on them. Nora counted six hardcover copies of *Trump* and several biographies of overaged heiresses and fading or dead movie stars. There were also a couple of paperback novels with banners proclaiming the number of weeks they'd been on the best-seller list.

It took Beatrice and Nora some time to make their way to two empty lounge chairs at the far end of the pool. Everyone knew that Bea's daughter was visiting. Everyone wanted to say hello. Except Max Miller.

Addie had gone to the eye doctor, a woman with a *Trump* book reported. "Her son's down and he took her. Such a nice boy," she added. And Nora, who'd been dreading meeting, under the noses of Beatrice and half the residents of the 1200 Building, the stranger with whom she'd just happened to spend the night, felt an unreasonable rush of disappointment.

She and Beatrice spread towels on the lounges and sunscreen on themselves. Then they went to work on each other's backs. Beatrice's flesh rippled in soft waves beneath Nora's hands. Her mother's bones felt close to the skin and fragile. Nora kneaded gently. She was afraid of damaging something.

Finally, Nora lay back on her lounge with half-closed eyes. All around her women talked and dozed and turned themselves like carcasses on spits. Sun-blackened flesh bulged over the top and out the bottom of vast expanses of Lastex. Cotton bathing suits hung on bones spindly as hangers. Nora stretched in the tropical sun. She'd never felt so smooth and lithe. She closed her eyes. When she opened them again, she was staring at a girl poised on the edge of the pool. Her brown toes curled over the cement edge. She sprang into the air and slipped into the chlorine-bright water in a single smooth arc. When she climbed out of the pool, droplets of water glistened on her firm brown flesh. Above a tiny white bikini bottom her stomach was flat. Small, pointy breasts held up the strapless top.

"That's Ann Safir's granddaughter," Beatrice said.

"Nubile little thing, isn't she?"

Beatrice shifted position on her lounge and tucked a quarter of an inch of thigh back into the leg of her bathing suit. "Sometimes I think we ought to have just one pool where no children or grandchildren are allowed."

Ann Safir's granddaughter dived into the pool again.

"She doesn't splash that much."

"Who's talking about splashing? She looks too good."

Nora started to laugh. "Only you could compare yourself to a seventeen-year-old kid."

"You're the one who called her nubile."

Nora turned her head and shielded her eyes with her hand to look at her mother. "I just assumed it stopped rankling after a while."

Beatrice closed her eyes. "You assumed wrong."

Nora turned back to the pool. That was when she saw him making his way toward them. It couldn't be anyone but the Sap.

The Sap was what Beatrice had christened Saperstein, the only widower in Building 1200 and one of perhaps two dozen in all of Palmetto Estates. A few months after Sam had died, Saperstein had let on to Beatrice that she could fix his fruit and cottage cheese for him any time she liked. Beatrice had reported this to Nora in a long-distance call with a mixture of pride at having won the contest and distaste for the prize. She said Saperstein was common. When he came down to the pool, he swaggered among the widows. And he wore a pinkie ring with a small diamond. "A very small diamond," she added. Sometimes it was hard to win with Beatrice.

But she was right. He did swagger. As he came toward them around the cement apron of the pool, Nora thought she couldn't have missed him. There was the pinkie ring and the cocky walk and the fact that there was only one other man around the pool that morning, and he had arrived with a walker and a black woman in a white uniform who settled him at one of the umbrella-shaded tables.

The Sap came toward them with outstretched arms. His pinkie ring caught the sun and shattered it into primary colors. His pink knit shirt and lime-green pants ran down his body and over his paunch like melting sherbet. His face was almost black and his shoes were white with little holes in them. They made Nora think of Cuban bandleaders.

He came to a stop at the foot of the two lounge chairs where Beatrice and Nora sat.

"So this is Bea's daughter. Well, I certainly heard a lot about you. I'm Charlie. Charlie Saperstein." He sat on the end of Bea's chair. "Glad to meet you. Nora, right? Glad to meet you, Nora. So, how long're you down for? Bea said a week, but I said, 'Leave it to me, Bea. I'll talk her into staying.' I mean, what's a week? Seven days. Seven days for a mother? A mother like this. That magazine of yours can wait."

He smiled. His caps hung on his gums like a string of perfect white beads.

"Yeah, I know all about the magazine. I saw your mother reading it around the pool one day. I said, 'Bea, what're you reading a magazine like that for?' Excuse me. I mean, it's a nice magazine. Beautiful. But I said, 'Bea, you think you got anything left to learn about decorating? Taste, you got plenty of. And when it comes to cooking.' I mean, Nora, you know your mother's apple pies."

He paused to savor the thought of Bea's apple pies.

"Are they as good as Grace Worken's rugalach?" Nora asked.

"Ach!" Saperstein groaned. "Poor Grace, she should rest in peace. I don't like to speak ill of the dead, but Grace's rugalach couldn't hold a candle—not a candle—to this woman's apple pies."

He patted Beatrice's knee. "The queen of the apple pies. So she tells me she's reading the magazine because her daughter is publisher of it. Publisher and editor-in-chief, she tells me. I said, 'Bea, you got some daughter.' And now I see I was right. Some daughter. Terrific to have you, Nora. Well, I gotta go. Time and tee-off wait for no man. Just wanted to stop by and say hello. See you later. Maybe we'll take a little swim. In the meantime, you need anything, don't hesitate to ask. Apartment Three-D. Charlie Saperstein at your service. You take care now, Bea." He patted

her knee again and was gone in a flash of sparkling diamonds and spiffy white shoes.

"The queen of the apple pies," Nora said as she watched
him making his way among the widows, nodding and
laughing and patting. "My God, you didn't do him justice."

"He was nervous," Bea answered.

"I'd be nervous too, if I had to walk around in those
shoes. What's the matter? Couldn't he get the rest of his
band out of Havana?"

Bea took a bottle of sunscreen from her canvas bag and
handed it to her daughter. "You better put some more on.
You know the way you burn."

Nora took the bottle from her mother and slathered the
white cream up and down her white arms and legs.

"Don't forget your feet," Bea said. "You always forget
your feet."

"I haven't forgotten my feet since I was sixteen."

"And you couldn't walk for days. Put a towel over them."

"Maybe the Sap will lend me his shoes."

"Don't be so quick to judge people. They haven't all had
your advantages."

"Since when did you start quoting Scott Fitzgerald?"

"What are you talking about?"

"What you just said. It's the beginning of *The Great
Gatsby.*"

"It's Daddy," Bea corrected. "He used to say that."

Nora didn't remember her father reading much, but
then, she didn't remember much about her father. She'd
never know where he'd got the piece of advice that Beatrice had suddenly, after all these years, passed on.

A little before noon, Nora noticed a change in the conversation around her.

"Maybe a little cottage cheese with a nice piece of
melon."

"I made a nice tuna salad yesterday. There's still some
left."

"I think I'll open a nice can of salmon."

"I've got a nice piece of chicken from last night."

Nora closed her eyes, but she couldn't shut out the images of all those solitary women sitting around their small tables picking at leftovers. She thought of the calendar on the desk back in her office. It was so dense with lunches that she relished the occasional free day when she could order a sandwich at her desk and work straight through.

The discussion went on for half an hour. Then they began to put on their terry-cloth and knit and flowered coverups and pack up their towels and suntan lotions and books and drift back to Building 1200. There were only a handful of people left when Max Miller showed up.

"There's Addie's son," Beatrice said.

Nora opened her eyes and saw Max Miller coming toward them. He'd gone upstairs to change when he'd come back from the doctor, and he was wearing nothing but a pair of swimming trunks. Nora was sorry the dusty Amtrak bedroom had been so dark. Addie Miller's son didn't spend all his time riding the rails. Nora was willing to bet he ran and swam and maybe even played squash. She was also willing to bet he was a little vain about the results.

"How's your mother?" Beatrice asked him.

"Fine." He stood at the foot of their lounges, and Nora had to squint up into the sun to look at him. "No cataract operation for the time being."

The news was so good that Beatrice decided she had to go congratulate Addie right away. Then she'd start lunch. "You stay for a while." She patted Nora's knee. "There's nothing to do but cut up a little fruit."

After Beatrice left, Max sat facing Nora on the empty lounge. He touched her thigh. When he took his index finger away, it left a white imprint. Then the color rushed back in. "You're getting burned."

"I have on sunscreen."

"You look as if you could use some more." He picked up the bottle. "Here, let me—"

"No!"

"I was only going to put suntan lotion on you."

"You see that woman at the end of the pool?"

"The one reading *Trump*?"

"Pretending to read it. She's actually taking notes for the

Palmetto Estates Gazette. Addie Miller's son and Bea Brickner's daughter caught in sunscreen slathering tryst."

"My mother says you're a nice girl."

"It seems to me she could have done better than that. My mother says you're a good-looking boy."

"Okay, she also said you've got good bones, and you dress well. Like your mother. So, why don't you come over for a drink this afternoon? My mother has her weekly beauty parlor appointment."

"Because with my luck she'd forget something or come home early, and we'd be caught in flagrante delicto, and your mother would think I wasn't a nice girl after all, and I can't do that to my mother, even if I'm not a nice girl but a grown woman with a responsible job and a life of her own."

He stood, walked the few feet to the deep end of the pool, and dived in. The pool was too short for his long strokes. He was back in minutes. With his hair slicked back from the water, his bony face wasn't quite so ordinary. He put on his sunglasses and sat on the lounge next to hers.

"As I see it, it's a problem of logistics."

"Try the pool at the club. It's Olympic-size."

"I was talking about us."

The last word, or at least the assumption, startled her. "That's not logistics, it's privacy. I really don't think I can deal with the entire Twelve hundred Building watching and speculating. Addie's son and Bea's daughter. Where do they go? What do they do? Is it working? Why didn't it work? Was it his fault or hers?"

"That's the fastest affair I ever had."

"I'm used to working on a monthly deadline."

"Do you like art deco architecture? We could drive down to Miami for dinner."

"I happen to be crazy about art deco anything, but I also happen to be here to have dinner with my mother. So are you."

"Okay, we'll be good kids. I'll have dinner with Addie. You have dinner with Bea. We'll play by the rules. But I just checked the rules." He gestured to the list of regulations posted at the far end of the pool. "And there's no law against midnight swimming."

* * *

"Ow!"

"I told you you were getting burned."

"It's not the sunburn," she lied. "It's this damn door handle. Why did you rent a compact anyway?"

"Because when I rented it, I was planning to drive in it, not . . ." His mouth let the sentence drift off into the curve between her neck and shoulder.

"Fuck in it."

"You editorial types have a real way with words," he said, but he didn't stop what he was doing.

She tried sliding farther down in the seat. Her knee hit the steering wheel. She had no idea what he was doing with his long legs. "This is ridiculous. We're both too tall. Not to mention too old."

"Do you want to go to a hotel?"

"In bathing suits?"

"Actually, I think you're enjoying this."

"I'm enjoying some of it."

They shifted position again. It was a little better. They stopped talking. She couldn't see very well in the dark, but she could still remember what his hands looked like, and she knew what they felt like.

"Ow!" she said again after a while.

"I warned you."

"No one likes an I-told— Ow!"

"Where does the sunburn stop? It's so damn dark I can't tell."

"Try braille."

He moved his hand. "Tell me if it hurts," he said.

It didn't.

Beatrice lay on one side of the king-size bed. The glass doors to the bedroom terrace were open because no matter how low she set the air-conditioning, it still turned the apartment arctic, and the crickets were sending up an awful racket. Sometimes she went for nights without hearing them, but once she noticed them, the sound became deafening.

She turned on her side. It didn't help. She ought to think

about having the cleaning woman turn the mattress. Ever since Sam had died, she'd clung to one side of the bed, as if she'd get lost if she ventured out into the center. Was this the way Susannah had felt?

Beatrice fought back the thought. It was no good thinking about Susannah in the middle of the night. Her mind switched to Nora. Beatrice had commented on the extra glass of wine and her daughter had asked how else you got to sleep. Beatrice had almost told her. She thought of Addie's son. He was a nice boy. She thought of that man, that Tony, who'd dragged on for years. Niceness wasn't likely to recommend Max Miller to Nora.

She forced herself to move toward the center of the bed, this vast wasteland of her old age. How had she got here? All those years, certainly, but all those years weren't so long ago. Sometimes they came back in flashes so intense that she felt if she only made a little effort, she could walk right back into them. At those moments she saw the glistening blue linoleum of the kitchen and felt the curve of the metal cabinet handles as she opened and closed the doors, taking out the yellow Fiesta dishes that had suddenly become collector's items. At those moments, she'd see Susannah and Nora sitting across from each other at the kitchen table, sometimes in cotton dresses with their small oxfords swinging a couple of inches above the floor, sometimes in woolen skirts and twin sweater sets and loafers with pennies stuck in the front, their heads bent over books, their soft hands smudged with ink. Then she'd hear the sound of a door closing. Sometimes it was the faint rattling of the windows on the side door because Phil always left his car in the garage and came in the side door calling her name. "Beatrice" would ring down the years like a carillon calling her back. Sometimes it was the more solid sound of the front door closing, because Sam always walked from the train station and came up the front path. "I'm home," he'd call, or, when the girls were still teenagers, "Is anybody home?" She'd see Phil in one of his dark, double-breasted suits coming into the kitchen through the breakfast nook because that entrance was closer to the side door, and Sam coming in from the front hall smoothing his thinning hair because he'd just hung up his hat and coat, and she'd know what it was to be literally heartsore.

The dull throbbing was worse than the pain from her arthritis. That was old age. Choosing between ailments, between the ache of muscle and tendon and bone and the curse of memory.

Only she didn't feel old. Inside, beneath the flesh that wrinkled under pressure and the joints that refused to perform, she didn't feel very different from the young wife and mother who moved through the landscape of her past, even from the girl she used to be before that. The other day when Charlie had said her new bathing suit was becoming, and there'd been admiration in his voice and something close to awe in his face, she'd walked around singing all afternoon. She'd thought age was supposed to make you immune to all that. It was supposed to dull the quickening excitement that came, like electricity, from a proper connection. It was supposed to bring peace and self-containment. Only it hadn't. Sometimes Beatrice felt as if she were still waiting to find out what it was like to grow up. Maybe that was the secret, the terrible bad joke. You grew old without ever having grown up.

Nora opened the apartment door gently and closed it softly. The surreptitiousness took her back. Years of creeping up the stairs after dates, months of sneaking into the guest room where Paul spent the night when he stayed over, stifled giggles, muffled moans.

It was hard to believe that after all these years she was still trying to spare Beatrice's feelings. But these were different feelings. Once Beatrice had wanted to protect Nora. Nice girls don't go too far. Nice girls don't go all the way. But Nora had known differently. Still, she'd been careful to protect Beatrice, or maybe she'd only been protecting herself. But now she wanted to protect Beatrice not from the knowledge that her daughter wasn't, after all, a nice girl, but from the reminder that Beatrice was a lonely old woman. It would be unnecessarily cruel to come crashing into the silent, bleached apartment, vibrating with the hum of recent sex.

4

When Nora was in her mid-twenties and struggling out of her marriage, she, like everyone else she knew, went to a psychiatrist. He asked her to tell him about herself. She mentioned her decaying marriage, her mother, her sister, and her stepfather. "My father died when I was seven," she added at the end. "But it didn't affect my life at all."

What she'd meant, she decided two years later when she left treatment with a supposedly heightened self-awareness, was that she hadn't had an unhappy childhood. Beatrice saw to that. So did Phil's admirable foresight. Beatrice didn't have to go to work. She could afford to devote herself entirely to her two daughters. The French-speaking Mary was replaced by a woman who came in to clean two days a week.

There were some terrifying months, perhaps the best part of a year. Nora, who'd always come home to that solid Harding-Coolidge Tudor as if to asylum, suddenly found reasons to hang around the playground or other kids' houses. Anything was better than walking in and finding Beatrice sitting at the kitchen table or on the edge of her bed with tears streaming silently down her cheeks. To Nora those thin watery streaks were torrents of responsibility. She shrank from them guiltily.

Then, one day Beatrice returned to the beauty parlor,

and after that on Thursday afternoons Nora came home to a familiar woman with shiny red nails that Nora admired inordinately and hair that curved like a question mark over one cheek.

Uncle Lewis's possessions gradually evaporated from the house. He married and had a little girl whom he named Phyllis after Nora's father. Nora hated the baby, but then Uncle Lewis went to practice in California, and by the time Nora saw Phyllis again, she'd forgot that she hated the little girl.

Nora finally got over the allergy that disfigured her forearms and the back of her knees and even, occasionally, her face for the year after Phil died. Beatrice took her to several doctors, but none ever figured out what Nora was allergic to. Eventually the angry red rashes just began to fade.

That spring Nora won first prize in the school flower show, thanks to Susannah. They were in the backyard choosing roses for the event. Both girls wanted red. Red roses always won. Halfway up the trellis a perfect flower spread its wine-colored petals. Susannah and Nora spotted it at the same time. Then Nora's eye wandered to the bud above it. It was red, too, and wrapped tight as a baby in bunting. The flower show wasn't until the following day. Nora knew about the transitory nature of life. She asked Susannah which rose she wanted and held her breath. Susannah chose the wine velvet one that hung heavy on the trellis. Nora could barely keep from jumping up and down as she cut the tight bunting-baby bud.

The next day Nora came home from school hugging the white satin ribbon that said First Prize and her own cleverness. By the time she found out Susannah had been just as clever but more generous, Susannah had a child of her own and Nora was working at *American Homemaker*.

"But if you knew the bud was going to open the next day, why didn't you take it?" Nora asked.

"Because you were my baby sister," Susannah answered. "Besides, the prize meant more to you."

The house couldn't have been sad, because by the time Susannah was in high school, it was always filled with girls, and kids don't gravitate to sadness. They gravitated to Beatrice.

They came because Beatrice was there and because—though Nora didn't realize this until much later—Phil was not.

Susannah's friends liked Beatrice. A few years later, Nora's friends liked Beatrice so much they occasionally hung around with her downstairs while Nora was upstairs doing her homework. Nora was the only girl she knew whose mother never told her to do her homework. Even Susannah couldn't claim that distinction.

Unlike other mothers, Beatrice didn't stretch invisible ropes across the various rooms of the house but let them sprawl as they wanted. In the winter the kitchen was always full of homemade apple pies and store-bought jelly rolls; in the summer the refrigerator overflowed with already washed fruit just begging to be eaten.

But Susannah's and Nora's friends liked Beatrice most of all because she was an authority on the two topics of consuming interest. Beatrice loved clothes. And she knew men, or at least how to get them. All the girls knew the story of those four fraternity pins.

For a while, the safe house turned into a sorority house. No man lived there, but the aura of men permeated every room. The air they breathed was thick with the fumes of romance.

Beatrice was a widow, but she kept her hand in. More than one of Susannah's friends turned to her for advice. Susannah herself needed no help, not with that silky blond hair that fell in the kind of curve other girls slept on rollers for and that classic oval face and that willowy but ripe body. Susannah was a natural, in the way she looked, and the way she treated men. She never worried about hurting their feelings or wounding their vanity or dashing their hopes, at least until Nick Demopoulis, but that came later. Susannah didn't give a damn about men, and they loved her for it.

Billy Blinkman, aka Blinker, later poor Blinker, loved her more than all the others, even Nick Demopoulis. Blinker appeared on the scene the autumn that Susannah turned sixteen and he entered Harvard, and didn't leave until he was in law school and Susannah was engaged to Nick Demopoulis. The last time Nora saw poor Blinker was at the engagement party.

He wasn't around consistently for all those years. Susannah dropped him at regular intervals. Occasionally, he disappeared for weeks or months at a time in desperation or despair. The longest hiatus was from mid-October through Christmas of one year. It was intended to bring Susannah to her senses, but poor Blinker hedged his bets by snaring Susannah for New Year's Eve before he disappeared. Susannah and Beatrice had a good laugh at that. Sometimes they laughed at his letters too, though Nora thought they were well written, and once or twice Beatrice listened in on the extension when he called from Cambridge. It never occurred to anyone, not even Nora till years later, that poor besotted Blinker wasn't community property. There wasn't much, including Nora's first real kiss, that wasn't community property in that household.

When Nora got her first love letter from a precocious adolescent known as Six-Eyes—his glasses were that thick —she refused to show it to Beatrice or Susannah. Dinner that night was a riotous affair. Beatrice and Susannah egged each other on, quoting imagined passages from the letter. As the veterans of so many letters of their own, they wanted to know what could be so special in Nora's that it had to be kept secret. Sam told them to leave Nora alone, but he was laughing when he said it. Finally, twenty-four hours later, after a second scathing dinner, Nora turned over the evidence. She had to admit that once Beatrice and Susannah had it in hand, they treated it with respect, and, Nora had the feeling, relief.

Gradually Nora learned to stand her ground. When her acceptance came from Smith, Beatrice followed directions and did no more than weigh the envelope speculatively until Nora called from school and gave her permission to open it. Of course, the letter was only from a college. That night Sam was the one who made the fuss at dinner.

Sam wasn't the first man to come along in the wake of Phil's death. After a suitable period of mourning, relatives

and friends set about turning up eligible men. Beatrice was
still, as everyone said, a young woman. Nora heard them
say it, but didn't believe it, any more than she believed that
Beatrice was beautiful. Beatrice was her mother. She was
also forty-one.

It was funny watching your mother go out on dates. For a
while there it was like having two older sisters. Nora didn't
exactly feel left out. There was plenty for her to do, what
with Merry Widows to hook and backs to powder and neck-
laces and bracelets to fasten. It wasn't so much being left
out as left behind. But Nora was catching up fast.

One Christmas Beatrice took them on a Caribbean
cruise. When they sailed at midnight, the small cabin on
the *Nieuw Amsterdam* was crowded with baskets of fruit
and flowers. Beatrice and Susannah went to sleep in the
lower berths, Nora in the upper. It took them the better
part of the next morning to unpack. They used the extra
upper berth to store shorts and sweaters and handbags.
They couldn't close the closet doors. Dresses and crinolines
burst out of them like rowdy celebrants. Dyed-to-match
pumps, sexy sandals, and sensible flat walking shoes
marched down the narrow hall leading to the cabin door.

In the morning the steward brought them breakfast
trays, and they sat in their bunks and giggled about the
night before. Susannah was breaking the heart of the son of the
dairy king of Westchester. Beatrice courted danger by
dancing with a man from their dining table after his wife
went to bed. Nora took a walk on the upper deck with the
junior shuffleboard champion, and he held her hand.

They shopped in St. Thomas and swam behind a barra-
cuda net in Grenada and had Cokes in Harry's Bar in Havana. When Susannah and the dairy prince went ashore
again that night, a Cuban stopped them on the street and
asked if they wanted a room. Beatrice was shocked, but
Susannah told her she could take care of herself, and by the
time the ship turned north, even Beatrice was laughing
about the incident.

When they came through customs on the way home, the
inspector thought they were sisters. As they stood on the
damp pier with the bleak January afternoon closing in

around them, he teased them about the three watches they'd bought, and the three gold bracelets, and the three pairs of earrings, though Nora's ears weren't pierced yet.

A few months later Sam Brickner turned up. He was Uncle Lewis's wife's cousin and came with Uncle Lewis's highest recommendation. He called to ask Beatrice to dinner, and they talked for a long time, considering they'd never met. After that, Beatrice walked around smiling until Saturday came.

When Sam rang the bell, Nora went downstairs to open the door. Even when Beatrice and Susannah were ready, they liked to send Nora down to answer the door.

She neither liked nor disliked Sam that night. It wasn't like poor Blinker, who, if he had any sense, would be crazy in love with Nora, who appreciated him. Sam was just another man who had too much forehead showing through too little hair and a lot of questions about how old she was and what grade she was in and all that other stuff they thought they were supposed to ask. The only thing she could say for Sam one way or another was that he wanted to know what kind of movies she liked. He told her he was crazy about British films. He called them films, not movies.

Nora said she'd never seen one. She didn't add that her mother would as soon go to an English movie as buy a dress made in Taiwan, and Sam never found out. By the time they married, Beatrice had become an Alec Guinness fan. She insisted she loved his movies—except for *The Captain's Paradise*. She didn't even smile at that one.

Sam began to show up every Saturday night, and then on other nights as well. The first time he came for dinner Beatrice had the cleaning woman stay to serve. He brought flowers for Beatrice, a book on British film for Nora, and the latest Frank Sinatra LP for Susannah. She said thanks for the record but not much else during dinner.

That Christmas Sam took Nora into New York to see *The Nutcracker*. He invited Susannah too, but she said she was too old. Nora supposed she was too, but she was flattered by the invitation. Sam had no children of his own, though he'd been married. Nora thought that was strange. All the married people she knew had children. Sam's wife had died young, just like Nora's father.

Beatrice told her daughters a few days later.

Nora and her mother were sitting at the small table with the leatherette benches in what Beatrice called the breakfast nook, when Susannah came down that morning. It was still Christmas vacation, and they were all in their robes. Susannah poured a cup of coffee from the percolator on the stove and carried it to the table. She'd just started drinking coffee, and Nora noticed that she always grimaced after the first sip.

There was an apple pie, Beatrice's favorite weekend and holiday breakfast, on the table, and Susannah broke off small pieces of crust with her fingers and chewed them thoughtfully as Beatrice debriefed her on the previous night. Poor Blinker was in disfavor again, and Susannah had gone to a party with one of his friends. Blinker's date had been wearing what had to be the ugliest dress known to womankind. Susannah described it in detail. And she had piano legs.

Nora was crushed. Wake up, Blinker! She wouldn't have worn an iridescent violet dress, and she didn't have piano legs.

Nora had already stood and carried her empty milk glass and plate to the sink, when Beatrice told her to come sit down again. "I have something to tell you," she said.

Nora knew what it was right off. You didn't have to get straight A's to put together Beatrice's funny little smile and *The Nutcracker* and the fact that marriage was a constant topic of conversation in that house.

"Sam and I are going to get married," Beatrice said.

Until then Nora hadn't known you could feel scared and pleased at exactly the same time.

Beatrice went on talking. They weren't going to move. Sam would sell his house, which was smaller, and come live with them. Nothing was going to change, except now there'd be a man around the house again.

"I'm not going to call him Dad," Susannah said. It was the first thing she'd said since Beatrice had told them.

"I'm sure he doesn't expect you to," Beatrice answered quickly.

"He's not as tall as Daddy," Susannah said.

"He's not Daddy," Beatrice answered, "but he's a very nice man."

"Just as long as he doesn't expect to take Daddy's place."

Beatrice reached across the table then and put one hand with its perfect red fingertips on each daughter's arm. "You have to remember one thing," she said. "No one comes before the two of you." Her dark eyes moved from one to the other of them. "Men come and go, but there'll always be the three of us."

Sam came for dinner that night. Susannah and Nora were in the dining room setting the table when he arrived. "Did you tell them?" they heard him ask Beatrice while he was still in the vestibule taking off his galoshes. Though he couldn't see into the dining room, his voice carried there. Beatrice told him everything was fine. "I've never been called Dad before," he said. Then he came into the front hall and closed the door behind him.

Susannah put down the knives and forks and went into the hall. She walked right up to Sam, who was holding his hat in one hand, and kissed him on the cheek.

"Congratulations," she said. "I'm going to call you Sam. Okay?"

Nora didn't make any announcements. Three weeks later her mother and Sam were married in a rabbi's study. After Beatrice and Sam kissed each other—chastely, Nora thought—they each kissed Susannah and Nora.

"Congratulations, Dad." Nora put the emphasis on the last word, so it came out as a kind of joke, and Sam laughed and said thanks.

5

*B*eatrice and Addie Miller had made all the arrangements before Nora was even up that morning. By the time she came out onto the terrace off the kitchen, her mother was sitting at the white wrought-iron-and-glass table with her second cup of coffee, making lists. The table was set for two, two plates, two mugs, two precisely folded paper napkins, each weighted down by a fork to keep the breeze from carrying it off. There were two kinds of jam, too, each in a crystal jar with its own small spoon.

Beatrice was wearing a white eyelet robe. A smudge of white talcum powder stood out against her tan chest. She was humming as she wrote. "I have to go to the market this morning," she said when Nora sat across from her. "We're having people in for drinks. Then Addie's son is taking us to the club for dinner."

"Why don't you just lock me in the linen closet with him? It would be more subtle," Nora said on her way back inside to answer the kitchen phone.

It was Lucy. Apparently the magazine wouldn't run all that smoothly in the event of Nora's keeling forward over her desk. There was a problem with a piece by a celebrated graduate of the Betty Ford Center. "She can't write it," Lucy said.

"Of course, she can't write it," Nora answered. "Why do

you think God created free-lance writers and junior editors?"

"I mean she can't put her name on it. She's on the sauce again."

Nora cursed, then told Lucy to move up the article on women in medicine. She was about to hang up when Lucy remembered one more thing.

"*CompuAge*'s crisis is our deliverance. At least temporarily. Wheeler had to go to Japan."

Will Wheeler had a whole new line on demos. He didn't give a damn that the population as a whole was getting older. All he knew was that brand-name consumers were getting younger. He worshipped the sixteen-year-old high-school kid with a part-time job who lived at home and could spend upwards of a hundred dollars a week on CD's, designer jeans, and acne medications. He was almost as smitten with the young mother who divided the family budget between disposable diapers and microwave dinners. His latest love affair was with the Japanese. Wheeler knew that Japanese women and children had no power, but Japanese venture capitalists and architects and PC users had a yen, millions of them, for information. In the past five years, Will Wheeler had cut a swath through Japanese culture that would have turned MacArthur green with envy.

For once, Nora was grateful for the obsession. It was unnerving to think of Lucy sitting in her place at a meeting with Wheeler. Nora wasn't afraid Lucy would usurp her job, only blow it.

Nora went back out on the terrace and asked her mother whether she had time for a swim before breakfast.

"The Winn Dixie isn't going anywhere," Beatrice said.

Max Miller was doing laps when Nora got down to the pool. He didn't stop when he saw her. They swam in opposite directions for a while. Even if she could have put her ear in the water, her form wouldn't have been as good as his. When he finished, she did two more lengths before she stopped.

They stood talking in the chest-high water. His long brown arms and legs wavered against the blue pool paint.

"Did they ask you about this little dinner party or just spring it on you?" she said.

"It was my idea."

"I think the sun is beginning to get to you."

"Nope. It's all very logical. My mother's a good woman. She was in labor with me for sixteen hours. She wouldn't wish such pain on her worst enemy. Since then she hasn't drawn an easy breath worrying that something might happen to me. All she's ever wanted is my happiness. If you don't believe me, ask her. She's a good woman. That's why I want you to have dinner with her. Because I've had a lot of good woman in the last few days, and I want to share the wealth. Besides"—he looked around to make sure no one had come into the pool area while they were swimming, then hooked a finger in the front of her bathing suit and ran it back and forth over her skin—"I've got a charley horse in my leg from that damn compact car."

"Are you planning on something in the club?"

"I thought it might be nice to have dinner with you. It'll make me happy. It'll make my mother happy. It'll make your mother happy. It's even going to make Charlie Saperstein happy."

"God! Is he coming too?"

"Male bonding. Besides, he's crazy about your mother."

"She can't stand him. She calls him the Sap."

Max shrugged. The water licked at his chest. "All I know is that they decided to invite him."

She started out of the pool. "Aw, shucks. The party of the century and I don't have a thing to wear."

"Just your diaphragm's enough for me," he called after her.

She figured only the front half of the 1200 Building had heard him.

Beatrice and Nora locked the car and crossed the hot pavement into the arctic supermarket air. Nora wished she'd listened to her mother and brought a sweater. She got a cart and followed Beatrice up the first aisle.

Her mother was a methodical shopper. They worked their way up and down all the aisles except the automotive one. Beatrice loaded the cart with three jars of mixed nuts, five different kinds of crackers, and enough club soda and tonic and bitter lemon to fill half the pools of Palmetto Estates.

"Just how many are you expecting?" Nora asked.

In the fish department, Beatrice and the man behind the counter debated how many pounds of shrimp five adults required to stave off starvation till dinner was served. The man gave her an estimate. Beatrice doubled it. The cheese department took even longer. Chèvre had hit south Florida with a vengeance, but Boursin and Brie were still holding their own.

"Let my daughter taste," Beatrice said as the clerk held the samples out to them. "She knows gourmet food. She's the publisher of *AH!*"

"I don't think the cheese man gives a damn where I work," Nora murmured, but she knew she'd signaled approval as if she were giving the royal nod.

By the time they got to the checkout counter the shopping cart was half full. Nora eased it into line behind a spindly woman with white hair and a back curved into a tragic osteoporotic arch. She'd put her groceries—a pint of milk, two bananas, a container of cottage cheese, and a jar of instant coffee—on the baby seat on the top of her cart.

As they waited for the line to move, Nora looked around at the carts on either side of her. In the next aisle a man transferred three frozen dinners and a container of ice cream from the baby seat to the counter with palsied fingers. Behind him a woman whose white hair, cotton dress, and low-heeled sandals were as impeccable as Beatrice's stood with a straight back. A single Styrofoam-and-plastic-wrapped chicken breast, a melon, and a bag of peaches sat on her baby seat. The selection wasn't so different from what Nora might buy at home. Nora looked up from the groceries and saw that the woman was staring at their cart. Not at Beatrice or Nora, but at their cart. There was a terrible longing in her face.

Without realizing what she was doing, Nora took her mother's hand. Beatrice, who'd been studying the groceries of the young mother ahead of them, turned and smiled.

* * *

Beatrice had put the cheese and crackers and nuts and little linen napkins with embroidered roosters around the living room by five. In the refrigerator the shrimp lay curled on a crystal platter. Nora opened the door to get the lemons and limes, and the silver bowl of blood-red cocktail sauce at their center trembled like a beating heart.

When everything was ready except the two of them, Nora went out on the terrace, sat in one of the white plastic upholstered chairs with her feet propped on the railing, and opened the latest trend report. According to one life-style analyst, the current demographic darling was a thirty-five-year-old woman, married to a man two years younger. She had been a corporate executive, but now she was planning to start her own business so she could stay home and raise the child she was about to conceive. Wheeler swore by trend reports. Nora didn't trust them. They always made her feel out of sync.

Beatrice came out on the terrace. "Don't you think you ought to shower?"

Nora looked at her watch. "You said they're not coming till six." The only time Nora ever had a drink at six was at magazine-related parties. Only those without a full work-load or with a flagrant disregard for their own livers would begin drinking at six, but then this wasn't exactly a drinking crowd.

"If you shower now, you can take your time. You're always rushing at the last minute."

"Sam used to say you could savor getting dressed the way a gourmet could a four-star meal."

They slipped back into the old tug-of-war so easily, as if neither of them dared drop the line because the other might keep pulling and topple over.

"I just want to look some things over." Nora went back to the trend report. "I won't be late. I promise."

Beatrice didn't exactly sigh, but as she left the terrace, the air trembled as if she had.

Nora wasn't late, but she came close. She was brushing her hair, which she'd just decided could no longer be de-

scribed as strawberry blond—prune would be the analo-
gous fruit these days—when the doorbell rang.

She was surprised. In her experience, when you asked
people for six, they didn't usually arrive with the prompt-
ness of the evening news, but Beatrice was ready for them.
She'd been ready for twenty minutes, and not because she
took her preparations lightly. Beneath the carefully tai-
lored linen dress with the tiny mother-of-pearl decorative
buttons running down the front, there were bras and girdles and stockings and slips to worry about. Her makeup
and jewelry required the care of the exquisitely understated. Her Italian pumps were neatly heeled and beautifully shined. Beatrice had a theory about shoes. If they
were well made and properly polished, you could get away
with anything, though as far as Nora knew, her mother
hadn't tried to get away with anything since those four
fraternity pins.

"Lovely, lovely." The Sap's voice boomed across the living room and down the hall into the guest bedroom. "You
look just lovely, Bea.

"Doesn't your mother look lovely?" the Sap asked as
Nora came into the room. The golf clubs on his yellow tie
matched his blazer, which was the color of strawberry dai-
quiris. He was wearing his white shoes again, and he obviously subscribed to her mother's theory, at least the properly polished part. As he crossed the room, a trail of chalky
white flakes disappeared into Beatrice's white rug.

"You're a pretty girl, Nora, but your mother . . . I tell
you. I seen three women in my life I'd call beautiful. I'm
not talking pretty now, I'm talking beautiful. Gene Tierney, my late wife, she should rest in peace, and your
mama."

He'd managed to move to the bar while he talked, and
now he began taking glasses down from the shelves and
filling them with ice.

"Can I make you ladies a drink? Beautiful, your mother
is, but she doesn't know from mixing drinks. I like that in a
lady. Apricot sour, Bea?" He didn't wait for an answer, but
started pouring sweet sticky things into a cocktail shaker.
"Now I'm a real mixologist. Name your poison, Nora. Whis-

key sour? Daiquiri? How bout a piña colada?" The *y* sound
in his "piña" reverberated like a guitar. "I make the best
peen-ya colada in Palmetto Estates. Correct me if I'm
wrong, Bea."

"Charlie makes a very good piña colada," Beatrice said,
and Nora didn't dare look at her mother, because she knew
the fine aquiline nose would be twitching with suppressed
laughter. When Nora finally allowed herself to glance at
Beatrice, she'd obviously got herself under control. She
was merely smiling at the Sap.

"I'll have a gin and tonic," Nora said. She watched the
mixologist pour a whisper of gin into a tall glass and fill it
with tonic. Then the doorbell rang again, and while her
mother and the Sap went to answer it, Nora poured out a
third of the drink and filled it with gin.

Addie had brought a plastic container of chopped liver
from the deli that made it almost as good as her own, in
case there wasn't enough food. Beatrice thanked her. The
Sap was taking drink orders again.

They were all talking at once now. Addie Miller, whose
soft accordion-pleated cleavage rose and fell in excitement, was warning that she didn't want her drink too
strong, because everyone knew what happened to her with
a strong drink. The Sap was arguing that no one ever got
drunk on his drinks. Addie's son was saying it was a nice
apartment and didn't it have a different exposure from
Addie's. Beatrice said it did and hadn't Max got a nice tan
in the short time he'd been down there.

"Poor Nora got a terrible burn the first day," Beatrice
said.

Max smiled at Nora over her mother's head. His teeth
were improbably white against his dark face, which was
completely unlined. He seemed to be getting younger
each day they were there. In his blue blazer and khakis he
looked like a goddamn undergraduate.

"Was it painful?" he asked Nora. "The sunburn, I mean."

"You should be more careful," Addie said. "All the time I
used to spend in the sun." She shook her head in regret. "If
I knew then what I know now about wrinkles."

Nora took the ice bucket into the kitchen to refill it.

Beatrice followed to get the confectioners sugar which the Sap called after her that she always forgot.

"It's nice to hear men's voices again," she whispered to Nora as they passed in the kitchen.

Nora suspected they didn't have to invite the Sap up to hear his voice. It probably carried from his apartment two floors below, but she didn't say anything. Besides, Max's voice was pitched to a lower key. And Beatrice's voice was the best of all. It had an excited catch in it that Nora seemed to remember from another time.

When Nora came back from the kitchen, they were all standing around the library table looking at the silver- and pewter- and brass-framed photographs. There was a formal wedding portrait of Beatrice and Phil, and a more informal wedding picture of Beatrice and Sam. There was an engagement portrait of Susannah, a snapshot of an infant Cornelia on a beach blanket flanked by Susannah and Nick, and another of a seventeen-year-old Cornelia in a cap and gown with Beatrice on one side and Nora on the other. There was a photograph of Nora that had appeared in the advertising column of the *New York Times* when she'd been made editor-in-chief and another formal portrait of an eleven-year-old Susannah and a seven-year-old Nora sitting on an ottoman in the living room of the old house on Byron Road. Many of the pictures were the same as those Nora kept on her own library table in New York, and several were different, but the strangest one, at least to Nora, was a snapshot that was neither identical to the one in her apartment nor entirely different from it. Both, if she remembered correctly, had been taken on the same afternoon at the beach house Beatrice and Sam had sold years ago, but they had been taken from different perspectives. In this picture, Beatrice and Sam and Susannah and Nick all stood with their arms around each other, while Nora sat on the grass with a baby Cornelia on her shoulders. They were all grinning blindly into the camera as if it were the sun. The only one missing was Nora's husband, Paul, but someone had to take the picture. The photograph on Nora's table in New York was more candid. In it Beatrice and Susannah were sitting side by side in canvas chairs, their heads tilted toward each other, framing a triangle of sunlight that shone on Cornelia, who was playing on the deck between them. A little distance away, Sam reclined on a chaise reading the newspaper. Nora was on a chaise next to him, her face almost hidden by huge sunglasses. She was reading a magazine, but there was a pencil in her hand. Behind them Nick stood with his back to the group gazing off toward the water.

Max picked up a silver-framed snapshot. In it Beatrice, Susannah, and Nora stood in one-piece Lastex bathing suits on the sun deck of the *Nieuw Amsterdam,* their arms twined around each other like plants that have become tangled in their common growth. "Your sister?" Max asked.

"I don't look anything like her," Nora said.

Max went on staring at the picture. "There's a family resemblance. Among all three of you. The high forehead." He dropped his voice. "And the body."

Nora decided he must be kidding. Either that or blind. The narrow hips were the same, and the legs, but in the bra department Susannah had been a four-letter woman while Nora had never even made varsity. In the old days it had killed Nora—witness the boned bathing suit that made her look as if she were wearing twin ice cream cones strapped to her chest—but somewhere along the way style had caught up with her. Or maybe she'd evolved with the style.

They settled into the white upholstery in the living room. Beatrice urged food on them. The Sap obliged. He ate the shrimp carefully, leaning over the coffee table and holding a napkin under each piece as he carried it to his mouth. The food slowed down his conversation, but not by much.

"Addie tells me you're a train buff," he said to Max.

"Did you notice his tie?" Addie asked.

They all concentrated on Max's tie. It was an ordinary club silk, red with small gold P.R.R. keystones on it.

"Me," the Sap went on, "I'm into stars."

"You mean like *People* magazine?" Nora asked.

"Astronomy," Beatrice said.

"I got a telescope on my terrace. Guess how much power I got in that thing." He paused for Nora to guess.

"I couldn't imagine."

"How much?" Max asked.

"Two hundred and fifty. That's what it magnifies. I paid a pretty penny for that scope, I can tell you. But it's not the scope. Forget the scope. Forget the money. It's the stars. I go out on my terrace,and I look up at all those stars, and I think the light I'm seeing is from millions and billions of years ago. I'm standing here today, but I'm looking at something that was sent out before man. Before he ever climbed up out of the water, like Mr. Darwin said. And I say to myself, Charlie Saperstein, what're you doing worrying about par on the ninth hole or what the market did today? What does it matter? What do you matter? You're nothing. *Nada. Gornish.* Not even a blink in the eye of the universe. I tell you, it makes you think."

He looked around the room from one to the other of them and smiled as if he was suddenly embarrassed. Nora noticed something then that she'd been too busy looking at his white shoes and constantly moving mouth to see before. The Sap had the soft, sad eyes of an ASPCA mongrel who's had some rough times.

"Ach! I'm getting morbid. Here I am with all these lovely ladies"—he winked at Max, and suddenly the sad, soft look was gone—"and I'm shooting off my mouth about light-years and telescopes. Who needs a drink? Charlie Saperstein, mixologist first class, at your service."

They walked across the golf course to the club, the Sap in front with one hand on Beatrice's elbow and the other on Addie's, Max and Nora behind with several respectable inches of night between them.

"If there were any truth in packaging," Nora said, "that man would be labeled 'hazardous to your health.' "

"He's just nervous," Max said.

"That's what everyone keeps telling me. What's he so nervous about?"

"You, for one thing."

"Me?"

"He wants Beatrice's daughter to like him."

"Beatrice doesn't even like him."

Max shrugged. "All I know is if the poor guy doesn't calm down soon, he's not going to have any hands left."

"What do you mean?"

"Didn't you notice his fingernails, or at least what's left of them?"

Nora, who liked to think of herself as observant, hadn't noticed the Sap's hands at all. Probably because she was too busy looking at Max's.

He put his hand on her shoulder. "I have to leave early tomorrow. Really early. And I want to turn the car in with a full tank, so I ought to fill it up tonight. Want to go for a ride after dinner?"

"It takes approximately ten minutes to fill up a gas tank."

He moved his hand over her shoulder to the back of her neck. It was as if she were sunburned all over again. "Not when all the gas stations are closed. Besides, the tank's already full."

"You're very good at this."

"If that's a question, the answer is no, I did not screw around while I was married."

"Funny," Nora said. "I did."

Immediately after dinner Addie hightailed it to the card room for her regular Monday night bridge game. Not even her tall, handsome, six-figure-a-year son could interfere with that. A little later Beatrice, who was not a card player, said she thought she'd call it a night. The Sap said he'd walk her home across the golf course.

"You two stay," Beatrice said to Nora and Max.

"Sure, have a nightcap," the Sap added. "Maybe a little B and B. Or some Amaretto."

Max started to explain about filling up the tank of the rented car, but no one was interested, no one, that is, except Nora.

Beatrice drifted out into the thick Florida night on the arm of the Sap, who was saying something about Orion's Belt. Nora and Max were just about to follow when Mrs. Gold caught up with them. It wasn't anything to be alarmed about, but Addie wasn't feeling well. Nothing, really, just a little heartburn.

Max sprinted into the card room. The other women at the table sprang into action. On his way out of the card room, Max told Nora he'd be right back with the car. Nora told him not to worry about her. She didn't add that she had nothing against the back seat of Max's rented car, except when the front seat was weighed down by his responsibilities.

Out on the golf course, Nora tried to pick out Orion's Belt. The best she could do was the Big Dipper. The lights of the apartments glowed brighter than the stars. Behind gauzy curtains and Levolors, an occasional single shadow moved. Through open terrace doors Nora picked up snatches of conversation. They were followed by laugh tracks. From one apartment far overhead, the strains of Glenn Miller floated like a plaintive cry through the thick night.

Nora used her mother's extra key to let herself in. Cold air smacked her in the face. The lobby smelled of antiseptic. She pressed the elevator button. The door opened immediately. Unlike her apartment building in New York, there was no waiting. She rode to five.

The hall was silent. Not even laugh tracks filtered through the closed apartment doors. Nora walked to the end of the hall. There was no sound from her mother's apartment. Beatrice was probably watching the news in her bedroom. Nora let herself in quietly on the off chance that her mother was asleep.

When Nora thought about it later, it was like an old silent-movie comedy routine, but at that moment there was nothing funny about the scene.

Beatrice and the Sap sprang apart. He managed to hit his shin on the coffee table in the process and he was holding his leg and grimacing. Beatrice jumped up from the sofa. Her face was almost as gray as her hair, and her dress— Oh, my God, Nora thought. The buttons down the front of her dress weren't just decorative.

Her mother was buttoning furiously. The Sap was no longer grimacing. He looked as if he was going to cry.

"I'm sorry," Nora said and kept walking, through the living room, down the hall, and into the guest bedroom.

She closed the door behind her and stood in the center of the dark room. She didn't know whether to laugh or cry. She realized suddenly she was trembling.

She heard whispers in the living room, then the sound of the front door closing. A moment later there was a knock. Beatrice came in. She switched on the light. They blinked at each other.

"At least someone in the family knows enough to knock," Nora said. "I'm sorry."

Beatrice stood in the doorway staring at her daughter. "You're shocked."

"Of course not," Nora lied.

"Look at your face. It's like the time after Daddy died when you had that awful rash."

"I'm not shocked," Nora insisted.

"You are," Beatrice said, "but the question is whether you're shocked because it's Charlie or because I'm an old lady."

Nora didn't tell her mother it wasn't an either/or situation.

6

*D*espite four fraternity pins and two marriages, Beatrice was not a worldly woman. Especially about sex. She knew, to paraphrase Cole Porter, that movie stars and café society and Aly Khan did it out of wedlock. Other people, people within Beatrice's immediate experience, waited till they settled down. Then, well, they settled down.

Given that particular world view, Beatrice's reaction to Susannah and Nick was admirable, perhaps even astonishing. Years later, when friends complained about their mothers, Nora always cited that incident with Susannah as proof of Beatrice's breadth as a woman and depth as a mother. Beatrice could be, when she wanted to, really something.

Susannah met Nick Demopoulis on the day after Christmas. The occasion was commemorated in her date book. Susannah kept a date book. Nora kept a diary.

Every December Susannah would pick up one of those little books Hallmark gave out free to those who cared enough. Her use of it was unorthodox. She kept a record not only of dates she made, but of those she refused. The entries were color-coded. Acceptances were written in black, rejections in red. Susannah's date book ran red as a broken heart. At least half the red entries mentioned poor Blinker. Years later, when Nora saw Billy Blinkman's name on the front page of the financial section of the *New York Times,* she still thought of him as poor Blinker. But on December 26 poor Blinker's name was in black. Susannah had agreed to let him take her to a party. She went to the party with Blinker. She even came home with Blinker. Susannah always played by the rules. But the phone rang five minutes after Susannah got rid of poor Blinker. At least, that was the way she told the story the following morning. No one had heard it ring, despite the fact that there was an extension on the night table on Beatrice's side of the bed. Susannah had been sitting in the sun porch with her hand hovering over the phone waiting for it to ring. She must have picked it up on the first vibration.

She and Nick talked for close to an hour that night. By the time Susannah came upstairs, her Kissing Pink lipstick was eaten away and her silky blond hair raked through with finger marks. Susannah usually came up from dates almost as pristine as she went down to them. Nick had got farther over the phone than poor Blinker and a couple of dozen others ever had in person.

The next night when he came to pick up Susannah, Nora knew why. Nick Demopoulis looked like an ad for retsina or a week on Mykonos. His lashes cast spiky shadows over his high cheekbones. His eyes were what were known at the time as bedroom. His smile was slow and premeditated as a striptease. Beneath the obligatory gray flannel and oxford cloth and herringbone, he had the body of—not to put too fine a point on it—a Greek god.

As Nick stood in the front hall waiting for Susannah, who'd been ready for ten minutes, he shook hands with Sam firmly and called him sir, admitted to Beatrice that he was in his last year of medical school, and turned Nora weak with pleasure when he pretended to think she was in college too.

Nick was a smart boy. He did all the right things. But the best thing he did, at least as far as Beatrice was concerned, was unintentional. When Susannah finally came down the stairs that night, Nick's face lit up like a hundred-watt bulb. He couldn't have dimmed it if he'd tried.

"Demopoulis," Sam said after Nick and Susannah left.

"Greek." It was an observation rather than a complaint. Susannah had said she wouldn't call him Dad, and he'd never tried to be one to her.

Beatrice followed her husband into the sun porch. "Only half. Susannah says his mother's Jewish." She sat in the other barrel chair facing the television set.

Sam fiddled with the channels. "I've heard of Italian and Jewish. Even Irish and Jewish. And, of course, Abe Gross's wife Belle is the daughter of a Baptist minister. But I never heard of Greek and Jewish."

"As long as his mother's Jewish. That's the half that counts."

Nora stood in the door to the sun porch, unwilling to join them, but unable to tear herself away from the scent of romance. "What do you mean that's the half that counts?"

"The law says if the mother's Jewish, the child is Jewish." Sam laughed. "Your mother, the Talmudic scholar."

Beatrice smoothed her skirt over her knees. "Just because I'm not religious doesn't mean I'm a *shiksa*. I know the law."

Beatrice's voice was firm with conviction. The sight of true love made her heart beat as fast as any fraternity pin. And the fact that Nick was going to be a doctor didn't hurt.

It was true love, and it didn't run smoothly. What could you expect with two strong-willed people, Beatrice observed at regular intervals during the next two years. In fact, Susannah's will wasn't especially strong. Life had bent to it so easily that it had never built up any muscle.

Nonetheless, they were two beautiful spoiled people who wanted two different things. Nick wanted Susannah. Susannah wanted Nick as a husband. He said she was the only virgin in all of Smith College. She said he wouldn't respect her. He quoted *Love Without Fear*. She quoted Doris Day.

They broke up repeatedly, and like poor Blinker, Nick always came back. Only he wasn't like poor Blinker. When he stopped calling, there was no prearranged New Year's Eve date to hang on to at the end of the silence. Susannah went crazy. You could almost see the nerves jangling just beneath her skin.

Then one night after a separation of eighty-seven days, Nick showed up at her house at Smith unannounced. It was during reading period. Susannah looked awful. At least, she told Beatrice and Nora she did. The wonderful thing was that Nick looked awful too, and not just from the strains of internship or the drive up from New York. While Susannah talked, Nora painted a picture. There's nothing like two beautiful people, drawn and ravaged by the lack of each other.

Susannah had an exam the next day, but she went out with him anyway. She'd always had her priorities straight. By the time she got back to the dorm—and she came closer to missing curfew that night than she ever had—it was on again.

Nora wondered what had changed. Beatrice said they simply realized how much they loved each other. But Beatrice didn't know the whole story, at least not yet.

That night during reading period, parked near Paradise Pond in Nick's secondhand Chevrolet, he didn't say anything about Susannah's proving her love. He didn't have to. The eighty-seven days had worn her down. She wasn't thinking about holding on to Nick. She wasn't thinking about marriage. For what may have been the first time in the twenty-year romance that was Susannah's life, she wasn't thinking.

And for the first time in her life she wasn't telling Beatrice everything. Even Susannah couldn't come home and say, "Gee, Mom, I lost my virginity in the front seat of Nick's secondhand Chevrolet last week."

Susannah came home for the summer. Nick practically moved in. He had so little time off from the hospital that there was no point in his wasting it driving back and forth after dates.

Once Nora came in late from a date of her own. She could have sworn she heard voices in the guest room, which now held some of the same medical journals that Uncle Lewis used to leave there. Nora stood in the hall listening for a moment, then went into her own room and closed the door. It must have been the radio. With Susannah, it would have to be the radio. Nora was another story. She'd already done one or two, but only one or two, things that Susannah had been telling her since she was twelve you definitely did not do.

In the fall Susannah went back to Smith. Nick was a resident now. There was no reason why he shouldn't marry. Now that Susannah was a senior, there was every reason why she should get engaged. They fought a lot that fall. And they made up a lot. In the back seat of Nick's car, in rented Northampton rooms, in the apartment Nick shared with another resident, they made up with a vengeance.

Of course, there was the pregnancy scare. Given the times and Susannah, there had to be a pregnancy scare. It lasted for two weeks. Then Susannah got her period, and Nick got his ultimatum.

Susannah was home for the Christmas holidays. It was just a week short of two years since they'd met. They were going to a party, as they had that night they'd met, only this was an engagement party. Among Susannah's friends, rings were sprouting like icicles that holiday season.

When Susannah and Nick got back to the house on Byron Road that night, she went into the living room and sat in one of the two chairs facing each other in front of the fireplace. Nick wasn't staying over because he had to get back to the hospital, and in any event Beatrice was discouraging his staying over these days, but they could have gone into the sun porch. As Nick pointed out, they used to go into the sun porch all the time. Susannah said she had her period. Nick started to say they didn't have to actually . . . but Susannah cut him off. She said she wanted to talk.

Nick sat in the chair opposite hers. His beautiful full mouth was a tight line. He knew what was coming.

"I'm ready for marriage," Susannah said. "All my friends are getting married. I want to get married and settle down and have children."

Nick started to say something about money. Susannah cut him off again. She'd get a teaching job right after graduation. Beatrice and Sam would help out. Money was not the issue.

"I'm interested in marriage," Susannah said, "and if you're not, then I don't want to see you anymore."

So far the scene had played exactly as Beatrice and Susannah had planned it, but they'd been conditioned by too many years of poor Blinker.

Nick stood. "Then I guess that's that."

Susannah was stunned, but she didn't show it.

They walked to the door. Nick put on his coat. Each waited for the other to say I'm sorry, I was wrong, I must be out of my mind. That was the way it worked in the movies. Neither of them said anything. Nick moved in to kiss her good-bye. Susannah moved away. She always used to let poor Blinker kiss her good-bye. Once she'd even cried while poor Blinker had kissed her good-bye forever. But she didn't let Nick kiss her good-bye. This time she cried after rather than before he left.

Poor Blinker was back on the scene in twenty-four hours. Susannah was so cruel to him this time around that even Beatrice called her on it. That was when Susannah broke down and began to cry again. That was when Beatrice got firm and said Susannah was just being silly. She'd get over Nick. And that was when Susannah finally burst out after months of unnatural reticence that she'd never get over Nick because she'd *sleptwithNick.*

They were in the car when she made the confession, driving home from the Millburn branch of Lord & Taylor. Beatrice was driving, Susannah was beside her in the front seat, and Nora was in back with a stack of boxes and bags, each imprinted with a single long-stemmed red rose. Outside the car windows, the New Jersey countryside was growing dark, and the colored lights of Christmas were beginning to go on.

Beatrice's foot must have come down on the accelerator at the news, because the car speeded up a little, then it slowed. Beatrice didn't slam on the brakes. She didn't pull over to the side of the road. She just kept driving the gray Cadillac that was the most recent in a long line of Cadillacs

Beatrice always drove because Phil had always driven Cadillacs.

"When?"

"Last spring. That night he showed at the end of reading period."

"Just that once?"

It took Susannah a while to answer, and when she finally spoke, she was almost whispering. "Don't be silly."

"You mean ever since then."

Susannah didn't answer.

Nora sat in the back of the car hugging herself. This was a terrible and a wonderful thing her sister had done. The images of it made her suck in her breath.

"Oh, my God!" Beatrice said, and Nora knew, though she couldn't see her mother's face, that Beatrice was crying.

The rest of the ride home they said only two more things.

"I'm sorry," Susannah mumbled.

Beatrice didn't answer. A few minutes later she said, "No wonder he didn't want to get married."

When they got home, Sam's car was already in the garage. Beatrice inched hers in beside it. The Cadillac was on the left, and Susannah would have to slide across the front seat. She couldn't get out until her mother did.

Beatrice didn't move. She just sat in the cold, dark car staring straight ahead at the garage wall that was hung with rakes and hoses and an old girl's bicycle. Nora knew that her mother was going to finish the thing out here. Sam wasn't going to be in on this. Beatrice hadn't lied that morning she'd told her daughters she was getting married again. Nothing came between the three of them.

"If somebody else told me about you," Beatrice said, still staring straight ahead at the garage wall, "I'd say, 'that tramp.'"

Susannah let out a terrible little noise. Nora wanted to put her hand on her sister's shoulder, but she was afraid to move.

"But you're my daughter, and I love you, so I'm going to try to understand."

* * *

There was fallout from the confession, for Beatrice, for Susannah, and even for Nora. That New Year's Eve Nora ended up on the sun porch sofa under a lanky Pingry senior named Barry Koenig.

Nora had gone out with him only a few times and knew the rules, Susannah's rules. By virtue of a few movies and parties they'd arrived at the light necking stage, with the emphasis on light. He was not supposed to touch any critical part of her body. The idea of her touching any critical part of his body was so unimaginable that Susannah never bothered to warn against it.

There had been a minor skirmish, but now Barry was playing by the rules. He was kissing her. True, his tongue was in her mouth, but that was one of the areas where Nora bent Susannah's rules. As far as Nora could see, there wasn't much point in kissing otherwise. But he was playing by the rest of the rules, the important ones. His hands were on her back. He'd made no feint at zippers or buttons. Then he did something that confused Nora. He rolled over on top of her. He was still kissing her, and there was a lot of writhing going on. There was also something hard poking into her stomach. If you took it all together—his tongue and all that writhing and the hard thing poking into her stomach—it was damn near the nicest feeling Nora had ever had. That was the tip-off. There had to be something wrong.

Nora tried to think it through, though the activities at hand weren't exactly conducive to thinking things through. His hands, the really dangerous things, were still on her back. Her clothes were twisted, but still on. And there was one more thing. It came to her just as she heard the faint metallic whoosh of the zipper that ran down the back of her good green silk dress. Even Susannah didn't play by Susannah's rules anymore. That was how Nora found out that you might have to be in love with someone to sleep with him, but there were lots of other things you could do with someone you just liked.

Poor Blinker was the beneficiary of the rest of the fallout. From the moment the three women climbed out of the cold gray Cadillac and carried their packages into the house, Beatrice couldn't have been nicer to him. He didn't have Nick's eyes or Nick's shoulders or Nick's charm, and Beatrice missed all that in a man. He was a lawyer rather than a doctor, which in Beatrice's hierarchy was second best. But he loved Susannah. More important, he respected Susannah.

For a while there during Susannah's senior year, as the snow began to melt and the sidewalks of Northampton became visible again, it looked as if poor Blinker was making progress. Susannah had put away her Hallmark date book along with other childish things. On the Metropolitan Museum of Art calendar Blinker had given her, his name was written several weekends in a row.

Then Nick did it again. One night he just turned up at the dorm. He looked like hell, again. Susannah, who'd just washed her hair because it was a Thursday night, looked sensational.

The girl who sat at the desk in the parlor called upstairs to say there was a man for Susannah. Susannah didn't even bother to ask who it was. She was a senior. It was a weeknight. The only men likely to turn up unexpected on a weeknight were other seniors from Amherst—Susannah didn't date at the University of Massachusetts—and they weren't what Susannah deemed eligible. She went downstairs in a pair of khakis and an old red shetland with a cigarette hole in the shoulder. Before Susannah ever learned to say the words "fuck you," it was her fuck-you uniform.

When she saw Nick pacing the hall outside the housemother's suite, she didn't even go back for her coat. She just signed out and kept walking. Outside the dorm Nick gave her his jacket. Then he turned up the heat in the car. By the time Susannah came back to the dorm, she was wearing a diamond ring on the third finger of her left hand.

At the engagement party a month later poor Blinker danced several times with Nora. She was a kid, but she was no longer a baby, and he needed consoling.

Nora was only mildly flattered. It was finally becoming

her turn, just as Beatrice had promised, and when you looked at poor Blinker rather than up at poor Blinker, he didn't look quite so wonderful. Nora hadn't even met Paul Moss, but she knew that he, or someone like him, existed.

7

Max postponed his depar-
ture for fourteen hours. He wanted to be certain it was
heartburn rather than a heart attack. Nora was at the pool
when he came to say good-bye. The sun was poised on the
roof of the 1200 Building, just about to slip behind it, and
most of the women and the handful of men had drifted
back to their apartments to parcel out the minutes of the
long night ahead. Except for another visiting middle-aged
child at the other end of the pool, Nora was alone.

"How is she?" Nora asked.

Max sat on the end of her lounge. He didn't look like an
undergraduate anymore. His tan only accentuated the
twin lines running from his nose to the corners of his
mouth.

"The doctor says she's fine. She says she supposes she's
well enough for me to leave. If I have to. I had to twelve
hours ago. I had a meeting in Washington this afternoon.
Damn!" He wiped a faint mustache of sweat off his upper
lip.

He should have left it at that, but he went on. "I'll give
you a call."

It was the end of every first date, Sunday night of every
college weekend, Labor Day of every summer at the
beach. It was all those things when you were sixteen years
old.

"Sure."

He stood looking down at her. "Well?"

"Have a nice trip."

"Don't you want to give me your number?"

"Oh." She reached for the canvas bag beside her lounge.
There was a folder of work in it, a bottle of sunscreen, her
wallet. She gave him a card from the wallet.

He looked at it, then back at her. "Does this mean you
want me to call for an appointment?"

She held out her hand for the card. He gave it back to
her. She scribbled her home number on it.

After Max left, Nora collected her towel, picked up the
canvas satchel, and went up to her mother's apartment.
Beatrice was on the terrace overlooking the pool. It wasn't
the coolest one at that time of day.

"I saw Max come to say good-bye. You gave him your
card. Very professional."

"I wrote my home number on it."

"I saw that too."

Beatrice said there was fresh iced tea in the kitchen.
Nora went to pour herself a glass.

"So," Beatrice said when her daughter came back out on
the terrace, "I guess he's going to call."

Nora sat in one of the tubular white chairs and took the
folder of work from her canvas satchel. It was like being
sixteen and coming home at the end of a first date, a college
weekend, Labor Day. The only thing missing was Susannah.

The next night Beatrice drove Nora to the airport. Her ear
infection had healed enough for her to fly back to New
York. The plane was predictably late. Nora told her mother
not to bother waiting until it took off. Beatrice said she
wanted to.

"But you'll get home late," Nora said.

"No one's waiting."

Nora wanted to say not even the Sap, or Mr. Saperstein,
as she fastidiously called him now, but she didn't. They
hadn't mentioned the incident since that night. The next
day at the pool the Sap's monologue had run a good five

minutes, and he'd had Band-Aids around two of his fingernails.

They walked to a corner of the waiting area. A couple of
teenagers sprawled, half asleep, their heads pillowed on
backpacks. Beatrice and Nora had to detour around them.

The two women sat side by side on molded plastic chairs.
The chairs were attached—the better to keep them sta-
tionary, orderly, and there—but Nora felt strangely dis-
tanced. Imminent loss separated them more than the actual miles eventually would. After all, once they were apart
again, they'd resume the old telephone connection.

Beatrice and Nora spoke at least four times a week, frequently more, and not for the regulation three-minute
check-in period either. Nora relayed tales of botched covers and advertising coups, as if her mother understood the
mechanics of running a magazine as well as her daughter's
need for approval, and maybe by this time she did. Beatrice reported on the way she spent her days and whether
she was sleeping at night. They plotted Cornelia's future
and retraced the past. They talked about the clothes they
bought, the movies they saw, the books and articles they
read, men Nora met, women Beatrice went places with,
whether the weather was good enough for Beatrice to
swim or Nora to run.

Other women marveled at those conversations. Mothers
who settled for Sunday duty calls that were as meager as
the Sunday dinners of welfare families envied Beatrice.
Daughters who begrudged those pathetic Sunday calls
were suspicious of Nora. Lucy, who spoke to her mother
every two or three months and hadn't seen her sisters in
more than a year, was simply amazed.

Not that the conversations weren't sometimes rocky.
That was another thing outsiders couldn't understand. If
Beatrice got off the phone shaking her head because it was
nine o'clock and her daughter had just got home to that
empty apartment to sit alone over some meager salad masquerading as dinner and too much wine after it, if Nora
hung up muttering to Lucy that her mother really ought to
find some charity work or continuing-education course to

take her mind off her solitary state, why did they call back
the next day?

It was a question Nora occasionally asked herself, but one
she'd never answered satisfactorily. Perhaps it was a reflex,
like Dr. Strangelove's hand, she joked to Lucy. It reached
for the phone as automatically as Peter Sellers's saluted
Der Führer.

But the unsatisfactory conversations were rare, at least
they had been in recent years, so it was odd that in the sick,
harsh light of the airport, they'd suddenly stumbled on an
awkward silence.

"Thank you for coming."

Nora felt her cheeks getting hot. "Don't be silly. Thank
you for letting me come. I had a nice time."

"Addie's son helped."

"Mother," Nora groaned.

"I know, I know. I'm not supposed to think that way
anymore, but I do think that way. You had a good time with
him."

"I had a good time with him," Nora admitted. "I also had
a good time with you. And I'm not going to wait so long to
come down again. I promise."

A disembodied voice announced that Delta's flight 76
was boarding. Beatrice and Nora stood.

"I don't want you to feel obligated," Beatrice said.

They started moving toward the line that was forming.

"I don't feel obligated. I love you." It was only half a lie.
Nora did feel obligated, but she did love her mother.

The line was inching toward the stewardess. Nora bent
to hug her mother. Beatrice seemed shorter. Her soft gray
hair tickled Nora's nose. Her shoulders were fragile as a
child's. She smelled faintly of Joy.

"Listen, Mommy," Nora began and stopped. She had no
idea what she wanted her mother to listen to, but she'd
heard her own voice. What kind of grown woman calls her
mother Mommy?

"Your boarding pass, please," the stewardess said.

"I'll call. I'll call you tomorrow night," Nora promised.

Beatrice reached up and patted her daughter's cheek.

"Call me tonight. Person-to-person for Nora Heller. Just so I know you got in safely."

Nora took a step beyond the stewardess. Beatrice moved in the same direction. A metal banister separated them now.

"And rip off N.Y. Tel.?" Nora said. A man jostled around her. His carry-on hit her legs from behind and made her knees go weak for a moment.

"It's all right," Beatrice said. "I'm a stockholder."

Another man bumped past Nora. There were only a handful of people left in line behind her.

"You'd better go," Beatrice said.

Nora started walking toward the door. On the other side of the railing Beatrice kept pace with her.

"Thank you," Nora said.

"Thank *you*." Beatrice put a sweet emphasis on the second word.

Nora stopped for a minute and stood staring at her mother. Then she peeled off into the boarding sleeve. She glanced back. Beatrice was still standing there watching her, as Nora knew she would be. Beatrice smiled and waved. Nora waved back.

Just before she stepped onto the plane, she turned back once more. She was relieved to see that Beatrice had started the long walk through the terminal to the parking lot. Then she noticed how her mother's fragile shoulders sagged under the stylish padding of her blouse.

They made up more than half an hour in flight, but Nora still didn't get home till after midnight. José, the doorman, took one look at her and said it really was a cold one out there tonight. Nora told him that was a suntan, pried a week's worth of mail out of the box, and went up to her apartment.

She'd turned off the radiators before she left. Now she went around turning them back on—the foyer, the living room, down the hall to her bedroom. She liked being home again. If the apartment wasn't exactly grist for the *Architectural Digest* mill, it at least told you something about the woman who inhabited it. What it told you, her interior designer friend Annie insisted, was that the woman's development had been arrested somewhere in the thirties—not hers, the century's. There was the ventilation grille in the shape of the New York skyline which Nora had found at a demolition site on the West Side. Her former husband, Paul, who believed that in design, as in emotion, less was more, had thought she was crazy. Worse than that, he'd thought she was garish. There was the Norman Bel Geddes cocktail shaker; the reproduction of the Jean Patou perfume bottle in the shape of the *Normandie* that Annie had bought, against her better judgment, for Nora's fortieth birthday; and the Rose Iron Works screen Nora had bid on at an auction and never expected to get. That time it was her insurance man who'd thought she was crazy. Nora wasn't a serious collector. She just had what Cornelia called "a thing" about art deco artifacts.

Nora continued on past her bedroom to Cornelia's room or the guest room or the study. The name changed according to other people's needs or Nora's mood, but the ambiance remained haphazard. Over the years the decoration in that room had progressed from early rock star groupie to fifties movies chic to, just before Cornelia went away to school, serious design. The graphic posters still hung on the wall, but now the past four years of *AH!* magazine filled one bookcase and a computer that could slip into a briefcase or be hooked up to the one in Nora's office stood on the desk. In a way, the study looked a lot like Nora's office, though she always insisted it said less about her than any room in the apartment. Annie, who was dying to throw everything in the room out and build everything in, said she wasn't so sure.

Nora went back down the hall to the front closet and hung up her coat, then into the kitchen. She cradled the phone between her ear and shoulder while she poured herself a scotch. "I want to place a person-to-person call to Nora Heller," she said. Was there an operator left who didn't know the ploy?

"She's not expected till tomorrow." Beatrice sounded tired but pleased.

Nora hung up the phone, put on a Billie Holiday tape,

and went back to the bedroom. In less than half an hour the laundry was in the white wicker hamper in the bathroom; her linen jacket in the closet in the study where she kept her out-of-season clothes; her makeup, toothbrush, and aspirins in the medicine cabinet.

She took the pile of mail to bed. There was barely room for her drink on the night table. It overflowed with books and galleys and other people's magazines—the competition. Nora's idea of nirvana was, for just once in her life, to be caught up. Her favorite day of the year was the last Sunday in October. It was twenty-five hours long.

She started to sort the mail. Except for the bills, most of it could have been addressed to Occupant. She got out of bed, crossed the room, opened her briefcase, and took out her appointment book. Now, like Susannah, she kept an appointment book. Standing there at her dresser with a drink in one hand, she turned to the current week. Meetings and lunches, reminders and obligations were scrawled in a rainbow of colored ink. There was barely any white left. She put the book back in her briefcase, finished her drink, and went to bed.

By six o'clock the next day she felt as if she'd never been away. She'd returned a couple of dozen calls. She'd given the go-ahead on first serial rights to a book called *Letters to My Lover*. Stop trying to talk to the sons of bitches, the author argued, since they don't listen anyway, and simply refer them to letters, indexed by number, that tell them what you don't like about their conversation, breath, or sexual performance. Nora found the idea simplistic, offensive, and, like most self-help, just practical enough to scare the living daylights out of her. She'd approved a new advertorial. The word still made her wince, but the revenues from those glossy inserts made her look good. She'd spoken to Wheeler, who was in Frankfurt. Nora always suspected Will Wheeler called her from regional sales offices around the world to remind her how small a cog *AH!* was in the magazine group's wheel.

He said it was snowing like hell. She said she was thinking about shopping for a new ad agency, one that could freshen the book's image a little.

"Yeah," he said, "Lucy told me."

Nora thought that was odd, since she didn't remember mentioning it to Lucy.

"It's about time you did something," he added.

The response was unfair. The last report was only the first that indicated a drop in advertising pages. But Nora refused to whine, or even argue.

"I'm going to let the old agency make a presentation too. They've done a good job till now."

"Till now isn't operative, Nora. It isn't even relevant." Nora imagined Wheeler scowling into the phone. When Will Wheeler so much as frowned, his low hairline met his bushy eyebrows, and his forehead disappeared. To look at Will Wheeler was to understand evolution.

"I still think we ought to give them a chance."

"It's your book," he said. "I don't care what you do—as long as it works."

Nora was in harness again. She dialed Cornelia's number in New Haven, leaned back in her swivel chair, and turned until she was facing the windows. As the phone rang, she stared out into the gathering dusk. Around and above and beneath her, the lights of other people's offices made random patterns in the night. The Chrysler Building, the most romantic art deco artifact of them all, cast a heartbreaking shadow against the darkening sky. She'd been looking at those lights and that building all her life. Once, from across the river, they'd been a long shot. Now she owned a close-up.

She swiveled the chair again until she was facing the office. One of the nice things about going away was that when you came back, you really saw things, at least for a while. Now for the first time in a long time, she saw her office again. On one wall a couple of framed awards hung. Not exactly Pulitzers, Nora always said, but what she didn't say was that she cherished them almost as much as if they were. One was for a series of articles on working mothers. Another was from a council dedicated to responsible advertising. Her favorite was for general excellence.

She turned to the bulletin board over her desk. It had been months since she'd noticed the personal mementos among the clutter of schedules and tearsheets. There was a caricature of Nora holding an issue of the magazine wrapped in a baby blanket, which the art director had sketched when Nora had become editor-in-chief. Beneath that was a bumper sticker Lucy had given her when she'd become the publisher as well. *Behind every successful woman there's a divorce.* Next to that Nora had tacked a postcard, one of those museum reproductions guaranteed to bring art with a capital A into every home and within the reach of every pocketbook.

Nora had picked up the postcard around the time Beatrice had moved to Florida and Cornelia had started Yale. On her way out of museums she often bought postcards to send to remind them that New York, and Nora, still existed, but she hadn't sent this particular card to either of them, though both would have liked it. Instead, she'd pinned it to the cork bulletin board above her desk.

The card was a print of a photograph taken around the turn of the century. In it a woman and a child stood framed in the doorway of a room. The woman was wearing a long white robe, and the girl, about seven or eight, was in a somber dress with a starched white collar and cuffs. The mother, curling toward the child like a pale Beardsley streak, was seen only in profile, but the daughter faced the camera straight on. Beneath a thick fringe of bangs her eyes were solemn and a little fearful, as if she knew that, no matter how good the preparation, going out into the world was a serious business.

Over the years, as Nora sat at her desk pouring old wine into *AH!*'s sleek new bottle, she'd written dozens of scenarios for that mother and child. Sometimes the woman was sending her daughter to entertain unseen guests. Shake hands, look people in the eye, avoid religion and politics. Others she was relaying a message to an offstage father. On days when Nora felt particularly cynical, the man waiting in the wings became a lover and the girl a knowing little accomplice. Nora had watched that mother teach that daughter dozens of different lessons.

But sometimes she sat and looked at the postcard not as symbol but reality. She was fairly sure the photographer hadn't posed a woman and child but captured a mother and daughter. Nora looked at the picture and thought that the vulnerable girl with the stiff dress and watchful eyes would be a grandmother now, if she were still alive. And she looked at the mother and grieved for guests and husbands and lovers who no longer came, for a willowy beauty who no longer existed.

Nora had thought she'd bought the postcard for its aesthetic value. As she sat listening to the phone ringing in Cornelia's room at school, she knew she'd had other motives as well.

"How's Grandma?" Cornelia asked as soon as she recognized Nora's voice.

"Fine. She has a beau."

"You're kidding."

"A white-shoed gentleman who mixes the best piña coladas in Palmetto Estates and thinks Beatrice is the greatest thing since Gene Tierney."

"You mean white-haired."

"That too. What there is of it."

"Do they do it?"

"That's your grandmother you're speaking of," Nora said, but she remembered the buttons down the front of her mother's dress that had turned out to be functional after all and wondered how she'd got to be the stupid one in the family.

"I'll check them out in a couple of weeks. A lot of hot young architects are working in Florida, and Andy and I want to see what's going on."

"I blinked and missed someone again. Who's Andy?"

"The best design guy in the whole school."

"Better than you?"

"Much better. That's the only thing wrong with him. You met him last Christmas."

"I thought you were hanging out with someone called Burt last Christmas."

"Kurt. He's a friend of Andy's."

"You take after your mother."

"Yeah," Cornelia said, "but I don't keep a date book of the ones I turn down."

When Nora got home that night, her answering machine glowed with a bright red "5." She rewound the tape and played it back. The machine was old and erratic. It sometimes swallowed the beginning of messages. But Nora recognized Annie's voice. ". . . hate to ask you, but Mark has some Japanese coming in over the weekend, and we're desperate for a hot Broadway ticket. Forget Pinter and Mamet. I'm talking moving chandeliers or barricades. Do you think you or your critic could pull a few strings? I know this damn machine is going to cut me off, so I'll call tomorrow and—"

The machine did, and Maude's voice took over. ". . . had lunch at Island today, and I'm still sick to my stomach. That actor—you know, the one from the Woody Allen movies whose name I can never remember—was at the next table. He was with this child. You've heard of 'young enough to be his daughter'? This was granddaughter material. They couldn't keep their hands off each other. I mean, I know it's not exactly a new story, but—"

The machine intervened again, then Maude's voice returned. "Listen, I've been cut off by classier machines than this. Give me a call. I have an idea for an article on growing old gracefully."

"It'll never sell," Nora said as she waited for the next call. All she heard was a dull buzzing sound, kind of like an electronic heavy breather. There was a time when those nonspeaking callers used to bother her, but over the years she'd come home to Spanish, Indian, or perhaps Pakistani, and lesbian obscene calls. She was jaded.

She got out of her public work clothes and into the worn woolen robe that was her private work uniform. Then she went into the kitchen, made herself a drink, carried it down the hall to the study, and upended her briefcase on the desk. She worked for forty minutes without thinking of anything else.

It was after nine when Max Miller called. He was at the airport. He said he'd called her twice from the plane. So much for electronic heavy breathers. He asked if she'd eaten yet. She said she hadn't. He said he'd be there in half an hour.

Nora showered, put on fresh underwear and makeup, and the dress she'd worn to work. She didn't want to look as if she'd fussed. Then she filled the ice bucket. She was just mopping up spilled water when José called from the lobby. Max Miller had got lucky again and made good time from the airport.

Afterward, she tried to figure out how it had happened again. He'd walked into her apartment, dropped a briefcase and carry-on bag, and taken off his coat. She'd asked if he wanted a drink. He'd said sure. The next thing she knew they were in bed.

"We've got to stop meeting like this," she said afterward.

She sat up and looked down at him. Stretched diagonally across her king-size bed, he covered a lot of territory.

"I know. It's just that all the way back on the plane tonight I kept thinking what it would be like in a real bed with enough light to see your sunburn marks."

Nora didn't ask what the verdict was.

Her silence seemed to make him uncomfortable. She had a fleeting understanding of masculine power, or at least one aspect of it.

"Listen." He sat up with his back against the headboard and took a swallow of the drink she'd barely had time to pour. "This isn't just this. It isn't just sex, I mean." He'd turned over the record. It was the other side of the I-got-lucky song.

She still didn't say anything.

"In case you were worried. That it was only this, I mean."

They never did get out for dinner that night. Max suggested sending out for something.

"What do you feel like eating?" he asked. "I don't even know what kind of food you like."

Nora said she liked all kinds of food—unless it came in grease-stained cardboard and foil takeout containers. She said she'd scramble some eggs.

He pulled on his trousers and followed her into the kitchen. As it turned out, Max made a mean omelette.

The alarm went off at 6:45. Nora turned off the buzzer, but left on the radio. It was fiercely optimistic Offenbach.

Max groaned, rolled over, and wound himself around her.

"Good morning," Nora said. Beatrice's sexual rules had crumbled, but her etiquette standards stood.

He opened one eye, squinted at the digits on the radio alarm, and closed it again.

"Don't you have to get to the office?" she asked.

"I could do without all that French cheer," was all Max said.

She reached over to turn the radio off and managed to extricate herself from him at the same time.

"I asked if you didn't have to get to the office."

"Not at this hour."

"What kind of a lawyer are you, anyway?"

"Corporate," he mumbled.

"I know that. I meant what kind of a lawyer doesn't hit his desk at dawn?"

He opened both eyes, but didn't look happy about it. "A grown-up lawyer. I get the work done. I just don't have to make a show of it."

"Blasphemy."

"You talk too much." He put a hand between her legs. It was the move of a half-conscious man. There wasn't a lot of finesse to it.

She put her hand on top of his, but not in encouragement. "I've got a meeting."

His hand stopped moving but didn't retreat. "At seven o'clock in the morning?"

"I've got to go over some stuff before it."

He rolled away.

She got out of bed. "You can go back to sleep, if you want."

He didn't go back to sleep. She gave him a towel and a disposable razor and went into her shower. He went down the hall to the other one. By the time she came out, he was standing in the kitchen drinking a cup of coffee. A fine dusting of dark hair fanned across his chest like wings and disappeared down his stomach into a towel monogrammed with Cornelia's initials.

Nora wondered if she should have tried to wing the meeting, but it was too late for second thoughts.

8

*S*hortly after Nora became editor-in-chief of *AH!*, she was asked to speak to a group of divorced women on the crisis of marriage in modern society. The topic was tired, but the speech turned out to be enlightening, at least for Nora. In passing, she made a comment about marrying the boy you'd dated in college and suddenly finding yourself living with a stranger. To her amazement, a room full of women burst into applause.

Nora didn't regret the marriage. In a way, like a war veteran, she felt she'd proved herself by the experience. Lucy was obsessed with statistics that proved she stood less chance of marrying than of dying in a plane crash. Still, Nora had married a stranger.

Smith wasn't the only school set up to encourage the practice. It just did a better job of it than most. There were stringent curfews, and limited overnights, and soft-chinned housemothers who combined the prurience of a *Playboy* reader with the zeal of a HUAC investigator. They were dreamy, fantastic women who sensed a man under every bed.

On special weekends, from two to five on Sunday afternoons, there actually were men sitting on if not under the beds. For the rest of the time the only male presence was an occasional stray father. At the first whiff of his presence, a girl would fly down the hall, her voice beating like wings, screaming, "Man on the floor! Man on the floor!" Then half-dressed girls shrieked, and doors slammed, and the stuffy, overheated air vibrated with excitement.

Gradually the girls returned to their books or their bridge games or their passionate attachments to amateur theatrics and poetry and politics. "Amateur" was the operative word. Only a handful of girls Nora knew talked about careers. The few women instructors thought of themselves as exceptions rather than role models. When Nora told her adviser, a dusty poet manqué with a fake Oxford accent whom all the girls lusted after, that she was toying with the idea of going to graduate school, he encouraged her. "Of course, I'll write you a recommendation," he said. "It'll be something to do until you get married."

Not that Nora and her classmates didn't take their work seriously. They had a duty to society and their future husbands and children to be widely read, well informed, and aesthetically astute. But they were only human. As the week wound down to Friday, appearances deteriorated. Hair grew limp and stringy, blouses lost their freshness, and the obligatory skirt for dinner—gracious living was still in the curriculum—was pulled on over a pair of Bermuda shorts or rolled-up khakis.

Then came Thursday night. The bright communal bathroom blossomed with the aromas of Prell and Halo and Breck. Suitcases were wrestled down from the tops of closets. There was a run on ironing boards.

On Friday mornings Nora sat in her History 101 lecture and marveled at the sea of shining hair that stretched before her. On Friday afternoon they marched, cashmere shoulder to cashmere shoulder, tweed to tweed, to the railroad station. By Friday night half the troops were gone. Those who remained readied themselves to surrender to the invading forces.

One Friday night Paul Moss invaded with them, and Nora's life changed forever, or so the official story went. Actually, Nora's life, like a scheduled train, was already on track. Paul Moss just happened to board it at the right station.

They were fixed up by mutual friends. Years later, Nora

observed she'd never been broken, but that was years later.

The blind date was a common if barbaric ritual. It entailed the pairing of two people of the opposite sex who didn't know each other by two people who did. Height and religion were the determining factors. Physical comeliness and school affiliation figured into the calculations. No one mentioned such dicey matters as character or common interests. If you had the same background and friends and couldn't eat peanuts off each other's heads, what more did you want?

The stated object of the ritual was a night, or for the terribly brave or the terribly desperate, a weekend of mutual pleasure. There was nothing mutual about the unstated goals. Girls were looking for love, which would, needless to say, lead to marriage. Boys were looking, as Max Miller stated it years later, to get lucky. That the ritual not only survived but flourished was astonishing.

Paul Moss came with a list of more or less verifiable credentials. He was tall—six feet one. He was cute—a word Nora didn't trust unless applied to small animals and children. He was pre-law at Dartmouth—only a two rating. Harvard and Yale were the schools of choice at Smith. Dartmouth was known to harbor animals. On Saturday nights they roved in packs, standing in the stairwells of the various houses and shouting up, "Who needs a date?"

Paul Moss was not an animal. He was a big gentle boy with a blond crew cut and blue-gray eyes that were too small for his face. As a result, he seemed to be always peering at something. The eyes gave him a misleading air of attentiveness. There was nothing misleading about his jaw and shoulders. They were both strong. Nora had a weakness for more aesthetic types, slender boys with hollow cheeks and consumptive airs, but she was openminded. Since she wasn't Susannah, she knew she had to be.

The blind date was a success. They found they had one or two favorite books in common. Paul's parents had threatened to cut off his allowance when he wrote a letter to the *New York Times* in support of some Soviet policy. On Byron

Road Nora was known as the house pinko. They both liked
sex, though neither was particularly experienced or profi-
cient at it.

Paul began coming down to Smith regularly. Nora saved
all her overnights to go up to Dartmouth. It was a life lived
on anticipation, at least for Nora. She had no idea what the
week was like for Paul. She thought about him constantly,
but only in terms of her life, not his.

They introduced her roommate to his best friend. By an
extraordinary feat of mitosis, now they were four. Usually
they were eight or sixteen or forty. At the rare times they
were alone, they fell on each other hungrily. They were
clumsy, but enthusiastic.

Once, during a school vacation, they went out alone.
Years later, when a steel-and-glass skyscraper stood on the
site of the dark French cellar where they'd had dinner, and
Nora could no longer recall the play they'd seen, she still
cringed at the memory of that evening. Eventually she
came to see it as emblematic.

She was supposed to meet Paul at the Plaza. In those
days, when the hookers hadn't yet elbowed the ghosts of
Scott and Zelda off the leather banquettes, the Oak Bar was
their place.

Nora had left Beatrice and Susannah in Bergdorf's and
was hurrying across Fifty-eighth Street toward the hotel. It
was the shortest day of the year. Nora blamed the moment
of shame on that. It never would have happened if it hadn't
been dark.

She was walking quickly because, though she wasn't late,
she wanted to go to the ladies' room off the lobby before
she met Paul. Nora knew the rules. You didn't face a boy
with six-hour-old makeup, uncombed hair, and wrists naked of perfume. In case she'd forgotten them, both Beatrice and Susannah had reminded her when she'd left
them on the fifth floor of Bergdorf's.

"A little more eye shadow wouldn't kill you," Beatrice
said and smoothed the beaver collar of Nora's dress coat.

"And put on your scarf before you go outside," Susannah
added. "Otherwise, your hair will get all kinky in this
weather."

Nora was wearing a scarf and hurrying across Fifty-eighth Street to put on more eye shadow before she met Paul, but suddenly Paul was running down Fifty-eighth Street toward her. His big arms were outstretched, and his tweed overcoat flapped around him as he ran.

Nora stood still on the sidewalk for a split second. This wasn't the Paul she knew. Then she opened her arms and began running toward him.

Over the years she saw that moment again and again. They were running toward each other with outstretched arms, her hair, or at least her scarf, streaking behind her in the winter night, his long, if slightly meaty, legs eating up the distance. It was the prototype of all those Vaseline-blurred commercials that would run in endless slow motion through the next decade.

They kept running toward each other, getting closer and closer. Then, just at the moment when they could reach out and touch each other, just as she lifted her face to his, he ran past her.

Nora turned in time to see him embrace another girl who'd been running with outstretched arms behind her. She dropped her arms and started walking toward the Plaza. Paul was waiting in the lobby. She wondered how she'd ever made the mistake. He was much more solid than the boy who'd come running down Fifty-eighth Street toward her.

The small blue-gray eyes peered at her. "Boy, is your face red! I didn't think it was that cold out."

When Nora finally managed to lose her virginity a few months later, she had a fleeting memory of that December night. Probably because it was so dark she couldn't see Paul's face.

For as long as Nora could remember, Beatrice had put out the same party line. Sex was disgusting before marriage, a thing of beauty, complete with violins and satin lingerie, after. Even before Nora took Philosophy 101, she'd spotted the fallacious reasoning. Both halves of that sentence couldn't be true. She decided the first half held the error.

No one but Nick Demopoulis could have convinced Su-

sannah to part with her virginity without a wedding band.
Nora had made up her mind long before she met Paul Moss
that she wasn't going to be a virgin when she married.

It was a point of honor. Beatrice might insist that people
in their world didn't indulge in sex out of wedlock, but
people in Nora's world—Lady Brett, Daisy Buchanan,
even Countess Ellen Olenska—did. Nora knew which circles she wanted to move in.

To her eternal mortification, it took her three tries to get
there. She started one night in February during semester
break. Paul's older brother and his wife were in San Juan
on vacation. Paul had a key to their house. Nora stood on
the back steps shivering in her camel hair coat as he used it
to let them into the house. They were afraid to turn on the
lights and alert the neighbors, so they crept through the
dark kitchen and into the living room, bumping into tables
and stumbling over chairs. They embraced clumsily, like
two toddlers in snowsuits. Between nervous laughs they
debated where to go. The master bedroom was needlessly
sacrilegious, the living room too pristine, the den too uncomfortable. There were twin beds in one of the extra
bedrooms. Paul took Nora's hand and led the way upstairs.

Beneath the bedspreads there were no sheets. Paul considered the problem. If they didn't use a sheet, they'd stain
the mattress. If they used a sheet or a towel, they'd have to
take it, have it laundered, and sneak it back. Nora wondered why neither of them had thought of the problem
before. She considered the aesthetics of losing her virginity
in the house of a slipshod housekeeper.

That, of course, was the solution. Nora pointed out that a
woman who didn't keep clean sheets on her spare beds was
likely to have a pile of laundry moldering somewhere in
the house. Since Paul knew the terrain better, he went to
look. Nora sat on the end of the bed to wait.

The heat had been off for four days. The longer Nora
waited, the more she shivered. She was still wearing her
coat. She put her gloves back on. Maybe Beatrice was right
about sex before marriage.

Paul came back with a towel. A pink towel, he pointed
out. He spread it on the bed. They got out of their clothes,

then, careful to keep the towel beneath them, under the bedspread. By this time they were both shivering.

Paul recovered first. He was ready but inexperienced. Nora wanted to tell him he wasn't supposed to poke so much—at least she didn't think he was supposed to—but she knew this was one area where you didn't give a man directions.

"You've got to relax." He was whispering.

"I'm trying to," she snapped.

He decided something to drink might help. He got out of bed, put on his overcoat, and crept downstairs again. He must have walked into something on the way back, because she heard him cursing in the upstairs hall.

It was the first time Nora ever drank scotch neat. There was no sour mix, no orange slice, not even ice. It tasted awful. She managed to get down several gulps. Paul took a few himself. They returned to the task at hand.

Paul was twenty-two years old. Though he'd been stumbling around in the cold and dark looking for a bottle and a glass and walking into furniture and walls for a good ten minutes, he hadn't lost his erection. He even knew what to do with it. He just didn't know how to get Nora to the point where he could.

Her nipples were rigid from the cold. The rest of her was just rigid.

They went on that way for some time. Finally, she began to cry and he gave up. Or maybe he gave up and she began to cry.

She cried off and on in the car all the way home. She didn't get it. How had all those dumb, feckless girls in high school managed to get pregnant, when smart, industrious Nora couldn't even manage penetration?

Paul said not to worry. He said it was the cold. He said it was the fear of being caught. He said it would happen next time. He sounded sincere. He didn't even seem upset.

It didn't happen next time. That night in Paul's room of the apartment on 118th Street he shared with three other law students they came so close that Nora thought it might have. Paul said, nope, it was only partial. She was still a virgin. She wondered why, if he knew so much, he couldn't get the job done.

They finally carried it off on the floor of the sun porch on Byron Road while Beatrice and Sam slept above them. There was a reason for the floor. It was covered with a patterned carpet. Nora was expecting an indelible sign of achievement, like the A's on her transcript.

The next night they graduated to the sofa. Afterward Paul said, as he had the night before, that he loved her. Nora said she loved him. He said he supposed they ought to get married. She said she supposed so.

Six weeks later Nora fell in love with Michael Simon. At least, she thought it might be love.

Michael Simon was a sardonic boy with vague literary leanings and a compact, agile body. Nora had known him since her freshman year. They'd dated a few times, then become friends. It was an era when the two were still thought to be mutually exclusive. They went to the movies and for beers at Rahars, dutch treat. The financial arrangement was a sure sign that it was only friendship. They talked about books. He introduced her to Henry Miller. She led him to Edith Wharton. They talked about life. He was going to live abroad after graduation, probably work as a journalist while he wrote his first novel. She talked about graduate school. He cited the thick yellow bourgeois streak that ran down her character and predicted a husband, three-point-two children, and a station wagon. When she got engaged to Paul, he claimed vindication.

Then one night after a movie and several beers, Michael kissed her. The car was stopped under a streetlight, and it was bright enough to see his face, not to mention that sparkling stone on the third finger of her left hand, but to Nora's horror, she kissed him back.

She said this was terrible. He agreed. They kissed some more. She reminded him that she was engaged. He said he'd made a big mistake during all these years. By now they were lying down on the front seat. After a while he said he loved her. Now she was in a quandary. It seemed impolite not to say she loved him back. It seemed unconscionable to think she did. She decided to say nothing, and just went on kissing him. Michael was a good kisser.

When he put his hand under her sweater, she didn't stop him. In fact, she'd positioned herself to make it easy for him. Though she hadn't been a quick study with Paul, she didn't forget something once she learned it.

But she was still a nice girl. When Michael's hand slid under her skirt and up her thigh, she struggled out from under him.

She said they had to stop.

He said she had to break her engagement.

Ten days of exquisite agony followed. Nora walked around in a black turtleneck sweater clutching a pack of Marlboros. Tides of black coffee sloshed back and forth in her stomach.

Michael kept driving over from Amherst. She'd say it wasn't fair to Paul for her to see him. He'd say he knew. He just wanted to go for a cup of coffee or a beer. They'd always gone for coffee or beer.

She'd admit they had and climb the four flights to her room to get her coat. They'd go for coffee or a beer. For an hour or so they'd talk in circles. The cheap glass ashtrays overflowed with her Marlboros and his Gauloises. Finally, Nora would say she had to get back to the dorm.

Michael would pay for the coffee or beer. Things had changed. They'd walked to his car. They'd drive to her house. They'd stop in the parking lot behind it. And every night it was the same.

It was hard to tell because she hadn't gone as far with Michael as she had with Paul, but it occurred to Nora one night that Michael had both more experience and more flair. The experience part didn't bother her. The innate gift was something else. She felt guilty for recognizing it, but not guilty enough to stop what she was doing. That was the night she took off the black turtleneck and the bra beneath it, or rather Michael did. If Nora had still believed in God, she'd have expected him to be waiting in her room on the fourth floor of the house that night.

The next night she decided not to study in her house. The libe, as it was cloyingly called, was safer. She even went to one of the carrels. For more than an hour she sat there staring into the gloom. Every time she thought of marrying Paul, she began to wonder about sleeping with Michael. Every time she thought of running off to Wales with Michael—he was going to write in Wales—she was knocked over by a bolt of love for Paul. She felt like the ass caught between two bales of hay in her psych textbook. As soon as that poor dumb animal moved toward one bale, the other bale made his mouth water. The ass eventually starved to death. Nora was close to tears for that ass by the time Michael found her in the carrels.

They went for coffee. He asked her what she was going to do. She said she didn't know.

They drove back to the dorm. He tasted of black coffee and cigarettes. It was the flavor of imminent exams, overdue papers, and suffering. Somehow her sweater and bra got lost in the shuffle again. Then Michael did something that Paul had never done and Susannah had never even warned her about. He opened his fly, took her hand, and put it inside his corduroys.

At first she was shocked. Then she was intrigued. She moved her hand experimentally. Michael put his hand on top of hers and offered guidance. She wondered why she'd never thought of this herself. She wondered why Paul, who hadn't had to worry about zippers and Jockey shorts, had never taken her hand and put it in such a logical place. Then she felt guilty for the thought and struggled up from under Michael. Her hand was sticky.

She was still thinking about her hand when she went into the phone closet on the fourth floor of the house and called home. Beatrice picked up the phone on her night table.

"I can't marry Paul," Nora said.

"What do you mean?" Beatrice asked.

"I have to break the engagement."

"Why?"

Nora leaned her head on her hand. Then she remembered where her hand had been and pulled it away. "I don't think I love him."

"You loved him enough to get engaged to him."

"That's what I'm trying to say. I think I made a mistake."

"Did you have a fight?"

"I haven't even spoken to him in three nights."

"Then what?" Beatrice was struggling to remain calm, but Nora heard the panic racing like a flood tide into her mother's voice.

"I think I'm in love with someone else."

The tide receded. Beatrice was a reasonable woman. "Who?"

"Michael Simon."

The flood came rushing back. "You've known Michael for years. Now all of a sudden you're in love with him?"

"I don't know."

"Come home."

"What good is that going to do?"

"Don't argue with me. Tomorrow's Friday. Sam will get you a plane reservation as soon as we get off. If worse comes to worst, you can take the train."

"I can't come home now. It's too close to exams."

"You'll study on the plane."

Beatrice had said someone would meet Nora at Newark airport. Paul was the first person Nora saw when she entered the terminal. He put a big shetland arm around her and kissed her shyly. His smile was so big that those small blue-gray eyes almost disappeared. There was no way Nora could give him up.

He took her hand as they started to walk. It was the same hand Michael had taken the night before.

"Your mother is a wonderful woman," he said. "She called this morning and said no engaged couple should have to go for more than three weeks without seeing each other. She said that was why you sounded so down last night."

Nora didn't have to ask if Beatrice had said anything else about the conversation. She knew her mother hadn't.

Beatrice sat at the head of the table nearest the kitchen. Sam sat at the other end. Susannah and Nick were on one side, Nora and Paul on the other. Sam picked up the carving knife and fork. They all held their breaths. He cut into the roast. The ends were beautifully charred the way Sam liked them, the center was pink for Nick and Paul. It was perfect.

"Did Mommy show you the silver patterns?" Susannah asked.

"After dinner," Beatrice said.

Susannah heaped a mountain of string beans on Nick's plate. "Choose Acanthus. That way, if we ever have more than twelve people, we can borrow each other's silver."

"She's right," Nick said. "Can you imagine if we had thirteen people to dinner and had to serve one of them with a different pattern? I'd probably be drummed out of the hospital." He pointed his knife at Nora. "Go for the Acanthus, kiddo."

"He talks a good game," Susannah said to Nora and Paul. Her voice was pitched an octave higher but in the same key as Nick's. This was no accidental duet, but a polished performance. "He pretends he doesn't care, but he cares."

"The Acanthus is nice," Beatrice said, "but so is the Monticello. You can look at them after dinner."

"Please, Bea," Nick said, "you know I can't eat when I'm excited."

"Very funny." Beatrice beamed at her son-in-law.

"Do you know where you're going on your honeymoon yet?" Susannah asked.

"If we do, we're not going to tell you," Paul said.

"Wanna bet?" Nick said. "My wife will get it out of Nora."

"Well, why not?" Susannah asked. "The only people you have to keep honeymoon plans from are animals like your old roommate." Her voice went only slightly flat.

"Gordo's a good guy."

"Good guys do not call the Plaza and do Groucho Marx imitations on someone's wedding night." Susannah turned to Nora and Paul. "Gordo's an animal."

After the three women had done the dishes, Beatrice went upstairs and brought down the samples of silver. She spread them out on the coffee table, and sat with her daughters on the sofa.

"I'm not sure," Nora said.

"Take the Acanthus," Susannah urged.

"I liked it when Susannah chose it," Beatrice said, "and I still like it. But it's up to you."

"What do you think?" Nora asked Paul.

He came and sat beside her on the couch. "It's nice. They're all nice."

"I guess I like the Acanthus," Nora said.

Beatrice began wrapping the pieces of silver in the gray cloth bags. "I'll call and order it tomorrow."

"But—" Nora began.

"You made your choice," Susannah said. "Now don't start driving us crazy by changing your mind. You're going to be happy with the Acanthus. I am."

She and Nick left a little later. They all stood in the front hall saying goodnight. Nick was behind Susannah, his arms around her waist and his shoulders hunched over so his chin rested on her shoulder.

"I'm going to take my wife home," he said.

"You want to play tomorrow?" Sam asked him. In clement weather, Sam played tennis every Saturday and Sunday on the local courts. During the winter months, he drove an hour every Saturday to play on indoor courts.

"Sure," Nick said. "Eleven okay?"

They went out into the night, Nick with his arm around Susannah, Susannah with her arms around a bag of leftovers. Beatrice and Sam went up to bed a few minutes later. Nora and Paul went into the sun porch.

"I missed you," he said.

"I missed you," she agreed.

After a few minutes, when they were still half dressed, Nora unzipped his fly. She'd never done that before. She reached inside. At first he was surprised. Then his response was exactly the same as Michael's.

Nora was sitting alone at the breakfast table when Nick came into the kitchen the next morning. "Where is everyone?"

"Mommy's out pillaging the A & P. Sam's upstairs. He said to tell you he'll be down in a minute."

Nick sat sideways on the leatherette banquette across

from her. His long legs stretched out from under the table. He looked at the half-eaten pie on the table, the sibling of the one Susannah had taken home the night before.

"I never had pie for breakfast until I married into this family."

"What'd you used to eat? Moussaka?"

"Very funny. Get much last night, kiddo?"

"God!" She stood, stepped over his legs, and walked to a cabinet. "Isn't anything sacred in this family?"

"It's sacred, all right. It's sacred as hell. It just isn't private."

"You want a piece of pie?" She wasn't looking at him, but she could feel his eyes on her. They weren't camera shutters, like Beatrice's, snapping away, but dark speculative disks, measuring her. And probably finding her wanting. She was no Susannah.

"Had some at home. You can come back now."

She put an empty plate in front of him. "In case you change your mind."

He was still staring at her. She tucked one side of her woolen robe beneath the other and pulled the sash tighter.

"That's your role in the family, not mine. The word's out. Nora's indecisive. Who's this Michael character, anyway?"

"I've known him since freshman year."

"And now you think you're in love with him?"

"I don't know."

"You go to bed with him?"

"Of course not!"

"Don't sound so shocked. If you think you're in love with him, maybe you ought to."

"What about Paul?"

"You tell me. It's not too late to change your mind."

"You think I shouldn't marry him?"

They heard Sam's steps on the staircase.

"I don't think anything, except that maybe if you're so mixed up about it, you shouldn't marry anyone. What's the big rush, anyway?"

Sam came into the kitchen carrying his tennis racket and a small duffel. He stood there looking at the two of them without speaking.

Nick stood. "Break precedent, kiddo. Graduate without a ring on your finger."

Sam still didn't say anything, but he was smiling.

"I don't understand," Beatrice said. "Last night you were picking out silver patterns. This afternoon you're telling me you still haven't made up your mind."

Nora twisted around to face her mother. They were having tea with Susannah in Lord & Taylor's Bird Cage. The chairs, each with its own tray like high chairs for adults, were arranged in awkward clusters. Knees and feet bumped, but faces never faced.

"I was picking out silver patterns because you two brought it up. Did you want me to tell Paul I wasn't sure in front of everyone?"

"Have you told him at all?" Susannah asked.

"No."

"You're sure."

A gray-haired woman in a pink uniform shuffled her wagon over. Slices of custard pie and pieces of frosted cake and molds of tinted Jell-O trembled expectantly on their plates. All three of them said they'd have the tea sandwiches.

"I don't like this Michael," Beatrice said. "This beatnik."

"It's not his fault."

"What do you mean it's not his fault? He knew you were engaged. Does he want to get married? Not that I'd let you marry the kind of boy who goes chasing after engaged girls. Next thing you know he'll be cheating on his wife."

Nora considered the answer. She and Michael had occasionally discussed marriage, in the abstract. He said since he didn't believe in God and had even less faith in the Commonwealth of Massachusetts, he didn't see the point.

"He says he loves me."

"That's not what I asked."

A girl in another starched pink uniform brought the tea sandwiches. They lay in limp brown and white crosses on the plates. A sprig of parsley made a pathetic stab at festivity.

"Nick says I shouldn't marry anyone. He says I have plenty of time."

There was a moment of silence. Nora took a bite of a cream cheese and watercress sandwich. Beatrice and Susannah exchanged glances.

"Since when did Nick become an authority on marriage?" Beatrice asked.

"He was only trying to help," Nora answered.

"You don't know Nick," Susannah said. "He was probably playing devil's advocate."

Beatrice took a sip of her coffee. When she put the cup down, there was a perfect crescent of red on the rim. "With all due respect to Nick, he's not exactly an expert on what's best for a young girl."

"All he was saying was that I didn't have to marry anyone."

"Am I telling you to?" Beatrice twisted around in her chair until she was facing Susannah. "Did you hear me tell her she had to marry someone?" She twisted back to Nora. "All I'm saying is you better make up your mind because I'll have to cancel the invitations, and we'll have to start sending back engagement presents. Besides, it's not fair to Paul. He's a nice boy, and he's going to make some girl a good husband. If you don't want him, someone else does."

By the time they piled the packages into the back seat of the new Cadillac, they were joking and laughing and debating their purchases again. Beatrice got behind the wheel. Susannah climbed into the passenger side. Nora got in back with the packages.

"Did Mommy tell you what happened to Nick at the hospital last week?" Susannah asked.

Beatrice giggled. "It's terrible."

Susannah was laughing too. "If it's so terrible, why do you start laughing every time I mention it?"

"I'm not laughing," Beatrice insisted, but when she turned to check a cross street, Nora could see her mother was trying to suppress a smile.

"What happened?" Nora asked.

Beatrice shook her head. "Nurses!"

Susannah turned to the back seat. "According to Mommy, Florence Nightingale was just the first in a long line of camp followers out for cheap thrills."

"And rich doctors. They think all doctors are rich."

"Tell me," Nora pleaded.

"Nick had just finished with an emergency," Susannah said. "He was standing at the nurses' station reading the chart. It was late and there was no one around but him and this one nurse."

Beatrice shook her head again. "A tramp," she said, but Nora could tell from her mother's voice that she was still smiling.

"So he's standing there studying this chart, and all of a sudden he feels this hand grabbing him. I mean . . . you know . . . grabbing his . . ." Susannah dropped her voice. "His penis."

Susannah and Beatrice were both giggling again.

"What did he do?" Nora asked.

"Went on reading the chart," Susannah said between snickers.

Nora thought but didn't say that her brother-in-law must have some power of concentration.

That night it was Paul who brought up the silver. They were in the car driving back from Manhattan, where they'd gone to dinner and a play with one of his roommates and the roommate's fiancée. Beyond the car windows, the red neon Budweiser bird flapped its wings over the dark New Jersey countryside.

"Did your mother order the silver?" he asked.

"Not yet."

"You better tell her to hurry. The longer she waits, the more time you'll have to change your mind."

"Paul." Nora's voice was a small squeak beneath the sound of the engine, like a faint noise that indicates mechanical trouble ahead.

"Yeah?"

"I'm not sure."

He laughed. "I knew it. Okay, I'm sure. Whatever that

pattern was you picked last night, the one Susannah has, that's the one we want."

"I mean about the wedding."

"Okay, I'm sure about that too. Your mother wants a big wedding. My parents want a big wedding. Susannah says you'll be sorry if you don't have a big wedding. We'll have a big wedding."

"I didn't mean the wedding. I meant about getting married."

He looked at her, then back at the road quickly. He didn't say anything.

"I mean, maybe we should wait a while."

"Why?"

"I don't know." Her voice trailed off, then came back. "Nick says what's the rush?"

"What's Nick got to do with it?"

"Nothing really. I was just talking to him this morning. I mean, what is the rush?"

This time he didn't even look at her. He just kept driving.

He pulled the car up in front of the house and killed the engine. She sat staring straight ahead, her hands folded in her lap.

He turned to her. "What aren't you sure about?"

It took her a while to answer. She couldn't tell him about Michael. She wouldn't tell him about that hollow black sensation she got when she thought about marrying him. It felt like Sartre's nausea, but Sartre was talking about freedom and she was thinking of marriage.

"I guess I'm just scared."

"Of what?"

"I don't know."

They sat in silence for a few more minutes.

"I don't know what to do," she said finally.

"I do," he answered. "We'll get married."

Years later, when she'd grown tired of chastising herself for letting him make the decision for her, she asked him why he'd been so hot to marry her. "I mean, I wasn't exactly stable at the time. She loves me, she loves me not. She wants to get married, she doesn't want to get married."

They were sitting side by side in an absurdly overpriced Chinese restaurant. After his remarriage and several years of silence, Paul had called and suggested lunch. She had a feeling he wanted to show her how well he was doing. That was okay. She deserved a little comeuppance.

His big face with the small eyes swiveled from the Peking duck to her. "What makes you think I was so much older and wiser than you? People told me it was just nerves. That everything would be okay after we were married."

"It wasn't."

He laughed. By that time they could laugh about it. "I noticed."

"By people, you mean Beatrice."

"Your mother. My mother. It was the prevailing wisdom of the day."

"In other words, I was like some overwrought neurasthenic maiden. All I needed was a good lay to straighten me out. But I'd already had a good lay."

The editor in her deleted the "good," but the woman at the table kept quiet. They'd both been young. There was no blame to assign, but there were plenty of feelings to hurt. Besides, there was one thing she was sure of by then. She could have chosen Michael Simon instead of Paul, and it wouldn't have made any difference. She would have known that even if she hadn't gone on running into Michael, who'd gone not to Wales but to the *Business Week* offices of the old McGraw-Hill Building on Forty-second Street. Chatting with him and his wife after screenings and before awards dinners and on random street corners over the years, she was sometimes able to summon up those heady, tortured days. But the memories that could still make her ache never had anything to do with the man she was talking to who merely made her nod and smile.

"That was part of it," Paul said. "I thought maybe you felt guilty. About sleeping together before we were married, I mean."

Talk about marrying a stranger.

9

That Friday night Nora called Max's office to say she was going to be late. When no one answered, she tried his apartment.

"Half an hour, at the most," she said.

"Then I won't start the soufflé till you get here."

"You're kidding."

"I'm kidding."

"Forty-five minutes tops."

"Okay."

"Make it an hour, just to be safe."

"What're you putting together down there, the Bible?"

"Both testaments. I'll see you in an hour."

She was only ten minutes later than that. He'd obviously used the time well. As soon as the elevator door opened on his floor, she picked up the scent of sautéing garlic. It led her straight to his apartment. He opened the door with one hand. He wiped the other on his khakis before he took her hand and led her inside.

In the seven years since Max Miller had divorced, he'd made a home for himself. The apartment, like most apartments in upper East Side postwar buildings, was an ordinary arrangement of boxlike spaces that any laboratory rat would know his way around. The furniture was what Annie called postmarital, the kind of inexpensive, undistinguished "contemporary" that a newly separated man could buy in a single day. The cleanliness level wasn't as high as a stockbroker's Nora had known several years earlier who'd stopped in the middle of sex to pick a white down comforter up off the floor, nor as low as a poet's whose toilet she'd never sat on without wiping it off first. Max's apartment lacked distinction, but, like Nora's own, it carried his mark.

He'd turned one wall of the living room into bookcases. She noticed some recent, highly respectable fiction—the last man she'd slept with who'd read fiction was the grubby poet—and half a dozen shelves of railroad volumes. Another wall was literally covered with framed photographs. Some were of railroad cars and engines; others were of a girl and a boy, sometimes posed with Max, at various stages of their development; and several were of groups of young men playing a variety of sports and working on what looked like a newspaper or yearbook and posing to commemorate their joint achievements. It was the wall of a man who had a past and a family and interests. None was extraordinary, but in Nora's experience, a man who took the time to collect, frame, and hang the pictures was rare.

"It's nice," she said. "I like the pictures and . . ." Her eyes flew over the numbingly mediocre furniture and came to rest on the rug. It was an old Oriental and deserved better. ". . . and the rug."

"Have you ever noticed how the Oriental rugs always outlast the marriage?"

"Fresh fruit outlasted my marriage," she said.

He took her into the kitchen and gave her a drink.

Nora looked around at the pegboard hung with a variety of pots, a wok, and two unpolished copper pans; the magnetic knife rack holding carving and paring and serrated knives; and the ceramic jars stuck with wooden spoons and spatulas and even a wire whisk. It wasn't a model kitchen. If it ever made the pages of *AH!*, it would be as a "before" picture. But it was clearly a room that was used.

She sat on a tall stool and sipped her drink while he went back to the garlic. Max cooked like a man, or at least unlike any woman Nora knew. He used enough butter and oil to give any nutritionally enlightened human being a figurative as well as a literal heart attack. He never used a single pot when he could dirty two or three. His movements were broad, noisy, and violent. Sauces slopped over saucepans. Fat spattered everything in range. Water thundered full force. Utensils clattered. Knives slashed. When he offered her a tasting from a wooden spoon, she jumped back.

They polished off one bottle of wine with dinner. He opened a second. By the time they finished dinner, it was after ten. Nora offered to do the dishes. He let her.

When she finished, she went into the living room. It was empty. She walked into the bedroom. His clothes were on the floor, the half-finished second bottle of wine was on the night table, and a familiar smile was on his face. He lifted the covers for her.

"Are you sure the scullery maid's allowed above stairs, or between sheets?"

"If you didn't want to do the dishes, you shouldn't have offered."

"It's a reflex. I was raised by a mother who believes a woman's place is in the kitchen and a man's isn't."

"Statute of limitations ran out. Are you going to take off your clothes, or do you want me to?"

Nora thought about the question for a moment. She sat on the side of the bed. She put her hand on his chest. There was only a fine dusting of hair. That was okay with her. She'd never understood the attraction of hairy men.

"I want you to."

They were down to her necklace and earrings when the phone rang. They stopped what they were doing, but they didn't take their hands off each other.

"I better answer it." He rolled over on his back and reached for the phone.

She stared at the ceiling and thought that a man with a responsible job, two minor children, and an aging widowed mother ought to have an answering machine.

"No, Mother," Max said. "You aren't interrupting anything."

"Thanks a lot," Nora whispered.

He put his hand over the mouthpiece. "You're the one who's hot on privacy.

"Fine," he said into the phone. "How are you?"

"Do you want me to go inside?" Nora whispered.

He shook his head no.

She pulled the covers over them and moved closer. He put his free arm around her. She put her hand on his penis. She didn't move it, just kept it there, kind of as a safeguard.

She lay with her head on his shoulder looking up at his face. It wasn't as interchangeable with all those other faces lurking behind the *Wall Street Journal* as she'd originally thought. There were distinguishing marks. A series of scars, like miniature railroad ties, ran beneath his chin. Max had spent a good portion of his formative years being raced to doctors' offices and emergency rooms, though he insisted he'd never stuck his chin out much. He had a vein at his left temple that, Nora had noticed that last day in Florida, was the billboard of his anger.

"Damn it," he said. "I forgot it was today. What did the doctor say?"

Nora waited in silence while Addie reported what the doctor had said.

"It makes sense to me. We'll just wait for a few more weeks."

There was another silence.

"Then get another opinion."

The silence went on longer this time. Nora took her hand away. Max put it back. He got off the phone. It rang again almost immediately.

"Christ!" he said to her. "Hello," he said into the phone, then there was another silence while he listened. Nora had the feeling from the physiological repercussions that he didn't like what he was hearing.

"This isn't a good time," he said. "I'll talk to him about it tomorrow."

Max hadn't used a name, but Nora recognized the tone, though she'd never heard Max use it before. She got out of bed and went into the bathroom. At least she didn't have to wipe off the toilet seat before she sat.

She stooged around in the bathroom for a while, brushing her teeth, combing her hair, taking off her necklace and earrings. By the time she came out Max was off the phone. He was lying on his back staring at the ceiling.

She got back into bed. He put his arm around her again, but he didn't stop staring at the ceiling. "That was my ex-wife."

"I figured."

He turned and looked at her. "You don't make a lot of demands."

"Because I go into the bathroom when your former wife calls?"

"And discreetly disappear when my mother has heartburn and wants attention."

"I take it from that call that your former wife does make demands."

It was starting, the confidences, the confessions, the unraveling of their pasts.

Max turned back to the ceiling and thought about it for a while. "She always did like to have her bags carried."

Nora turned on her side and measured her body against his. "That's not so terrible. You carried my suitcase in Florida."

He turned and looked at her again. "It was an image." He laughed, finally. "What the hell kind of an editor are you, anyway, if you can't spot a genuine, A-number-one, literary image?" He put a hand on her hip. "Did I ever tell you about my journalism career?"

"Your high-school newspaper."

"Condescending bitch. The *New York Times.*"

"You worked for the *Times*?"

"First job I ever had. I was in high school."

"What did you do?"

"Airbrushed pinstripes."

"What?"

"You know those society wedding pictures? The bride and groom coming out of the church or at the reception at some club or something. The grooms were always wearing cutaways or morning jackets or whatever the hell you call them. With pinstripe pants."

"I don't get it."

"You know what happens to pinstripes when you get a hard-on? They get wavy."

"You're kidding."

"Scout's honor. My job was to straighten out the crooked pinstripes."

"I don't believe it. I mean, how many men came out of church or stood around at their wedding receptions with an erection?"

"Enough to keep me working one summer. Don't forget that was before the sexual revolution." He took her hand and held it against him. "A helluva time to grow up."

"The story seems to have restored your spirits. Either that, or you're lying, Pinocchio."

"Neither. I just decided to take the phone off the hook."

They showed off for each other that night. On the musty train to Florida, in the rented compact car, in Nora's king-size bed, they'd proved proficiency. Now they were shooting for greatness. By the next morning, Nora felt as if she had beard burn all over. It wasn't an unpleasant sensation.

She felt him behind her before she was entirely awake.

"You've been telling lies again," she mumbled.

He didn't bother to answer. She turned over. Her nose hit his chest. He smelled of sex. Like brewing coffee, it was an encouraging aroma to wake up to.

She burrowed into it. That was when it happened. Again. The phone on his night table sounded like an alarm. He obviously didn't know about the dial that turned down the volume.

He froze. She worked her way up till her face was on a level with his.

"That'll teach you to put it back on the hook," she said. He picked up the phone. She rolled away.

The conversation was brief. Max told someone called Fraser to look in the file and hung up. She rolled back into the circle of his arm.

"Who's Fraser?"

"A little brown-noser who wants to make sure I know he's working on Saturday."

"There's nothing wrong with ambition."

"There's something wrong with that kind of ambition.

One night I ran into Fraser in the elevator. It was just before Christmas. He was carrying a whole bunch of packages. That's why he dropped his briefcase. It opened. You know what the little prick had in it? A package of peanut butter cheese crackers. Not even a newspaper. Just those damn crackers. But he's terrified one of us is going to see him going home without his briefcase. What a world! If I had any guts, I'd pack it in."

"You'd miss it."

"Like hell I would."

He sounded sincere. She was shocked.

"What would you do?"

He rolled over on top of her. "Think of all the lines I haven't ridden." His hand started its own journey. "South America. China." He was gathering momentum. "India."

The law of averages was with them. It shouldn't have happened a fourth time. But it did. The phone rang. He rolled away and picked it up. She rolled out of bed. The last thing she heard before she turned on the water in the bathroom was Max reassuring his mother that she hadn't awakened him.

By the time Nora had come out of the bathroom, he'd hung up the phone and was sitting up with his back against the headboard.

Nora got back into bed. He didn't move. She sat on her own side and pulled the covers up over her chest.

"What now?"

"Ostensibly a question about her health insurance."

He was staring at the wall. Nora was staring at him.

"And the real reason?"

"Because, like Everest, I'm here."

That, Nora decided, was a debatable point.

He got up and went into the bathroom. He was still tan from Florida, except for a crucial area that glowed white, like an animal in mating season.

She rolled over and took the phone off the hook. If he noticed it when he came back, he didn't object.

It wasn't the first time they'd got up together, but it was the first time without the imminence of mothers or the press of jobs hanging over them. He gave her the less shabby of two robes, though it was a close tie. He produced croissants he'd had the foresight to buy the night before and coffee that put hers to shame. She put place mats and napkins and butter and jam on the dining room table. He brought in the paper. They sat down to breakfast.

Nora stood outside herself and watched them. This was what Beatrice called companionship. Another image flashed through Nora's mind. It was one of the classic montages in film history. Citizen Kane and his first wife sat at the breakfast table. Even in black and white, they were rosy with the glow of newfound happiness. They went on sitting at that table as the film ran and their smiling mouths shriveled into bickering and finally froze in silence. Nora had always thought it was a brilliant piece of filmmaking and a terrifying object lesson.

"Listen to this," Max said. "Thirty Haitian men are suing the U.S. government for using an insecticide to delouse them. They allege it led to gynecomastia."

"Okay, I'll bite. What's gynecomastia?"

Max looked at the paper again. " 'A condition in which men grow female breasts, and, in its most severe form, lactate.' "

Nora thought of Max's mother and former wife and kids who had to be talked to about something. He hadn't stumbled across that article. He'd been set up for it. The only thing she couldn't figure out was how a man like Max had ever managed to walk out on a wife and two children. He told her.

When Max had been married only a few years, he'd had to fly to Chicago on business. Since he'd finished early on a Friday, he'd decided to take the old Broadway Limited back. As he told it, he'd gone to bed early, then awakened around two or so. By that time he decided he might as well stay up to watch the horseshoe curve.

"Jesus, that's a sight. All those cars lit up like some over-size diamond necklace snaking around the curve."

Nora told him to skip the background color and get on with the story.

Max didn't know whether it was the thrill of the horseshoe curve—i.e., everything he was missing in life—or too much to drink or what, but he started writing. "A kind of letter."

"To your wife?" Nora asked.

"To myself."

He listed all the things wrong with the marriage, and they weren't matters like leaving the cap off the toothpaste tube. Apparently, he just didn't like his wife. Not that he blamed her, at least not entirely. He catalogued his own betrayals.

"You told me you hadn't screwed around."

"Betrayals of the heart and mind."

Nora wondered again how a man like Max had managed to leave.

He went on with his story. He wrote several pages that night. By the time he reached the end, it was all there in black and white. He had to get out.

The train got into Penn Station early the next morning. Max took the shuttle to Grand Central and a local train out to Westport. His wife met him at the station. She told him on the ride back to the house. She was pregnant.

"And you were trapped," Nora said, but she'd forgotten about those men with gynecomastia.

"I was ecstatic. For a while."

Eleven years and two children later, Max was cleaning out the locked drawer in his desk and found the letter. At first he didn't remember writing it, but he knew he had. In fact, he could have written it the day before. When his wife found it, she thought he had written it recently.

"Wait a minute," Nora said. "I missed something. I thought you were the one who found it."

"I didn't know what to do with it, so I stuck it in my briefcase."

"Didn't you know she went through your briefcase?"

"We'd had a fight about it the week before."

Nora didn't say anything. And she didn't ask why he'd married a woman he didn't like. She'd known the answer to that one even before she'd seen *Citizen Kane.* Emotions, like the people who inspired them, were unreliable.

She offered to do the dishes again. There were only a couple of mugs and plates anyway.

He followed her into the kitchen with the coffeepot in one hand and the butter in the other. He said his kid was coming into town for the afternoon. They were going shopping for a tennis racket. He said maybe she'd like to stick around. She could meet Dan and help them pick out a racket for his birthday.

She said thanks but she had an office full of work that had piled up while she was away.

He shrugged, mentioned that Dan would be in town for only a few hours anyway, and went into the dining room to get the jam.

When he came back to the kitchen, she said she'd probably be finished by five or six.

He put the butter and jam in the refrigerator and said they could make an early movie and dinner. He hadn't seen the new Woody Allen yet.

"Not Woody Allen. I always save them for Maude."

"Who's Maude?"

"A free-lance writer. We met on our first job. We've been going to Woody Allen movies together ever since we left our first husbands. My only husband," Nora corrected herself.

Max said there were plenty of other movies in town.

Several weeks later Cornelia spent a night in New York on her way back from Florida. It took her less than an hour to turn the extra room back into her room by the sheer force of her messiness. Nora wondered, again, how someone whose ambition was to create harmonious spaces to shelter the body and elevate the spirit could thrive in such disorder.

The dresser was covered with an array of gadgets, bottles, and jars that testified to the American flair for creating a need, then filling it. A pair of jeans lay in a corner of the floor, a couple of sweaters hung over the back of the rocking chair, a silk camisole dangled by one narrow strap from a doorknob. The *AIA Journal*, a book on Palladio, and several magazines cascaded over the bed.

Nora sat with her feet propped on the desk and watched Cornelia pull things from her duffel. The room was a disaster, but her niece was something else. Cornelia's adolescence had been a steady ascent of the slopes of her parents' beauty. It seemed to Nora that her niece had finally reached the peak. She had Susannah's mouth, wide, full, so sensual it sometimes looked bruised, and Susannah's high brow. It was a poet's brow, or perhaps only a romantic's. Her eyes were her mother's too, dark blue spheres of intelligence, or at least vigilance, but they were all the more startling under Nick's fringe of heavy black lashes. Her hair was Nick's legacy too, dark, luxuriant, a little wild.

Nora went on staring at her niece. She wondered if her love for Cornelia would be unadulterated by envy if the girl were really hers, if the beauty had come from her body, the perfection from her passion.

She remembered an afternoon, shortly before Cornelia had come to live with her. It was a Sunday, and Nora had been to the Metropolitan. She didn't mind going to museums alone. She preferred it. You didn't have to accommodate your pace to anyone else's. You didn't have to listen to fatuous comments, or hear yourself make them. She was walking up Fifth Avenue, feeling pretty good, if she remembered correctly, when she noticed another woman walking alone in front of her.

Nora watched the Sergio Valenti label bounce and ripple obscenely as the woman moved. Beneath the polyester knit top, her bra carved a deep furrow between rows of soft flesh. As they walked, one behind the other, Nora tried to place the woman. She didn't come from one of those irreproachable apartment houses with gleaming brass canopies. She wasn't carrying a bag from the Metropolitan or the Guggenheim or the Cooper-Hewitt. Nora guessed she'd wandered a few blocks west from one of the last lingering enclaves of Slavs and Irish who were being driven into the East River by developers and boutique owners and restaurateurs and people like Nora.

Suddenly a girl of about eight or ten came swerving up on a skateboard and cut the woman off. She was a leggy, coltish kid with long, silky blond hair and a face that hovered around the edges of perfection.

"Mom!" the girl wailed.

Nora couldn't believe that child had come from that mother.

"You didn't even care!" the girl went on. "I fell and you didn't even care."

The woman quickened her pace. Nora watched the Sergio Valenti letters bounce.

"Mom!" The girl picked up the skateboard and ran after her. "Mom!" Her thin body vibrated with frustration.

The woman stopped and turned on the girl. Nora saw the mother's face. It was pasty and puffy and twisted with rage.

"What d'ya want from me?" she screamed. "You got your friends. Your doormen. Every day you come home and tell me. 'I know all the doormen. All the doormen say I'm the best skateboarder. All the doormen say I'm so pretty.' So go to your fuckin' doormen."

Nora had come abreast of them by now. The girl was drooping, her head hanging forward, her silky hair hiding her face. The mother hunched over her like a hammer, hitting her again and again with the words.

Suddenly she noticed Nora staring at them. The women's eyes met. The mother's were like hard bits of glass. They dared Nora to interfere. Nora kept walking.

The scene had jolted her. She'd been watching and listening idly, as she often did when she was alone among people. She hadn't expected to stumble on something dangerous. A dirty little secret. A dirty little secret of motherhood.

Cornelia tossed a white lace garter belt on the bed.

"Where on earth did you get that?" Nora asked.

"Grandma bought it for me when I was down there."

"I should have known. I used to hate the damn things. Torquemada designed the prototype."

Cornelia sat on the side of the bed and held up the garter belt with one finger. "I think it's sexy."

"You're your grandmother's granddaughter, all right."

"Andy thinks it's sexy too."

"That's because he's never worn one. I hope."

"Grandma liked him."

"Your grandmother's like Will Rogers. She never met a man she didn't like. What'd you think of the Sap?"

"I think he's cute. They're cute together."

Nora glanced at the confusion of magazines Cornelia had tossed on the bed. On top of the *AIA Journal* a fashion magazine lay open to an advertising slice of life. A boy and girl with enough gray on their hair to paint a battleship but not to make them look like a mature man and woman were embracing. He looked down at her, she looked at the ring on her finger, and Nora looked at the caption. "These days I can afford to show her how much I care."

Nora would have run the ad—she'd run worse in *AH!*—but she wouldn't buy the message.

"Sometimes I wonder how I got mixed up with this coven of dewy-eyed romantics."

"What's wrong with Grandma liking to have a man around?"

"Nothing," Nora admitted.

"She says it keeps her going. Gives her strength and makes her more energetic."

"Kind of like those African tribesmen who eat their dead enemies' flesh."

Cornelia stared at her aunt, then shook her head in amazement. "I don't believe you said that."

"I'm sorry. I was just being a smartass."

Cornelia went on staring at her for a moment, then went back to pulling things from her duffel. "You know, sometimes when I look at this family and think about the sins of the mother being visited, I get really scared."

10

Beatrice was not a good mother, if being a good mother meant entering the world of children. When Susannah and Nora were small, she arranged their doll carriages for them, then lost patience when they messed them up. She never played Monopoly or built a sandcastle or a snowman. She had no patience with games or fantasy, unless, Nora liked to say in later years, it was the game of love and the fantasy of happily ever after. Beatrice didn't want to enter the world of children. She preferred to bring her children into her own world. When Nora was a child, she loved to play going to the vault.

As Nora followed Beatrice's clicking heels across the vast marble expanse of the old bank, tellers looked out from little brass cages, and behind a polished wood fence, men glanced up from their desks and nodded with smiles that came too quickly. Next there was the big steel circle that led into a secret cave made up of dozens and dozens of boxes. You needed two keys to open each one, your own key and Mr. Natwick's. That was where the scary part came in. Mr. Natwick had an eye that followed you no matter where you went, but never seemed to see you. Beatrice said it was a wall eye. While he took the key from Beatrice, and opened the locks, and slid the long metal box out of its nest, his eye rolled around like a renegade marble.

Mr. Natwick always put the key on top of the box and carried it into one of the small rooms that opened up off the long hall. Beatrice followed him, and Nora walked in her mother's footsteps.

For the rest of her life, the ritual of going to her own safe deposit box always made Nora realize that she was, despite inner turmoil and certain outer indications to the contrary, a grown-up. She hadn't forgot the secrets her mother had taught her. There were little velvet-lined boxes and suede and satin bags in her vault too. There were no coupons to clip, but there were stock certificates and the deed to her apartment. And there was a scrap of paper that she sometimes forgot, from visit to visit, that she'd saved.

#553310

Moss, Nora   Dr. Kauffman
> URINE PREGNANCY
> POSITIVE
> Total charges $6.00

Nora didn't go to graduate school. During her senior year she'd come to realize that despite good marks and faintly bookish interests, she was no scholar. Graduate school would have been, as her adviser had pointed out, simply something to do until she got married. She was already married.

She decided to get a job. Beatrice thought she ought to teach. Susannah had taught for a while after she graduated from Smith. It was something to do until you got pregnant. It was also something to fall back on, Beatrice said grimly. "In case."

"In case" was shorthand for a multitude of tragedies that ranged from having your husband, like Phil, die prematurely, but, unlike Phil, impecuniously, to having him leave you for some tramp or lose his job. Of course, any sensible girl hedged this last possibility by marrying a professional man who worked for himself.

Nora said she'd rather die than teach. Imagine Daisy Buchanan or Lady Brett teaching.

*   *   *

The woman who hired Nora told her she was lucky. "You'll be working with writers."

The woman's voice fell to a hush on the last word. She and Nora might have been in church.

Nora's first meeting with David Meadow threw her. For one thing, David looked exactly like Lenny the Letch, who owned the neighborhood liquor store. He had the same broad-nosed fleshy face, the same heavily lidded eyes, the same weight of chins sinking into thick neck. It was disconcerting to think the mind of a writer might be lurking behind the facade of a heavy-breathing liquor merchant with a nasty habit of running his finger across Nora's palm every time she tried to pay him. For another, David Meadow was in a wheelchair.

"Wellesley," was the first thing he said when she turned up in his office.

"What?"

He wheeled back from his desk, balled up a piece of paper, and shot it into the wastebasket across the room. "I was guessing that you went to Wellesley."

"Smith."

"The last researcher I had from Smith wanted to know where she could get hold of a writer named Trotsky. She was trying to track down a quote."

"Did you tell her to check the Mexico City phone book?" He wheeled back to his desk. "You just might do, Foyle."

"My name's Moss. Nora Moss."

"You'll always be Kitty Foyle to me."

Nora had to look up the reference. Only years later did she understand it.

David went on staring at her and rubbing his chins roughly. "Though, God knows, you look as if you fit the mold."

"What do you mean?"

"You've just joined an exclusive club. The magazine isn't exactly an equal opportunity employer when it comes to researchers. We hire Seven Sisters graduates. Not that it seems to do much good. Witness the Trotsky incident. We hire what we euphemistically call 'girls from good families.' That way we don't have to pay them a decent living wage. How's your lineage, Foyle?"

"Not exactly the Adamses, but no record of embezzlement or incest. We're not so sure about insanity."

He nodded. "And we hire lookers. The writers insist on it.

"This isn't a magazine," David explained when she'd been there about a week. "It's a womb."

They were in his office. She was still a little drunk on that office. Piles of books stood everywhere. Not only the familiar great books that had lined the offices of Nora's professors and sat on the shelves Paul had sanded and painted in their apartment, but new books with shiny jackets and glossy pictures of authors who were still alive and paper-covered editions of soon-to-be published books that David called bound galleys. Nora spent a lot of time on the phone calling publishing houses asking for books David wanted. At first she'd felt funny calling up that way and asking for handouts, but after the first few calls, she learned that as soon as she mentioned the name of the magazine, the voice on the other end of the phone sounded as if Nora were the one doing the favor. "Do you want me to messenger it over?" the voice always asked. It was Nora's first taste of power, even reflected power.

Besides the books, there were stacks of magazines, an old manual typewriter, and a maelstrom of works in progress. Various drafts covered every surface and hung from the cork bulletin board. There were no photographs or personal mementos.

In the close to two years that Nora eventually worked for David Meadow, she learned that he had a wife no one had ever met, two children, and a house in Connecticut to which he commuted in his custom-made car with hand controls for brakes and gas. She never learned how he'd ended up in that wheelchair, though there were plenty of stories, just as there was a lot of speculation about the extent of the damage. Nora's favorite version of the tragedy was that he'd been wounded on the last day of World War II. She preferred that one not only because it was the most romantic, but also because, given the rumored ages of his children, it meant that David wasn't entirely paralyzed. The thought of a life without sexual promise terrified Nora.

She asked Nick about it once. He said conditions varied from case to case, though there were certain givens. Paraplegics tended to have shorter life expectancies. Other systems, like the urinary tract, tended to kick out. Nora never asked Nick about it again.

"What do you mean, a womb?" she asked David.

"They feed us. Wait till you see the buffets they lay on when everyone's pulling all-nighters to close the book. They keep limos waiting downstairs to take us home. They advance us money to pay our debts. They send us to discreet little hospitals to dry out. They even, God bless their paternalistic souls, tell us what to write. There are guys who turn up here with the ink still wet on their diplomas and don't leave until they're carried out feet first."

"Cynicism is cheap," Paul said when she repeated David's lesson that night.

They were in the kitchen of the one-bedroom apartment they'd rented in a vaguely seedy brownstone on West Ninety-sixth Street. It had a fireplace that didn't work, a bathroom that opened into the kitchen, and a parquet floor that listed so badly a tennis ball dropped at one end of the living room rolled straight to the far end of the bedroom. Paul loved to demonstrate the tennis-ball trick for guests.

"If he's so dissatisfied, why doesn't he quit and do something he believes in?"

Nora didn't know it at the time, but they'd just fired the first salvo in the battle for her soul.

Nora stood staring through the hospital nursery window at a little old man wrapped in a pink blanket. The baby looked different today. Then she realized the nurses had rearranged the cribs. This little old man wasn't her little old man.

She tried to read the labels on the cribs. It took her a few minutes to find Baby Demopoulis. She didn't look much different from the first little old man Nora had been staring at.

Susannah and Beatrice came up beside her.

"She's gorgeous," Nora said.

Susannah laughed. "You don't really think so, but I do."

The women went on staring into the nursery more greedily than they'd ever looked into any shop window.

"You know," Susannah said after a while, "it's scary. I was up in the middle of the night thinking about it. Worrying about it."

"About what?" Nora asked.

"That something terrible might happen to her. Or to Nick." Susannah stood staring at her daughter and shaking her head in disbelief. "I can't be this happy."

"Shh," Beatrice warned. "Don't give it an *ahora.*"

Like generations before her, in moments of fear Beatrice found religion, or at least superstition.

Cornelia's eyes began to focus. She smiled. Her black hair fell out, and a new head of equally dark hair grew in. She rolled over, and her mother and grandmother and aunt, who just happened to be there at the time, applauded as if she'd won a gold medal for the decathlon.

Nora learned that she wasn't afraid to hold the baby. Beatrice carried her with aplomb. Susannah wore her like an appendage.

"It's amazing when you think about it," Beatrice said one rainy spring afternoon when Cornelia was three months old. She was sitting with her daughters and her grand-daughter in the kitchen of the house Susannah and Nick had bought with a small down payment, a little help from Beatrice and Sam, and a big mortgage.

"What's amazing?" Susannah shifted the baby to her other breast.

Beatrice put her cup of coffee down on the new blond wood table. There was a kiss of lipstick on the rim. A bottle of Susannah's nail polish sat beside the sugar bowl in the center of the table.

"Birth?" Nora asked.

"More than that. When you think about it, the baby's nothing more than Susannah."

Susannah and Nora laughed. "Nick had something to do

with it," Susannah said. "A miracle substance called sperm."

"Of course," Beatrice answered. "But since then, she's all you. She grew in your body, on your body. And since she was born, she's had nothing but your milk. She's grown and changed and gained six pounds from nothing but her mother."

Susannah bent to kiss the baby's fuzzy head. Her mane of light hair fell like a curtain separating them from the rest of the world. "I never thought of it that way." She kissed Cornelia again.

Out in the car, backing down Susannah's driveway, Nora wondered if she had that much to give.

She thought of her mother and sister and niece sitting in the color-coordinated kitchen of Susannah's new house. The first few times Nora had come to visit she'd had a hard time finding the house. It looked so much like one next door and two across the street. They all had the same spindly pillars in front, which was why they were called the Colonial, as opposed to the Elizabethan, which made a passing stab at half-timbering, and the Californian, which had pillars, half-timbering, and a red tiled roof. Each house was set on a full four-fifths of an acre of land, but beneath thin lawns, the soil looked raw and wounded, as if it were grieving. The builders had left a single tree in each front yard, though there were a few more in back, and pointedly ignored sidewalks. The lack of sidewalks saved a bundle and screamed cachet.

Oak Hills was one of the most expensive new developments in northern New Jersey. It was also only twenty minutes from Byron Road.

Nora told Paul the fake colonial split level in that raw suburb offended her sensibilities. In fact, it merely flew in the face of her acquired prejudices.

Paul said it was a good buy and a sound investment. He said he liked the idea of living in the country.

"Oak Hills is about as close to the country as that colonial is to Tara."

"There're no sidewalks."

"If that's the way you feel, we'll move to Venice."

But Nora had to admit, to herself if not to Paul, that for all its aesthetic shortcomings, there was something real about that house with its humming kitchen appliances and fourth bedroom that Nick used as a study, its laundry room and family room, its linen closet stocked with towels and sheets and months' supplies of tissues and toilet paper in decorator colors. It wasn't as much of a bastion as that solid Tudor of her childhood. Instead of brick and stone there were bay windows in front and glass walls in back. Instead of thick doors that closed with resounding thuds there was flowing space. But the house was still a refuge. It was certainly more secure than that one-bedroom walk-up with the handsome but badly listing floors. Nora wouldn't be caught dead living in her sister's split-level—she could imagine what David Meadow would think of it—but she always looked forward to going there. Then, a few hours later, she couldn't wait to get away.

"Christ!" David backed his wheelchair away from his desk, balled up Nora's report, and lobbed it into the wastebasket across the room. "Didn't they have something called freshman English at Smith?"

"I was exempted," Nora admitted in the half-embarrassed tone she reserved for such statements.

"God knows why. Unless the faculty thought an inability to use active verbs showed a certain delicacy of spirit. Very ladylike, I'm sure."

Nora smoothed her skirt. Her poet-manqué adviser had never ridiculed her like this.

"It's just a researcher's report. I didn't think you'd care how it was written."

David rubbed his chins. Except for his massive muscled arms, his upper body was soft. It flowed and rippled with each movement. Sometimes Nora found herself staring at David with morbid fascination.

"I don't care, Foyle, but you ought to."

Nora tried harder on the next report.

"He's not God," Paul said when he stumbled into the living room one night and found her still working. She purposely hadn't crumpled up the rejected drafts, because she didn't want to wake him.

"Just another minute," Nora said. "I promise."

"You really broke your ass on this one, didn't you?" David asked the next day. He was whizzing down the hall, one hand propelling the wheels of his chair, the other holding her report, and she was racing behind him.

"I tried." She sounded just the way she had when she'd admitted she'd placed out of freshman English.

"Yeah, I could tell. You must have had a hell of a time getting this many adjectives into a two-page report."

Nora swore she wasn't going to mention the incident to Paul.

She spilled it that night before he'd even taken off his jacket and tie.

"If he knows so damn much, what's he doing writing for that right-wing rag?" Paul hadn't yet moved to the right himself.

He dropped his jacket and tie over a chair in the living room and came back into the kitchen. The refrigerator jutted out into the small space, and it was almost impossible for them to keep from bumping into each other.

"Anyway, everyone at Smith thought you were a good writer." Paul took the oil and vinegar from the cabinet and started making the salad dressing. Among their friends Paul was known for his salads, or maybe only for the fact that he made them. "Where'd this guy go to school, anyway?"

"Harvard."

Paul finished making the salad dressing in silence.

Her next report was clean as a whistle.

"Better," David said.

Nora went home and told Paul.

"You don't need him to tell you you write well. We've been telling you that for years."

"You and Sam aren't exactly objective."

Still, Nora figured she was learning.

The next morning the phone was ringing when she reached her desk. "Get your ass in here!" David shouted as soon as she picked it up.

He was jerking his chair back and forth with short furious movements. When he saw her, he wheeled across the office, slammed the door behind her, and rounded on her. His soft fleshy face was crimson.

"What kind of village idiot reads some ass a piece about himself over the phone? *My* piece!"

"I didn't think—"

"You can say that again. Christ, the cleaning lady has more sense. You didn't even interview the guy for me. What I can't figure out is how he tracked you down."

"You gave me that essay to read. You said I could use your couch."

"So when some asshole calls and asks you to read him an article that hasn't even run yet, hasn't even been approved yet, you give him everything but the punctuation."

"I'm sorry."

"They assigned me a cretin as a researcher. A fucking cretin." David had never said "fuck" in her presence before, though the other writers did with numbing regularity.

"I said I was sorry."

"Sorry! You ruined one of the best damn pieces I ever almost rammed through this place, and you think all you have to do is say you're sorry!"

The tears behind her eyes were hot. She blinked. She swallowed. She had no defense, except her own stupidity. She took a deep breath.

"All I can say is that I just didn't know I wasn't supposed to. I mean, the article was on him. I suppose I should have known, but I didn't. Now that I do, I promise it'll never happen again."

He sat looking up at her for a while, then whirled around and wheeled back to his desk.

"Get out of here." He never mentioned the incident again.

She took the story home to Paul the way she would have a skinned knee to Beatrice. He said all the right things. To Nora's amazement, they didn't make it stop hurting. Instead, she and Paul ended up fighting about it.

"It isn't as if you gave away state secrets," Paul said without looking up from his law journal.

"It was a dumb thing to do."

"The guy ought to have some self-control. I'd never yell at my secretary that way."

"I'm not a secretary."

Now Paul looked up from the journal. "Maybe it'd be better if you were."

"What's that supposed to mean?"

He went back to his journal.

"I asked what that was supposed to mean."

He met her eyes again. "It means you get worked up over nothing. It's only a job."

"I'll remind you of that next time you come home bitching about some client."

"That's different."

Nora didn't argue. She knew he was right. She wasn't the one supporting them. She wasn't the one with the important future. She was just dabbling. Not even "in case." Just "until."

The more Nora talked about David, the less Paul liked him. She couldn't figure it out. Susannah said he was probably jealous, but that didn't make sense. If Paul was going to worry about one of the writers, it should have been Tom St. John.

St. John had white blond hair, cheekbones that could shave wood, and excessive literary pretensions, even for that crowd. He looked, and often sounded, like the issue of an aberrant coupling between a California surfer and Edna St. Vincent Millay. In an office riddled with intramural affairs—David insisted they wanted to prove they didn't have to leave the building for anything—Tom St. John was rumored to have slept with more researchers and secretaries than any writer in the history of the magazine. There was another rumor about St. John. It was that he'd started the first one.

Nora brought home all the stories about Tom St. John, including the one about the night he and a secretary were having at each other on his floor and one of the editors

appeared in the doorway of St. John's office. As the story
went, St. John kicked the door closed without missing a
stroke. But Paul showed no jealousy of St. John, not even
when he took Nora to lunch.

David wasn't so broad-minded. "You'll never sleep your
way to the top around here," he told her that afternoon.

Nora was genuinely surprised. "I'm married!"

David snapped his thumb and forefinger together as if
he'd just remembered something. "I forgot. Married people never screw around. Anyway, you won't get out of the
harem that way."

"What?"

"The harem. The golden gynie ghetto. The researchers,
Foyle. You can leave them, but you can't rise from them."

Nora hadn't thought of doing either, though Paul had
begun to make noises about getting out. His former roommate's wife was pregnant. Nora's former roommate was
trying.

Nora's IUD gnawed at her insides like a guilty con-
science.

Every writer at the magazine worth his salt had a book
under contract. David's was on the Kennedy administra-
tion. It was called *Failed Promises.* One day he asked Nora
if she'd like to help him with it. "Survey some of the litera-
ture. Track down some facts."

Nora shivered with pleasure. She hoped David hadn't
noticed.

"What's he paying you?" Paul asked. He was shaking
grated cheese into the salad.

Nora was horrified. "We didn't talk about money. Anyway, I'll do most of the work on magazine time."

"That's dishonest."

"Everyone does it. They're all working on their own
books."

"That doesn't make it right."

"It's good experience," Nora quoted David.

"For what?" Paul laughed at his own joke. "I mean, come
on, Nora, just what does this guy think he's preparing you
for?"

* * *

David finished his manuscript. He took Nora to lunch to celebrate.

That night Paul wanted to celebrate too. He decided to go for broke and make a real Caesar salad.

"From now on," he said as he mashed anchovies, "I'm going to ask not what you can do for David Meadow but what you can do for us."

The next day David said he had another free-lance job for Nora. "This one even pays."

She asked what it was.

"Editing."

"I'm not an editor."

"In other words, you want to be a researcher all your life."

"But I don't have any experience."

"This is your chance to get some. I have a friend. A sportswriter. Which is to say that he can string together thirty or forty violent words at a sitting. Somehow, he managed to sell a book. Now all he needs is someone to organize it and clean up his deathless prose."

"I don't know anything about sports."

"Christ, Foyle. It's a YA. Young adult. Great sports heroes of the ages. Don't tell me you've never heard of Jesse Owens or Jackie Robinson."

"They played football, right?"

"You're the girl for the job," David said.

"But you don't know anything about sports." Paul didn't look up from the contract he was reading when he spoke. The habit drove Nora crazy.

"I told David that. He said it doesn't matter. It's YA. Young adult. This time I'm going to get paid."

Paul looked up. "It isn't as if we need the money."

"David says it'll be good experience."

This time Paul didn't ask experience for what.

David was banging on his old manual typewriter when Nora got to his office. He used the hunt-and-peck system, but he used it with a vengeance.

"When you asked me if Jesse Owens and Jackie Robinson played football, I thought you were kidding."

"I was."

He stopped typing and turned to her. "That was a joke. My old buddy is pleased. More to the point, his editor is pleased." He wheeled back from the typewriter and crossed his arms over his soft chest.

"What do you want to do, Nora? Write? Everyone around this place is a closet writer."

"I don't think so."

"You want to be an editor?"

"I don't know."

"You want to stay with magazines?"

"I haven't really thought about it."

"Christ! 'I don't think so. I don't know. I haven't thought about it.' It must be nice to have all the options in the world. But it must be hell to be so stupid you don't even consider them."

He wheeled out from his desk and across the room until his withered knees were almost touching hers. "You better start thinking about them, Foyle, because they close in before you know it."

Nora stood in the vestibule of the brownstone holding the slip of paper. She'd stuffed the other mail back in the box and torn open this envelope as soon as she'd seen Dr. Kauffman's return address. The nurse had told her on the phone the test was positive, but Nora had to see it in writing. No matter how hard she tried to imitate David's cynicism, she couldn't get over her respect for the written word.

She slipped her hand inside her coat and put it on her stomach. There was something in there. Someday it could be a separate being, riding its bike and going off to school and fighting with her. But not yet. Now it was all hers. Her body, her baby, her responsibility.

She told herself to stop being melodramatic and climbed the stairs to the apartment. Paul said it wasn't a baby yet, just a fetus. Nick said it was a simple procedure. Even Beatrice and Susannah said she couldn't take the chance.

They'd both heard stories of babies conceived with IUD's, stories so horrible they couldn't repeat them.

Paul wasn't afraid to repeat them. His former roommate knew about this couple. The wife had got pregnant even with an IUD. They'd decided to have the baby. It had been born with the device imbedded in its forehead.

Somebody on Nora's floor was cooking something funny for dinner. It wasn't cabbage, but it was close. That was one of the things Beatrice hated about apartments. She said there was something indecent about smelling everyone else's dinner and having them smell yours in return.

Nora let herself into the apartment and closed the door behind her. There was no smell of cooking here, only the scent of ammonia and lemon wax. The cleaning woman had been in today.

Nora switched on the light. The apartment was immaculate. When she crossed to the bedroom, her shoes made marks on the newly vacuumed area rug.

She opened the top drawer of her dresser and put the slip of paper under the pile of handkerchiefs. Then she sat on the side of the bed, picked up the phone, and dialed the doctor's number.

Her hands and feet were like ice. No sensation. Her body was shaking with the cold. No, not with the cold. Her body was shaking with sobs.

A face swam into view above the stretcher. A coarse-grained older man's face with black stubble over the chin and cheeks. "You're all right," he said.

Nora's body went on shaking.

"Stop crying! You're all right."

But she couldn't stop crying, any more than she could stop shivering.

"Maybe this will teach you," the black hole in the stubbled skin opened to let the words out. "Maybe next time you'll be more careful." The face disappeared.

When Nora came to again, the man was gone. She never did find out whether he was a doctor or a nurse or an orderly. All she knew was that he was unfair. Unfair and wrong. She had been careful. And it wasn't all right.

* * *

Beatrice and Susannah took her home from the hospital.
They put her straight to bed, though she insisted she felt
fine. The cramps weren't even as bad as they'd been when
she'd had the IUD put in. That night she'd writhed in pain
and drugged herself with Darvon, and the next morning
Susannah had explained that she'd actually had labor pains,
or at least a facsimile thereof. Now she suffered from nothing more than twinges.

"I never did like the idea of that thing," Beatrice said as
she brought in a tray with three cups of tea.

"Nick says they're safe, but I don't trust them," Susannah
agreed.

Beatrice put the tray on the bed and sat in the rocking
chair beside it. Susannah was on the end of the bed. They
passed milk and sugar and the plate of cookies.

"I'm finished with IUD's," Nora announced.

"It's about time," Susannah said.

"There's no rush," Beatrice insisted. "Take a few months
off. Get back your strength. In the meantime, if it happens,
it happens. The more you think about it, the less it happens. Look at all those couples who can't conceive. They
adopt a baby, and the next thing they know, bang, she's
pregnant."

Nora looked at the set of galleys on her night table.
David had mentioned her in the acknowledgments. Even
Paul had been impressed. Nora loved seeing her name
there as if carved in stone. And it was her name. Not Nora
Moss, but Nora Heller Moss. David had been fastidious
about that.

"I'm going on the pill," Nora said.

A couple of years later when Nora was packing to move to
her own apartment, she found the slip of paper she'd se-
creted in her top drawer under the handkerchiefs. That
was when she locked it away in the safe deposit box she'd
just rented in her own name. Not Nora Heller Moss, but
Nora Heller.

Every time she went to the bank to get out some moder-
ately valuable piece of jewelry or less than crucial legal

document, the paper was there waiting for her. It was like the reminders of unfulfilled expectations that came at random moments. He'd be in nursery school by now. I suppose I'd cry on the first day. She'd be turning thirteen. We'd probably fight about piercing her ears.

But even at her most self-deluding, Nora never blamed the divorce on the abortion. Paul did for a while. Beatrice and Susannah were convinced of it. But Nora knew differently. She never regretted the divorce. She frequently grieved for the baby.

11

*B*eatrice said it as if she were making the most ordinary request in the world.

"Would you call Dr. Kauffman and make an appointment for me?"

"What's wrong?" Nora's tone was so sharp that Lucy, who was sitting on the other side of Nora's desk, looked up from the fit printout sharply.

"Nothing's wrong. I'm due for a checkup."

"Don't you have a doctor down there? I mean, I'd love to see you, but shouldn't you have a doctor down there?"

"I did, but I don't trust him. He gave Belle Gross a clean bill of health. A month later she found a lump."

Nora said she'd make an appointment for her mother.

"Besides," Beatrice said, "I haven't been to New York since last summer. I thought we could go to the theater. Maybe do a little shopping."

Beatrice got in late Tuesday night. On Wednesday morning she was up before seven. Nora heard her mother padding around the second bedroom trying to be quiet. She got out of bed, put on a robe, and went into the living room.

Beatrice was sitting at the dining table with a mug of coffee. Beneath her robe, she had on everything except her dress. She'd even put on earrings and makeup. Only the lipstick was lacking.

"I'm sorry," Beatrice said. "I didn't mean to wake you."

"You didn't," Nora lied and went to the door to get the paper.

"You know you don't have to go with me this morning," Beatrice said.

"I told you. I'm not going with you. I was due for a checkup too. And if I have to spend time cooling my heels in the waiting room, I'd rather do it with you than back issues of *Harper's Bazaar* and *Mother and Child*." Nora had always suspected that Kauffman's refusal to subscribe to *AH!* was personal.

Years ago Nora had followed her mother's and sister's footsteps into the offices of Dr. Arnold Kauffman. He was, Nick assured them, one of the best ob-gyn men in New York. Then, two months after Nora left Paul, she asked Kauffman for a diaphragm. Her life didn't seem regular enough to warrant the pill any longer.

Kauffman's eyes had focused on the ceiling as they did when he was concentrating on an examination, though he wasn't examining then. "Well, Nora," he said with a little laugh that she supposed was meant to be avuncular. It sounded more like Woody Woodpecker. "You have to be careful."

"I know," Nora answered. "That's why I want a diaphragm."

"I mean about men. I don't like to badmouth my own, but most of them only want one thing."

"Thank God for that," she said.

Kauffman's eyes snapped down from the ceiling. He told Nora that if she wanted a diaphragm, he'd give her a prescription for one. She'd never filled it. It would be just like Kauffman to give her the wrong size as divine, or at least Kauffman's, retribution. A year later, she'd switched to his associate.

At least fifteen women were loitering in the small waiting room when they arrived. Beatrice and Nora squeezed into a loveseat in the corner.

There were no clocks in the room. The women looked at their watches repeatedly, but the gestures were empty.

The morning was stuck somewhere in timelessness. They'd all put their lives on hold. Every so often a woman looked up from a dogeared magazine and sighed. Several prospective mothers sat with hands folded over swollen stomachs and joked familiarly with the receptionist. A lone man huddled in a straight chair in the corner. The woman beside him was reading *Vogue,* but he couldn't focus on the magazine on his lap. His eyes circled the room frantically in search of a place to land.

"They're making a sexist statement," the woman crushed into the loveseat on the other side of Nora said. She wore her hair in a crew cut and there were diamond studs in her ears. Nora found the combination jarring. "They're saying our time isn't as valuable as theirs."

"What they're making," Nora said, "is a lot of money. They book three patients for every time slot." Nora's early training at the hands of printers had taught her to read upside down.

Beatrice smoothed the pleats of her skirt. "My time isn't as valuable as theirs."

The woman gave Beatrice a shocked look and went back to her book. Nora sneaked a glance at the cover. It promised the equivalent of a Harvard Business School education in six minutes.

Half an hour later a nurse came out and called Beatrice's name. She sounded like a railroad conductor announcing an imminent station. Nora's followed a few minutes later.

The examining room, small, white, and immaculate, was designed to instill fear. Everywhere Nora looked, metal surfaces threw back distorted images of herself. The nurse ran through the familiar instructions in a bored voice. Take off this, put on that, follow instructions, be a good girl. Nora did as she was told, then sat on the end of the examining table, swinging her legs over the side and waiting for the doctor as if for judgment. On this turf, sex really was destiny.

She pictured Beatrice waiting in a similar antiseptic cubicle, wearing an identical skimpy white gown. Her brown arms and legs would be arranged in a semblance of composure, but her age-slackened stomach would be tense with expectancy. Nora wondered if the fear grew worse with each passing examination or if you were gradually lulled into a confidence of immortality.

She stared at the chart on the cold metal counter across the room. With a single exception, it told a neat, unexceptional story. No problems, everything in order, as Gray and before him Kauffman pronounced at the end of each appointment. When would the story take a turn for the worse? She sat there conjuring up cells that grew more secretly than a child, disorders that disordered lives. She thought of Beatrice lying in the next examining room like a wall between Nora and the unwanted discoveries.

They went out for a ladies' lunch. Annie joined them. As in the old days on Byron Road, Nora's friends still liked her mother. After lunch Nora went to her office, and Beatrice headed for the radiologist's. If she got the mammogram out of the way that afternoon, she'd be finished with doctors for another six months.

Beatrice was up early again the next morning, but she was still in her robe when Nora left for the office. They agreed to meet for lunch.

A little before noon Beatrice called Nora's office. Her secretary said she was in a meeting. Beatrice left a message for her daughter to meet her at Bergdorf's instead of the restaurant. "Tell her I want her opinion on a dress," Beatrice said.

The dress was exquisite. It was also gray chiffon.

"It's beautiful," Nora said, "but where are you going to wear it? Don't tell me. Cousin Phyllis is getting married again. Always a bride, never a bridesmaid."

"Not that I know of, but it's on sale, and I like to be prepared."

"You and the marines. *Semper paratus.*"

"That's the Coast Guard. The marines are *Semper fi.*"

Nora sat on the spindly chair holding her mother's dress and coat and handbag as well as her own trenchcoat and handbag and looked at her mother's reflection in the three-way mirror. She was a stylish triptych in gray chiffon.

"How do you know something like that?"

Beatrice shrugged.

There was a knock on the fitting room door; the saleswoman opened it without waiting for an answer. She was a big, handsome, tired-looking woman, the clone of dozens of women who'd waited on Beatrice and her daughters over the years.

"What does your daughter think?"

"I think it's beautiful," Nora said.

Encouraged, the woman stepped into the fitting room and examined Beatrice's reflections.

"It's perfect. All you need is your basic pearls. Or maybe a diamond clip." She took another step toward Beatrice and smoothed the fabric over the shoulders. "I can't get over the fit. You could walk down the aisle in that today."

"Now we know where you can wear it," Nora said. "Your next wedding."

"I told her it was your basic second-time-around dress," the saleswoman went on. "But she said it's the third. You want to take it or should I send it?"

Beatrice said she'd take it.

The saleswoman unzipped the dress and lifted it carefully over Beatrice's head. The neat gray hair emerged from the yards of gray chiffon, but Beatrice didn't look at her daughter.

Nora passed her mother her handbag. Keeping her head down, Beatrice fumbled in it for her wallet. It was fat with plastic cards. She rummaged through Saks and Bonwit's and Bloomingdale's.

"The lavender one," the saleswoman said.

"I know, I know." Beatrice handed the woman the card. The woman folded the dress carefully over one arm and took the card in her other hand. "You're going to be a lovely bride," she said and left the fitting room.

Nora sat under the pile of clothing, staring at her mother. Beatrice stood in the middle of the room in her thin silk slip, staring back.

"It's not a joke, is it?"

"Charlie wants me to marry him."

"And you're going to?"

"Why not?"

"Why?"

"Because he's a good man."

"Since when? You used to call him the Sap."

"Shh."

Nora looked around at the pale peach walls and the reflection of her mother and herself that went on into infinity. "Does he have the room bugged?"

"A person can change her mind. A diamond pinkie ring isn't a criminal offense. I was too quick to judge, like Daddy used to say. I was too critical."

The heap of clothing on her lap was making Nora sweat. She noticed that her mother was shivering. She handed Beatrice her dress.

"Listen, Mother, did it ever occur to you that you don't have to be married? I mean, you lucked out twice. Why not quit while you're ahead?"

"It wasn't just luck." Beatrice slipped the dress over her head. "Besides, I like being married. It's what I'm good at. The way you're good at your magazine."

"Thanks."

"I meant that as a compliment."

"Bullshit!"

Nora had never in her life said "bullshit" to her mother.

Beatrice turned her back. Nora zipped up her mother's dress in silence. Beatrice took her coat and handbag from her daughter and started out of the fitting room. The mirrors reflected a parade of fragile old women marching away, their skinny shoulders squared to a military correctness of courage.

Nora dragged herself up off the spindly chair. Her own reflection looked like an army of women in flight. She slammed the fitting room door on it.

Beatrice was standing at a desk signing the charge slip. Nora noticed that she formed the letters precisely. Her monthly statement wouldn't be littered with unintelligible scrawled names that might or might not be Beatrice Fine Heller Brickner, soon to be Saperstein.

"I'm sorry," Nora said.

Beatrice handed the slip to the saleswoman and took the

box from her. The woman thanked Beatrice again, pressed a card into each of their hands, and told Nora if she needed a dress for the happy occasion, she'd be glad to help her.

"I just want to know one thing," Nora said, and Beatrice stopped at the top of the escalator. Nora wasn't sure whether her mother was waiting to hear what she wanted to know or hesitating because at her age with her arthritis you didn't hop on and off things without some calculation. "Why did you have to let a saleswoman tell me?"

Beatrice put one foot, then the other on the first step. "I wanted to tell you. Ever since I got here."

Nora followed her. "Then why didn't you?"

"Because you didn't want to hear."

There were mirrors on either side of the escalator. Two familiar women kept pace with them. Nora could have run down the moving steps, but one of them would have followed her.

"Look," she said and moved down a step to stand on the same level as her mother. "I'm happy for you. Really I am."

They stepped off the escalator together. The images disappeared. Nora started to laugh. "Just don't expect me to call him Dad."

"You're late," Lucy said when Nora got back to her office. "I hope it was a power lunch, because Wheeler was down here looking for you."

"What did he want?"

"To tell you he noticed the ad pages were down again this month. He told me instead."

"Thanks."

"*Nada.*"

Nora's head snapped up at the word. Reminders of Charlie lurked everywhere.

She leaned back in her chair. "What do you think of a freestanding supplement devoted to multiple weddings?"

"Multiple weddings?"

"We've done the whole wedding etiquette bit. Last June. What about second weddings, or third, or tenth? We won't get as much advertising. The silver and china and crystal accounts won't come in as heavy, but there's clothing and furniture and travel. And all the linen accounts. No one wants to sleep on old sheets with a new husband. What do you think?"

"I think you're talking blasphemy."

"People get remarried all the time."

"I wouldn't know about that. I'm still working on the one without the prefix. But that's beside the point. Or maybe it is the point. No one wants to think about that prefix. No one wants to remember the last time or worry that there might be a next. Come on, Nora. You know as well as I do, beneath *AH!*'s glossy facade beats the heart of *American Home-maker*. Screw the statistics. At this book we still believe in true love."

The voice came booming over the phone. "Nora! Good to hear your voice. Good to hear your voice. So, how are you? Having fun with your mama? I bet you two girls are shopping up a storm. I said, 'Bea, why do you have to go to New York to shop? You got all the stores you need down here. Saks. Bloomingdale's. Even Martha.' See, I know my stuff. She says, 'Charlie, it's not the same. New York is where it's at, stylewise.' "

It was a sentence Nora doubted her mother had ever spoken.

"So, did she get a dress?"

"She got a beautiful dress." Nora hesitated a moment. Her chest hurt. "Congratulations." It took her another moment to force out the rest of the words. "I hope you'll be very happy."

"So she finally let you in on the secret. I don't mind telling you, Nora. I was a little worried. You marry a woman, you want her children to like you. Because if they don't, they can make everyone miserable. But as soon as I saw you with your mama, I knew. 'Bea,' I said, 'it's going to be okay.' She wasn't so sure, but me, I knew. 'Bea,' I said, 'we got nothing to worry about because your daughter and me, we got something in common.' She asks me what, like she's expecting me to tell her I found out you're interested in astronomy or you like to play golf or something. 'Bea,' I said, 'that daughter of yours and me, we both want to make you happy.' Correct me if I'm wrong, Nora."

She didn't correct him.

"And one more thing, Nora. I don't want you to worry."

"About what?"

"Maybe it's not my place to tell you, but your mama and me, we signed one of those things. A prenuptial agreement."

It was the one thing Nora wasn't worried about, not because she was so high-minded, only because she knew her mother. Beatrice was the most deceptive kind of romantic, a practical one.

"I don't want to come between you and her. Financially, I mean."

"I never thought you were after her money."

Nora heard a slapping sound at the other end of the phone. She was willing to bet it was Charlie hitting his head with his hand.

"You're right! What am I saying? As if someone would be after her money, a woman like that, with so much on the ball. All the same, I just wanted you to know."

"I appreciate that."

"So, did she tell you when the big day is? June. Maybe you think it's funny at our age, but your mama said she always wanted to be a June bride. Isn't that something? I mean, what can I give her? She's got the engagement rings and the diamond wedding bands. Both her husbands, they should rest in peace, took good care of her. But Charlie Saperstein's going to make her a June bride."

That night Nora and her mother watched the late news from Nora's bed. There was a segment about the new marine corps. Nora stared at the children masquerading as men who marched across her small screen.

"Was Charlie ever in the marines?" she asked.

"How did you know?"

Nora thought of the way her mother had looked that afternoon as she'd debated the wisdom of buying a gray chiffon dress. "*Semper paratus,*" Nora had said, and Beatrice had corrected her.

"A wild guess."

"During the war."

"You always said Daddy was too old for the war."

Beatrice was still looking at the screen, but Nora saw the grin that teased at the corners of her mother's mouth.

"Charlie's younger than I am. Four years."

Nora started to laugh.

"It's not that funny," Beatrice said.

"I was thinking of the latest trend report. You're a with-it woman."

Will Wheeler was standing hunched over his desk, his short arms planted solidly on top of it. Nora thought again of all those evolution exhibits in the Museum of Natural History.

"I wanted to talk to you about Millie Chase's memoirs," he said before she even sat.

Millie Chase was a formerly unimpeachable judge who'd been indicted on bribery, conspiracy, and several other counts. It was a sordid story that costarred an on-the-make attorney seventeen years her junior.

"We didn't bid on them," Nora said. "They wanted a fortune for first serial. Besides, I'm sick of stories about successful women undone by love."

"Your readers aren't."

"I thought we tried not to pander to the lowest common denominator."

"What do you call 'Fast Track'?"

"Fast Track" was a regular feature in the book. Each month the magazine profiled a woman who was, as the copy always said, a trendsetter in her field. The careers varied from month to month, but the tone of breathless overachievement remained the same. A cosmetics tycoon roused her children at six each morning so they could share twenty minutes of quality family time a day. An investment banker put in twelve-hour workdays, accompanied her venture capitalist husband to at least six black-tie events a week, and lived on a diet of Maalox and Advil. A trendy dress designer, who managed to turn out four pieces an hour working on a computer rather than a model, tucked a laptop into her backpack when she went mountain climbing in Nepal. Advertisers loved those "Fast Track" profiles. Readers fantasized over them. Publicists fought and schemed for them. And every time Nora read one she felt like a failure.

The old features—"Is This Divorce Necessary?" and "The Heartbreak of Motherhood"—had whined "Be glad you're not me." "Fast Track" screamed "Don't you wish you could be me!" Millie Chase's memoirs would put a new spin on both messages. All over America, women would open the article with shivers of titillation and close it with smug smiles.

"Anyway, I've already cut the deal," Wheeler said.

Nora was shocked. "For how much?"

"Six hundred thousand."

Now she was horrified. "Do you have any idea what that's going to do to our budget?"

"Chase's name on the cover will up the circulation. Maybe even the advertising."

Nora never did find out why Wheeler was determined to run Millie Chase's memoirs. Someone said the judge had been a friend of Wheeler's mother. Someone else said Wheeler's wife had sat through every day of both the Jean Harris and Bess Myerson trials. All Nora knew for sure was that it was the first time Wheeler had ever made her print anything. It was the first time he'd ever interfered in the editorial side of the magazine.

Nora was late getting to the restaurant that evening. She spotted Max and her mother at a table across the room, shoved her coat at the sullen would-be actress in the coatroom, and started toward them before the maître d' could even reach her. Max caught sight of Nora over Beatrice's head and frowned. Nora knew that frown. It said the movie line's begun to move inside, or the curtain's about to go up, or in one more minute I would have struck up a conversation with that woman at the bar. Then he couldn't help himself. He smiled. Nora knew that smile too. It meant that she was late, but she was here, and Max was a reasonable man who didn't hold a grudge.

Nora slid into the chair the waiter held for her and apologized. She said she'd got held up in a meeting with Wheeler.

"Sometimes I think she puts that magazine out single-handed," Beatrice said.

"Sometimes I think she thinks the same thing," Max said. They smiled at each other.

Nora stopped with the drink Max had ordered for her before she'd arrived halfway to her mouth. She felt like a woman who suddenly realizes that her best friend and her lover have been meeting behind her back. Only the meeting in this case was of the minds.

"Doesn't he usually stay over?" Beatrice asked after Max had let them out of the cab in front of Nora's apartment house.

"Is this my mother speaking? The woman whose favorite expression was 'He won't buy the cow if he gets the milk for free.' If ever there was an adage designed to drive a woman to promiscuity."

Beatrice just laughed. "The whole world has gone through a sexual revolution. What makes you think I'm standing like the Rock of Gibraltar?"

Nora thought of the linen dress with the decorative buttons that had turned out to be functional after all. "Nothing."

When Nora walked into the bedroom, the bright red "1" was glowing on her answering machine.

"How much do you want to bet it's Charlie?"

Beatrice followed her daughter into the bedroom. Nora pushed the button, and they stood waiting for the tape to rewind. Then she pushed another button. A strange voice identified itself as Linda in Dr. Kauffman's office.

"The doctor wants to talk to Mrs. Brickner about her test results."

Beatrice and Nora stood on either side of the night table staring at each other.

"He never used to call," Beatrice said. "Just sent those cards with the negative box checked off."

"Maybe somebody's raised his consciousness," Nora said, though she knew that his associate still sent postcards.

Beatrice sat on the side of her daughter's bed. "Of course, if it weren't negative, he'd have to call."

Nora sat beside her mother. "You're jumping to conclusions. It's too soon for the results of the Pap smear, and you said they told you it takes a week to hear about the mammogram."

"That's what the secretary said this time. Last time I went, she said I'd hear in a week, unless something was wrong. Then it would be twenty-four hours."

"But in that case the radiologist would call."

"No, he tells Kauffman and Kauffman tells me."

"I still think you're jumping to conclusions."

"I haven't said anything."

"I know what you're thinking."

"Kauffman wasn't making a social call."

"He took a lot of tests. Maybe you have high blood pressure."

"They can see that right away."

"Blood work. Maybe they're calling to tell you you have syphilis."

Beatrice managed a smile. "Sure. He took a urine specimen, too. Maybe I'm pregnant."

"Do you want a drink?" Nora asked.

Beatrice said she didn't, but told Nora to have one.

Nora went into the kitchen and poured a lot of scotch and very little soda into a tall glass. She took the drink back to her room and stood staring at the answering machine. Goddamn machines. Goddamn doctors. And their goddamn secretaries. They should have more sense than to leave a message like that.

She sat on the side of the bed and put her head in her hands. The message wasn't really enigmatic. No doctor, no matter how callous, would leave disastrous news on a machine.

She was still sitting that way when her mother walked into the room. Nora dropped her hands and looked up guiltily.

"I'm not worried," Beatrice said. "Really. And I don't want you to."

"I'm not."

They remained that way for a moment, forcing smiles into the teeth of each other's lies. Nora was still sitting on the side of the bed, and her head came only to Beatrice's chest. For a moment she felt like the little girl who used to fling herself against that thin body. Those small endangered breasts had offered oceans of comfort.

"Besides, even if they've found something," Beatrice said, "and I still don't think they have, it's not the end of the world. It may not even be malignant."

"Of course."

"Dorothy Gittler had a mastectomy, what, fifteen, twenty years ago. Then, two years ago they took off the other breast. I see her swimming, playing tennis, even jogging."

"Don't even think about a mastectomy. There are all sorts of new treatments."

The sound of the phone ringing made them both jump. Nora reached for it before it had a chance to ring a second time. She didn't know why. Even Dr. Kildare wouldn't call at ten-thirty at night, and she didn't rate Kauffman that high on the humane scale.

"Nora! It's Pops. Just kidding. Just kidding. Bea told me what you said about not calling me Dad. She said it's an old family joke. From when she married her second husband, he should rest in peace. I said Nora can call me anything she wants so long as she doesn't call me late for dinner. Just kidding. So where's the bride? I waited to call cause I knew you two were going to be out on the town. Bea told me. With Addie Miller's son. Nice. Nice."

"I think she may have gone to sleep," Nora said, "but I'll check."

"Sure, you go. I'll hang on."

Nora put her hand over the mouthpiece. "It's Charlie," she whispered. "I can say you're asleep."

"Why would you do that?"

"You really want to talk to him? At a time like this?"

Beatrice reached for the phone. "I'm going to marry the man, Nora. If there's anything wrong, it'll be hard to keep it a secret from him."

Nora handed over the phone. Then she left her mother

alone in her bedroom and went back to the kitchen for
another drink.

They passed in the hall in the middle of the night. Beatrice
was coming from the guest bathroom. Nora was going into
it because there were no aspirins in her own medicine
chest.

"Are you okay?" Nora asked.

"Are you?"

"Just looking for some aspirins."

"You have a headache?"

"I shouldn't have had anything to drink when I came
home."

"You want to come to my room for a while?" Beatrice
asked.

"Get in bed with Mommy?" Nora laughed nervously.
Then Beatrice did too. The sound was a cold rattle in the
three-o'clock darkness. They went back to their separate
rooms.

Beatrice was up even earlier than usual the next morning,
but this time the noise didn't wake Nora. She was up too.

They sat at the table in the living room drinking too
much coffee and passing sections of the *Times* back and
forth between them. At seven-thirty Nora announced she
was going to call the doctor.

"The office won't be open yet," Beatrice said.

"There must be a service. They'll tell us when it does
open."

"I'm glad neither of us is nervous."

The answering service said the office opened at nine-
thirty.

"Goddamn bankers' hours," Nora said.

At a little after nine, Nora called her own office and told
her secretary she'd be in later. Jenny asked when, and Nora
looped crazily through the day ahead. What would they do
once they got the news? Go back to the doctor's for more
tests? Sit in the apartment crying? Go through the motions
of a normal day. She told Jenny she'd let her know.

The phone rang as soon as Nora put it down.

"Listen, Nora, I'm sorry to call so early, but I thought maybe Beatrice could have some news." Charlie's decibel level was almost normal.

She told him the doctor's office didn't open till nine-thirty.

"They shouldn't do a thing like this. Leave a message to drive you half crazy overnight. How's Bea?"

This time Nora decided not to run interference. She handed the phone to her mother and went into the bedroom to get dressed.

Nora sat staring into her closet. She swore she wasn't superstitious, but just as there are no atheists in foxholes, so there are no rationalists waiting for medical test results. If she put on jeans to sit around and mourn, would she outsmart fate? If she put on a suit to go to the office, would she tempt it? She decided only Beatrice's daughter would find a correlation between what she wore and the news she was likely to get, closed the closet door, and went back inside.

Beatrice was just hanging up the kitchen phone. The clock on the stove said nine-twenty. They went back into the living room. At nine-thirty Nora stood.

"Maybe we should give it a few more minutes," Beatrice said. "In case they don't get in on time."

"Then we'll call again."

They went into the kitchen. Beatrice dialed. Nora could hear the busy signal from where she was standing.

"Christ!" she said. Beatrice didn't say anything.

She dialed again. This time Nora heard it ringing.

"This is Mrs. Brickner." Beatrice's voice sounded small and thin after the ringing. "I got a message to call about test results."

Nora couldn't hear the secretary's answer.

"Brickner. Beatrice Brickner. 'B' as in boy, R-I-C-K-N-E-R."

There was another silence.

"Yes, I'll hold. She's getting Kauffman," Beatrice whispered to Nora.

There was a longer silence. The refrigerator defroster went off. Nora hadn't noticed the noise till it stopped. Outside a horn screamed and brakes screeched. Nora waited for the crash, but none came. Through the air duct she heard a puppy crying. The young couple above her had bought a King Charles spaniel, though they were rarely home with it.

"What in hell is taking him so long?" Nora said.

Beatrice held up her hand with her palm toward Nora. "I'm fine, Dr. Kauffman. How are you this morning."

Nora could practically hear her mother's heart pounding beneath the polite formula. She turned her back and walked to the other end of the kitchen. It took only two steps. Then she walked back and stood facing Beatrice.

The silence went on for longer this time. Nora watched her mother's face. Beatrice's eyes were focused on the floor as she listened. Her lips were pressed together as if she were blotting lipstick.

"I see."

"What?" Nora asked.

"I see," Beatrice repeated.

Beatrice put her free hand on her forehead and rubbed the skin above her eyebrows with her thumb and forefinger.

"No," she said. "I'll have it done up here. My daughter's up here."

Life didn't stop. Nora had known it wouldn't as she'd sat staring into her closet that morning. She went to her office. She sat in on meetings. She approved articles and artwork and expenditures. She even went to an awards dinner.

"Go," Beatrice said. "You'll have a good time."

The advice came back to Nora from a hundred adolescent arguments. "Go, you'll have a good time," Beatrice used to say, and Susannah and Nora always argued that they weren't likely to have a good time with a boy who had bad skin or sweaty palms or parents who were "very fine people." Nora didn't tell Beatrice that the odds against her having a good time were even longer now. She didn't have to. Beatrice knew. They both knew, and they were both pretending.

So Nora put on her long black silk, and Max put on his black tie, and they went down to the New York Public

Library, where they sat at a table in the great hall eating mousseline of salmon and listening to Mrs. Wheeler talk about Jean Harris and Bess Myerson and Millie Chase. Max was good. He even discussed the legal niceties of the Millie Chase case as if it were a juridical problem rather than a tabloid writer's dream.

There were speeches during the grapefruit sorbet. Someone talked about the need to fight illiteracy and presented an award. Someone else accepted the award and talked about what he'd done to promote literacy. The guest of honor assured them he wasn't special, but just an ordinary CEO of a Fortune 500 company who'd liked to read as a kid. He quoted a little Kipling to prove it.

" 'We have forty million reasons for failure . . . ,' " he boomed out over the hall. Then something extraordinary happened. The timing was uncanny. At least, it was uncanny for Nora. The guest of honor probably didn't agree. He found it merely inconvenient.

Somewhere behind her Nora heard a thud, a small cry, excited whispers. She turned. At a table near the door, a few people were standing. Waiters had rushed over. Nora saw two black-clad legs and a pair of patent-leather evening pumps sticking out from the tablecloth.

"Give him room," she heard a woman cry.

" '. . . but not a single excuse,' " the speaker went on.

"Give him air," another hushed voice insisted.

The waiters had made a phalanx around the table, blocking it from view.

The speaker went on. He assured them he couldn't have done it alone. He named names.

Behind the phalanx, Nora saw several other waiters moving out of the hall. From the way their shoulders hunched forward, they must have been carrying something, or someone, heavy.

Nora turned back to the speaker. The other guests already had. He just wanted to say again how proud and grateful he was.

On the way home, Nora and Max shared a limo with Wheeler and his wife. Wheeler said he had to give the guest of honor credit. It was really something the way he just kept going when that guy in the back collapsed.

"Why not?" Nora said to Max when they'd dropped the Wheelers off at their apartment. "Strokes or heart attacks or whatever the hell he had are a dime a dozen, but it isn't every day five hundred people turn out in black tie to tell you you're a helluva guy."

It was the first time she cried in front of Max.

12

*B*eatrice was pleased, generally speaking. Both her daughters were married. Both her sons-in-law were good men with gilt-edged futures. More important, they were good husbands. If Beatrice's heart fluttered a little more for Nick, she breathed more easily around Paul. When she thought about it, and she thought about it often, she decided it was a nice balance. Susannah could handle Nick. Nora needed more of an anchor.

Then there was the next generation. Though Beatrice had begun to look forward to grandchildren the day Phil had died, sometimes, when she looked at Cornelia, the sheer joy of that small amalgam of the familiar and the new almost knocked Beatrice over. She was glad Susannah was trying again. Beatrice had always known Susannah would have two children. It was a tribute, to her daughters' closeness, and to the family Beatrice had forged.

Of course, there was that business with Nora and the abortion. Beatrice didn't like to think about that. She never had approved of that device, that IUD. But Nora would get over it. Beatrice knew women—friends, and friends of friends—who'd had abortions, and that was in the days before they were legal. The women hadn't been girls in trouble, either, but wives and mothers who'd decided for one reason or other that another child was out of the ques-

tion. Beatrice couldn't have done it herself, but she didn't
blame the women who did. They'd got over it, and Nora
would too. In six months or a year, she'd go off the pill.
Beatrice didn't like the pill any more than she did the IUD,
but what could a mother say? Then Nora would get pregnant and quit her job and settle down. It was only a matter
of time.

Generally speaking, Beatrice was satisfied. Not that she'd
come out and say such a thing. It didn't do to tempt fate. It
didn't do to give it an *ahora*.

The man Nora was in love with said something in French.
Beneath his nose, flattened like a kite against his battered
face, a subtitle translated.

"How many men have you slept with?"

The man waited. Nora held her breath. Beside her in the
torn leather seat of the Thalia movie theater, Paul
crunched a handful of popcorn between his teeth.

Jean Seberg held up one finger, then another, a third,
fourth, fifth. Nora sat absolutely still. Seberg raised her
other hand. She held up her thumb and forefinger. Seven
fingers were splayed on the big screen.

Nora gasped. Paul passed her the popcorn.

On the street the April drizzle had softened into a mist.
Empty cigarette packs and discarded papers lay like dirty
rags on the sidewalk. Car tires made a sizzling sound in the
wet oil slicks as they cruised down Broadway.

"How about some Chinese?" Paul asked.

Nora tried to picture Belmondo and Jean Seberg in Joy
Gardens. "We always go for Chinese food on Sunday
night."

"I know. That's why I suggested it."

She couldn't fault his logic.

They started walking up Broadway.

"Sheltered," she said. "I am so fucking sheltered."

She felt Paul's big frame list a little away from her. He
hated it when she said "fuck," but he didn't like to sound
prissy. "For a lit major, you have a real command of the
English language."

They opened the door to the aroma of tired cooking oil. Ever since Beatrice had declared White Castle off limits in Nora's youth, her mouth watered at the smell of cheap food in the making. They slid into a booth. Nora's slicker stuck to the redplastic banquette. She wrestled it out from under her while Paul studied the menu. She didn't know why he bothered. With his photographic memory, he could probably recite the whole thing by heart.

The waiter came. Paul ordered at length. None of this combination plate stuff for him. Nora chewed on a handful of dried noodles.

"I've never gone anywhere or done anything," she said when the waiter had left.

"You want to sell newspapers on Paris street corners?"

"It beats coming up with fifty ways to find more storage in your kitchen."

"I told you not to leave. You went from a reputable news weekly to a piece of fluff you pick up at the grocery check-out counter. Like razor blades or batteries."

"You've got us mixed up with *Family Circle* and *Woman's Day. American Homemaker* has a subscription circulation." She chewed some noodles. "Besides, I thought you were glad. Now I have normal hours."

Paul didn't say anything.

She took another handful of noodles. "Besides, David said I'd never get anywhere if I stayed."

"Where's anywhere?"

Nora dipped a dried noodle in the duck sauce. "That's what I'm trying to tell you. I don't know."

The waiter brought the eggdrop soup. Paul spooned some out for her, then himself.

"All right, you don't want to find new storage in your kitchen. You don't want to be a researcher. You don't want to sell newspapers on Paris street corners. You don't want a baby."

"Yet."

"Yet," he agreed. Paul was nothing if not fair. "What do you want to do?"

Nora didn't answer.

"Have an affair with a murderer? Is that it? I ought to

warn you though, most of them aren't like Belmondo. I know whereof I speak."

In his younger, more gullible days, Paul had spent a summer working for a criminal lawyer.

"It has nothing to do with murderers." Nora wasn't sure whether it was connected to lawyers who used terms like "whereof I speak."

"Just with having an affair."

"I didn't say that."

He poured tea into her cup, then his own. "You've implied it in the past. Who can forget that winning line about being in a library and reading the same book over and over?"

The waiter brought the spareribs and took away the soup.

Paul picked up a rib, but didn't start to eat. Nora watched him. He was holding it as if it were a gavel. She knew that behind the birdlike eyes a legal mind was at work. He was devoted to the principle of civil liberty. And he believed in carrying ideas to their logical conclusion.

"Individuals," he said finally, "shouldn't infringe on each other's rights. If it's that important to you, maybe you ought to have an affair."

Nora never blamed Paul. At the time she even admired his sophistication. Only years later, after the divorce, did she begin referring to him as the coldest man in America.

Still, it wasn't Paul's fault. If she was going to blame anyone, besides herself, it would have to be David.

For once Beatrice and Susannah were impressed. For once they took Nora's job seriously.

"You'll have to tell me what he's like," Susannah said. "I swear by him. Him and Spock."

"I used to listen to him on the radio, when you were both babies," Beatrice added. "He made sense. As much sense as experts ever make."

Dr. Leon Welch was the grand old man of pediatrics, second only, as Susannah had pointed out, to Spock. Welch, Nora later learned, didn't agree with the ranking.

When Monica Storch handed Welch over to Nora, she

was surprised. For one thing, it was a plum editorial assignment, or so she thought. For another, Nora had assumed
Welch had been dead for years. When Welch's article came
in, she decided she hadn't been far off. If the ideas and
language hadn't given him away, the paper would have. It
was yellowing around the edges and separating along the
folds. Apparently Dr. Welch hadn't heard of Xerox machines.

Nora told her mother and sister about it at lunch. They'd
come into town shopping.

"I can't believe he thought he could get away with it,"
Nora said.

"He's a very important man," Beatrice warned her.

"Even Nick is impressed," Susannah added.

"But he must have written the thing twenty years ago.
The paper looks like the Dead Sea Scrolls."

"Don't make trouble," Beatrice warned.

"Mommy's right," Susannah said. "You can't question a
man like Welch."

Nora went back to her office and called David Meadow.
"He may have written it twenty years ago," David said. "As
long as he didn't publish it twenty years ago."

"He couldn't be that stupid."

"He probably figures since he's forgotten, everyone else
has too."

Nora went down to the magazine's library. Over the
years, Dr. Leon Welch had written several articles for
American Homemaker, but though the ideas bore an uncanny resemblance to those in the piece he'd sent her, the
sequence of words wasn't exactly the same.

It came to her on the way back to her office. She retraced
her steps to the library and began lugging out old *Readers'
Guides*. She found the piece in a 1958 issue of *Ladies'
Home Journal*.

Nora went back to her office bristling with indignation.
"Quack," she muttered as she dialed Dr. Welch's office.
"Charlatan."

She managed to hang on to her outrage while a woman's
voice said she'd see if the doctor was free. Then the voice
that Beatrice had turned to on the radio for guidance and

reassurance came rolling over the phone and undermined Nora's anger.

The tones were thick and syrupy as cough medicine, the kind that's prescribed for small children. He called her Nora, though they'd never met or even spoken. He confided that Monica had said wonderful things about her. He promised that it was going to be a joy working together.

She told him she'd just read the article. She apologized for bringing it up, but mentioned that it was exactly the same as a piece he'd published in *Ladies' Home Journal* in 1958.

Welch chuckled. "There are certain eternal truths in life, Nora. And you'll find many of them in that article. Children haven't changed since 1958. Though I've updated a few things."

She couldn't argue with him there. He had actually crossed out a paragraph about sex-appropriate behavior for preschoolers. The pressure of the pencil had torn the paper.

"But, Dr. Welch, *American Homemaker* can't publish a piece that already appeared in another magazine."

Now Welch was the indignant one. "I never planned to, Nora. I assumed we'd work on it together. You are an editor, aren't you? Or did I hear Monica incorrectly?"

Nora cringed. Beatrice and Susannah had been right. A man like Welch wouldn't try to get away with anything. Nora had been dumb. And disrespectful.

They made an appointment to meet at his office.

Nora was accustomed to the sterile school of doctors' office decoration—a few polite museum reproductions in the waiting room, the requisite diplomas in the consultation room, a Norman Rockwell knockoff meant to soothe the nerves in the examining room. Dr. Leon Welch subscribed to a different design philosophy. Every inch of wall space was covered. There were idealized paintings of children, and saccharine sketches of children, and adorable photographs of children. There were also pictures, hundreds of pictures, of Dr. Leon Welch and children. In the spaces among all the pictures were aphorisms, scrolled and lettered in elaborate, leafy script, about the innocence and transience and joy of childhood. Dr. Leon Welch's office was a temple to immaturity.

Nora sat in the waiting room going over her notes. She'd prepared carefully for this meeting. She wasn't going to blow it again.

"Nora." The word came down from a godlike height. Nora looked up from her notes. Tall, gaunt, white-haired, terrifyingly paternal, Dr. Leon Welch filled the door to his consultation room.

She stood. The papers on her lap slid to the floor. She stooped to pick them up. Dr. Welch, patience incarnate, stood waiting.

Papers in one hand, her briefcase in the other, she crossed the room to him. That was when she realized she couldn't shake hands. She put down her briefcase and transferred the papers to her left hand. She held out her right. He took it, drew her into his office, and indicated a chair beside a massive desk. He took the throne behind it.

Nora looked around the room. The mawkish pictures and sayings were replaced by foot after foot, yard after yard of diplomas and awards. Hospitals and societies and entire nations acclaimed Dr. Leon Welch. On the desk a brass plaque that no one would call small proclaimed him Father to a Generation. And Nora Heller Moss had called him a plagiarist, albeit a self-plagiarist. No wonder Beatrice and Susannah had been shocked.

He leaned back in his throne. A small garden of white hairs flourished in his nostrils.

"Do you have any children, Nora?"

She said she didn't and mentioned her time in grade at the other magazine and the past months at *American Homemaker*. She didn't dare tell him how little editorial experience she'd had.

He didn't seem interested. Nora glanced around at the walls full of accolades and awards. No wonder he wasn't impressed.

"I'm looking forward to working with you," she said. "Working together, I'm sure we can bring a fresh voice to the material." She'd been rehearsing the line for days. She

knew the importance of the editor-writer relationship.
She'd read about Max Perkins.

Welch peered through his rimless glasses at her, then
leaned back in his throne and made a church steeple of his
liver-spotted fingers. "Can you guess how many children
I've examined in my life, Nora?"

She said she couldn't.

"I calculated the number once. Fifty-two years of clinical
practice. At least half a million children. White children,
black children, brown children. Asian children, African
children, Indian children. Healthy children, sick children,
starving children."

Nora was trying to think of a nice way to tell him she got
the point. "I noticed the pictures. With all those children,
we shouldn't have trouble finding case histories." She'd
decided case histories were crucial. She wanted the piece
to have the ring of authenticity as well as the stamp of
authority.

"Case histories," he repeated. "I have more than half a
century of case histories." He waved one long arm in the
direction of an old pine file cabinet. The two drawers
didn't look as if they could accommodate more than a
couple of hundred children. Nora was beginning to worry
again.

"Maybe if you gave me some appropriate files," she said
sweetly, "I could put together the case histories myself."

Welch pushed his throne back from his desk and stood.
She assumed he was going for his files, but he didn't move,
just stood looking down at her from the heights of altruism,
celebrity, and a still unshrunken frame. He took a deep
breath. The white hairs in his nose danced in the breeze.

"I've enjoyed talking with you, Nora."

"But your files . . . ," she began.

"I couldn't possibly violate doctor-patient confidential-
ity."

"I'm not going to use the names!" She hadn't meant to
sound so impatient, but did he think she was an idiot?

"This has been useful, Nora." He took her hand, drew
her up out of the chair, and began steering her to the door.
"Most useful."

"But the article . . ."

". . . is in your hands. I have complete confidence in you."

It was the first of many editorial conferences Max Perkins hadn't prepared her for.

Nora called David to report on the meeting.

"So you're going to tell them you can't handle the first real assignment they give you," he said when she finished.

"What am I supposed to do? There's no article. There're no case histories."

"When are you going to learn, Foyle?"

"I know. I'm naive."

He told her to meet him for lunch the next day, and he'd explain everything.

David wasn't at the restaurant when Nora arrived, though the maître d' said Mr. Meadow had made a reservation. He didn't offer to seat her. It was an era when women lunching alone anywhere but Schrafft's were potential hookers. It was also an era when women lunching with men on business slipped their credit cards beneath the table to spare their colleagues' pride and the waiters' embarrassment. Nora tried to make herself small in the tiny entrance area beside the bar, while waiters elbowed her into the wall and men alone and in groups bustled past to their tables.

David came wheeling through a group of them. They scattered like billiard balls. Nora had seen it happen before. David's presence threatened men.

"Why didn't you wait at the table?" he asked. His breath was short from wheeling the few blocks from his office.

"He didn't suggest it," Nora said.

David just looked at her for a minute, then backed his chair a couple of inches to let her go in front of him.

"You'll have to do a major rewrite," he said as soon as they'd ordered. "His old wine in your new bottle."

"I can't write his article for him."

"We're talking about some fluff on child care, Nora, not a philosophical treatise on the nature of thought."

"What about the case histories?"

The waiter brought her salad and his steak. David peered at the meat, then at her.

"Make them up."

Nora's eyes flew up from her own lunch. "That's lying!"

"It's illuminating a point. You're doing the reader a service, helping an old man, and saving your own ass. Notice, I didn't list them in order of importance."

"They aren't going to fire me because he's too senile to write an article."

"They're not going to promote you either." David sliced off a piece of steak. "Listen, Foyle, this guy's published a lot of books and articles over the years. I'll bet there's a whole damn society of editors and ghosts who have been making up his material. Rewrite the junk. Make up the case histories. You'll be in good company."

Nora made up the case histories. When she finished, she was proud of her handiwork.

Paul was scandalized. He predicted legal repercussions and moral ramifications.

"But David says everyone does it."

Paul looked up from his law journal. "That doesn't make it right." He sounded exactly as Beatrice had when she used to say she didn't care what other mothers thought. She didn't approve of ankle bracelets or boys who didn't open car doors for you or girls who hung out in front of the White Castle.

Monica Storch was delighted. She called Nora into her office.

"How'd you do it?" Monica asked. "I had a friend who worked with him at *McCall's,* and she said he hadn't been *compos mentis* in years. He just keeps submitting the same old pieces again and again."

Nora shrugged. "I have to admit I did a heavy rewrite. It's not all his."

Monica laughed. "I'll bet. Anyway, the case histories are terrific. How'd you pry them out of him?"

Nora remembered Paul's warnings. He'd been right. The jig was up.

"I . . . uh . . . fabricated them."

Monica pressed her heavily lipsticked mouth into a thin line. "You mean you made them up?"

Nora hesitated, then nodded.

Monica was still staring at her.

Nora waited for the ax to fall.

"Good for you," Monica said finally. "I wasn't sure you'd think of it."

Nora started to laugh. She was saved. Paul had been wrong. David was right. "I didn't. A friend of mine did."

David groaned when she told him about the conversation. "I'm glad you can scan a poem and bake an apple pie, Foyle, because you sure as hell don't know anything about the real world. When are you going to learn to keep your mouth shut?"

"Don't worry," Nora said. "I didn't tell her who you were. I didn't even mention your magazine."

He groaned again. "That's not what I meant. You should have taken credit for thinking of it."

"Even when I didn't?"

"This is going to come as a shock to you, Nora, but the world, unlike Smith College for Women, doesn't run on the honor system."

For once Paul agreed with him. Not about making up the case histories. He was still appalled at that. But about taking credit. Guys did it all the time, he said. It was called getting ahead.

Susannah went down the few steps from the kitchen to the family room. Nick was stretched out on the sofa, a medical journal open face-down across his chest. His eyes were closed, his mouth half open. He and the television hummed.

Susannah turned off the television, then walked to the couch and stood looking down at her husband. Except for the small snoring sound, the house was silent, a safe cave in the spring night. Cornelia slept upstairs. Nick dozed here. She watched over them.

She sat on the edge of the couch, rubbed her nose against his, then kissed him. He made a noise. It wasn't exactly a groan. In fact, Susannah thought it sounded more like one of Cornelia's whimpers.

She kissed him again. This time he did groan. She shook him gently. She needed him awake, at least for a little while. According to her basal thermometer, her temperature was up.

"In a minute," he mumbled.

"Come on, Nicky."

"I'm coming," he said without moving.

She put her hand on his fly. Now the sound was more like a purr, but he still didn't open his eyes.

She unzipped his trousers. "Come on. You've got your work cut out for you."

He refused to move, but he couldn't do anything about his involuntary muscles. He put a lazy hand on top of hers to stop her, but she pushed it away.

"You want to sleep or you want to make a baby?"

"Sleep," he said.

She knelt beside the sofa and bent over him. "Bet I can make you change your mind."

Nick changed his mind. It didn't take long. And Susannah stopped in time. It wasn't that she minded the taste, despite the jokes to the contrary, only that she had no intention of wasting valuable sperm in frivolous ejaculations.

No one understood why Nora was upset. So, a communications conglomerate had bought the magazine. So, there were rumors of a bloodbath ahead. So what?

"The worst thing that can happen is they'll fire you," Paul said. "Then you'll either get another job or"—he permitted a pregnant pause while he sprinkled dried mustard on the salad—"you'll stop working."

Beatrice and Sam and Susannah and Nick said the same thing, though they were appalled at the prospect of grown men suddenly out of work. They were less horrified by the idea of grown women in the same position.

"It just goes to prove what I always said," Beatrice insisted. "A Jewish boy should never work for anyone else." In moments of crisis, Beatrice always found religion.

"Don't they have tenure or anything?" Nick asked. Until then, Nora had considered her brother-in-law the worldly one in the family.

"You'd be quitting soon anyway," Susannah said. "You're not getting any younger."

David Meadow was the only one who thought Nora had something to worry about.

"Just sit tight," he said. "Whatever you do, don't ask anybody what's going on."

"Why not?"

"Because that gives the bastards an opening. 'Well, now that you brought it up, Nora, I'm sorry, but you're fired.' "

"Oh."

"Just do your work and keep a low profile. If all else fails, head for the ladies' room."

"What do you mean?"

It was the one time he told her a personal anecdote. As a young man, David had worked briefly for an advertising agency. During his first month there, the agency lost a major account. "The first thing they did was can all the top account executives and copywriters and art directors who'd worked on the account. But that wasn't enough. The personnel V.P. came gunning for more. It was a Friday afternoon. I disappeared into the men's room and didn't come out till after six. By Monday morning the dust had settled."

Nora followed David's advice. When new management walked in, she was still there. So, miraculously, was Monica Storch. From that day on, Monica regarded Nora as a fellow war veteran.

Nora waited for a few weeks to make sure that, in David's words, the dust had settled. Then she called to thank him for his advice. She gave the switchboard operator David's extension.

"Who do you want to speak to?" the operator asked.

"David Meadow."

"He's not here." There was something too human about the tone for it to be coming from a switchboard operator. Nora should have known something was wrong.

"You mean he's not in today?"

"He's not here anymore."

"You mean he left the magazine!" Nora was incredulous.
David wouldn't just pick up and change jobs without telling her.

"He passed on."

All Nora could think about was the words. She didn't
dare let in the meaning.

"Are you saying he died?"

"He passed on," the operator insisted.

"If you mean he died, say it, goddammit!"

"David Meadow is no longer with us," the operator said
and severed the connection.

Nora dialed Beatrice's number.

"That's terrible," Beatrice said. She meant it. She knew
the tragedy of death, especially young death, but there was
a catch to Beatrice's sympathy. Though she'd never met
David Meadow, she hadn't liked him. At least, she hadn't
liked his influence on her daughter.

"What did he die of?" Susannah asked on the extension.

"I don't know. I didn't think to ask." Nora remembered
Nick's explanation. Paraplegics have shorter life expectancies. Other systems tend to kick out.

She went down to the library of *American Homemaker*
and went through the last weeks of the *Times*. David
Meadow had died of complications.

She went back to her office and called Maude Phillips.
Maude had left the magazine a few weeks before Nora.

"Gee, that's awful," Maude said, but there was no conviction to the words. Maude had never worked for David. To
her he was just another writer, and she'd resented the
writers.

Nora left her office early that day. When she got home,
she went straight to the bookcase and took out her inscribed copy of *Failed Promises*. She opened it to the acknowledgement page. Nora Heller Moss. As if carved in
stone. She leafed back to the title page. David Meadow.
The name was written in big block letters, almost as big as
the title. She closed the book, carried it into the bedroom,
and lay down on her side of the bed on top of the spread.
Then she pulled her knees up to her stomach as Beatrice

had taught her to when she had menstrual cramps. Gradually the apartment disappeared into darkness. She was still lying on her side with her knees pulled up, clutching David's book to her, when Paul came home.

He switched on a lamp in the living room, walked into the bedroom, and turned on the overhead light. They blinked at each other.

"Are you sick?"

"David Meadow died."

There wasn't even a beat of disbelief. "I'm sorry."

He took off his jacket and loosened his tie. "What did he die of?"

Nora wondered why everyone kept asking. It didn't make any difference.

"Complications."

Paul went to the closet and hung up his jacket and tie.

"I didn't even know," Nora said. "He died last week, and I've been walking around all this time thinking he was alive."

Paul sat on the side of the bed and put his hand on her hip. "I don't suppose you picked up anything for dinner. That was a question, not an accusation," he added quickly. "Do you want to go out?"

"For Chinese food?"

"If that's what you feel like."

She started to cry. "It's a joke, Paul. Sam always says the only reason Jews pay condolence calls is so they can go out for 'Chinks' afterward."

"We have to eat," he said.

Nora didn't agree, but she went into the bathroom and washed her face and brushed her hair. They walked over to Joy Gardens.

Paul was kind. He let her talk about David all through dinner. And he couldn't help it if his eyes kept wandering. After all, he was facing the door, and Joy Gardens did a brisk business on Thursday nights.

Two weeks after David Meadow died, a week after Nora found out about his death, she went to bed with Doug Andrews. The sex wasn't much different from sex with

Paul, but though Nora didn't know it, she wasn't in it for the sex.

Doug was, as anyone who knew Nora might have predicted, an artist. While waiting to burst upon the art scene, he supported himself by doing free-lance work for the magazine. When he came into the office to pick up and deliver assignments, he wore jeans and work shirts. It was June, and sometimes there were dark blue sweat stains under the arms and in the small of his back. Nora hadn't seen anything as sexy as those sweat stains since she'd sat with Paul in the Thalia movie theater and watched Belmondo run his thumb back and forth across his lower lip.

Doug had a squalid apartment over a grocery store on Third Avenue. It was filled with canvases. They fell into two categories—paintings of horses with human heads, and paintings of humans with horses' heads. On initial viewing, the first two or three canvases had some shock value, but the effect paled quickly.

Nora, however, wasn't going to the apartment for its cultural advantages. If anyone had asked her, though no one did because no one, not even Susannah, knew, she would have said she went there for love, but even Nora knew she wasn't in love with Doug Andrews. One lunchtime as they lay in bed watching a roach work its way up a canvas of fillies, one of them with curly strawberry blond hair and a nose that was a little too long and thin, he said something about her leaving her husband and going to Paris with him. She could sell the international edition of the *Herald Tribune*.

Nora watched the roach make its way to another canvas. Several women stood as if posing for a group portrait, their horses' heads perched delicately on long slender necks. The figure in the center had a red mane and red pubic hair. Nora had never been a muse before.

She didn't answer, and Doug never mentioned Paris or her husband again, but for the next several days Paul thought his marriage was working out after all.

* * *

Nora swung down from the train. The July heat radiating from the cement platform felt good after the brutal air conditioning. She'd picked out Susannah's car through the train window. Now she headed for it.

"Hey, lady, did you rent that kid and dog and station wagon, or are you the real thing?"

"The real thing. Get in before Cornelia and Coco crawl out to get to you."

Nora got into the car. Cornelia tried to squirm out of the car seat into her lap. Coco pawed deliriously at the back of the front seat.

They drove home by way of the cleaners and the liquor store and the shoe repair man.

"It's a shame Paul had to work this afternoon," Susannah said. "Nick and Sam are playing tennis. They could have found a fourth."

"He used to say the only reason he worked on Saturdays was because I had to."

"Don't complain. He's doing it for you."

"He's doing it for himself. But I'm not complaining. I just want to know why everyone feels sorry for Paul for working so hard, but when you and Mommy came into town shopping, and I couldn't meet you for lunch because of that ASME meeting, you were both annoyed."

"ASME? Isn't she the heroine of that Salinger short story? You know, the one with love and squalor."

"God! How did I ever end up in this family? That's Esmé. This is the American Society of Magazine Editors."

Susannah turned the car onto Woodland Drive. "I was teasing you, Nora. I know what ASME is. We do listen, you know."

Beatrice's car was in the driveway. She was just getting out of it. Beyond her, the swimming pool that she and Sam had given Susannah and Nick as an anniversary present shimmered like a perfect chlorine-colored kidney.

Susannah pulled the station wagon into the attached garage. She lifted Cornelia out of her car seat. Nora let Coco, the brown poodle, out of the back, then went to help her mother unload packages from the Cadillac. There were two grocery bags of fruit from the local produce stand and a pie, a bulky box wrapped in paper with colored balloons, which Cornelia spotted immediately, and two bags from Saks.

In the kitchen Beatrice handed one Saks bag to each of her daughters, then turned to help Cornelia unwrap her present.

Susannah took a beige silk nightgown trimmed with coffee-colored lace from her bag. "It's beautiful," she said.

"It was on sale," Beatrice explained. "I thought it might be good luck."

"Maybe it is," Susannah said. "Promise you won't tell anyone?"

"Who're we going to tell?" Nora asked. "We're both here, and my editor-in-chief isn't interested."

"I'm ten days late."

"Shh," Beatrice said. The nightgown had been a charm, but she wasn't about to tempt fate.

Nora opened her own bag. Her nightgown was coffee-colored with beige lace. She didn't ask if it was supposed to bring her good luck too, and neither Beatrice nor Susannah suggested it.

The women changed into their bathing suits and went out to the pool. They were still there, melting over the tubular steel lounges in the last rays of the afternoon sun, when Sam and Nick came back from their tennis game and Paul arrived from town.

At sunset the breeze died. Beatrice was upstairs bathing Cornelia. Susannah was in the kitchen. Nora floated around the pool in a Styrofoam and metal chair.

Susannah had turned the heater up and the water was warm. The filters made a gentle gurgling sound. Nora closed her eyes. Maybe this was what life in utero was like.

She opened her eyes. Nick was demonstrating his new gas grill to Sam and Paul. All three of them were wearing alligator shirts and Bermuda shorts. Nick and Paul had drinks in their hands. Sam's was on the grass. They might have stepped out of an illustration in *American Homemaker*. "The Gas Revolution Sweeps America's Backyards." Only they weren't in a studio and the grass wasn't Astroturf and the sunlight electric. This was real life.

The chair floated to the side of the pool. They'd moved from gas grills to insurance. Nora closed her eyes again and went on drifting. Doug's apartment had been broken into the previous week. The thief was a philistine. He hadn't touched the paintings, but he'd made off with a variety of small electronics. Doug said he could live without the television but was really going to miss the stereo.

"Don't you have insurance?" Nora asked.

He looked at her, then started to laugh. "You gotta be kidding, babe."

Nora paddled to the shallow end of the pool and climbed out. She left a trail of wet footprints across the pool apron to the grill. She put her arm around Paul's waist. He put an arm around her shoulders as he went on talking. It was a reflex rather than a gesture. She stood on her toes to whisper in his ear.

"I love you."

Paul went on nodding. She wasn't sure whether he was agreeing with the men or with her, but that was all right. It made her feel better just to say the words.

As the summer wore on, the crowd around the pool grew thicker. Nick called it the Oak Hills Country Club. Friends drifted over with bottles of gin and vodka and changes of bathing suits for the kids, and joked that you couldn't beat the dues. There was always a woman putting towels in Susannah's dryer and a man putting hamburgers or hot dogs on Nick's gas grill and a terry-cloth-wrapped child with blue lips asleep on the porch.

On Saturday night of Labor Day weekend, the last Saturday night of the official summer season, after the children had been taken home and the baby-sitters had arrived, traffic at the Design Research wagon that served as a bar got heavy, and there were moral casualties. Betty Kagin went skinny-dipping with Jerry Richmond.

"I'm glad Mommy isn't here," Susannah said when she came back to the pool with two bath sheets.

"If she were, it never would have happened," Nora said.

She went upstairs to change out of her bathing suit and opened the guest room door on Myrna Richmond and

Roger Kalman. Myrna must have gone upstairs to get out of her bathing suit too, because she was wearing only the bottom.

Nora went back to the kitchen, where Susannah was making a pot of coffee.

"The party's getting rough," she said and told her sister about the scene in the guest room.

"You're kidding," Susannah said.

"Scout's honor. Actually, I couldn't see Roger's face, but I'd recognize his back anywhere. He always looks as if he's wearing a sweater in the pool."

"But Myrna! You can eat off her floors."

"That wasn't where his mouth was," Nora said.

Nick came into the kitchen carrying an empty vodka bottle and a couple of soggy towels. "Coffee. Great. Now we'll have wide-awake drunks." His consonants were thick with alcohol.

Susannah repeated Nora's story. "I can't believe it," she said. "And it started out as such a nice party. Everyone was having such a good time."

Nick bent over to pick up a crumpled cocktail napkin from the floor. For the first time Nora noticed that his hair was thinning. "They still are," he said. "Only now they'll be sorry in the morning."

"Just don't tell Mommy," Nora said. "Or she'll have Sam drive a cement truck up to the house and fill in the pool."

Sometime in September Nora stopped seeing Doug Andrews. She wasn't sure when, because the affair dwindled rather than snapped. One day she opened the bathroom door to a population explosion among the roaches. Another she arrived at the apartment to find Doug painting a saddle on one of the fillies. But mainly she didn't have the time. Monica was giving her more to do. The morning after Nora found out about David Meadow's death, she got her first novel to condense. Nora had never worked on fiction before. The editor who usually did was angry.

It was grueling work, paring eight hundred manuscript pages and four generations from the peat bogs of Ireland to the corridors of Washington power down to thirty thousand words, but it absorbed Nora completely. She cut characters and deleted scenes, wiped out lives and obliterated history. It was like playing God. The only time she thought of David Meadow was when she worked on the World War II scenes.

Nora made a discovery. The first time she'd gone to bed with Doug, she'd been thinking about David. The second and third and times after that, she stopped thinking about David. Sex worked. But work worked better.

Susannah was sitting at the table when Nick came into the kitchen that night. The sound of cartoons drifted in from the family room. That was the first sign that something was up. Susannah usually restricted Cornelia's television watching to an hour or two in the morning. The second sign was the raw pink look of Susannah's eyes.

"I got my period," she said before he'd even taken off his cord jacket.

"I'm sorry." He patted her shoulder and kissed the top of her head, then walked into the hall to drop his jacket over the banister. "You want a drink?" he asked as he came back into the kitchen.

She shook her head. "That's the second time in three months I was late and then got it."

He took one glass from the cabinet and filled it with ice.

"I think we ought to see a doctor," she said.

"You're looking at him."

"I'm serious."

Nick turned back to her and took a swallow of the drink before he spoke. "Susannah, we've been trying for eight months."

"Nine and a half."

"And we already have Cornelia. Don't you think you're overreacting?"

"You call it overreacting. I call it an intelligent, informed response to a medical problem. If I had constant stomachaches or you had chest pains, we'd go to a doctor."

"It's not the same thing."

"It's exactly the same thing, only this particular problem

threatens your masculinity. Your wonderful Greek masculinity."

"According to your mother, not to mention my mother
who's responsible, I'm Jewish."

"Not about this."

He stood leaning against the counter staring at her. "You
really think I'm an asshole, don't you?"

"I think you're being unreasonable."

"And I think you're being impatient."

"You don't live with the waiting."

He turned his back to her and slammed his hand down
on the counter. "Christ! Why don't you go to Saks or Lord
and Taylor and buy yourself a baby? Better yet, call Beatrice and ask her to buy you one."

There was a moment's silence. He stood with both hands
on the counter and his head down. Behind him he heard
her blowing her nose. He turned to face her again.

"I'm sorry."

She didn't say anything.

"It's just that I'm a little tired of the discussion. And the
thermometer and the charts and the goddamn schedules."
He carried his drink to the table, pulled a chair out, and sat
facing her. "Look, Susannah, what if we don't have another
baby? It's not the end of the world. We have Cornelia."

"I thought you wanted a boy."

"I also wanted a Lamborghini."

"That's different."

"I know it's different. I was joking."

"I always wanted two children."

"Okay, maybe it's not a joke. I always wanted a Lamborghini."

"I just don't see why you're so stubborn about going for
tests."

He pushed the chair out from the table and stood.
"Okay. We'll go for tests. They'll check you out and I'll jerk
off into a bottle. Now are you happy?"

"Yes."

* * *

Nick was right. There was nothing wrong. The doctor told Susannah to relax. Susannah told Beatrice she was supposed to relax. Beatrice suggested a vacation.

She and Susannah checked the calendar. Beatrice took Cornelia for the weekend, and Susannah and Nick went to a country inn to watch the leaves turn.

Two weeks later she got her period, again.

Beatrice had made Nora's wedding. Paul had chosen their first apartment. Susannah had handed down the inexpensive newlywed furniture to fill it. Nora was determined to take care of the divorce on her own.

Paul wasn't particularly eager for it, but he offered to find Nora a lawyer. It was, he believed, the only decent thing to do. She said thanks, but she'd already got a name from a newly divorced woman in her office. Paul disapproved. He believed in credentials, not hearsay.

When Beatrice and Susannah finally realized they weren't going to change Nora's mind, they both offered to go with her to the lawyer's office. Nora said she'd go alone. They pursed their lips and shook their heads.

A year later Paul called to tell her the divorce was final. He asked her if she felt like having dinner. She said why not. She should have known why not. They both should have.

He suggested she come by for a drink beforehand. She'd never seen his new apartment. She said why not again.

The apartment was exactly like several thousand other low-ceilinged, postwar rabbit warrens on Second and Third avenues. The bedroom was dark and barely big enough for the new king-size bed—Nora had kept theirs—on which they ended up. They were both surprised by the fact, though, again, they should have known better.

"I guess," Paul said, "we ought to get married again."

It occurred to Nora that she'd heard the sentence before, minus "again." She sat up in bed. "You really are a glutton for punishment."

"You mean this was just a celebration?"

She couldn't imagine how he could think she was that callous. "I don't believe in celebrating divorces. But you wouldn't want to commemorate the occasion with a stranger, would you?"

He got out of bed and put on the seersucker robe Beatrice had given him a few birthdays ago.

"Tell me something," he said. "Was that artist the only one?"

There it was. She'd been honest. Now he was going to throw it up to her.

"Of course."

"What about David Meadow?"

"Don't be ridiculous."

"Why is that ridiculous? You thought he was God."

"He was in a wheelchair."

"And you always said everyone wondered if he could get it up. I was just asking if you found out."

"He's dead."

"That makes him dead, not a saint."

"Nothing ever happened with David."

"What about Nick?"

"My brother-in-law!"

Paul sat on the side of the bed. "I'd hate to have to diagram your moral universe."

"He's my sister's husband."

"*I* was *your* husband."

"You said you didn't care. Anyway, Nick's crazy about Susannah."

Paul stood and left the room. He hadn't said another word, but there was a smile on his face that Nora had never seen before. It wasn't a nice-guy smile.

She grabbed his shirt from the floor and pulled it on.

He was standing in the kitchen putting more ice in his glass.

"What are you smirking about?"

"I'm not smirking."

"You are smirking. Because I said Nick's crazy about Susannah."

He just stood there staring at her with that smug grin on his face. She wanted to hit him. Once, when they'd been married, she'd actually punched his arm. He'd just gone on looking down at her, like some goddamn judge looking down from the bench.

"Just because you're pissed at me, don't take it out on my family."

"I'm not taking anything out on anyone."

"You're implying Nick's unfaithful."

"I'm not implying. You're inferring." The grin grew a little wider. "You're supposed to be the editor."

She went back into the bedroom, took off his shirt, and put on her clothes. On her way out she had to pass the kitchen. He was still standing there in the seersucker robe Beatrice had given him.

"While you're on this divorce kick," he said, "did you ever think of leaving Mommy and Susannah?"

It was a nice parting line, but Nora missed it because Paul still hadn't raised his voice.

13

All hospitals smelled the
same, a thick stench of institution food and eye-watering
antiseptic. It didn't matter whether they were new or old,
large or small, urban or suburban. Every hospital was located in the same place. Limbo.

Across the street from this hospital, the park was turning
from a tentative budding green to a darker shade. The
forsythia had already rioted. On the paths, cherry blossoms, ground down by thousands of pairs of running shoes,
lay like rumpled pink sheets.

Just a little more than a week ago Nora's own Sauconys
and Max's Nikes had trampled those blossoms heedlessly.
Afterward, she'd felt sweaty and vibrant and unusually
proud because she'd finally managed to keep up with him.
That was because she'd finally caught on to him. Max had a
habit of asking her about work as soon as they started
around the reservoir. That way he was entertained and she
was out of breath for at least one lap and often two. But that
had been ten days ago. Now the only sign of spring that
permeated the grime-streaked hospital windows was a
shaft of watery city sunshine. It illuminated a room that
didn't cry out for light. Black scuff marks smudged the pea-
soup-colored linoleum. Two prints, one of a bowl of fruit,
the other of a vase of flowers, hung on walls of the same
dispiriting green. Molded plastic chairs of orange and yel-

low and that pathetic green stood at crazy, unplanned angles to each other. A few old copies of *People* littered a Formica table. Somebody had drawn a mustache on Princess Diana. It was the kind of thing you did as a kid. Nora wondered whether a child had been waiting out a parent's surgery or a parent's surgery had turned someone back into a child. She tried to remember a time when she hadn't felt like this lonely, aging woman wrapped around a hollow of fear. It seemed impossible that only a week ago she'd sat in the doctor's examining room, thinking of her mother down the hall. The worry, she knew now, had been all pretense. She hadn't really believed anything could happen to Beatrice.

Daddy can't die.

And it wasn't only fear for Beatrice. As Nora had sat in the examining room that day, swinging her legs from the end of the table and staring at her distorted image in the cold metal surfaces, she'd thought of her mother, sitting on an identical table in an identical examining room, forming a wall between her and unwanted discoveries. The wall was crumbling. Nora was scared.

She looked at the ragged black ink mustache hanging from that royal upper lip. Somebody had been pissed.

She scrawled a note in the margin of the memo on her lap. "Trite. Tired. See last September's issue. How about some new ideas!" She drew three angry ink lines under the word new.

Across the room Charlie put down a coverless magazine he'd just picked up. He folded his hands in his lap. There was a Band-Aid on his right index finger and another on his left pinkie.

"You want some coffee?"

Nora shook her head. The last cup was still rising dangerously in her throat.

"A bagel?" he insisted. "A Danish?"

She shook her head again. He stood, walked down the hall, came back, sat again.

Nora kept her eyes on the papers on her lap. She hadn't asked for Charlie's company, but Charlie was not a man who waited for invitations, or even brooked obstacles.

"Don't worry where I'll stay," he'd said to Beatrice over the phone. "I got a daughter on Long Island, a son in Westchester. They got hotels in New York. What's money for, if I can't come stay in a hotel to be near you now? So you just tell Nora not to worry."

He came to be near Beatrice, to cheer her up, to be—and he used the word—supportive.

"So, what's the big fuss?" he said as soon as he arrived. "Dolly Parton you're not, Bea. Dolly Parton loses a breast, you'd notice. You should excuse me for saying it, Bea, especially in front of your daughter, but with you it's not going to make such a big difference."

Nora started to say something, but Charlie went on.

"I'll love you just the same."

Charlie picked up another limp magazine, put it down again. "So, maybe it'll be benign after all. A little biopsy, and we're all finished."

Nora didn't answer. The doctor had said he was virtually certain the lump was malignant.

Nora stood. Charlie was on his feet in a minute. "You need something? What can I get you?"

"I'm just going to call my office."

"You got change?" He began going through his pockets. "I have change."

"Here." He held out a handful of quarters, nickels, and dimes. "Just in case."

Nora walked down the hall to the pay phones. A woman was on one of them. "He turned up this morning," the woman said. "Out of the blue."

Nora dialed her office number.

"Nobody's seen him for two years, maybe three."

"How's your mother?" Jenny asked.

"But now that she's dying, he turns up."

"She's still in surgery," Nora said. "No word yet."

"Like a bad penny."

Nora put her hand over her free ear and asked what was going on in the office.

"Everything's under control," Jenny said and ran down a list of messages.

Nora said she'd call in again this afternoon. Then she

held down the lever until she got another dial tone, dropped in one of Charlie's quarters, and dialed Max's office.

"Now that she's dying, and he thinks there's some money."

Nora held her hand over her ear again.

Max's secretary put her through immediately. Nora could tell from his voice that he wasn't alone. "You have someone there."

"It's okay," he said. "Any news?"

"It makes me sick to my stomach."

"She's still in surgery," Nora said.

"It hasn't been that long," Max answered.

"But you know her. He was always her favorite."

"Do you need anything?" Max asked.

Nora said she was okay.

"Let me know," Max said. "As soon as you hear anything, let me know."

Nora held down the lever again and dropped in another of Charlie's quarters. She started to dial Annie's number.

"He's not going to get away with it!" the woman hissed into the phone. "It's not right. It's not fair."

Nora pressed the coin return, collected Charlie's quarter, and went back down the hall.

Charlie sprang to his white shoes as soon as he saw her. "Everything all right?"

Nora nodded.

"Good." He rubbed his hands together. "Good."

Nora crossed the room to the chair where she'd left her briefcase. Charlie followed and sat beside her.

"I was sitting here thinking. While you were gone," he said. "Even if it's . . . you know . . . even if it's malignant . . ." His voice fell to a terrible hushed croak on the last word. "It's not the end of the world. Not even a mastectomy, the doctor said. Right?"

"Right," Nora agreed without looking up from her papers.

"I mean, I joked about that, but I tell you, it's not an easy thing. Me, I wouldn't care. But for Bea. A woman who takes such pride in her appearance. It's not an easy thing."

Nora tried to concentrate on her work.

"Now this other operation, this lumpectomy. That's not such a big deal. Oh, sure, it's still major surgery. You gotta have a general and everything. But taking out a lump is not like the other."

Nora didn't say anything.

Charlie stood. "You sure you don't want coffee, something?"

"No, thanks," Nora said and read the first sentence of a memo for the third time.

"You should put something solid in your stomach. At least a piece of toast."

It was close to eleven. A surly Hispanic kid in a wrinkled hospital uniform shuffled past the door pushing a steel cart. The stench of hospital food rose from it like noxious fumes.

"I'm not hungry," she said.

"I'll go down and get something from the coffee shop anyway. You'll see it here, maybe you'll eat it."

Charlie took a few steps across the room, then stopped. Nora looked up from her papers. The surgeon stood in the doorway. His face was long and bloodless as a cadaver's. His eyes, behind rimless glasses, were dead.

Nora sat waiting.

"I was right," he said. "It was malignant."

Nora felt herself collapse into the hollow of fear. A strangled sound came from her throat. Then she started to cry.

The surgeon's long, bloodless face swiveled from Charlie to Nora. "That's exactly the kind of behavior that isn't going to help her."

Nora took a handkerchief from her handbag and wiped her eyes. "I'm sorry," she mumbled. Fuck you, you cold-blooded bastard, a voice inside her head screamed. My mother has cancer, it went on howling.

"The lumpectomy went beautifully. Now we just have to wait for the tissue reports. We should have them in a few days." He turned and left the waiting room.

"Thank you," Charlie said to his receding back.

Nora went and stood in the window with her back to the room. When Charlie turned away from the doctor, he saw her shoulders shaking.

"Go ahead," he said. "You go ahead and cry." He took a step toward her. "What does he know?" He took another step. "He could have the best hands in the business, but no heart."

He stood behind her and put a hand on her shoulder. She clamped her teeth together to keep from pushing it off. He talked about Gene Tierney and Beatrice's apple pie and the fact that he'd still love her with only one breast, but if something happened . . . If! The voice shrieked in her head again. Something was happening. And Charlie would go on. Nora saw him nodding and patting and smiling his way around the widows of Palmetto Estates. Who would be next? Addie Miller? Mrs. Gold? And he had the nerve to offer comfort.

She thought of Susannah. Susannah would have understood. She wanted Susannah here now. Susannah's hand on her shoulder was the only one she could permit. Charlie's was worthless. Worse than that, Charlie's was an intrusion.

Nora took a step away. Charlie's hand fell from her shoulder.

When she turned, she saw his face. It was a lumpy yellow blob. Black lines ran between his eyebrows and from the corners of his mouth to his chin. She started to cry again. The tears obliterated his face.

Beatrice lay small and gray in the hospital bed. Her skin was gray, her hair a tangled gray web on the pillow, her mouth a gray hole in her wrinkled face. Nora thought of the gray chiffon wedding dress hanging at home in her guest room closet. The sharpest colors on the bed were the black and blue marks on Beatrice's arm. It lay on top of the white covers hooked up to life.

Beatrice opened her eyes. Nora moved to the side of the bed and took her mother's hand. It rustled against hers like tissue paper. Beatrice tried to smile. She moved her eyes to the other side of the bed, where Charlie was standing. Then she closed them again.

"She smiled," Charlie whispered.

Nora nodded.

They went back to their chairs in opposite corners.

A nurse came in, went to the bed, and checked for life signs.

Charlie averted his eyes. At first Nora thought he was being delicate. Then she saw how white he'd gone beneath his tan. His eyes kept darting to the IV bottle, then veering away in a panicky arc.

Nora went back to work. After a while she heard the faint sound of Charlie snoring. His head had fallen back on the chair. It inched down on the plastic upholstery. It fell forward. He sat up, startled, then glanced around the room guiltily.

He looked at his watch. The gold band glinted watery yellow like the sun outside the grimy windows.

"It's after three, Nora. Go downstairs. Get yourself a bite. Your mama wouldn't want you to starve."

"I'll wait."

"You don't want to leave, right? In case she opens her eyes again. Okay. I'll go down and get you a sandwich."

"I'm not hungry. Really."

"I insist. Bea would want me to. What do you want?"

"Anything."

"A hamburger? Some tuna fish?"

"It doesn't matter."

"Maybe turkey. Roast beef I don't think would be so good in a hospital coffee shop. Pastrami I wouldn't let you have."

"Whatever."

"Turkey then. You want it on rye. With a little tomato and lettuce?"

"Fine."

"Unless you'd like a salad."

The voice came in a faint rasping sound from the bed. It floated in the room like the particles of dust caught in the streaks of sunshine filtering through the windows.

"Chicken salad," Beatrice whispered. "She loves chicken salad."

Nora and Charlie turned to the bed. Beatrice's eyes were still closed. They both started to laugh.

* * *

The head of the bed had been cranked up a little, but Beatrice was still dozing. Nora shifted position in the chair she'd been in for the last seven hours. Her body was sore and her temples ached, but at least the room was quiet. Charlie had gone to have dinner with his daughter and son-in-law.

When Nora looked up from the proposal she was trying to read, she saw Max standing in the doorway. She got up and went into the hall with him.

"This was nice of you, but I don't think she's ready for visitors."

"I didn't come to see her. I came to see how you were."

"I'm okay."

From the way he looked down at her, Nora knew she didn't look okay. She was suddenly aware of the stale, metallic taste in her mouth.

"How much longer are you going to stay?"

She looked at her watch. "They'll throw me out in another hour or so."

"You want some dinner?"

"Please! Charlie's been trying to stuff food down me all day."

"Then a drink? I don't mind waiting around."

"Thanks, but I think I'll just go home and go to bed. Sleep."

"I knew what you meant."

She walked him to the elevators. Max pushed the down button. They stood waiting.

"I'll give you a call tomorrow. If she feels up to it, I'll stop by tomorrow night."

"Thanks."

The elevator doors opened. Max put his arms around her. She stiffened. He squeezed her shoulders for a moment, just till he felt her relax, then released her.

He stepped onto the elevator and raised one hand to her as the doors closed between them.

Nora was back in her mother's room when she realized what was so strange about that embrace. It was the first asexual physical contact she and Max had ever had. It took

another few minutes for Nora to realize that Beatrice had
had to undergo surgery to bring it about.

Cornelia called the hospital every day. Then she called
Nora's apartment at night. Nora sat on one side of her bed
with a drink on the night table and a stack of office papers
on her lap. For the first time in her life she was having
trouble working. At the other end of the line Cornelia sat
in her room in Timothy Dwight College. The single bed
was covered with discarded sketches. When she shifted
position, the papers crackled beneath her. Cornelia's pencil went back and forth furiously, defacing the facade of a
fantasy house that would never be built. Nora's scribbled in
margins.

"Is she really okay?" Cornelia asked.

"She's doing beautifully. When I got there this morning
she was putting on makeup."

"Grandma's some piece of work."

They talked about the reports then. Nora drew aimless
circles on the paper on her knees. Cornelia crushed the soft
point of the pencil into the drawing.

"It'll be all right," Cornelia said.

Nora didn't answer.

"Grandma's indestructible."

Nora still didn't answer. She was more like Beatrice than
she knew. It didn't pay to tempt fate.

Daddy can't die.

"What do you think?" Cornelia pleaded for reassurance.

"I think we'll have the results of the tests in a day or
two."

The long-distance connection was silent for a moment.
Nora sipped her drink. She heard the faint sound of papers
crackling as Cornelia reached for the mug of coffee on the
floor beside her bed.

"You want to hear something weird?" Cornelia asked.
"There's this girl in the architecture school. We worked on
a project together last year. Well, her mother died a couple
of months ago."

Cornelia hesitated. At the other end of the line, Nora
waited.

"Everyone was really upset. I mean, it was weird to watch. Because they weren't only upset for her. They were scared. For themselves. You know, for their own parents. But here's the weirdest part of all."

This time the silence went on longer.

"What?" Nora asked finally.

"I felt smug. Like I was safe."

Nora knew the sensation. It was the deep breath after the panicky hyperventilation of death. You walked around thinking the worst had happened. There was a certain security to that. The worst had happened. You were safe. Then along came something like this, and you realized the worst could happen again and again. It was a heartless permutation calculated on the number of people you loved.

Nora heard the sound of her niece blowing her nose.

"It's no fucking fair," Cornelia said.

"Who ever told you life was going to be fair?" Nora had once taunted Susannah.

"Beatrice," Susannah had answered without a moment's hesitation.

Max came by just before the end of visiting hours. The night before he'd brought a plant. Now he was carrying several magazines.

"He's very thoughtful," Beatrice whispered when Nora bent to kiss her goodnight.

Outside the hospital a cool breeze slid over Nora's skin. It came from the park and smelled of damp earth and vegetation. She hadn't realized how stuffy the hospital room was.

She stood on the sidewalk between Max and Charlie.

"Would you look at those stars," Charlie said. He put an arm around Nora's shoulders even though he had to reach up to do it. "I tell you, everything's going to be okay." He squeezed her shoulders. "You two kids have a nice dinner now." He turned and walked away before Max could even suggest that he join them.

They went to a neighborhood restaurant near Nora's apartment. Scotch had never tasted so good. It wandered through Nora's body like fingers, kneading the kinks and aches out of her muscles. She didn't finish her burger, but she had three drinks.

Walking out of the restaurant, she felt weightless. Beatrice was still there, but not so heavily.

They walked the two blocks to Nora's apartment. They were farther from the park now, but she thought she could still smell spring.

"Do you want me to go home or do you want company?" Max asked.

"I want company."

In fact, she didn't want company. She wanted sex.

She assumed Max found some pleasure in it. She even went through the motions of giving pleasure. She put her hand here. She put her mouth there. It all came automatically. But she wasn't interested in Max that night. She wasn't even interested in pleasure. She was looking for affirmation. Or maybe it was only escape.

As soon as it was over she felt guilty. Her mother was lying in a hospital bed. Inside Beatrice's body death might be growing. Nora wondered how many cancer cells reproduced in the amount of time it took two healthy adults to fuck.

She turned on her side with her back to Max, drew her knees up in a fetal position, and thought about her mother. The tears ran into the sheets Beatrice had helped her choose. She kept her fist in her mouth as she cried. She didn't want Max to hear her. If he heard her, he'd move across the bed to hold her. It wouldn't be as bad as having Charlie's hand on her shoulder while she cried, but it wouldn't help.

Nora held her breath against the hospital smell. It was the fourth day she'd spent there, but the thick odor still made her queasy. She wondered if you got used to it if you worked in a hospital. She thought of Nick.

Sitting up in bed, Beatrice didn't look like herself, but she did look better. The day before, Nora had shampooed her mother's hair. They'd joked about how Nora, as a child, used to scream when Beatrice had washed her hair.

"Now you know how I used to feel," Nora had said when

the shampoo had run down Beatrice's forehead toward her eyes. Nora had mopped it up just in time.

"Now *you* know how *I* used to feel," Beatrice had answered.

The table with Beatrice's breakfast tray was still across the bed. She'd eaten a little oatmeal and half a piece of toast. Nora slid the table into a corner. She was just about to straighten the covers when the surgeon came into the room.

"How are you feeling?" he asked Beatrice. "You can wait outside," he said to Nora.

Nora went into the hall and stood leaning against the wall. An old woman in a cotton robe and velour scuffs shuffled by on the arm of a younger woman in street clothes. They looked alike, only the younger woman looked disgruntled and vaguely familiar. Then Nora remembered where she'd seen her before. At the pay phones the morning Beatrice had been in surgery. Nora averted her eyes.

The surgeon came out of the room and walked past Nora without a word. She caught up with him.

"About the lab report . . . ," she began.

"I discussed it with Mrs. Brickner," he said and kept going.

Nora went back into the room. Beatrice was sitting up in bed. There was no telling from her face what the news was.

"What did he say?"

"That my scar was beautiful."

"I mean about the report."

Beatrice's face sagged a little. "We'll know tomorrow."

"He said three days. Today is the fourth day."

"He said a few days, Nora."

They decided to go for a walk. "The doctor said I should get as much exercise as I can," Beatrice said.

Nora helped her mother out of bed and into her robe and slippers. She offered her arm, but Beatrice said she didn't need it.

They walked slowly, down corridors, through closed doors, past nursing stations. At first Nora thought they were ambling aimlessly, then she realized her mother had a destination. They reached the maternity ward.

On the other side of the nursery window cribs stood at random angles. There was a sea of tiny heads, some round, some long, some beautifully shaped, some still pinched and deformed, some bald, some topped by a crop of black or brown or blond hair.

A young couple came up beside Nora and her mother. He was wearing a pin-stripe suit, but the stripes were a little too wide to pass muster. She was in a robe and slippers.

"There he is," the woman said. "Sean Gregory. Wave to Daddy, Sean."

"Over my dead body," the man muttered.

"I'm not going to call a baby Frank."

"It's good enough for my father."

"That's my point," the woman said and walked away. The man stood for a moment staring at the baby, then turned and followed her.

Beatrice and Nora went on gazing into the nursery. Small red faces slept or sucked hungrily at the air, whimpered or howled. Tiny fists clenched and unclenched and pummeled space.

Beatrice could still remember how she'd felt the first time they'd put Susannah in her arms. The terror had washed over her like another wave of ether. The baby was so small, so fragile. Those fingers ending in minuscule milky nails had practically broken her heart. Nothing could be that tiny and survive. It's all a mistake, she wanted to scream. I can't take care of her.

The nurse had saved her. It was a Catholic hospital, and the nurses were all nuns. Beatrice was afraid of those women in white with their stiff wimples and rimless glasses, their deceptively soft faces and iron wills. She knew they didn't like her, because she was a Jew and because she was a woman in labor.

"It can't hurt that much," one nun had snapped at Beatrice when she'd howled at a contraction.

"How would you know?" Beatrice had shot back and surprised herself more than the nun.

Beatrice never saw that nurse again. Another nun brought Susannah in for the first time. There was no line of resentment to this one's mouth. She stood beside the bed for a while after she put Susannah in Beatrice's arms.

"Don't worry," she said, though Beatrice hadn't mentioned her fear. "She's not breakable."

And, of course, she hadn't been. At least not as a baby. Beatrice had overcome her fear. By the time a lay nurse— it was a different hospital—put a newborn Nora in her arms, Beatrice was an old hand. Familiarity had blunted the sharpness of all the emotions, if only a little.

"Do you ever regret it?" Beatrice said after a while. She'd never dared ask the question before, but since the doctor's secretary had left that message on Nora's answering machine, Beatrice was living by new rules.

"The abortion?" Nora asked.

Beatrice was surprised. She'd forgotten the abortion. "No. You couldn't have had that baby. I meant do you ever regret not having a child?"

Nora didn't have to think about the answer. The words came out automatically. "I have Cornelia."

"That's not—" Beatrice caught herself. She'd been about to say that it wasn't the same, but if Nora didn't know that, there was no reason to tell her.

Charlie was waiting in Beatrice's room when they got back.

"We were in the nursery," Beatrice explained.

"Your mama was afraid to go yesterday," Charlie said. "She thought they might not let us in. But I told her what's the big deal. Just act like you belong there. It'll cheer you up."

Nora said she had to get to her office. She'd be back later in the afternoon. That was when Beatrice remembered the transistor radio and Nora realized she'd forgotten it.

"That's okay," Beatrice said. "I just thought I'd like a little music at night. After everyone leaves."

"I'll stop at the apartment on my way back here and pick it up," Nora said.

Beatrice insisted it was too much trouble.

Nora said it wasn't any trouble at all.

"I'll get it," Charlie interrupted. "Give me your keys, Nora. I'll go while Bea is napping and get the radio."

"It's in the guest room," Beatrice said. "The top drawer of the small chest of drawers."

Nora took the keys to the two locks on her apartment off her key ring and handed them to Charlie.

"Now everyone's happy," he said.

The next morning Nora called the hospital before she left the apartment, as she always did, to find out if Beatrice had thought of anything else she wanted.

"I'll talk to you later," Beatrice said. "The doctor just walked in."

"Call me," Nora said. "Call me as soon as he leaves."

Nora hung up the phone in the kitchen. She went inside and made the bed. The handful of pennies, nickels, and dimes Max had left on the table the other night were still there. He always left his small change, as if he were too good to carry it. The habit annoyed the hell out of her.

She went back into the kitchen and put her coffee cup and plate into the dishwasher. Then she wiped the counter.

She stood staring at the phone remembering the last time she'd stood in the kitchen waiting for news. Beatrice had been with her then. And the news hadn't been good.

She went back to the bedroom, combed her hair again, and put on lipstick. The goddamn doctor had spent three minutes with Beatrice yesterday morning. What in hell was he doing now?

Nora knew the answer. Explaining the results. Laying out a prognosis. She wondered if he'd be falsely optimistic or brutally frank. She wondered if his eyes were dead because he spent his life giving bad news or if he'd chosen a life of giving bad news because he was dead.

The phone rang. Nora sprang for it.

"It didn't spread," Beatrice said.

Nora sat down hard on the side of the bed and began to cry.

* * *

Nora didn't know why she was surprised. Beatrice had told her. Charlie had told her. Would it, as e e cummings had told her in her more impressionable days, take "a piece of the old Third Avenue El in the head" to tell her?

"You're still going through with it!" she said.

Holding a small mirror in one hand and a tube of lipstick in the other, Beatrice looked across the hospital room at her daughter.

"Why wouldn't I?"

"I don't know. I just assumed . . ."

". . . that Charlie wouldn't want to marry me now?"

"No. Charlie's not that dumb. I thought you might want to postpone it."

"Why should we postpone it? I'll be out of the hospital in a couple of days. That gives us a few weeks to get ready. You won't have to do a thing."

"I wasn't worrying about myself. What about the chemo-therapy?"

"There's no law that says you can't get married while you're undergoing chemotherapy. Anyway, the treatments probably won't start until after the wedding. Charlie's figured it all out. We can sublet a place for the summer. Half the apartments in New York go begging for the summer. Charlie said we won't have any trouble. And this way you won't have to worry during the treatments. Charlie can take care of me."

"Sure."

Beatrice knew she should ignore her daughter's tone, but then she'd never been able to keep from picking up the pieces of food Nora had thrown from her high chair when she went through that particular stage either.

"He's here all the time," Beatrice said.

"Which is one of the reasons you're so tired."

"I'm not tired."

"He talks so much you can't even nap."

"Hospitals make him nervous."

"I make him nervous. Hospitals make him nervous. What does he want for a wedding present? A giant-size bottle of Valium."

Beatrice closed the lipstick she was still holding and put

it and the mirror on the night table. When she turned back to Nora, the freshly applied makeup couldn't hide the ravages of the past few weeks, and longer. Those eyes that had never missed anything were sunken beneath soft, sadly drooping lids. The flesh of her chin hung loosely. If a dress had fit that badly, Beatrice never would have worn it.

"You're right, Nora. Charlie isn't much good in a crisis. But I don't need him in a crisis. I have you. It's the other times, the other things I need him for. Now when I see something funny in the paper, I have someone to read it to. I can eat dinner with him instead of Dan Rather. And when I get dressed to go out, Charlie's there to tell me I look nice or my slip's showing."

Nora felt her face beginning to collapse the way it did when she was about to cry. "You've never in your life left the house with your slip showing."

"I'm serious. So never mind about his pinkie ring or that he talks too much or doesn't know which fork to use. You can teach a man those things. Especially a man like Charlie who wants to learn. And never mind that medical problems scare him because he spent two years sitting in a hospital watching his wife die of cancer. Charlie's there for the things I need him for. The rest you overlook."

Nora supposed she hadn't noticed it before because she hadn't gone into the study in several days. By the time she got home from the hospital at night, she didn't have the energy left to go to a desk, though she frequently read in bed. The room was neat, exactly as Beatrice had left it, except for the small chest. The middle two drawers were open a few inches. The top one had a scarf caught in it. Nora knew Beatrice wouldn't leave a chest of drawers like that. Then she remembered the transistor radio. Charlie had been here.

Nora opened the top drawer to tuck in the scarf. That was when she found it. A small piece of paper with a message scrawled in a felt-tip pen.

"Welcome home. Love, Charlie."

Nora tucked the paper back in the scarf, closed the top

drawer, and opened the second one. A second note nestled among the bras and girdles.

"I missed you. Love, Charlie."

She opened the third drawer. This note was tucked into a slip.

"I love you. Charlie."

In the fourth drawer the note lay on top of her mother's blue sweater. Nora picked it up to read it.

"I finally got into your drawers. Love, Charlie."

Nora replaced the note, closed the drawer, and went back to her own room to change for Max's partner's dinner party.

"I'm forty-one years old," Nora said to Max in the cab. "You're forty-four."

"Are you gloating?"

"I'm thinking. When we were kids fumbling around in the back seat of someone's car—"

"Like a couple of months ago?"

"I mean it. And our parents were this age, we thought they were over the hill."

"Shows what we knew."

"Do you think when we're in our seventies we're going to be eating our words again?"

He took her hand. "I hope so. Words or something else."

The dinner party was in one of those enviable old Park Avenue buildings where the walls are thick as vaults and the guests get lost going to the bathroom. Not that these guests didn't know their way around. Nora could tell from the real buttonholes on the sleeves that three of the five men were wearing custom-tailored suits. The two holdouts were Max and the husband of an attorney.

The husband sought Nora out after dinner. He said it was an amazing coincidence running into her this way. He made it sound as if they were Siamese twins who'd been separated at birth.

Nora managed an innocuous if not intelligent smile. She didn't get it, but she was trying to be nice. After all, Max had put in all that time discussing Millie Chase with Wheeler's wife.

"I'm Lee Banahan," the man went on.

Nora kept smiling.

"Of Bananas. I've been trying to reach you for weeks."

Nora had heard of a new advertising agency called Bananas. She was even more familiar with the pile of pink phone slips that had been mounting alarmingly on her desk while she was in the hospital giving shampoos and visiting maternity wards and chasing doctors. "I've been out of my office a lot lately."

"Lucy Greer told me. I've been working with her. She set up a meeting for this Thursday morning. We've got a campaign that's going to turn your book around."

Nora said, through the pasted-on smile, that she was looking forward to seeing it. She didn't bother to add that the book didn't need turning around, only fattening up with a few more advertising pages. Nor did she mention that on Thursday morning she and Beatrice had an appointment to talk to the team of doctors. Three different agencies had already pitched the account, and none had come up with anything fresh. Nora had just about decided to stay with the old agency. She'd let Lucy handle Bananas.

Outside the air was ripe with spring, or as ripe as it gets on Park Avenue. Max suggested walking home. They started north. She launched into a postmortem of the party. Maude said postmortems were the only reason for going to dinner parties. Annie said postmortems were one of the reasons for staying married. Nora believed postmortems were, at the least, a reward for good behavior.

Max called her a hypocrite. "The hostess thought you were crazy about her. She said she'd never had such immediate rapport with any . . ." He hesitated.

"With any of the women you've dragged to these things over the years," Nora finished for him. "Of course, we had rapport. You didn't expect me to get into a serious disagreement with a grown woman, a furious grown woman, who tells me now that the children are grown her husband's job is to work, hers is to play. Anyway, she's married to one of

your partners. One man's hypocrisy is another woman's
diplomacy."

Max said he appreciated the effort. Nora said it was nothing.

They covered another block in silence. Her hand was in
his, though she wasn't sure who'd made the first move.

"It looked as if you had immediate rapport with Lee
Banahan too," Max said.

"His agency is going to pitch the account this week."

"If that's your story, you stick to it."

They took another block in silence. It suddenly occurred
to Nora that Max wasn't kidding. He wasn't angry or upset,
but he wasn't kidding.

She told him he was cute when he was jealous.

"Mad. The line is 'You're cute when you're mad.'"

"How would I know? You don't get mad."

"You sound disappointed."

She wasn't, but she knew from his voice that women in
his past had been. Just as some of her friends were. Not
Annie. Annie said Max was the best thing that had happened to Nora in years. Nora told Annie she wouldn't say
that if she'd seen Max's apartment. But other friends who
hadn't even met him weren't so sure. At lunches and dinners, they leaned forward, clutching wineglasses, and
asked about this man she'd met, this Max she was seeing.
The gesture was eloquent. Dish, it said. Tell all. But Nora
couldn't. She wouldn't talk about the sex. She didn't know
how to explain the rest. "He's nice," she'd say. "We get
along."

It was clear from their faces she'd let them down. They
wanted more from her. The romantics hungered for tales
of sexual prowess and a blood-boiling need for each other.
Of course, they were willing to pay with their own orgasm
counts and anecdotes of hearts beating as one and minds
functioning in uncanny extrasensory sync. The angry
craved stories of violent words, slammed doors, and as-
sorted victimizations. This was the group that, with
straight faces, called Tony Demarco the great love of
Nora's life. And the practical pressed for lists of cleverly
planned evenings and expensive gifts. Most of these were

appalled at Max's penchant for travel by rail, but a few found hope in his repeated calls from airplanes and were willing to reserve judgment until Nora's birthday rolled around.

Nora didn't entirely blame them. They were looking for flash and drama, the stuff of which good stories are made. The rest of it—the jokes that were so small and fragile they'd die if exposed to the elements; the silences that had, surprisingly, become comfortable as a worn sweater; the first stirrings of trust—didn't play as well. They were the things you deleted from a novel when you were condensing it for first serial.

"Nope," she said to Max. "I admit there was a time when I thought a childish temper was a sign of love or passion or, —God help me—a sensitive nature. But now I recognize it for what it is."

"What's that?"

"Just a sign of childishness." Nora was startled at her own voice. For a moment there it had sounded exactly like her mother's.

14

"How could you?" Susannah demanded. "In my own backyard."

Nora kicked her door closed. The phone had been ringing when she walked into the office.

"Actually, it was Betty Kagin's front yard," Nora said. "She was picking up the morning paper at the end of the driveway in a pink terry-cloth robe—you ought to tell her terry cloth makes her look dumpy—when Ron and I pulled out of the driveway. It must have been a little before eight, because he dropped me off in time for me to get the eight-fourteen into town. I figure Betty was back in the house and on the phone to you in thirty seconds." Nora looked at her watch. "Which means you've been dialing at one-minute intervals for the last hour and twenty minutes."

"For God's sake. He's one of Nick's best friends."

"Yup. That's how I met him."

"Why can't you see him in New York? Take him to Max's Kansas City or one of those places you go with your other friends."

Nora knew that if Coco was in the room with her sister, the dog had pricked up her ears at the word "friends." Susannah had made it sound that menacing.

"You're impossible to please. All those months you were screaming about Tony Demarco. At least Ron's divorced."

"That doesn't mean you have to come out here and flaunt what you're doing."

"It's the middle of August, Susannah, and Ron's wife left him with a house that has a pool. Just like yours."

"Right down the street from mine."

Susannah moved from the kitchen table to the stove. The extra-long telephone cord followed her like a tether. She thought of the other argument. Forget me. What about you? You're ruining your life. Running around with all kinds of people. Going to bed with a lot of different men. But they'd been through those arguments too many times. The discussions didn't do any good, and they always got muddled. Your life became our life. Morality became Beatrice's arbitrary middle-class rules. And Nora became irrational.

"I can take care of myself," she always ended up screaming. "I've got my own job and my own money and my own apartment. I don't have to rely on anyone."

That was exactly what Beatrice and Susannah worried about.

"Are you going to marry him?"

"Christ, Susannah, I barely know him."

Susannah carried the fresh cup of coffee back to the table. "You know him well enough to sleep with him."

"This is going to come as a shock to you, but these days two consenting adults—especially two consenting divorced adults—frequently go to bed without knowing each other well. There's a sexual revolution afoot."

"Not in Oak Hills."

"More like Hypocrisy Hills. Don't forget I've been to your pool as well as Ron's."

"You're exaggerating."

"You think so? At your last July Fourth party I went up to my room to pass out quietly. I admit I had too much to drink. The next thing I knew I opened my eyes and Roger Kalman was standing beside the bed with his pants open chanting like some whacked-out Hare Krishna, 'Put me in your mouth, baby. Put me in your mouth, baby.'" Nora heard the sharp intake of Susannah's breath. "I think it was the 'baby' that offended me more than anything else."

"You mean if he'd called you Nora, you would have done it?"

"What makes you think I didn't?"

"Nora!"

"Come on, Susannah. I may be a woman of easy virtue, but I'm not a hooker. I don't do breezies."

"Breezies?"

"Quick and dirty blow jobs. On demand."

"I have to go," Susannah said.

"Sure. Don't keep your foursome waiting," Nora answered and slammed down the phone.

It rang again immediately. Monica Storch's secretary said Monica wanted to know if Nora could stop by her office. It wasn't really a question.

Monica sat behind her desk. One hand with long blood-red nails lay on top of some papers. Monica's nails always surprised Nora. They reminded her of Beatrice's and Susannah's. They were beautiful, but they weren't serious.

Ted Gilmann was on the sofa. Ted was the vice president in charge of marketing and research. Except for the interior design editor, who liked to think of himself as one of the girls, Ted was the only man at the book. He called himself Uncle Teddy. The editors called him the hit man, though never to his face. If God were selling first serial rights to the Book of Genesis, Ted would have produced studies showing that the average reader served her husband two-point-six snacks a day and the apple industry was responsible for point-eight percent of the book's advertising revenues. Then he would add that it was a damn shame because any fool could see there was quite a bit of literary value in the Book of Genesis, but you had to pay attention to the bottom line, and the bottom line was circulation and advertising, not necessarily in that order.

"Ted's worried about this proposal of yours." Monica's talons tapped the memo on her desk.

Ted took the pipe out of his mouth. He'd once taught English in a private girls' school and still took the five-forty-seven to Princeton every night. "Concerned," he corrected Monica. "Just a little concerned, Nora." He put the pipe back in his mouth and puffed thoughtfully.

Nora slid into the chair across from Monica's desk.
"What's the problem?"

"This family planning group you want to profile," Ted
said. "They believe in zero population growth." He puffed
again. "That doesn't quite fit our image."

"Zero population growth doesn't mean *no* children,"
Nora explained.

Ted smiled his avuncular smile. He chuckled. "I know
that, Nora. But our latest reader profile study showed that
our typical reader has three-point-eight kids."

"That's a lot of kids," Nora said.

"Right you are. Higher than the national average." Ted
sounded proud of the fact, as if his sperm were doing the
job.

"Then maybe our readers need this article."

Ted puffed again. "You might think so, Nora. I might
think so. But I'm not sure our readers think so. Our last
attitude study showed that ninety-three percent of our
readers regard motherhood as a woman's highest calling."

Nora looked at Monica. Monica stared back. Her face was
impassive, her long fingernails drummed on the desk.

Ted unbuttoned his tweed jacket and stretched his arm
along the back of the sofa. The jacket was gray herringbone. Nora would have put money on the likelihood of
finding a Brooks Brothers label inside. Sam had a jacket just
like it. Nick did too. The last time she'd seen Paul, at least
the last time she'd seen him dressed, he'd been wearing
his.

"I know what I sound like, Nora. Keep 'em barefoot and
pregnant. But you can't go against your readers' convic-
tions. Or"—he sucked on his pipe—"your advertisers' interests. Do you have any idea what percentage of our advertising pages go to child care products?"

Nora didn't.

The avuncular smile came into play again. "Thirty-eight
percent. Gerber's and Beechnut and J & J fork over a lot of
advertising dollars. I appreciate your position, Nora. I ad-
mire it. I'd like to fight world hunger myself."

His foot swung in a measured movement. He wore jodh-
pur boots with a strap and buckle. Nora's uncle Lewis used

to wear boots like that. If the jacket hadn't done her in, the shoes would have.

"But I don't think undermining the book's positioning vis-à-vis advertising is a way of fighting world hunger." Ted stopped smiling and looked at her a little sadly, as if she were a gifted but truant student. "Do you?"

"I never thought of it that way."

He tapped his pipe into the ashtray on the end table, stood, buttoned the tweedy jacket. "I knew I could count on you to see reason, Nora. Keep up the good work," he added on his way out the door.

"Then that's it?" Monica asked after Ted left. Unlike the summons to her office, it really did sound like a question.

"He made sense."

"Twenty-six percent of our advertising comes from child care products. Not thirty-eight. Twenty-six and falling. Just like the birth rate. His figures are out of date."

"Why didn't you correct him?"

Monica drummed her gaudy fingernails on the desk. "Because I don't have to learn to stand up to the guys, Nora. You do."

It was one more lesson Nora never got around to thanking Monica for.

Through the glass wall of the breakfast room Susannah saw Betty Kagin crossing the backyard. She was wearing shorts and an overblouse that wasn't quite up to the camouflage task. Nora was right. Betty was getting dumpy. She was also carrying a coffee mug.

Betty opened the back door and stuck her head, enclosed in a helmet of frosted hair, into the kitchen. "Feel like company?"

"The coffee's on the stove," Susannah said, as if Betty didn't know where the coffee was at this time of morning.

"I saw Cornelia getting on the day camp bus. You got her that Florence Eiseman shorts and top outfit." Betty sat across the table from Susannah. "I wish you hadn't. Every time Cornelia gets something new, both my girls want the same thing."

"That's what you get for being so fecund." Susannah managed a smile.

Betty broke off a piece of the untouched doughnut Cornelia had left on her plate. "Did you talk to your sister?"

Susannah walked to the stove and poured herself a third cup of coffee. "I talk to Nora all the time."

"What did she say? About being seen coming out of Ron Herman's house at eight o'clock on a Monday morning, I mean."

"She said it was a little before eight."

"You ought to tell her to be careful. Seth says Ron's gone through an awful lot of women since Gloria left."

Susannah said nothing.

Betty broke off another piece of doughnut. "Seth says Ron will never remarry."

"What makes you think Nora wants to marry him?"

Betty shook her head. The helmet of frosted hair didn't move. "Come on, Susannah, he's one of the biggest dermatologists in northern New Jersey."

Susannah sat staring at the mustache of crumbs on Betty's upper lip. Betty finally took the hint and reached for a napkin. Susannah smiled. Nick called it her reigning monarch smile. All it was missing, he said, was that little wave of the hand.

"Nora's ex-husband is a partner in one of the biggest firms on Wall Street, and she walked out on him. So I don't think she's unduly impressed with Ron Herman's credentials."

Susannah was late getting to the courts. The other three women were volleying aimlessly.

"What took you so long?" Myrna asked.

Susannah wondered how many people Betty Kagin had called that morning.

At five o'clock Cornelia came banging in the back door with a canvas bag full of wet towels and clothes and a fresh Band-Aid on her knee.

"Lisa got one too, but mine's bigger. Can I have supper at Lisa's? They're going to McDonald's."

Susannah said she'd have to check with Lisa's mommy. She dialed Faith Sherman's number. If it weren't for the hedge between the houses, she could have seen Faith answering the phone in her own kitchen. When they'd first moved in and the shrubbery had been sparse enough to see through, it had been like looking into a mirror. Despite the lack of privacy, there had been something reassuring about that view.

Faith said she had no intention of cooking on a night when Howard wasn't coming home for dinner. "Send Cornelia over. What's one more? It must be bliss having an only child. She goes out, and you're on vacation."

"Bliss," Susannah said and wondered whether Faith was being bitchy or merely dumb. "I think I'll make Nick take me out to dinner."

Susannah sent Cornelia next door and dialed Nick's office. His new receptionist answered. Brigitte, who'd worked for him since he'd gone into practice, had married and left to have a baby. Susannah didn't like Stacey as much. "Doctor's with a patient," she said. Her voice was too thin for arrogance, but it had a certain childish nah-nah quality to it. "He's running forty minutes late. Do you want me to give him a message?"

Susannah decided to drive to his office and surprise him. She said there was no message.

Upstairs in their bathroom, she took off her shorts and shirt, covered her hair with a plastic shower cap, and stepped into the stall shower. While she shaved her legs, she debated whether she should tell Nick about Nora right away and get his opinion on what to do, or wait until they got home. They rarely went out to dinner without other people, and she hated to ruin the occasion.

She got out of the shower, dried herself, and powdered profligately with Norell. Back in the bedroom she took fresh bikinis and a clean bra from her second drawer. She decided it was too hot for pantyhose. Beatrice still insisted a lady never went anywhere without stockings, but Nora even went to her office barelegged. Not that anyone would call Nora a lady these days.

Damn it. She'd managed to forget her sister for a minute.

Now she was back. Up the road, in the house where Susannah had gone to parties and dinners, in the bedroom where she'd helped Gloria Herman choose curtains and a bedspread, in bed with a friend who referred patients to Nick and to whom Nick referred in return.

What had happened to Nora? They used to agree on everything. Well, maybe not everything, but at least they'd never fought. Susannah remembered how Nora used to love to come into her room and sit on the white canopied bed. A couple of months ago when Susannah had talked about buying a canopied bed for Cornelia, Nora had asked if she was going to bind Cornelia's feet and give her a clitorectomy too. That was the way she talked now. Like that line about breezies. Even Nick said she'd turned into the world's oldest living adolescent.

It came to Susannah while she was teasing her hair. Nick would speak to Ron. Man to man, older brother to friend. Nora was still a rebellious kid, despite the fact that she was a twenty-eight-year-old divorced woman. They had to protect her. Not from Ron—Nick would make that clear—but from herself.

Susannah zipped up the sleeveless cotton dress and examined herself in the mirror on the back of the bedroom door. Maybe she should have put on pantyhose after all. The dress stopped several inches above the knee, and there was a fine network of veins, like a purple spiderweb, on the inside of her left thigh. It hadn't been there the summer before. Nick had teased her about it, but she'd said those weren't varicose veins, only a few stray hairs that had fallen out of his head. He hadn't teased her again.

Looking to both sides and in the rearview mirror for kids, Susannah inched the station wagon out the driveway. They'd leave her car in the parking lot behind Nick's office and pick it up on the way back from dinner.

She wondered if they ought to go to the new French place out beyond the golf course. Or, if Nick felt like driving, they could go to the shore for lobster. She'd let him suggest that, though. She didn't want to ask him to drive if he was tired. God knows he put in long enough days.

Maybe he wouldn't want to go out at all. He must have

had an emergency. The receptionist said he was running forty minutes late. She'd said it in that snippy tone that implied Susannah was just one more hypochondriacal woman wasting the doctor's precious time. Susannah missed Brigitte, who always asked about Cornelia and offered to drag Nick out of the examining room to come to the phone, though Susannah never let her.

The lot behind Nick's building was almost empty. Susannah parked the station wagon next to his old Buick. She never noticed it in the garage, but out here in the slanting light of the setting sun, she saw how beat-up it was. Nick was right. They needed a new car, and if he thought they could afford a Mercedes, then he ought to have a Mercedes, though Beatrice and Sam would disapprove. They didn't believe in buying German products.

She locked the door on the passenger side of the station wagon, then got out and locked the one on the driver's side. Normally, she would have left it open, but they'd be gone for several hours.

She walked carefully across the parking lot. It hadn't been repaved in years, and the loose gravel bit at the heels of her shoes.

The door to the office was unlocked, but the waiting room was empty. The receptionist and all the girls had already left. Susannah walked down the hall to Nick's private office. It was empty too. She tried to see the room as a patient would. Nick's medical school diploma, his license, his board certification, the F.A.C.P. certificate, all beautifully framed in dark wood, hung on two walls. A picture of her and Cornelia stood on the desk. On a third wall were photographs of the stand of trees behind the pool taken by Nick in the four different seasons. The colors in the autumnal one were breathtaking, but Susannah liked winter best. Nick had snapped it after a snowstorm. You could feel the peace in that picture. Susannah thought the series was a nice touch. Like the picture of Cornelia and her on his desk, it said just enough about the doctor.

The door to the last examining room at the end of the hall was closed. If he was still with a patient at seven-thirty, he was running more than forty minutes late. Susannah walked back to the waiting room.

The receptionist's desk was clear except for the telephone and a large appointment book. At least Stacey was neat. Nick insisted she was more efficient than Brigitte, but Susannah still didn't like her. Susannah flipped open the book. Hour after hour, day after day of names, all of them dependent on her husband. There were several she recognized, more she didn't.

She took the latest issue of *Time* from one of the tables and sat down to wait. She heard the faint sound of Nick's voice, but the examining room was too far away to make out what he was saying. She flipped backward through the magazine. Kirk Douglas, Natalie Wood, and Nancy Sinatra had been taken by some oil swindler. There was a picture of Burt Reynolds with two bare-breasted girls. You could even see the nipple on one of them. In an article on teen-age sex, an eighteen-year-old New Jersey girl was quoted as saying, "It sure can clear up the blues." Maybe Nora was right about the sexual revolution. But Susannah was right too. They weren't mounting the barricades in Oak Hills.

There was a soft moan from the direction of the examining room. Susannah tried to shut it out. Her knees went weak at the thought of what Nick might be doing to the patient. There was another moan, louder this time. She felt a trickle of sweat run down her side. She tried to concentrate on "The Jewish Swing to Nixon," but despite the air-conditioning, her hands stuck to the pages of the magazine.

The moaning was louder now, "Ohhhh." It came rushing down the hall at her like a river of pain. "Ohhhh."

Susannah sat perfectly still. The sweat running down her sides felt like bugs crawling down her skin. She knew that sound. It wasn't pain. And it wasn't from a patient.

"Ohhhh," Nick always moaned, like a train whistle announcing that the ride was coming to an end. "Ohhhh," he'd cry a few more times, and then, when he actually came, "God!" and "Susannah," as if they were equally responsible.

She stood and started down the hall toward the examining room.

"God!" The word wēnt off like an explosion behind the closed door. Susannah stood dead still in the hall, the sweat still running down her sides. "God," Nick said again.

"Right on," a thin, whining voice answered.

There were only three cars left in the parking lot, Susannah's station wagon, Nick's Buick beside it, and a red Ford beside that. Susannah tried the door to the Ford. It wasn't locked. She pulled it open. There were some crumpled tissues, a pack of Marlboros, and a pocket comb on the front seat. A box of tissues stood on the dashboard. Susannah reached across the front seat and yanked open the glove compartment. She began pulling out maps and papers, a flashlight, one winter glove, a package of Dentyne gum. She chewed gum. God! There was no registration or insurance card, but there was a postcard with a picture of Mickey and Minnie Mouse in front of a sign that said Disneyland. Susannah turned the card over. It was addressed to Miss Stacey Cole. Someone named Megan was having a wonderful time and wished Stacey were there.

Susannah didn't bother to put the things back in the glove compartment. Let the little bitch think someone had tried to steal her car. Let the little bitch get scared. Susannah climbed into the station wagon and turned on the ignition. She grazed the fender on Nick's Buick as she pulled out.

She stopped at a phone on the turnpike. Her hands were shaking as she dialed Faith Sherman's number. "I'm going to take you up on that offer to keep Cornelia overnight."

"Give a woman dinner out with her husband, and she turns it into a second honeymoon."

Susannah swallowed the sob.

"Are you okay?" Faith asked.

"Fine. I have to go into the city, though."

"Is anything wrong?"

This time Susannah caught the sob before it reached her throat. "Just my sister Nora. Another crisis."

"I hear she's seeing Ron Herman."

"That's not the crisis."

"Maybe if you're lucky, she'll marry Ron and settle down again, and you and your mother can stop worrying."

"Listen, Faith, I really appreciate this." Susannah's voice vibrated like the strings of a musical instrument.

"It's nothing. I just hope your sister's okay."

Susannah dumped more change into the phone. Her hands were still trembling. As she dialed Nora's number, she wondered what she'd do if her sister wasn't home. What she'd do was go to Beatrice, but she wasn't ready for that yet.

Nora answered her phone on the fourth ring.

"Can I come see you?" Susannah asked.

"What's wrong?"

"Nothing. I'll tell you when I get there."

"Where are you?"

"On the turnpike. I'll be there in twenty minutes."

"Just don't speed," Nora said.

That's my line, Susannah wanted to scream.

"It's not the end of the world," Nora insisted.

"It's the end of my world." Susannah sat slumped under the weight of the pain. Her skin, beneath the tan, was a waxy yellow. Her eyes, rimmed by smudged makeup, had the glazed look of the mentally ill.

Nora felt the way she did when she read in the paper about plane crashes or murders. The instinct was to find a logic to the disaster. The instinct was to distance herself. They shouldn't have flown a charter. He shouldn't have been jogging before it got light. She shouldn't have trusted Nick.

He called a little after ten.

"Faith said Susannah's there. What's the crisis this time? It must be good, because she didn't even leave a note."

Nora handed Susannah the phone and went into the bathroom. She even ran the water in the sink, but she could still hear Susannah crying.

The doorbell rang at a little after eleven. Susannah jumped as if something had backfired.

"You don't have to be afraid of him," Nora said. "He can't hurt you."

Susannah looked at her sister blankly. "Of course he can."

"Only if you give him the power to."

"For God's sake, Nora."

Nora went to the door. It was the first time she'd seen Nick frightened.

"This is stupid." He spoke past Nora to Susannah, who was huddled in a corner of the couch.

Nora went into the bathroom and turned on the water again.

Half an hour later, she came out. Susannah was still huddled in a corner of the couch. Nick was sitting in the middle, holding one of Susannah's hands in both of his. They glanced up when Nora came into the room. Susannah's skin still looked like tallow. There were smudges of dark eye makeup beneath her eyes. The clean line of Nick's jaw was gone. His chin sagged softly.

"We'll get out of here and let you get some sleep," he said.

"Susannah can stay if she wants," Nora said.

"We're going home," Nick insisted.

"I might as well," Susannah said. "That way I can see Cornelia before the bus picks her up for camp. We're not going to settle anything tonight."

"Everything's settled," Nick said.

He stood. He was still holding Susannah's hand. He tugged her up off the sofa. Her dress was a maze of wrinkles. She moved as if her body ached.

"I'll call you in the morning," Nora said.

She stood in the doorway and watched them go. The stairs were narrow, and Nick had to drop Susannah's arm to let her move ahead of him, but he kept his hands on her shoulders as if he were steering her.

The phone was ringing again when Nora walked into her office the following morning.

"Tell me exactly what happened," Beatrice said as soon as Nora picked it up.

"Didn't Susannah?"

"She started to, but then she began to cry and that Betty

Kagin walked in—don't Susannah's neighbors have homes of their own?—and we had to get off."

Nora talked for some time. When she finished, all Beatrice said was that she had to hang up.

"Are you going to call Susannah?"

"I'm going over there."

Beatrice didn't exactly take over. She merely stepped in to help, as she would have in the event of any family illness. She walked with a quiet, solemn step through the rooms of the house she'd helped buy. She whispered behind closed doors. She took Cornelia on jaunts to get her out of the way. She made sensible suggestions. First there were the surgical procedures. Stacey would be cut out. Nick would give her two weeks' pay and tell her not to come in the following day. Then there was the recovery process. Nick must prove his repentance. Susannah must work at forgiveness.

Susannah wasn't sure she wanted to forgive.

"What do you mean?" Beatrice demanded as she and her daughters sat around the pool one September Saturday. It hadn't been vacuumed in days, and a handful of leaves, faded a dispiriting yellow, floated on the surface. "You don't throw away ten years of marriage because of some little tramp," she insisted. Her voice was no longer hushed. The immediate crisis had passed. It was time to get the patient out of bed and on her feet.

"Because of Nick," Susannah corrected her mother.

"Mommy has a point," Nora said. "I told you, it's not such a big deal."

"That's not what I said," Beatrice insisted.

"Not a big deal for you," Susannah said.

Nora stood and walked to the shallow end of the pool. She felt like a street kid who'd been given a day in the country by two well-meaning but naive women.

A thin film of decay coated the surface of the water. She sat on the steps. A dead leaf floated over her foot. She thrust her legs deeper into the pool.

When she went back, they were still talking.

"You think raising a child alone is a picnic?" Beatrice asked.

"People remarry," Susannah said.

"People also get jobs and make lives for themselves," Nora said.

"You're a thirty-two-year-old woman with a child," Beatrice reminded Susannah. "They're not going to be beating down your door."

"You were forty-one with two children when you married Sam," Susannah said.

"The art director at the magazine is divorced with two kids," Nora said. "She insists the kids are happier now than when their parents were together and fighting all the time."

"And don't think it was easy." Beatrice shook her head. "The men I went out with before him. Playboys. Gold diggers. And I worried about you two, too. You don't bring a man into a house with two teenage girls and not worry. I was lucky."

"Maybe I'll be lucky too," Susannah said, but she didn't believe it. She'd lost her faith, in Nick, in her own luck, in Beatrice's promises.

15

Nora's first thought was who in hell had invited Wheeler. He was standing at the head of the conference table smiling so broadly that his forehead had disappeared entirely. Standing beside him, Lucy was smiling too. Nora knew who had invited Wheeler.

Nora went on standing in the doorway looking at the director of the magazine division and her executive editor. The aura of satisfaction was so thick it was almost postcoital.

Papers littered the table. Storyboards and mock-ups of print ads were propped on the ledge that ran around the room halfway up the wall. They touted the new *American Homemaker.*

Nora looked again. *AH!* was nowhere in sight. The book is dead. Long live the book.

"How was the presentation?" Nora asked.

"Hot," Wheeler said.

Lucy ducked her head, as she did when she was embarrassed. Nora suddenly realized that she'd always found the gesture a little phony.

Nora glanced at the ads again. In one a mother and child sat on the porch of a Victorian house. The woman was a bony, beautiful Madison Avenue version of *American Gothic,* the kid was so cute she made Nora's teeth ache, and you couldn't touch the house for less than half a million. In a second, another Grant Wood beauty stood in front of a Tudor house. Behind her on the lawn a cunningly cute boy and girl sat cross-legged. That house reminded Nora of the one she'd grown up in on Byron Road. A storyboard showed mothers and fathers and children coming home to front hallways and kitchens and porches and yards. No matter where Nora looked the same line jumped out at her. *AMERICAN HOMEMAKER'S* COMING HOME.

"Hasn't anyone around here read Tom Wolfe?" she said.

"That guy who always wears those ice cream suits?" Wheeler asked.

Nora let it go. "Is this the hot campaign?" She tried not to sound incredulous.

"What do you think?" Wheeler asked.

Nora looked around the room slowly. She was trying to give it a chance. She really was. "I think it looks a little tired. I think it looks more than a little like the stuff we were running twenty years ago."

Wheeler's eyes swiveled from the ads to Nora. "I didn't realize you'd been here that long."

"I haven't. But I've seen the ads."

"What goes around comes around."

The last of the Australopithecines speaks.

"Are you going to bring back 'The Heartbreak of Motherhood' and 'Is This Divorce Necessary?' too?"

"The American woman is tired of materialism, Nora, and we've got to cash in on the fact." Wheeler frowned. The effect was even more disastrous than when he smiled. Nora tried not to think about that display in the Museum of Natural History.

"We've got the oldest median reader of the top eleven women's magazines," Wheeler said. "The fifth oldest of all twenty-three women's magazines. Old ladies don't buy. They have. I want a girl with money in her pockets. Money burning a hole in her pockets."

"And you think this is the campaign to get her."

He stared at Nora for a moment. Lucy dropped her eyes. "You represented the feminists, Nora. After you came the yuppies. What we're looking at now is a whole new ball game. What Lucy calls the New Feminines."

"Lucy?"

Lucy raised her eyes, then ducked her head again.

"Yeah," Wheeler said. "She and research came up with the target market. The tastemakers among the baby boomers. Careerists. Incomed. But not afraid to be feminine. Wife and mother aren't dirty words anymore."

"No one ever said they were."

Wheeler raised his eyebrows. They met his hairline. "I didn't read them much in *AH!* American women are going back to the old values, and we've got to go with them. More to the point, we've got to lead the way. Lucy took a couple of brainstorming sessions with the guys from Bananas. She even came up with the tag. *American Homemaker*'s coming home. She's a real gem, Nora. Hold on to her."

Nora looked at Lucy, then at Will Wheeler. "I wouldn't let her go for the world."

Before Nora left the office that evening, she called Max and told him not to bother to stop by the hospital.

"Beatrice is coming home tomorrow." Beatrice, *American Homemaker*, everybody.

"I'm crazy about Beatrice, but I was coming to pick you up. We were going to dinner. The Washington contingent, remember? You were going to do your hypocritical act again."

She'd forgotten about the people from Washington. Anyway, Max had admitted he didn't need her along, he just liked to have her along.

"Actually, I have to work. There's a crisis here."

"What kind of crisis?" Max's voice wasn't exactly bored, merely unconcerned. Nora thought of one of Beatrice's favorite fables, the boy who cried wolf.

"While I've been sitting in the hospital, they've decided to revamp the book. According to Wheeler, I'm two trends behind the time."

"What does two trends behind the time mean?" Max's voice had changed. Nora took it as confirmation of her fears.

She thought of Monica Storch. One of Will Wheeler's
first moves had been to fire Monica. Of course, Monica had
been close to sixty. She'd gone up to his office one morning,
and come down from it five minutes later with two security
guards. They'd stood in the door to her office, while she'd
packed a silver pen, a leather Mark Cross blotter and calendar set, a few cosmetics from her bottom desk drawer, an
umbrella, a sweater, and a pair of rubber boots. If there'd
been a bottle of rye in that desk, she'd left it. They hadn't
let her take her Rolodex. Nora had called Monica's apartment that night. A man's voice answered. Nora tried to
imagine it ordering "steady as she goes" or "ten degrees
north." The voice sounded too old and frail. It said in a sore,
impatient tone indigenous to houses of mourning that Miss
Storch wasn't taking calls. Nora had never telephoned
again, though when she thought about it, she always felt a
twinge of guilt.

"It has to do with a rebirth of the old values. Not to
mention the birth rate. Apple pie and mom. I don't qual-
ify."

"What are you going to do?"

"That's what I have to figure out tonight. I want to go
over the stuff they sprang on me today."

Max said he'd be home by ten if she wanted to talk. And
he didn't say she had nothing to worry about.

Nora didn't recognize him at first. For one thing, her mind
was on *American Homemaker*'s homecoming. For another,
she'd grown accustomed to strange men in sanitized white
coats and expressions to match turning up in her mother's
hospital room unexpectedly. This one wasn't young
enough to be in training. He was one of the sleek older
specimens, practitioners of related specialties, purveyors
of begrudged second opinions. But he was a doctor for
sure. He had the smooth, smug look of a man accustomed
to being waited on and agreed with and deferred to. "Doctor will see you now." "Whatever you say, doc." "You're
the doctor." It was the look of the uncrossed, the unop-
posed, the unassailable. It was indigenous to the breed.
Max didn't have it. She supposed lawyers went up against

their own too often. Businessmen didn't have it. They were too busy figuring the odds and staying one step ahead of the competition. Editors sure as hell didn't have it. She was living proof of that. The only ones who came close to having it were teachers, especially teachers of small children. They too were masters of the unfairly matched encounter. But if teachers had the smugness, they couldn't afford the polish. This particular doctor had the kind of tan that came this early in the season only from weekends spent on his own tennis court or boat deck. Beneath the white jacket he also had a custom-made shirt and the right Hermès tie. When he reached out to take Nora's hand, she saw the discreetly minuscule monogram on his cuff. NAD. Nicholas Alexander Demopoulis. It wasn't that she hadn't recognized him. She'd seen him a few years earlier at Cornelia's graduation. Only that she hadn't been expecting him.

He pointed to Beatrice, who was dozing in the hospital bed, then motioned Nora outside.

"What are you doing here?" Nora asked when they were in the hall.

"I have privileges," Nick said, and it took Nora a minute to realize he was talking about access to the hospital rather than the story of his life. "Cornelia told me Beatrice was here. I thought I'd stop by to see how she was. But I suppose it's just as well she's sleeping."

Nick dropped his eyes. The gesture made a hairline crack in the smooth veneer. He knew he was on dangerous ground. He and Beatrice had never been able to stop liking each other. They were like two beautifully polished surfaces that shone a little more brightly in each other's reflections. But they'd never been able to forgive each other either.

They talked about Beatrice for a moment. Nick really didn't have to ask how she was. Doctor to doctor, he'd got more information from the surgeon than Nora had been able to get blood from that particular stone. He said things looked good. Nora thanked him for his concern. She meant it. She'd never been able to stop liking Nick either.

He stared down at her. "How're you holding up?"

It was a familiar feeling. She always felt that he wasn't just looking at her, but comparing her to Susannah.

"I'm okay."

"You look a little tired."

American Homemaker's coming home. Only you couldn't.

"I have a mother in the hospital," she said, because she didn't want to go into the rest of it.

"Can I buy you a cup of coffee?"

She made a few excuses. The usual hospital overdose of caffeine. The need to be there when Beatrice awakened. The press of time. She should have stopped at one. It would have been more convincing.

"Please."

As they walked the long halls to the cafeteria, Nora knew she'd joined the long line of women who'd been unable to say no to Nick Demopoulis.

The cafeteria smelled like the rest of the hospital, only more so. They found a table in the corner. He brought a tray with two cups of coffee. A nurse at the next table looked up.

"Hi, Dr. Demopoulis," she sang.

Nora recognized the tune. Nick knew from the way she looked at him that she had. For the second time that evening, the veneer cracked and he dropped his eyes.

Nora asked about his wife and son. She didn't think of it as pressing an advantage, only being polite. Anyway, the son part hurt, though she supposed it was better in the long run that there'd been only Cornelia. The trouble was that the long run didn't matter until it was too late.

"How's my daughter?" Nick asked.

"Fine. I talked to her last night. For close to an hour."

Nick closed his hands around the coffee cup. He had nice hands, not as nice as Max's, but nice just the same.

"She have anything to say?"

"Nothing much."

"For close to an hour?"

Nora shrugged. "You know our family."

"I hadn't spoken to her for a couple of months, until last

week. Then she only called because of Beatrice. She wanted a crash course in breast cancer."

"She wanted reassurance."

He'd been staring into his coffee cup. Now he looked up at her. "Thanks for the instruction."

"I'm sorry. Do you call her? I mean she doesn't call me all that often. I call her a lot."

"She's never there."

"You can get her late at night or early in the morning before classes."

"Early in the morning I'm in my office or at the hospital."

Nora didn't say anything.

"You know the last time she came home?"

Nora started to answer, then realized he meant his house, not her apartment.

"Christmas vacation. She spent spring vacation in Florida with Beatrice. I understand she stayed with you for a weekend, too."

"She went to Florida with Andy."

He slumped back into the cheap plastic chair. "Who's Andy?"

"The current contender for the title. You probably met him last Christmas. She tells me I did."

"Just because she introduced him to you doesn't mean she did to us."

"Anyway, you don't really think you can compete with young love, postmodern architecture, *and* a tan. Those are the real reasons she stayed with Beatrice."

"I would have taken her south. Brenda wanted to go to the islands."

Nora didn't answer.

"Brenda even sent her some brochures. We were willing to take Timothy out of school for a week so we could go during Cornelia's break."

"And have him miss Coloring 101? Wow!"

He stared at her for a moment, as if she'd caught him off guard, then shook his head slowly. "That's exactly what Cornelia said when I made the offer. The only thing I can't figure out is why I'm surprised."

"Spring vacation is over. Why are you telling me all this?"

"Who else should I tell?"

Nora took a sip of her coffee. It had started out bitter. Now it was cold and bitter. She had a mother lying upstairs in a hospital bed. She had a career slipping away from her. She didn't need an embittered father gunning for her.

"I'm sorry if you're having problems with Cornelia, but that's between the two of you."

Nick just sat staring at her.

"I mean, it has nothing to do with me."

He went on staring.

"You act as if I'm one of those crazed women who bundle kids out of carriages in supermarkets and shopping malls."

"If the shoe fits . . ." It was another of Beatrice's favorite adages, but Nora was sure Nick didn't remember that.

"Cornelia was old enough to decide where she wanted to live."

"With a little help from her grandmother and aunt."

"She didn't need help. Not after Brenda—"

"Bullshit!"

The pert nurse turned to stare at Dr. Demopoulis. Nick didn't notice.

"Don't give me that cheap psychological garbage. Sure, Cornelia resented Brenda. All over America teenage girls are resenting their stepmothers."

Nora started to say something, but Nick cut her off.

"Even stepmothers who are young enough to be their older sisters, so don't give me that crap either. But most of them get over it. If Cornelia had stayed, she would have got over it. If you and Beatrice hadn't stepped in, she would have got over it."

Nora pushed back her chair. It made a screeching sound on the linoleum floor. She saw Nick shudder. She stood. He looked up at her.

"I'm sorry," he said. "This isn't what I had in mind. I really did want to talk to you about Cornelia. Sit down. Please."

This time the "please" didn't work. He went on staring up at her. His face, behind the perfect tan, was smooth. His perfect shirt wasn't wrinkled. His perfect tie was in place. But there was something else going on underneath. She supposed that was why she still liked him.

"I'm sorry, too, Nick. But you don't want to talk to me. You want to blame me. Beatrice and me. I understand how you feel. God knows, there were times when I wanted to blame you."

"You mean you didn't?"

She didn't want to think about that. Not now. That was in the past. New things were crumbling. But not Cornelia.

"I never meant to take Cornelia away from you. I couldn't. Hell, you're her father. I leave scratches. You leave scars."

"Thanks."

"I'm sorry. Again. I don't seem to be striking the right note today. Cornelia's fine. Terrific. But if you miss her, keep calling. Take time out from a patient in the morning. Or get away from Brenda at night." The rest came out before she realized it. "God knows you're good at that."

"So you do blame me after all?"

"No, I didn't mean that."

"The hell you didn't. I just don't understand where you get off being so holier than thou. What about that artist? The one who had a thing about horses."

"How did you know about him?"

Nick smiled, silvery as a mirror reflecting all the old confidence. "There was a time when Susannah and I got along, you know."

A wave of exhausted nausea almost knocked Nora back into her chair.

"That was the difference. Paul didn't care. Susannah did."

"Are you sure of that?"

"He just about told me so."

"I wasn't talking about Paul. I was talking about Susannah."

"Are you kidding? She was wild about you."

"Or at least the idea of me."

Nora knew what he meant. Over the years she'd watched Susannah spinning out, and Beatrice holding to the course, and herself floundering, and wondered the same thing. Beatrice said she liked having a man around. It gave her strength. And Nora accused her of cannibalism.

She did something then that she'd never intended to do. Half an hour earlier, when he'd glided into Beatrice's room, as shiny and unscratched as a new car, she never would have dared. Now she reached out and touched his cheek.

He looked as startled as if she'd slapped him.

It came back then. God, how she'd idolized him. They all had. Only Nora had never got close enough to lose it. She and Nick had never screamed; accused; turned angry, wounded backs to each other in bed.

"No; Nick. You."

She dropped her hand. He still looked startled.

"I have to get back now. I don't like to leave Beatrice alone for too long. Call Cornelia. Keep trying till you get her."

When Nora got home that night, she changed into her robe, made herself a drink, and got into bed with the file for the new ad campaign. She'd seen the numbers before. Now she started to go through the focus group reports. Nora had never put much faith in focus groups, though Wheeler swore by them. She didn't trust women who bared their souls, or even gave their opinions, in exchange for ten dollars and all the cheap Danish they could eat.

"I was working ten hours a day, making six figures a year, and all of a sudden I found myself running around looking in baby carriages."

"After a high-powered day competing with corporate men and women, I want to come home to something soft and warm."

"I want to be the kind of woman my grandmother was. I want to live in a big old house, and bake my own bread, and sit on the porch with my husband and children and grand-children."

Lots of luck, Nora thought. Just wait till the mortgage payments on the big old house come due, and you've got no job, and your husband is sitting on another porch with his second wife and new family.

Nora thought of Nick. Her arm reached for the phone. "God, am I glad you're there," she said when Cornelia answered.

"What's wrong?"

Nora heard the alarm in Cornelia's voice.

"Nothing. Grandma's fine. I didn't mean to frighten you. She's coming home tomorrow. I left her at the hospital with Charlie. They were watching sitcoms and planning to live happily ever after."

"Then why do you sound so wired? If I didn't know you better, I'd swear you were putting something funny up your nose."

Nora lay back on the bed with the phone in one hand and put the other over her eyes. She'd come to motherhood unprepared, uncertain, and, as Nick had pointed out, unauthorized. Once or twice, during difficult times, Cornelia had reminded her she wasn't her mother. Nora had always known she had to be more than a buddy.

Even if she'd opened her eyes, Nora could still see the scene. It had happened in this room.

Cornelia must have been thirteen or fourteen. By that time she'd been at her new school long enough to risk having a party. There'd been some discussion of where Nora ought to be while the rock blared and the pizza was ground into the rug. Cornelia thought the movies sounded like a good place. Nora was all for the scene of the crime. They compromised on her bedroom.

It hadn't been much fun sitting there huddled on her bed, trying to read while the floors and walls vibrated to the beat, kids screamed, and she tried not to think about Coke stains on the upholstery and coke on some kid. But the worst part of the evening had occurred when Stephanie Salander had come into the bedroom and asked if she could use the phone. Stephanie was one of those girls who look two or three years younger than their age and, perhaps as a result, act two or three years older. She wasn't precocious, just mature.

Nora moved to the other side of the bed, the one away

from the phone, and pretended to go on reading. There
was no way she could keep from eavesdropping.

"Come on, Mom," Stephanie said, "it's only ten o'clock."

An old-fashioned mother, Nora thought, and wondered
if she was too permissive with Cornelia.

"He can still call," Stephanie went on. There was a silence. "Anyway, he didn't say he'd call tonight. He just said
he'd call."

Nora read a sentence for the third time.

"Look, Mom, you said you had a good time. If you did, he
probably did too."

Stephanie sat on the side of the bed with her back to
Nora.

"Well, he seemed like he had a good time this morning. I
mean, I heard him singing in the shower." There was a
brief pause. "Yeah, he sings Beatles' songs."

This time the silence went on for longer.

"Do you want me to come home?"

Stephanie's small body hunched forward.

"Sure, I'm having a good time, but I'll come home if you
want me to."

Nora fought the urge to grab the phone out of Stephanie's hand. "Okay, then, hang up. He could be trying to get
you right this minute."

Stephanie stood.

"Listen, Mom, don't worry. He'll call. And I'll be home
early."

Nora had made two resolutions that night. She'd never
again serve food or drink in primary colors to adolescents.
And she wouldn't cry on shoulders that weren't fully
grown. It made no difference that Claire Salander had
been worrying about a one-night stand and Nora was sick
to her stomach over a twenty-year career. They were both
adult terrors. X-rated. The young had to be protected.

Nora and Cornelia stayed on the phone for less than
twenty minutes. It was a short conversation, for them.
When Cornelia asked how things were going at the magazine, Nora said okay and changed the subject.

"I saw your father tonight. He came to the hospital."

"How is he?"

"Worried about you."

Cornelia didn't say anything.

"Why don't you give him a call?" Nora suggested.

Nora went back to the demos. She didn't swear by them, but she knew how to use them. Tonight she'd made up her mind. Tomorrow she'd get research working on it. And she'd call Maude. Nora had been wrong about that article on aging. Maude had sold it. Now she was working on a book about aging in American society.

Nora would get all the ammunition. Then she'd make her move. She didn't mind going over Wheeler's head, especially if it meant saving her own neck.

16

Just as, given the times and Susannah, there had to be a pregnancy scare, so, given different times and another Susannah, there had to be a retaliatory affair.

Harvey Koch was the heir to Koch Brothers, a chain of jewelry stores that stretched across the northern part of the state like the heavy gold chain he wore around his neck. It was just about the time when men like Harvey were beginning to wear chains like that, and he was coining change on the phenomenon. Harvey had a lot of money, a modicum of good looks, and a shortage of intelligence. Susannah's affair with him was proof of a fundamental law of extramarital sex. Women like Susannah don't screw around, they screw down.

Some instinct in her recognized that. Some relic of the old Susannah resisted it. For several months she patched things over. When Nick was late coming home from the office, she accepted his explanations and buried her own suspicions. When he took her hand or put his arm around her, she fought the urge to pull away and faked the old effortless affection. When he referred to her as "my wife," she tried to hear the half-pride and ignore the half-depre- cation. When they lay on the sheets monogrammed with that tangled emblem of their marriage and he turned and put a hand on her breast or stomach or thigh, she tried not to think of his hands on that twenty-year-old breast or stomach or thigh. But she was no good at compromise. Maybe because she'd never had to be. She ached with festering resentment.

One morning she lay rigidly beneath him while he went through the motions of sex. She couldn't believe he was doing any more than going through the motions. Not that he wasn't still skillful at them. He knew what she liked. He knew where to touch, what to do. She lay there wondering if that twenty-year-old who chewed gum and talked with a childish nasal accent had the same tastes. Or had Nick had to learn new tricks?

The harder he worked, the more she thought about it. The image of him and that girl in the examining room stopped the first tremor of an orgasm in its tracks. Had they undressed or just removed strategic articles of clothing? She tried to remember if there were stirrups on the examining table. Nick would get a kick out of that.

He'd given up on her now. It was every man for himself. "Ohhhh," Nick, the Little Engine That Could, moaned. "Ohhhh," again, and then, "God!" and "Susannah."

He collapsed on top of her. She looked down at the head on her chest. Pillowed on her breast, if you wanted to believe the poets. His hair was messed, and the small thinning spot was more noticeable.

"Right on," she said.

He pulled away so quickly he hurt her. Then he stood, walked into the bathroom, and slammed the door.

That was Sunday morning. On Sunday evening they went to the annual art show to benefit the local hospital. Nick didn't take her hand or put his arm around her or refer to her as "my wife." She didn't give a damn.

Though Harvey Koch wasn't an intellectual giant, he was no dope, at least about certain things. He noticed a change in Susannah Demopoulis that night.

There were several pictures of children with huge sooty eyes. Almost everyone knew enough to laugh at those. Most of the charitable types drifting through the gallery weren't so sure about the Pollock and Rothko and Stella spin-offs. Once again Harvey was just smart enough.

He idled up to Susannah. "You know the old line? 'I don't know anything about art, but I know what I like.' I don't even know what I like. What the hell do you see when you look at this stuff?"

The Smith art history major stepped out from behind the deceived wife. Susannah told him. Harvey listened. It was a long time since anyone had looked at her that way. Nick used to. She wondered if he'd looked at the twenty-year-old gum-chewer that way. She let Harvey bring her another glass of white wine.

They talked for so long and so well that it didn't seem odd, or at least outrageous, when he called her from one of his stores the next morning.

He suggested they have lunch. Just lunch, he assured her. He liked talking to her, he said.

She had to drive forty minutes to get to a dark fake-wood-and-red-leatherette-glorified diner near the farthest outpost of Koch Brothers, Inc. The bartender poured drinks with a meager hand. They used the same restraint in pouring out their hearts. Things weren't quite right at home, but neither went into detail.

Outside in the parking lot, Harvey held the car door open, then got in after her. For a moment Susannah wondered what this strange man was doing behind the wheel of her station wagon. There was some tipsy grappling. Neither of them was accustomed to drinking at lunch. Mouths. Tongues. A hand trying to figure out how to get inside her double-breasted trench coat. Another hand clawing at the crotch of her pantyhose.

Susannah pulled away and sat with her back against the passenger door. Her eyes were as big and accusing as those in the awful paintings in the art show. She explained that this wasn't what she had in mind. He'd said he just wanted to have lunch. She'd taken him at his word.

Harvey straightened his tie and smoothed his hair. He said he'd got carried away. How could he help it? He was crazy about her. But they'd take it any way she said. He was dying to go to bed with her. She must know that. But if it was just going to be this, if they were just going to be friends, he'd settle for that. It took two more lunches before she went to bed with him.

Harvey couldn't believe his luck. Susannah was the prom queen who wouldn't look at him in high school, the Smithie who wouldn't give him a date in college, Marilyn Monroe —"only," he liked to say, "with more class." Susannah never did make him understand that the word was a sociological category rather than a compliment.

From Susannah's point of view, Harvey's feet were more firmly rooted in clay. Besides, she wasn't made for infidelity. After the thrills of being once again adored and finally revenged wore off, she found herself mired in the minutiae of finding time and covering tracks and remembering lies. The affair took on the aura of household drudgery without any of its subsequent feeling of a job well done. Finally she told Harvey she couldn't see him anymore, except, of course, at dinners and parties and around the pool where they'd all go on seeing each other. Then she told Nick about the affair.

Nora had warned her not to, but then Nora wasn't exactly an authority on marital relations.

Nick got angry, then, with the help of his new receptionist, even. Susannah consulted a divorce lawyer. He was an old-fashioned fatherly type who told her to think it over.

Beatrice hadn't been so furious since that day during Christmas vacation when they'd driven home from Lord & Taylor, and she'd called her daughter a tramp.

"I forgave you then," Beatrice said. "You can forgive Nick now."

Susannah hadn't told Beatrice about Harvey. It was the first of a good many things she never got around to telling Beatrice.

"Think of Cornelia," Beatrice argued.

"He'll marry that tramp," Beatrice added, though by that time it was clear to Susannah and Nora, if not Beatrice, that there was more than one tramp.

"You think it's easy to be a single woman with a child in this world?" Beatrice asked.

"Who's going to want you? A thirty-four-year-old woman with a child," she repeated.

Susannah thought she knew the answer. For months after that night she'd driven down to Nick's office, she'd walked around feeling as if her life were over. Now she saw at least a glimmer of promise.

Maybe it was because of Harvey—Nora had told Susannah that she'd walked differently at the beginning of her affair—but men were coming on to her again. They'd never really stopped, but now they were more serious. Or maybe she was. Syd Gabriel, who commuted to Wall Street, asked her if she could ever get away for lunch or dinner in town. He'd joked about it before, but now he actually took her aside at a party and pleaded with her. He had the sweetest look in his eyes when he did. And one day when she'd gone into the city alone because Beatrice and Sam were away on a cruise, a strange man had tried to pick her up on the train coming home. He lived in the next town; belonged to the older country club, the one that refused to admit Italians and Jews; and dropped the middle syllable in the word "restaurant" when he suggested they meet at one.

"He wanted a little ethnic action," Nora said. "The flip side of all those terrible JAP jokes is a whole class of men—most of them with boarding-school diplomas and crooked teeth—who think Jewish women give better head."

"For God's sake, Nora, I tell you about a casual conversation on a train, and you immediately have me in bed with him."

"Sorry, I should have known you had nothing more than a Great Books discussion in mind."

Susannah didn't tell Beatrice about the man on the train, but she did tell her mother she couldn't go on living a lie. Beatrice told her to stop talking like a grade B movie. Nora admired her mother's editorial instincts, but understood her sister's drift.

Susannah told Nick they couldn't go on this way. He said he supposed not.

Nick moved out of the house on Woodland Drive. Then he began coming home again. He came to pick up Cornelia. He came to pick up legal papers and skis and sweaters. He came to pick up threads that neither of them could cut.

"He shouldn't be hanging around your kitchen," Nora said. "At least, not if you're serious about a divorce."

"Look who's talking," Susannah answered. "The woman who went to bed with her ex-husband the night her divorce became final."

Nora wondered again how her mother and sister could accuse her of keeping secrets.

"That's how I know," Nora insisted. "A clean break is best in the long run."

"I'm not thinking about the long run," Susannah said. "It's nine-thirty at night, and I'm thinking about getting through to tomorrow morning."

They both knew the line was a cliché. But clichés apply only to other people. When the same facts hit home, they're known as truths.

Nora wondered how her sister did it. Nora had her job. Her job had perks and social repercussions. She went to parties and openings and screenings. She met people for lunch and drinks and dinner. She was once again spending two nights a week in her apartment with Tony Demarco.

Nora had discovered Tony Demarco at a party. His dark, silky looks were vaguely menacing. She gravitated to them instantly. His view of masculine honor and feminine duties had been shaped somewhere in the hills of Sicily several centuries earlier. She was outraged, and fascinated.

They left the party for a murky bar. Tony was no ethnic stereotype. He drank too much and badly. Nora chalked it up to his profession. He was a writer.

They went back to her apartment. They'd already taken off each other's clothes when he warned Nora he'd never leave his wife. Nora was surprised, not because she'd thought he might, but because she hadn't known he had a wife.

It was a classic love-hate relationship. Tony Demarco was everything Beatrice hated in a man. Nora fell in love.

They began seeing each other two nights a week. Tony would come to her apartment straight from his class at The New School. He hadn't exaggerated when he'd said he was a writer. Several years earlier he'd published a slim volume of misty reminiscences about growing up Italian in Brooklyn. Since that time he'd been working on his novel and teaching. He was known for his course called "Mining Your Ethnic Heritage." He referred to himself as the Italian Philip Roth, but told Nora he preferred "melon-breasted Jewesses from New York"—Thomas Wolfe, in case she missed the reference—to blond *shiksas*. She pointed out that in her case lemons were the applicable fruit. He said, yeah, he knew that now, but her kinky, ethnic hair had turned him on. A few weeks later Nora put away both her oversized rollers and blow-dryer.

Five months after that, she ended the affair. The immediate reason was a pregnancy scare. Mrs. Demarco's, not Nora's.

Several months later Tony turned up in Nora's office one evening. Monica Storch had just left it. She'd come in to tell Nora about her promotion to senior editor.

"Congratulations," Monica said, and Nora caught a whiff of rye.

Tony waited in the hall until Monica left, then slouched into Nora's office. He said he'd been in the neighborhood and decided to take a chance and drop by. He took off the dark glasses he wore indoors as well as out and looked into her eyes. He said he'd missed her and that her hair looked great, as if someone had run barefoot through it.

She said it was easier to take care of this way and told him about the promotion. He said they had to celebrate. She thought of Monica's rye-scented breath and said she supposed they did.

They took a cab to the Village. Tony had two rules about restaurants. He never ate or drank above Fourteenth Street if he could help it, and he always sat with his back to the wall.

Nora talked about her new job all through dinner. Tony listened and questioned and made suggestions. He said maybe she'd like to speak to his classes sometime. He reminded her that if she wanted a piece on growing up in the bosom of an old-fashioned Italian family, he was her man. It was good foreplay.

This time Tony didn't mention his wife, but as he was getting dressed to go home, he brought up his son. He'd leave as soon as little Tony was grown, he said.

They went back to their two-nights-a-week routine. That was about the time Susannah and Nick went out for dinner a couple of times. Nora knew without asking that they went to bed as well. She also knew it wouldn't do any good.

"You don't know everything," Beatrice said.

Nora let it go. Those evenings with Nick weren't going to save the marriage, but they might get Susannah through a few nights. She'd told Nora about lying on her back in the king-size bed, staring at the shadows of trees on the ceiling. When the wind was up, the shadows rioted like a menacing crowd.

But Susannah was okay. She was tracking. She began reading the want ads. It was a discouraging pastime. There wasn't exactly a crying need for women with B.A.'s in art history who wanted to be home by three o'clock in the afternoon, but Susannah kept at it, and everything else. The house was orderly. Cornelia had clean clothes to wear to school in the morning, a hot meal on the table at night, and help with her homework when needed. In fact, Susannah watched her daughter like a forest ranger on twenty-four-hour duty in a dry season. Again and again she chanted the catechism of divorce, as if she were doing penance. "Mommies and daddies leave each other but they never leave their children."

"Then why doesn't Daddy live here anymore?" Cornelia asked around the time Susannah's fatherly attorney filed the divorce papers.

"He hasn't left. He still comes to see you. He takes you to dinner and the movies and all kinds of things. You stay at his apartment."

"Could I stay there all the time if I wanted to?"

"Do you want to stay with Daddy all the time?" The words, like icy food, made Susannah's sinuses ache.

"Could I, if I wanted to?"

The throbbing spread up Susannah's forehead and down her nose. "I don't know. We'd have to talk about it."

Later that night, when Susannah was sitting up in bed

staring at the inflated faces with their frozen smiles that came and went on her television screen, murmuring yes-johnny-it's-great-to-be-back-johnny-you-said-it-johnny, Cornelia padded barefoot into the room and crept across Nick's side of the bed. Susannah lifted one arm and Cornelia nested under it.

"Mom . . . ," Cornelia whispered above the chorus of johnnies.

"Mmmm?" Susannah answered, trying not to sound too eager.

"I don't want to live with Daddy all the time."

Susannah hugged her daughter to her. "Then you don't have to."

Susannah got a job with Dottie Bell Design. At least it sounded like a job. It sure didn't pay like one.

"I'm counting on your connections," Dottie Bell said. "I'll pay you fifty a week to answer the phone, type a few letters, kind of watch the office when I'm not there. I know it isn't much," Dottie went on before Susannah could protest. She hadn't been about to protest. Though she'd grown up hearing that she was precious, she had no idea of her value. "Any of your friends who come in to redecorate—and I mean at least a full room, none of this re-covering the couch bullshit—I'll give you a piece of the action. In the meantime, you'll be learning the business."

The conversation was Susannah's first encounter with sisterhood.

"Who're you going to meet sitting in an interior decorator's office all day?" Beatrice asked. "If you volunteered at the hospital, you'd meet a doctor."

"She met a doctor," Nora pointed out.

Susannah met Nancy King, who worked in the boutique downstairs from Dottie Bell Design. All Nancy and Susannah had in common was the prefix *ex* before the word *husband*. It was enough. After a few weeks, Nancy suggested they go out the next time their respective kids spent the night with their respective fathers.

Susannah recognized the scene as soon as they arrived. She'd seen it on dozens of television programs. She'd also seen a Vietnamese police officer shoot a man point-blank on television. That didn't mean she wasn't outraged.

A trio of lugubrious but loud musicians pleaded with her to call them mellow yellow. Strobe lights turned the room that color as well as green and blue and red. The men fell into two categories. The older ones wore gold chains—Harvey must still be turning a profit—and body-hugging shirts. The younger ones wore even tighter jeans. The women were more elaborately dressed. Susannah shuddered to think of the number of woman hours that had gone into making up those faces that were trying desperately to pass off terror as hauteur.

Susannah spotted the Kid, as he would eventually become known, immediately. He was wearing the tightest jeans in the room and a pair of lethal-looking cowboy boots. "When I saw him start toward me," she told Nora later, "I knew my life was turning into a cliché." As he got closer, the cliché got worse, or maybe better. He had a cleft in his chin and ice-blue eyes.

The Kid was a photographer, which meant he worked in the local camera store and owned some fancy German and Japanese equipment. He had no darkroom, Susannah learned when they ended up back at his place. For one thing, it was closer than Susannah's. For another, Nancy had warned her it was safer. "No one ever rapes and dismembers on his own turf."

It had taken Harvey Koch three lunches and several years of neighborliness to get Susannah into bed. It took the Kid one drink and a couple of dances. Following him to his apartment in her own car, Susannah had renewed faith in her mother. One of Beatrice's favorite adages was "The first time it's a sin. After that it's a habit."

He called her babe. He called it balling. He called the cigarette he offered her first a joint. He said he'd call her sometime. By then she was standing at the door with her coat on, and he was lying naked on the mattress on the floor.

"Do you think he meant it?" she asked Nora over the phone the next morning. Her fingers beat a nervous tattoo on the table beside her third cup of coffee.

"I don't know. More to the point, I don't think he knows. Things have changed since you used to date."

"Thanks for the news flash."

The Kid did call. Nick had just brought Cornelia home, and he and Susannah were standing in the kitchen discussing car insurance when the phone rang. Susannah picked it up.

"Yo, babe."

"Uh," Susannah said. "Hi," she added.

"You like the Doors?"

"No. Uh, I don't know. Listen, can I call you back?"

Nick stood waiting while she jotted down the number.

"You could have talked to him while I was here," he said, but he drew himself up when he spoke, as if he were making an effort to be correct.

Susannah called the Kid back after Nick left. It took a little effort. She'd never called a boy before.

He answered the phone with a grunt. He said he was just hanging out. Maybe she felt like hanging out, too. Smoking a joint. Listening to the Doors. Getting it on.

"I'd love to." Susannah cursed the trill in her voice. He'd asked her to drive half an hour to smoke an illegal substance, listen to discordant music, and screw. He hadn't invited her to the prom. "But I can't. My daughter just got home."

This time she cursed herself. What kind of a mother would rather do all those things than spend a quiet Sunday night with her child, especially after she hadn't seen the child all weekend?

"You got a kid?"

Susannah owned up to the fact.

"Hey, that's really something. Why don't I drive over to your place?"

"No!" Susannah snapped. "Not tonight," she added.

"Yeah, well, maybe some other time."

When? Susannah wanted to scream. I can get a babysitter. We could make plans to go out.

"Later, babe," he signed off, as if it were an answer to her question.

By the following Thursday he still hadn't called.

"He probably thought I was too old for him," Susannah said to Nora. "Maybe he'd never seen stretch marks before. Maybe he thought I was too straight."

"You can go on speculating for the rest of your life, Susannah. You'll never know what he thought. From the sound of him, he doesn't think. So why do you care whether he calls?"

But the question was rhetorical. In the days after her divorce, before she'd come to rely on Tony Demarco for two nights a week and *American Homemaker* for the rest of her life, Nora had sweated out the answer dozens of times herself.

"Because," Susannah said, and for a minute Nora thought her sister was going to cry, "I wasn't made for rejection."

"Then don't," Nora said as gently as she could, "set yourself up for it."

The next morning, for the first but not the last time in her life, Cornelia called her mother a bitch.

Cornelia was sitting at the table with her chin in her hand and a mean expression on her face. Susannah was trying to ignore the expression.

"If you don't finish your cereal, you're going to miss the bus."

"You can drive me."

"Then I'll be late for work."

"Big deal."

"My job may not mean anything to you, but it does to me. Who do you think puts that cereal on the table?"

"Daddy."

"Eat your breakfast, Cornelia."

"I don't want it."

"You can't go to school on an empty stomach." It was another of Beatrice's home truths.

"Who says so?"

"Several generations of nutritionists. I'm their spokesman. Woman. Person."

"I don't feel like it."

Cornelia began to push the bowl away from her. Anticipating her movement, Susannah put her hand out to push the bowl back. The milk slopped onto the table and over the side to the floor. A few drops landed on Susannah's skirt. She jumped up as if she'd been scalded.

"Now look what you've done!"

"You're the one who pushed it."

"Stop talking back to me."

"Stop screaming at me. It wasn't my fault. You're always blaming me. You . . . you . . ." Cornelia whipped her head back and forth. The black hair lashed at her eyes. "You bitch!"

Susannah's hand came up, then fell to her side. They both began to cry.

17

"**G**o," Beatrice said again on her second night home from the hospital. "You'll have a good time."

It wasn't a good time Nora was worried about. It was time. Research had sent her a lot of material. Maude had given her a lot of ideas.

"Besides, you owe it to Max," Beatrice went on. "He went to see Cornelia with you."

One Sunday several weeks earlier Max had driven to New Haven with Nora. Of course, that was different. Andy had come along for lunch, and afterward Cornelia had taken Nora aside and said she thought Max was great. "He doesn't pull seniority."

"What do you mean?"

"Andy's parents act like we're about twelve. I keep expecting his mother to cut his meat for him. But going out with you guys, it was just like, well, like four people."

Nora thanked Max on the way home. He said he'd enjoyed it. Then he told her about the detour. The Branford Trolley Museum was just a few miles out of the way. She was going to love it. That was the night Max finally agreed to watch Nora's tape of *Dodsworth*.

Nora didn't like to think of it as owing Max something. She wasn't keeping score. But she told him she'd love to have dinner with his daughter.

"Skip the hyperbole," Max said, "and just knock off work about seven-thirty. We'll pick you up at your office. Amy's dying to see it. She was just elected editor of *Calliope*."

"Kids in Connecticut must be big on epic poetry."

"What?"

"Calliope. The muse of epic poetry."

If Amy Miller had been dying to see Nora's office, she did a good job of hiding it. She entered clutching her father's arm and balancing the chip on her shoulder. It was no easy feat.

Max suggested that Nora show Amy the mechanical on her desk. Amy said she knew all about production from her work on *Calliope*. She added that someday she was going to work on a serious magazine. Her voice made it pretty clear where she rated *AH!* on the frivolity scale.

Max asked what kind of food they felt like for dinner. Nora said anything but Indian.

"That's the first thing all Daddy's girlfriends learn," Amy said.

Nora would have bristled at the term "girlfriend" if the "all" hadn't tripped her up first. Amy had drawled it as if she were auditioning for Scarlett O'Hara.

"That he hates Indian food," Amy went on.

Things didn't improve in the restaurant. Amy sat next to her father on the banquette. Nora took the chair across from them. Amy was a pretty kid with big brown eyes. They didn't leave Nora's face for a minute.

"Do you always drink scotch?" Amy asked after Nora had ordered a drink. It was less a question than an invitation to a recital of the AA creed.

Nora explained that she drank gin in the summer and wine all year round.

"Mom drinks Stolis. Daddy used to. When I was little, they kept a bottle in the freezer. It was always there when I went for ice cream."

Just the way Daddy was. I'm sorry, Nora wanted to say, but it's not my fault.

If things hadn't got better in the restaurant, they got worse outside it. Amy had an excuse. She was a suburban kid. But

Nora should have known better. She braved the streets of
Manhattan daily.

Max was walking between Nora and Amy. They were
crossing Third Avenue. The cab came careening up it. Max
saw it first. He shouted, grabbed Nora's arm, and yanked
her back. Amy sprang forward. The cab made it through
the intersection, and the rest of the traffic stopped for the
red light. Standing alone in the middle of the street, Amy
turned back to her father. Max dropped Nora's arm.

A week later Rita Banner, née Saperstein, called Nora at
her office to ask if she and Beatrice needed help with the
wedding. Obviously Rita knew nothing about her new
stepmother. If there was one thing Beatrice didn't need
help with, besides clothes and men, it was weddings. Three
leather-bound volumes attested to her expertise.

They started with pictures of the bride walking down
the aisle. First Beatrice, then Susannah, and finally Nora,
all in that same bias-cut satin dress. It was, Nick had said
when they were sitting around looking at pictures one
night, as if once you'd walked back up the aisle with that
dress, you'd married all three of them. Susannah had told
him not to be such a smartass. It was a beautiful dress, and
some day she hoped Cornelia would wear it.

Then there were the photographs of the ceremony.
Dimly lighted rooms; long-robed rabbis imitating Charlton
Heston imitating Moses; the twin backs of a man in a white
or black dinner jacket and that white satin dress with the
long train; the *chuppah,* which some of Nick's relatives
insisted on calling the gazebo, groaning under a weight of
hothouse flowers.

Finally there was the reception, pages and pages of people, smiling into the camera, toasting the camera, hugging
for the camera, mugging for the camera. Some faces were
still familiar, others belonged to names it took a minute or
two to remember, and too many were dead.

Finally, on the last page Beatrice and Phil, and Susannah
and Nick, and Nora and Paul, in street clothes, looking less
formal but still not natural, walked arm in arm through a
door.

Professional photographers had sold Beatrice those albums, but they hadn't sold her a bill of goods. A picture wasn't worth just a thousand words, they'd argued. It was worth a thousand memories. It captured the occasion. It let you relive the day again and again. And best of all, though no one ever mentioned it, it never followed Beatrice and Phil, or Susannah and Nick, or Nora and Paul beyond the perfect frame of that door.

There'd be no professional photographers at this wedding, but Charlie's son was bringing his videocamera, and one of his grandsons had some state-of-the-art German equipment for stills, Rita Banner reported. "And I'd really like to help," she went on. "Pop told me how busy you are with your job and Bea just out of the hospital and all. I'm still on sabbatical. I took the year off to make the twins' bat mitzvahs."

"What kind of a woman takes a year off to make a party?" Nora asked her mother that evening.

Beatrice's fine nose twitched as it did when she was trying not to laugh. "Twins. Maybe it's twice as much work."

"She didn't say sabbatical from what. Is it brain surgery or the presidency of IBM?"

"She teaches kindergarten. It's not like running a magazine."

Nora winced. She hadn't told her mother about *American Homemaker*'s homecoming. Somehow, around Beatrice, it didn't seem like such a life-and-death problem.

"She wanted to know if I needed the name of a good caterer," Nora went on. "Listen, it's entirely up to you. I mean, it's your wedding. But just how much fuss are you planning?"

"You mean if I have to do this disgraceful thing, can't I at least have the decency to do it in secret?"

"That's not what I meant."

"It is, but to answer your question, we'll try not to embarrass you. I'd like my daughter and my granddaughter there. Charlie wants his children and his grandchildren. That isn't exactly a cast of thousands."

Nora agreed that it wasn't.

"And I invited Max."

"When did you speak to Max?"

"Last night. He said he'd expected you for dinner almost an hour earlier, and you weren't in your office."

"I was in a meeting."

"There were no phones?"

"Do you have any idea how it looks to leave a meeting to call and say you're going to be late for dinner?"

"It looks like you have consideration for other people."

"Not a highly marketable commodity."

"It also looks like you have a real life."

Nora didn't answer. The meeting had run till after seven. But it wasn't the time of the meeting, it was the tenor. Nora had got into a fight with Gary Court, the advertising director, over an ad for the September issue. It showed a man in a pair of vicious-looking riding boots ravishing—that was the only word for it—a woman bent backward over a banister. Thanks to the massive square staircase, the male model's hunting jacket, and the silk dressing gown the female model was almost wearing, the tone was very English country house, but the message was pure rape. And the Great Dane in the background didn't help. Nora said the ad was demeaning to women. Gary said it was sexy. She argued it went beyond official taste guidelines. He countered that it would sell perfume. The dispute wasn't unusual. The only difference was that this time Gary didn't back down.

"Lucy thinks it's feminine," he said.

Lucy isn't running the magazine, Nora wanted to scream, only she didn't, because she wasn't going to fight the battle here. She'd picked her time and place. She had a meeting with McDermott on Monday morning, the day after the wedding.

Nora looked at Lucy. Lucy ducked her head.

Nora turned back to Gary. "If they refuse to reshoot it, tell them to airbrush the line between the bodies. I want his thigh out of her crotch. And get rid of that damn dog. The English don't even like Great Danes. If they have to have an animal, why don't they get a couple of King

Charles spaniels or a corgi? Doesn't the Queen raise corgis?"

"The Queen's dead, Nora. Princess Di and Fergie are in."

Nora thanked Gary for the information and went on with the meeting. And now Beatrice was reprimanding her for it. Her mother sat in her apartment, cashing her dividends and clipping her coupons and planning her weddings, and lectured Nora about real life.

Cornelia came home for her grandmother's wedding. She camped out on the living room sofa while Beatrice spent her last single nights in the guest room. Dresses hung from the tops of doors, lingerie spilled over dressers and chairs, and different shades of makeup mingled in the bathrooms. It reminded Nora of that stateroom she and Beatrice and Susannah had shared on the *Nieuw Amsterdam*. It reminded her of the New Feminines.

"I'm so glad you could make it," Beatrice said when Max arrived at Nora's apartment that Sunday afternoon.

"I thought you might need a male member of the family to give you away," Max joked.

He bent to kiss Beatrice on the cheek. She went up on the toes of her gray pumps to receive it. Then she took Max's arm and led him into the living room. "I want you to meet Charlie's children."

Nora stood in the hallway watching Beatrice lead Max around the room. Her mother always had been a sucker for a pretty face and a well-cared-for body, Charlie Saperstein notwithstanding. From the way her hand remained tucked in Max's arm, anyone might have thought he was the groom. And from the way Max smiled and shook hands and beamed into upturned faces, he might have been.

The doorbell rang again, and Nora went to answer it. She knew it was the rabbi, though she'd never met him. He didn't say hello, he intoned it.

Nora led him into the living room. Charlie came rushing over.

"You're late, rabbi. I was getting worried. I said to my

bride, he's not here in ten more minutes, we're gonna start without him. Just kidding. Well, what're we waiting for? Let's get going before Bea changes her mind."

Charlie's voice had hammered them all into silence. The rabbi crossed the room and stood with his back to the big windows. He motioned Beatrice and Charlie into place in front of him. The others fell into a loose semicircle behind them. They all had to squint into the light to look at the rabbi. Nora was willing to bet that was no accident.

Cornelia stood on Nora's right, their shoulders touching. Max was on her left. The rabbi cleared his throat. Charlie nibbled a cuticle. Beatrice stood, absolutely quiet and waiting.

The rabbi cleared his throat again. Cornelia leaned a little into Nora. The movement was barely perceptible, just a faint pressure of one shoulder against another, but it pushed Nora back almost three decades. She and Susannah had stood exactly the same way at Beatrice's last wedding. Nora felt the bottom of her face collapse the way it did when she was about to cry. She clenched her jaw against it.

From where she stood she could see Beatrice's profile. What did you think about at your third wedding? The long line of ceremonies that had gone before? The long line of loss that came after the perfectly framed shot of the happy couple walking through the door on their way to life? Phil? Sam? Susannah? Of course, Susannah. Nora knew her sister was always on her mother's mind, just beneath the surface, like a half-exposed root you'd trip over if you tried to run away.

Max shifted position next to her, and Nora realized she'd been listing away from him toward Cornelia.

The ceremony was winding down now. Charlie took Beatrice's thin hand with the cruelly curled arthritic fingers. His nails were painfully short, but there were no Band-Aids. Nora realized suddenly that there was no pinkie ring either. Maybe that was what Beatrice was thinking about. Not Phil or Sam or Susannah. She'd spent days and nights thinking of them, years thinking of them. They didn't require thought anymore. They existed in Beatrice. She couldn't have left them behind if she'd wanted to. But she was moving on, changing Charlie, shaping her own destiny. A few weeks earlier she'd been lying in a hospital bed recovering from surgery to remove a mass of cells. Death. A familiar battle for her, only on new ground. She'd fought the first skirmish, come through with flying colors, the bloodless surgeon had said, and managed to climb out of the bed. Now she was going on.

Charlie slipped the plain gold ring on Beatrice's finger. Beatrice looked at the ring, then at him, and her mouth curled, not in triumph, but in a small courageous crescent. The new ring on the third finger of her left hand was an assertion of herself against the conditions of her existence. Just as those four fraternity pins had been, so many years earlier.

They were getting to the end now. The rabbi bent to put on the floor the inexpensive glass that Charlie had bought for the occasion and Nora had wrapped in one of her dinner napkins. Charlie raised one short leg and came down on it with gleeful force. Beatrice was married again.

They broke out the champagne and the hors d'oeuvres that Nora had managed to order without Rita's help. The room grew noisy with excited relief. Charlie's son circled with his videocamera. Charlie's grandson held the microphone. Charlie told posterity how happy he was.

Nora went into the kitchen to tell the out-of-work actor she'd hired for the occasion to open more champagne. He gave her an arrogant look that read like a bumper sticker. "I'd rather be auditioning."

Suddenly the arrogance burst into sunshine. He was trying out for someone. Nora turned. Cornelia was standing behind her in the door to the kitchen. Nora tried not to take it personally. She tried to think of it in terms of demos and target groups. Then she wished she hadn't. The New Feminines.

"I've never been to a wedding before," Cornelia said.

"You forgot your father's."

They looked at each other for a minute.

"I think the word is 'repressed,'" Cornelia said. "Anyway, this is fun."

"I'm glad you think so," Nora said. "With Beatrice as a grandmother, you're likely to attend a lot of them."

"God, are you cynical." Cornelia held her glass out to the out-of-work actor. He managed to get a lot of business into the act of pouring a little wine. Cornelia turned back to her aunt. "What does *mehr shoen bei dir* mean?"

Nora held her own glass out to the waiter. He made a cursory pass over it with the bottle, then started for the living room.

"Loose translation is 'It should happen to you.'"

They went back to the living room.

"You throw a hell of a wedding," Max said.

"And I didn't even have to take a year off to do it."

Rita closed in on them. "It's a lovely wedding." She leaned closer. Nora knew something conspiratorial was coming. Perhaps Rita wanted to know where she'd bought the caviar or the name of the haughty actor circling with the champagne. Rita's eyes flickered up to Max, then back to Nora.

"Mehr shoen bei dir," Rita said.

Nora looked back at her. Rita was about Nora's age. It was disconcerting. You couldn't tell the old feminines from the new, even with a scorecard.

Beatrice and Charlie had gone to their sublet pied-à-terre. Cornelia had taken the train to New Jersey to spend a few days with her father, her stepmother, and her half-brother. The actor had done a respectable cleanup job. The guests were long gone. Nora pictured Rita—her new sister, Charlie had joked after his second glass of champagne—somewhere on the Long Island Expressway, stretching, yawning, patting her husband Shelly's thigh, saying well-that's-that with the conviction of a job well done.

Nora wondered what it felt like to be Rita: to go to sleep thinking of a job completed; to get up in the morning and make breakfast for Shelly and the twins; to chauffeur the girls around; to drive to the market, the tennis courts, the swimming club; to come home at five or six o'clock and start still another meal; to sit for a couple of hours in front of the television; to shake Shelly awake so he could go into the bedroom and fall back to sleep.

Years ago Nora had asked Susannah how all that felt, and Susannah had said it felt great. Then a few years after that Susannah had asked Nora how she got through the night.

Nora went into the bedroom. Max was sitting up in bed with a copy of volume one of *Southern Pacific Daylight; Train 98–99.* It weighed at least ten pounds. Nora wasn't sure when it had taken up residence in her apartment. Max closed the book.

"You want to talk about it?"

"The wedding?"

"The meeting."

She sat on the side of the bed. "I don't know. Sometimes I think I've got it all on wires. Others, I don't think I stand a chance."

"You stand a chance."

Nora wondered if Max meant to sound ominous. She told him about an incident that had happened a few days earlier. The food editor wanted to do a spread on tea parties. There was a recipe for sandwiches.

"You take an unsliced white bread, cut off the crusts, slice lengthwise in a couple of layers, and slather with cream cheese, deviled ham spread, and sliced pimento olives."

"No peanut butter?"

"I told her we'd stopped running that one the year after I came to the magazine. Do you know what she told me?"

Max waited.

"That atavistic foods were in. Mashed potatoes. Salisbury steak. Fucking Jell-O! Foods that remind us of our childhood."

"What'd you tell her?"

"That she ought to consult our nutrition column and that I was thinking of buying first serial rights to a book on women and eating disorders. In other words, that a lot of medical progress has been made and a revolution fought since we ran that recipe."

"You're gonna knock 'em dead tomorrow."

"Or at least go down in flames."

* * *

Nora had always fought for sexual equality in the work-place. Equal pay for equal work. Promotion according to achievement rather than gender. But that night she dis-covered there were sexual differences when it came to job performance. She'd recently read an article in a pop-psych magazine about middle-aged executives who'd been fired. Impotence was high on the list of repercussions. At least there were some areas where she was fail-safe.

Beside her now, Max, for all his concern, slept the sleep of the professionally unendangered. Her head was still in the crook of his neck. His carotid artery beat against her mouth. She could almost taste his pulse. It was steady.

Nora eased herself out from his arm. He stirred, mut-tered, went on sleeping. She got out of bed quietly, put on a robe, and closed the bedroom door behind her.

There was a half-empty bottle of champagne in the re-frigerator. She didn't like the implications of flat cham-pagne. Still, she had to get to sleep. She poured some scotch into a glass. The club soda was as flat as the cham-pagne.

She carried the drink down the hall to the guest room Beatrice had just vacated or Cornelia's room or the study. Nora always said the room took its identity from its func-tion. Like her.

She sat behind the desk. It was a strictly Grand Rapids version of art deco that she'd picked up on Third Avenue before the secondhand furniture stores had changed their names to antique shops. The desk had no pedigree, only associations. Nora had spent a good part of the past eigh-teen years at that desk. She'd hunched over it while she'd made up Dr. Leon Welch's case histories. She could still remember that night. At first she'd been frightened. She was sure she couldn't possibly pull it off. But once she'd started, she hadn't been able to stop. The children had crowded around her desk begging to be included in her article. She'd been like a new mother choosing names. David. Susannah. Paul. Then she'd whipped them into shape. One or two had fought her, but she'd finally got them under control. By the end of that night, she'd felt like a proud parent.

When she and Paul had broken up, she'd moved the desk to her new apartment. She'd worked her way up the masthead of the magazine working at that desk, until finally, one night, she'd sat there turning the pages of the first issue of *AH!* Her hand had stroked the glossy stock. "Nora Heller, Editor-in-Chief," it said at the very top of the masthead. Her name and the title were nicely centered, one under the other, so they balanced perfectly.

Nora tried to remember what she'd done the night she'd become editor-in-chief. She'd had no special celebration. The achievement was celebration enough. Then she remembered. It had been one of those perfect October days that inspire the fashion editor to wax eloquent about tweeds and the interior design editor to talk about decorating with boughs of autumn leaves and the food editor to get misty-eyed about snapping crisp new beans into a hearty stew. Nora had walked home, all forty-four blocks from her office to her apartment, swinging her briefcase beside her. Somewhere on Madison in the seventies she'd stopped to look in a window. She didn't remember what was in the window, but she did remember thinking that she could buy it if she wanted, but she didn't have to. She didn't have to buy anything. The feeling was that heady.

Michael Simon had caught up with her while she stood in front of that window. He was still working for *Business-Week,* and they'd been running into each other at irregular intervals ever since college.

"I've been following you for a couple of blocks," he said.

"Why didn't you call?"

"I was having too much fun watching you. I don't know where you're coming from, Nora, but you were walking like a woman who just climbed out of bed. An illicit bed."

"I was walking," she said, "like a woman who just made editor-in-chief."

It had been nice watching her reflection flicker and grow in his horn-rimmed glasses.

She pushed herself away from the desk, turned out the light in the study, and went back to the bedroom. Max's breathing made a soft sighing sound in the darkness, less than a snore, more than silence.

She thought about death. She thought about her meeting with McDermott tomorrow morning. She thought about someone else running the book. It was funny how the most incontrovertible facts of life were the hardest to believe.

18

Susannah sat on the hard cement at the side of the pool. The air felt so clean she might just have taken it, warm and fresh-scented, from the dryer. The foul exhaust from Nick's car had evaporated before Nick and Cornelia were even out of sight. The sun was a hard golden disk. The sky was eggshell blue. She wondered why they called it eggshell. She'd never seen a blue egg. Maybe it had something to do with robins. That was it. Robin's-egg blue. She'd had a dress that color when she was at Smith. An Anne Fogarty dress with yards and yards of skirt and a deep scooped neck. Somebody had said something nasty about that neck. No, not about the neck, about her. Something about a look-but-don't-touch mentality. Not Nick. Certainly not Blinker. Someone.

Anyway, the dress was the same color as the sky. Or the sky was the same color as the dress. They were both the color of a bird's egg she'd never seen. There were no clouds. Beyond the stand of trees—the same stand that was immortalized in all seasons on the walls of Nick's consultation room—a ceiling of eggshell blue stretched forever. Even through dark glasses the color dared her eyes to believe.

There was a breeze from the general direction of the golf course. It carried voices. Not intelligible words, just sounds.

All of them male. Women weren't permitted to play on weekend mornings.

Susannah leaned back on her elbows—the terry-cloth robe cushioned the cement—and stared at the sky through the dry crystalline air. There'd never been a Labor Day like this. A new front, the radio kept saying. A flag-waving Labor Day. Susannah looked around her pool. There were no flags waving.

Behind the dark glasses she closed her eyes against the brassy disk of the sun and tried to remember other Labor Day pool parties. They ran together into one long orgy of celebration. Nick at the grill in his Brooks Brothers madras swim trunks. Nick in the kitchen hunting for rolls or ketchup or tonic. A film of perspiration glistening on his sun-blackened chest. Her own tongue, quick and smug as a salamander, darting up his chest. The taste of salt, like the rim of a margarita. Cornelia naked in Nick's arms, the blue water lapping at her fat baby body. Cornelia and Lisa Sherman and the Kagin girls tottering on short brown legs that rose to an explosion of soft white diaper. Cornelia and the other kids learning to swim and dive and watch younger siblings.

Susannah opened her eyes. This morning Cornelia had sat in the passenger seat of Nick's car staring straight ahead as he backed down the driveway. She looked nervous, like a too-young girl on a date.

Susannah had almost asked Nick not to take Cornelia this weekend. Standing there in the driveway beside his old Buick, hugging the blue terry-cloth robe to her, she'd opened her mouth to talk about their daughter and the word Seconal had come out. "Just a couple," she said. That was what happened when you divorced a doctor. You went on asking him to heal the pain.

He stood there looking down at her with clinical detachment.

"It's not as if I'm going to do anything with them," she said. "What could I do with a couple of lousy Seconals?"

There'd been more than a couple in the house those two years before they'd separated. They'd both taken too many to get through those years. But when Nick had left, he'd taken the medication with him.

He said he'd think about the Seconals.

She took off her dark glasses and rubbed her eyes. The sky was still eggshell blue. The sun was still a golden blaze. The air was still immaculate. Betty Kagin had luck. In weather like this it would take a total absence of alcohol or an aberrant guest peeing into the pool to ruin the party.

Susannah stared at her own pool. The sun bombarded the water with hard beads of light that collided like molecules in fission. She could hear the sound of things breaking up in the silent air. She sat staring at the crashing, careening beads of light until her eyes hurt and the yard swam around her. The mirage of destruction mesmerized her. When she finally dragged herself away from it, she was still dizzy.

Inside the house she went around straightening furniture, plumping cushions, aligning things on tables. There was a white princess phone on her night table, a pink one on Cornelia's, a beige desk phone in the den, and a white wall phone in the kitchen. There was even an antique brass phone on the table in the entrance hall, though she never used it because it made you sound as if you were talking from the bottom of a deep pit. Moving from room to room, she kept her eye on the phones, circling them at a wary distance as she would a house pet she didn't entirely trust.

But she was the untrustworthy animal. She was the one who picked up the phone. She was the one who was always calling people. Beatrice, Nora, old friends, new acquaintances. She pushed the buttons furiously, muttered at busy signals, raged at rings that weren't answered. But when they were, when she finally got Beatrice or Nora or Faith or Betty or Nancy on the phone, she couldn't wait to get off. She'd lie about burning food or imminent appointments and hang up abruptly. Then she'd pace around the house for a while. Minutes later she'd find herself calling someone else.

Back in the kitchen, she took the phone receiver off the wall and dialed Beatrice's number.

"We were just talking about you," Beatrice said, and

Susannah pictured her mother and Sam sitting on the screened-in porch worrying about her. "Sophie called. She wants us to drive to the shore to see her and Bill, but I told her I didn't think so. All that holiday traffic. By the time we get there we'll have to turn around and come home. Unless you want to go."

Susannah said she didn't.

"Do you want us to drive over there?" Beatrice asked.

"I thought you were worried about traffic."

"Twenty minutes on back roads. It's not like getting on the Parkway to the shore."

Susannah thought about a day around the pool with her mother and Sam. The impatience churned. She carried the phone to the glass wall overlooking the backyard. From this distance the light dancing on the pool didn't make her dizzy.

"I have to go to the Kagins' party."

"We could come over later. You're always depressed after those things."

Susannah paced back to the counter. "Thanks, but I'm a big girl now, and you can't kiss it and make it better."

Beatrice sighed. Susannah tapped her fingers on the Formica.

"I wish I could."

"So do I. Listen, I have to run. I've got a million things to do. Go to Sophie and Bill's. And don't worry about me. I'm fine."

She went upstairs, took off her robe, and put on the new black bikini. It was skimpier than the bathing suits she used to wear. She wasn't trying to prove anything. It was just that times had changed, and she was thinner.

She sat on the side of the bed. Her arm reached for the phone. Her fingers raced through the digits of Nora's number.

"What's up?" she asked when Nora answered the phone, though she knew that nothing could be up since nine o'clock the night before, which was the last time she'd called.

Susannah's foot kept time to a nervous beat. She watched

the flesh of her thigh jiggle. "Listen, are you sure I should wear the black bikini to this thing?"

"I'm not sure you should go to that thing, but if you're going, wear the bikini. It looks great."

Susannah's foot stopped keeping time, but her fingers took up the beat. "What else am I supposed to do?"

"You could spend the day with Mommy and Sam."

"I don't want to spend the day with Mommy and Sam! I want to have a good time, goddammit!"

Susannah heard her sister take a deep breath.

"Come into town. We'll go to a movie, or a museum. I'm not seeing Tony till tonight."

"What kind of a married man gets away on a holiday night?"

"The kind who's flying to a writers' conference the next morning, but tells his wife he has to leave the night before."

Susannah pictured a woman somewhere in Brooklyn packing a bag for her husband. She stood and began pacing the carpet beside the bed. "Listen, I'm okay. Maybe I'll even have a good time. I mean, it's a party." She caught a glimpse of herself in the mirror over the dresser. "I'm just not sure about the bikini."

Nora groaned. "I told you. It looks great."

Susannah sat on the side of the bed again. "I'm almost forty years old."

"Thirty-six is not almost forty."

"I read somewhere that every day after twenty-one, or maybe eighteen, is a day of deterioration."

"One thing I've learned as an editor, Susannah, is never to take seriously any statement that begins with I-read-somewhere."

"But it's true."

"Sure, if you're a baseball player or a dancer with the New York City Ballet."

"Or a woman."

"I don't believe we're having this conversation. A nubile body isn't everything. What about your mind? That's not deteriorating. I can name lots of women who make you look like a baby who don't think they're over the hill.

Editors. Writers. A consumer advocate we're doing a pro-
file of. Go to the library and take a look at *Who's Who of
American Women,* "Nora said as if she were speaking of the
King James Version of the Bible.

Susannah stood and began pacing again. "I don't want to
turn forty alone."

In Beatrice's world promises were reflexes. The baby will
come. The marriage will work out. Daddy can't die.

"You won't," Nora said, though she should have known
better.

They were the words Susannah needed to hear, even if
she no longer believed in the family gift of prophecy. She
thanked Nora and hung up the phone.

Nora sat holding the receiver in her hand. All through
childhood and youth, Susannah had been the older sister.
Then one summer night Susannah had called Nora from
the New Jersey Turnpike to say she was on her way, and
they'd switched places. Suddenly Nora had become the
one who knew the rules, the one who got places first. But
now Susannah had cited bare numbers and restored the
old sequence. She was almost forty, she'd said in the voice
of a woman who was sure she had nothing to look forward
to.

Susannah walked into Betty Kagin's kitchen to deliver the
pies she'd made.

"Look good enough to eat," Seth said, and his eyes slith-
ered over Susannah's face and down her body. She didn't
bother to take offense. Seth belonged to the contingent of
Oak Hills husbands who drove the kids to Sunday school so
their wives could sleep in and talked football in the corner
when men like Roger Kalman began asking other men's
wives to dance. His only sin was an inability to get through
two consecutive sentences without a smutty double enten-
dre. Nick used to say that Seth had never done half the
things he joked about.

Susannah put the pies on the counter and went out to the
pool. She could have found her way around even if she'd
never been there before. The house was a mirror image of
her own. The pool was identical. Only the light here was

different. No beads of sunlight crashed and shattered on the water. Instead, people stood waist-deep holding glasses or trod water hanging on to the side of the pool or pulled off a few lackadaisical strokes before returning to the business at hand. The pool churned with activity. The air vibrated with shrieks and laughter and desperate enthusiasm. Maybe that was the secret. In the quiet of her own pool, everything was breaking up. Here it held together by some mad centrifugal force.

Susannah crossed to the bar and cabana at the far end of the yard. The cabana was new, and, she thought, tacky, especially the long bar with the high rattan stools. Who were they expecting? Dorothy Lamour? She and Nick had always used a Design Research cart that glided in and out of the house on large bicycle wheels. Even if she had the money, which she didn't anymore, she'd never build anything as flashy as that cabana.

Susannah didn't so much join the group at the bar as lay siege to it. A few heads turned in her direction. A few greetings glanced off her skin and fell to the scratchy green outdoor carpeting. Two women edged closer together. Their shoulders made a suntanned wall shutting out Susannah. The men looked at her, then away uneasily. Later, when their wives drifted off or their alcohol level drifted up, they'd risk a few words, a couple of jokes, an arm around the shoulder, a quick pat on the ass, but not now, not yet. It wasn't worth the hassle. She wasn't worth the hassle.

She took a tall plastic glass from the bar and filled it with ice. No one offered to make her a drink. Until two years ago, she'd never made a drink for herself. As it turned out, she was a quick study. She reached for the gin bottle, then noticed the pitcher of margaritas on the bar. It was a pale green ocean of comfort. She filled the tall glass, but decided to skip the salt. As the wife of an internist, the ex-wife of an internist, she knew the danger of too much salt in your diet.

She went back to the shallow end of the pool, where a group of neighborhood mothers had arranged themselves over the pool furniture like towels stretched out to dry. As she'd always told Cornelia, the mothers were a safe haven. "If I'm not around, you can count on one of them." Faith Sherman shifted her legs to make room for Susannah. Everyone else listed imperceptibly in the other direction. Susannah sensed rather than saw the move and understood it instinctively. Women who carried Lysol when they stayed in motels and spread paper on toilet seats in public rest rooms weren't likely to risk contact with a recently divorced woman.

Susannah got up and went back to the bar. As long as she was there, she topped off her glass.

Harvey Koch was standing alone in front of the door to one of the cabana dressing rooms. The gold chain around his neck glinted in the sun. She leaned against the wall next to him. He seemed to shrink a little.

Harvey had taken her separation hard. She'd run into him in the supermarket one Saturday right after Nick had moved out.

"I felt just terrible when I heard," Harvey had said. He was clutching a package of Thomas's English muffins to him. "I hope it wasn't because of . . ." His fingers kneaded the muffins. ". . . us."

"It wasn't," Susannah said.

"Good. I'm glad. Because I was always, you know, up front, about, you know, that."

"That?"

His hands were kneading the English muffins again. She remembered that he didn't have a light touch. "It's not Harriet, but the kids."

Susannah had asked how the kids were. Harvey had said they were fine and made his getaway. Harriet must have wondered what hit the English muffins she'd sent him to the store to get.

"Some party," Harvey said.

Part of her wondered how she'd ever gone to bed with this man. Another part of her knew.

Harriet joined them. "Did you see what Harvey bought me for our anniversary?" Harriet fingered the fine gold chain splintered with small diamonds that looped several times over her chest. "He said the fifteenth isn't diamonds.

That's one thing about being married to a man in jewelry. He always knows which anniversary is which. But I told him I didn't care." She went on stroking her necklace. The obscene gesture triggered something in Susannah's memory. Harriet didn't like to have her breasts touched. Susannah had been shocked when Harvey had told her that. She'd assumed all women were like her. Harvey never should have told her that about Harriet. It was disloyal. But then having an affair with your neighbor's husband, not to mention your husband's neighbor—she was still married to Nick then—wasn't exactly going to win her the probity sweepstakes either.

She looked up and saw Harvey watching her watching his wife's breasts. Did he remember what he'd told Susannah? He put his arm around Harriet's shoulders. Harriet put her arm around his waist. Susannah excused herself and walked away.

She refilled her glass and carried it to the shallow end of the pool. There were only a couple of the younger kids hanging around the stairs. The older ones drifted in for hot dogs and soda, then disappeared to other yards and pools and television rooms. They wouldn't be caught dead spending the day with their parents.

Susannah sat on a middle step. The water lapped around her waist. She sipped her drink and stared from behind her sunglasses at the party. Things were warming up. Faces glowed like dangerous embers in the hot sunshine. Mouths moved up and down taking in food and spewing out words. Adam's apples undulated as gin and vodka and rum and tequila slid down throats. She took another sip of her drink. There was only an inch left in the glass. She tried to figure out how she could refill it without getting out of the pool. She had no intention of moving for the rest of the day.

She felt the pressure of a pair of knees behind her shoulders. The glass was taken from her hand and another icy one pressed into it.

"How you doin'?" her host asked.

"Fine. Terrific. Terrific party." The words fell out of her mouth and skipped over the water like stones.

"Seth," Betty screamed. "We need more ice."

"It's in the basement freezer," he called back, but the knees moved away from Susannah's shoulders, and he went to get the ice.

Susannah took a swallow of the new drink. Say what you wanted about Seth, he knew how to make a margarita, though he'd put salt on this one.

Someone had put on music. Roger Kalman and Myrna Richmond were gyrating on the patio next to the new cabana. Myrna's breasts bobbed up and down in time to the music. They had more rhythm than Roger.

Susannah saw Myrna's daughter Kim watching. The girl turned to Lisa Sherman and let her tongue fall out of her mouth as if she were about to vomit. Then the two kids turned and walked down the driveway.

Susannah watched them go. Little bitches with their empty bikini tops and sharp ribs pushing against smooth brown skin, their narrow hips and sweet breath and fine soft pubic fuzz. They were Cornelia's age, Cornelia's friends.

Susannah held the glass to her forehead. It had started then. She hadn't been wrong the other day. That had been disgust in Cornelia's eyes when she'd looked at Susannah modeling a new dress. And incredulity that anybody would make the effort with that aging flesh. And pity. The little bitch. Only the little bitch was her little bitch.

Myrna went on bumping and grinding. Her breasts bounced and her thighs quivered and orange blusher oozed down her face.

Susannah felt the greasy weight of her own eyeshadow on her lids. She sucked in her stomach. She hitched up her bikini top. Why had she let Nora talk her into this bathing suit? She should have heeded the message in Cornelia's eyes.

"Give up, Mom. A gunnysack, Mom."

Faith Sherman sank to the step above Susannah's. Everyone always laughed at Faith's cotton bathing suits with their proper little-girl skirts. Susannah wasn't laughing at her now. The pink and white gingham floated around Faith's chubby thighs with graceful modesty.

"How was that blind date the other night?" she asked

Susannah. "I saw him walk up your front path. He didn't look bad."

"Looks are deceiving." Susannah moved to the bottom step. The water lapped at her chin. "He told me he never goes on blind dates, but he owed my uncle a favor."

"Okay, so manners aren't his long suit."

Susannah took another swallow of her drink. "He said he didn't go out with women who had children either."

"Scared of the responsibility?"

"Put off by their bodies. Stretch marks disgust him. And they're not as tight. If I knew what he meant, he said." Chlorinated water lapped over Susannah's chin and into her mouth. She spat it out and took another sip of her drink. "I knew what he meant."

"I don't know how you do it. I couldn't go out on a blind date again, if my life depended on it."

Susannah let her chin float dreamily in the water. "The funny thing is, it isn't 'again.' When I was young, I never had a blind date."

"You were lucky."

Susannah lifted her chin to let the margarita flow in without pool water. "You're right, on both counts." She polished off the drink. "I was lucky. And now my life does depend on it."

Faith put a hand on her shoulder.

"Fuck," Susannah said.

Faith took her hand away. After a few minutes, she got up and drifted back to the mothers on their lounges.

The pool was half in shadow now, though the steps were still in sunshine. Susannah sat contemplating her empty glass. Suddenly Ron Herman took it from her. He was back in a minute with a fresh drink and a strange woman in a string bikini. He introduced the woman as his woman. She smiled down at Susannah and said she'd gone to school with her sister. "Nora was a senior when I was a freshman."

Susannah managed a smile. A trickle of chlorinated water ran into her mouth.

The shadows were getting longer. They reached almost to the steps. Seth started putting steaks on the grill beside the hot dogs and hamburgers. Women began bringing out bowls of salad and platters of corn on the cob. Myrna Richmond tripped and dropped a tray of buns. Two men got down on their hands and knees and began picking them up and putting them back on the tray. Somebody screamed about ants and somebody else told her to shut up.

Faith came back and asked Susannah if she didn't want to get out of the pool. Susannah said she didn't. She dropped her head back in the heated water. Her hair floated out around her.

This time Roger Kalman refilled her drink. He sat on the top step and ran his toes up and down her leg under water. The hair on his back and chest and arms was beginning to turn gray. She wasn't alone in growing old. But she was growing old alone.

"How you doin', baby?"

She lifted her head out of the water. "Babe," she said. "People say babe now. Baby is old-fashioned. Like from a thirties gangster movie or World War Two or something. I mean, it may sound like meaningless semantics to you, but you are what you say."

He didn't say anything, just kept running his toes up and down her leg. Susannah looked around the pool. They were the only ones left in it. Maybe everyone thought she'd contaminated it.

"Divorce Susannah," she said.

"What?"

"Like Typhoid Mary. I'm Divorce Susannah. A carrier. That's why no one else is in the pool."

"You're just feeling sorry for yourself."

"My solar system is broken."

"What?"

"It won't heat anything."

"Call Johnson's. They're expensive, but they'll do it right the first time."

"I think the pool filters are going too."

"Maybe they just need cleaning."

"I can't get rid of that poison ivy behind the mimosas."

"I need a drink," Roger said.

She watched him make his way to the bar. He flung a hairy arm around Myrna Richmond's shoulders.

Susannah sipped her drink and thought of the magazines of her youth. *Seventeen. Glamour. Mademoiselle.* Thousands of words, millions of advertising dollars spent teaching her "How to Talk to a Boy."

This time Seth brought food with her fresh drink. He leered down at her and waved a hot dog back and forth in front of her face. "Nibble on this for a while."

Susannah took a bite. The roll was wet and tasted of chlorine.

"You sure you don't want to come out?" he asked.

"I'm sure."

Seth sat on the step above her. His slope shoulders disappeared into the water. He stopped leering. He narrowed his eyes and pressed his lips together as if he were debating something. "We go back a long way together," he said finally.

She let go of the hot dog. It sailed off and sank like a dud torpedo. "Mmm."

"My pool. Your pool."

"All God's children got pools."

"I've always had the feeling we had this special bond."

"You have?"

"Couldn't you sense it?"

Susannah laid her head on the surface of the pool again. Her hair floated out around her. The water rushed into her ears. She felt as if it were flooding her brain. She lifted her head. Seth was still talking. She couldn't hear him above the sound of the water still roaring in her ears. She smiled and nodded. He kept talking. She kept smiling and nodding.

The sky was dark now. She didn't remember the day fading. Someone turned on the lights in the pool. She looked down at her body. No matter how still she sat, it went on wavering in the illuminated water.

Seth stopped talking. At least his mouth stopped moving. She couldn't hear any sound over the water rushing around her brain. Or maybe that was the margaritas. He stood and hitched up his swimming trunks. He seemed to think his waist was somewhere in the area of his armpits. Susannah started to laugh.

He reached down, circled her arm with his hand, and dragged her out of the pool. The air was cold. She shivered. He took a towel from one of the chairs and wrapped it around her. It was as wet as she was.

She wondered what happened to her drink. She looked down and saw a plastic glass floating on the shimmering blue surface of the water. She looked around her and saw brown faces floating in the night. Glittering eyes in wet white orbs. Red mouths open to sharp teeth and fat slithering tongues. And brown flesh. Arms and legs and stomachs and chests and backs and breasts. Miles and miles of damp flesh giving off fumes of perfume and after-shave and suntan lotion and chlorine and alcohol and sweat and lust. The margaritas surged back up her throat, then subsided again. People were slipping back into the pool. She wondered dimly if they'd just been waiting for her to get out of it. Their bodies undulated in the electric water.

She was still shivering. Her bladder ached. She started across the yard. Seth put a hand on her arm. She twisted away and slipped out of his grasp.

A bunch of kids were hanging around at the end of the driveway. They stood holding the handlebars of their bicycles, legs braced on either side of the wheels. Instinctively, she looked to see if Cornelia was among them. Then she remembered. Cornelia was away. Nick had taken her away.

She crossed the street. Her house was a shadow in the darkness. She'd left no light for anyone. No one had left a light for her. Coco began barking before Susannah reached the back door. When she went inside, the dog danced around in circles, torn between Susannah and freedom. Finally, she made a dash for the yard.

Susannah went upstairs to her bathroom. She sat on the toilet hugging the wet towel around her. When she came out, she saw the phone sitting on the night table, a dull white glow in the darkness. She sat on the side of the bed and began to dial Beatrice's number. She pressed down the button before she got to the last digit, then dialed half of Nora's number and changed her mind again.

She jumped up and stood staring at the bed. What was

she doing sitting on the quilt in a wet suit! She smoothed the damp stain she'd left, then dropped the towel on the floor and peeled off her wet suit. She put on her blue terry-cloth robe, but couldn't stop shivering.

She went down to the kitchen and began turning on lights. There was a noise at the back door. She opened the door to let Coco in. Seth was standing on the porch.

He asked if she was okay. He asked if she wanted him to make some coffee. He kept talking. She tried to follow the words, but they kept slipping away from her. His mouth kept moving. Shivering. Hot shower. Hot coffee. Brandy. She thought she was shaking her head.

They were standing beside the kitchen table. He was still talking about cold and hot. He put an arm around her shoulders. She started to cry. He put his other arm around her. She laid her head on his gently sloping shoulder and cried harder.

"I love you," he said.

She lifted her head like an animal who's just picked up the scent. She wasn't sure she'd heard him right. Or maybe she just didn't understand the words anymore. She hadn't heard them in so long.

She knew all the other sentences. Great lines in a divorced woman's life. She'd learned them quickly.

You've got great tits.

Want another joint, babe?

Have you ever made it with a guy and another woman?

Seth reached out and turned off the light. Then he tried to kiss her mouth. He hit her left nostril.

She tried to remember if he'd really said the words. She wanted to ask him, but he'd finally located her mouth. His lips were rubbery. They reminded her of Play-Doh. She pulled away. That was when he said them again.

"I love you."

They went upstairs. Nick had been right. Seth didn't do half the things he talked about. It was over in a few minutes. At least it was over for him.

He got out of bed, pulled on his swim trunks, hitched them under his arms. "I better get back. Betty's going to wonder what happened to me."

He suddenly noticed that he was standing in front of the window. He jumped away from it, though the room was dark. Neither of them had wanted any light.

"I'll stop by tomorrow."

She didn't say anything.

"You okay?" he asked, but he didn't wait for an answer.

She lay in the dark room staring at the white phone. It glowed like a candle. Next to it on the night table the illuminated hands of her alarm clock carved a narrow wedge from the night. It was only a little before ten.

Beatrice would still be up. But she'd hear the slurred words oozing out of the phone. Beatrice didn't approve of drunks. She especially didn't approve of her daughters as drunks. Beatrice was entirely capable of rousing Sam, getting into the car, and driving over to make coffee and shake her head in confused silence.

She could call Nora, but Tony was there tonight. Maybe she ought to call Tony's wife. They could commiserate.

There must be someone she could talk to. Her hand reached for the phone, then drew back. She had to stop. She'd already heard the frustration in Beatrice's voice, the impatience in Nora's. But she couldn't stop. Someone had to help. Someone had to make it stop hurting.

She got out of bed, went to the bathroom, and switched on the light. Her hair was tangled and her eye makeup smudged. Those were the only marks Seth had left. Not even a beard burn to remember him by.

She opened the medicine cabinet. The bottle stood behind the box of Band-Aids. Nick thought he was so fucking smart. He should have known her. After all the years, he should have known how practical she was. She always saved for a rainy day. She never ran out of paper towels or dishwashing detergent or milk. A fresh roll of paper always appeared on the back of the toilet before the old one expired on the holder. He should have noticed those things. He should have paid attention. He should have known she'd save the Seconals for a rainy day.

She didn't even take all the pills. She left four in the bottle. For another rainy day. Then she turned out the light, went back into the bedroom, and got into bed.

The memory surged over her like the nausea from the margaritas. She'd got into bed once before tonight. With Seth Kagin. She'd gone to bed with Seth Kagin. She'd fucked Seth Kagin. For a moment she was sure she was going to throw up the margaritas. Then the nausea subsided again.

The phone was still glowing on the night table. Next to it the slice of time had grown slimmer. It was five of twelve. She wondered how it had got so late. But the time didn't matter. She could call as late as she wanted. She could bother Beatrice. She could interrupt Nora. She could even call Nick. She had a reason now. She wasn't just complaining. She was dying. Literally dying. She reached for the phone and started to dial.

When Faith Sherman found her the next morning, she still had the phone in her hand.

19

The call came as Nora was on her way out of the office. It was from McDermott's secretary.

If Lilian Surrey had been born thirty years later, she might have been sitting behind McDermott's desk, rather than outside his office. Lilian was smart and quick and willing to make decisions. There was a rumor that during the crash of '87 when McDermott had been out of reach at an inn near Japan's inland sea with Will Wheeler, Lilian had taken responsibility as well as his broker's calls and saved McDermott a bundle.

Lilian had once told Nora that she was the only publisher or editor-in-chief, female or male, in the magazine group who didn't condescend to her. The confession came at a Christmas party, and Nora supposed the fact that she was talking to Lilian proved it was true. Nora genuinely liked Lilian. She also knew there wasn't much Lilian didn't know.

Lilian said that Mr. McDermott was running late. He'd see Nora this afternoon instead of this morning.

Nora hesitated. Just because Lilian knew all, didn't mean she was willing to tell all. It was best to approach obliquely.

"Is he back yet?" Nora asked. She had no idea whether McDermott had been out of town, but it was a safe assumption.

"He got back yesterday," Lilian said. "He's closeted with Mr. Wheeler."

Nora had been standing up when she took the call. Now she sat down in her chair hard. She should have known Wheeler would get there first.

She remembered a lunch she'd had with Maude last week. She'd told Maude the story about atavistic foods. Maude free-lanced for a variety of magazines. She could write in half a dozen different styles. She knew how to make accommodations. Maude had chewed her steamed vegetables thoughtfully while she'd listened to Nora's story. "Run it," she'd said finally. "God knows you've run worse things than stomach-turning recipes."

"Sure," Nora said shoveling her own vegetables around the plate. "I can run the cream cheese loaf. I can appeal to the New Feminines. But why would Wheeler want me to when Lucy can do it better?"

Nora stood now and walked to the door of her office. Men and women—boys and girls, really; fresh out of college and glowing with their own promise—were typing away at their word processors, calling the tunes of their own futures. The room hummed with the whisper of the keys, the gentle buzz of the machines. No earthquake, not even a tremor, just everyday business going on around her.

She could see across the open area into Lucy's office. Lucy sat behind her desk, her forehead resting on one hand, the other clutching a phone to her ear. It seemed to Nora that her own phone hadn't rung all morning, except for Lilian's call. But that was ridiculous. Of course, it had rung. She tried to remember the calls she'd taken. She tried not to jump to conclusions. Wheeler could be talking to McDermott about eighteen other magazines, twenty-seven if you counted Japan and Sweden.

Nora's phone rang, and her secretary picked it up. "Nora Heller's office." Jenny's tone was crisp and efficient. Nora had always preferred the smart, on-the-make future editors to the professional secretaries. As a result, she'd had three different ones in the four years since Monica Storch had gone up to Wheeler's office and come down five minutes later with two security guards.

Nora felt a wave of dizziness. She went back to her desk and sat behind it. How had she forgot about the security guards? She saw herself walking down the hall between the two men in pseudo police uniforms who'd been smiling her in at the desk in the lobby each morning and signing her out at night for years. One was beefy; the other had the undernourished pasty look of an alcoholic. The undernourished one was always deferential, the beefy one salacious. She wondered if their attitudes would change now. She pictured them standing in her office while she packed her extra umbrella, the old pair of shoes she kept for sudden showers, the art deco box Cornelia had given her for paper clips. She imagined the beefy one's face when she took the box of Tampax from her bottom drawer. She wondered if she ought to start packing now. A streak of larceny told her she could slip her Rolodex into her briefcase, and they'd never know.

She looked around the office. She'd have to leave the awards on the far wall. They belonged to the book. The caricature of her holding the magazine in a baby blanket didn't look so amusing now. She'd never noticed how sharp the art director had made her nose, how long her chin. The only mother he'd had in mind in that sketch was a wicked stepmother.

Her eye moved to the bumper sticker Lucy had given her. *Behind every successful woman there's a divorce.* She wondered if she'd ever stop hating Lucy. She wondered if Monica Storch still hated her.

The dizziness had passed, but she was still holding on to her desk. She tried to remember the old movie—was it a silent?—where the actor clutches the table while all the props in the room bounce around him. It was the Hollywood version of an earthquake. She couldn't remember which movie it was. Maybe it was more than one. This kind of thing happened all the time. That was what she'd told Susannah about something else. Not to me, Susannah had answered.

Nora stood and took down the museum postcard of the mother and daughter. She knew she'd have to rush once the security guards were there. She put the postcard in her briefcase. It was a meaningless thing to do. Worse than that, it was a silly thing to do. Still, in a way, it was something to hold on to. Not like her desk.

She sat again. This was ridiculous. She'd be okay financially. They'd have to buy out her contract. She had savings and investments. Her job was only a job. She was the same person with or without it. Only she wasn't.

Lilian barely looked up from her desk as Nora passed. If Nora hadn't been feeling so sorry for herself, she would have felt sorry for the secretary. Lilian couldn't face her.

The door to McDermott's office was open. Before she was even inside, Nora saw Wheeler sitting on the long leather sofa. So much for the twenty-seven other magazines. So much for going over Wheeler's head.

McDermott asked if she'd mind closing the door behind her. The over-mayonnaised chicken salad she'd eaten at her desk turned over in her stomach. She closed the door and sat in one of the two armchairs across from McDermott's desk.

McDermott's office was on the forty-second floor. When you sat, the only view was celestial. Beyond his head, murky yellow streaks smeared a polluted sky. Nora preferred the view from her own window. She could look up from her desk and see the Chrysler Building. The thought cut. She might never look up from her desk to that silvery promise again.

She looked around the walls. Framed covers of the various magazines hung like so many Rubenses and Renoirs and Picassos. There were a handful of vintage covers done by famous illustrators or commemorating historical events, but most of them were more recent. McDermott had even changed several since she'd been to the office last. Nora searched for her baby. Last October's cover, one of her best, hung in its familiar place. Then Nora's eye caught something on the table beneath it. She stared at a mock-up of *American Homemaker*. That damn *American Gothic* beauty and her insufferably cute children stared back at her. Talk about writing on the wall.

Nora forced herself to look at McDermott. He was of medium height and medium build, with medium brown hair and eyes. His mouth smiled a lot, though the smiles had no effect on his eyes, and he always repeated a name when he was introduced and never forgot it after that. McDermott was corporate man writ, by definition, not large, but medium.

"I hope you don't mind." McDermott had only the faintest Midwestern accent. "Will asked if he could join us."

Nora looked from McDermott to Wheeler. Wheeler smiled. His forehead almost disappeared. She thought of the Museum of Natural History, but somehow it wasn't funny.

"Will is worried about the drop in advertising pages." McDermott's voice was unruffled. He might have been implying that Wheeler was a dangerous hysteric, but that he for one was unconcerned. Only Nora knew he wasn't.

She told him that was what she wanted to talk to him about. She had a new campaign in mind.

McDermott's eyes flickered to the mock-up, then back to her. "Yes, I've seen it." His voice gave no indication of what he thought of it.

"Not that one," Nora said. "That campaign's already out-of-date."

"That's the point," Wheeler said. "By going back to the basics, we're going after a younger market."

"We're going after a shrinking market." She still refused to look at Wheeler. "According to current census projections, by 1990 there'll be more adult women over forty than under it." She finally turned to Wheeler. "What year are we in, Will?"

He didn't answer.

Nora leaned forward and handed McDermott a study she'd had Research put together. The graphics were primitive but eye-catching. Four lines ran in boldface across the top.

BETWEEN 1990 AND 2010 THE UNDER– 40 MARKET WILL DECLINE. ALL GROWTH WILL BE IN THE 40–PLUS MARKET.

Nora turned to Wheeler and apologized. She said if she'd known he was going to be here, she'd have brought copies for him.

McDermott handed Wheeler the report. Will glanced at it briefly, then back at Nora. He was frowning so intensely his forehead had disappeared entirely. "The Census Bureau doesn't buy space to advertise, Nora. You can spout numbers till you're blue in the face, but I know two things for sure. Old people don't buy new products. And no one wants to look at pictures of old broads."

She handed McDermott another report. "The first page is a list of new products that have been developed for the older market in the last five years; the second estimates the advertising dollars that will be spent to promote existing products to that same market."

Again McDermott handed Wheeler the report, and again he barely glanced at it. "Then how come all those geriatric magazines—*Leisure Years, Retirement,* all of them —are losing money or barely breaking even?"

"Because you're right," Nora said.

Wheeler looked as if he didn't trust her for a minute.

"In America 'old' is a dirty word. And those magazines came out screaming they were going after the old market. Even the names are depressing. But who says we have to announce we're going after the forty-plus market?" She turned back to McDermott and launched into her plan. She talked about a campaign and a magazine that blurred age distinctions. She reminded him that the name *AH!* had been chosen because the sound implied excitement and serendipity and life breath. She added that the under-forty market, the shrinking under-forty market, she repeated, was already crowded. *AH!* had carved out a niche for itself. They ought to be building on that. She just happened to have the figures for a regional edition of *AH!* "We'd be

targeting women with an MHI of close to ninety thousand
dollars."

But Wheeler hadn't got where he was by giving up easily. "I still say you're overlooking an important market."

"I have no intention of overlooking the New
Feminines." For the first time she realized the term
sounded like a name-brand sanitary napkin, but she kept
going. "There's a proposal on your desk for a quarterly
spin-off of *AH!* It'll be called *New American Homemaker,*
and it'll be devoted to traditional values in contemporary
society." She looked at Wheeler. "I was thinking of putting
Lucy in charge of it."

Nora was finished, but the sound of her own voice ech-
oed in her ears. She sounded as if she were trying to sell
them one of the city's major bridges.

She looked at the two men. Wheeler was still frowning.
McDermott was wearing one of his zero-level expressions.
Nora had no idea what he thought, but she had some idea
what he knew. He knew those census figures. You'd have to
be an idiot to be working in the magazine business and not
know them. He also knew what you could do with numbers. Nora had a point, but she didn't have the only point.

McDermott looked from Nora to the papers on his desk,
then back at Nora. "You have some interesting ideas." He
hesitated again. "I'd like to think about them. And I'd like
to discuss them with Will after he's had a chance to go over
your proposal for that new quarterly."

She was dismissed.

Outside McDermott's office, Lilian was talking into a
phone tucked into her shoulder and typing at the same
time. She didn't look up as Nora passed. She still couldn't
look Nora in the eye. Or maybe she was just busy.

When Nora got back to her desk, there was a message
asking her to call Max.

He asked how it had gone. She told him, in detail. He said
it sounded promising. She said she wasn't so sure.

"Sixty, forty," Max insisted. "If he didn't like it at all, he
would have told you then and there. If he's leaning toward

it, he's got to save Wheeler's face." He asked her if she felt like going out for dinner.

"I'm not very good company."

"As opposed to the barrel of laughs you've been for the past few weeks. It's okay," Max went on before she could protest. "You bitch a lot, but beyond that you're easy."

"I know. I don't make a lot of demands. If you ask me, that's a hell of a basis for a relationship."

"I've heard of worse."

Nora knew she wouldn't hear from McDermott for several days. She'd steeled herself for the wait. But the next afternoon, as she was leaving for a meeting, Jenny stopped her and said Wheeler was on the phone. Nora went back into her office.

"I keep forgetting to mention it," Wheeler said.

Nora wondered what he kept forgetting to mention. That she was fired? That if she ever went over his head again, he'd crucify her?

"Remember that business about my club last winter."

Nora remembered all right. Wheeler's club was one of the handful still restricted to women. Nora had argued that the policy was in conflict with the law of the nation, not to mention her need to do business. Wheeler had said it was nice to have a place where boys could be boys.

"You win," Wheeler said. "They voted to admit women."

"They didn't have much choice after the Supreme Court ruling," Nora pointed out, but her mind was skimming ahead. It wasn't like Wheeler to call just to concede defeat.

"I'm going to put your name up."

"Ah!" Nora said. It was an expression of surprise. It was also the name of her magazine. Again. Or still.

"That is if you're interested in joining."

Nora knew the principled course of action. It was the reverse of the old Groucho Marx joke. She shouldn't want to belong to a club that didn't want to admit her. The only thing to do was tell Wheeler thank you but no thank you.

"Thank you," she said.

"So now you can play with the big boys."

* * *

Nora didn't even hang up the phone. She just pressed a button to get another line and dialed Max's number.

"I'm taking you to dinner," she said.

"I gather from the tone of your voice that you won."

She told him she hadn't heard from McDermott, but Wheeler was putting her up for his club.

"You won," Max said. "Does this mean I can retire?"

"It means you can choose the restaurant tonight, and next time I'll take you to my club."

20

The Irish linger drinking over their dead, and WASPs permit a polite interval for viewing, but Jews hurry their own into the ground, as if they're ashamed. They buried Susannah so soon after her death that the new front was still holding. The sun was warm, the air thin and clear. There was a light breeze. People in somber summer-weight clothing trudged from their cars up the gentle slope of the cemetery. The ground was firm but not hard beneath their feet. The workmen had had no trouble digging the grave. The faint scent of turning leaves held less hint of decay than promise of a new season. Nature rebuked them.

Nora and Sam walked with Beatrice between them. They each had a hand on her elbow. The idea was to support Beatrice, but there was nothing there to support. She seemed to have lost substance in the last two days. Beatrice and Nora wore sunglasses, as if they thought they could hide something.

Nick and Cornelia walked in front of them. He kept his head down. Even when people clasped his hand or murmured words of consolation in his ear, he refused to meet their eyes. At the funeral home he hadn't been able to face Beatrice.

Beside him Cornelia was fragile as a twig. His hand on her shoulder covered half her back. She kept her eyes down too. When they reached the grave, she collapsed into him. They remained that way through the service, a tall man forcing the pain in his eyes into the ground along with his wife's coffin, and a thin girl leaning against him as if he were a tree.

Nora forced herself to look at the plain pine box. Supported by two mechanized straps, it hovered over the opening in the earth. The coffin was the same pale wood her father had been buried in, the same color Susannah's hair used to be.

The mourners made a ring around the open grave. Faith Sherman was biting her lower lip. Betty Kagin cried noisily into her husband's gently sloping shoulder. Roger Kalman stood thin-lipped and chastened, his hairy hands clasped in front of his dark blue suit, like a codpiece. Harvey Koch took a handkerchief from the breast pocket of his own dark blue suit and blotted his eyes. Myrna Richmond checked her earring between thumb and forefinger, than ran her tongue over her upper teeth in search of errant lipstick smudges. Nora dropped her eyes. She'd been raised to believe you weren't supposed to feel hatred at a gravesite.

The rabbi began to chant something in Hebrew. He was forcing his voice up from deep down in his diaphragm and projecting it out over the crowd. He had a good crowd today.

There seemed to be no place for Nora to put her fury. She tightened her grasp on her mother's elbow. Beatrice put a hand over her daughter's.

Nora heard the soft whirring of a motor. The coffin began to descend. Beatrice gasped. Inch by inch, the box sank into the raw hole in the earth. Nora could feel her mother shaking, though she made no more sounds. Or maybe that was herself she felt shaking. She couldn't tell which. Grief had blurred the demarcation between them.

The box had disappeared into the earth. Though the motor was still whirring, only the lid was visible, and that only to the people standing right beside the grave. The rabbi picked up a fistful of dirt from the mound piled next to the hole in the ground and tossed it onto the coffin. Nora caught a whiff of fresh earth, a fragrance she associated with walking into a florist shop or potting plants. There was a dull thudding sound as the dirt hit the coffin lid.

The rabbi took a step toward them and murmured something to Beatrice. She shook her head no. The rabbi hesitated, obviously dissatisfied. Sam leaned over. "No, rabbi," he said.

The rabbi moved to Nick. Without raising his eyes from the grave, he too shook his head no.

Nora caught on. The rabbi wanted them to follow his example. He wanted them to throw dirt on Susannah's coffin. He wanted them to bury Susannah.

The rabbi hesitated for a moment in front of Cornelia. Nora was ready to spring. Before the rabbi could speak, Nick pulled Cornelia closer to him and shook his head again.

The rabbi turned to Nora. She shook her head. He gave up.

Nora realized that the noise of the motor had stopped. Believers would say Susannah was at rest.

Nick announced he was going to move back into the house and live there with Cornelia. Everyone agreed it was the best plan. Nora had only one request. She wanted to be the one to go through her sister's things.

"You can have anything you want," Nick said.

Nora didn't bother to tell him she knew that. Nor did she bother to tell him that wasn't the point.

There was no point. She knew that too. She just wanted to do it.

Beatrice and Nora went through the house together. They worked in tandem, driven by the same need.

They chose a day when Cornelia was at school and moved quickly and methodically. Each of them wanted a few articles of clothing, pieces that they pictured Susannah wearing when they thought of her. The rest would go to Goodwill. Nora took some books. Beatrice said she'd put the jewelry aside for Cornelia. Nora took a gold bracelet from the jewelry box. She had one that was identical. So did Beatrice. They'd bought them on that cruise. Susannah had

gone ashore in Havana with the dairy prince from Westchester, and a man had offered them a hotel room. Beatrice
had been appalled, but Susannah had said she could take
care of herself. She'd told them the same thing on the
phone that Sunday afternoon. And they'd believed her.

The following summer Nick sent Cornelia away to camp.
There was some debate about that. Beatrice said she was
too young. Nora said she was too old. Real campers started
at eight or nine or even younger. By the time they were
twelve, friendships were sealed, cliques formed, outsiders
excluded. Nick listened to them both and made up his
mind. Cornelia went off to camp, the housekeeper went to
visit her family in South Carolina, and Brenda moved in.
By the time Cornelia returned home in August, Brenda
had taken over.
   A year of living with her father and spending weekends
with her grandmother or aunt had taught Cornelia her way
around. One afternoon she came home from school, took
money from the top drawer where Nick kept extra cash for
emergencies, and called a cab to take her to the railroad
station. In New York she took another cab to Nora's apartment. Her aunt was still at work, but the doorman knew
Ms. Heller's niece and let her in. She was waiting when
Nora got home from work. Nora wasn't entirely surprised.
The doorman had warned her. But she wasn't exactly prepared either.
   It was a smaller apartment, not the one they'd eventually live in, and Cornelia was sitting on the living room
couch that opened up to her bed when she stayed over. In
the regulation jeans and sweater she'd worn to school and
the regulation long straight hair, she looked like any
preteen kid, not a small adult who'd lifted some money
from her father, braved mass transit, and talked her way
past a New York doorman to find her way home.
   "Can I stay here?" was the first thing she said.
   "Of course."
   "I mean for good."
   Nora never did know whether she played that scene
correctly. Did she hesitate too long before she answered?

Did Cornelia spot the doubt and fear and selfish reservations that crowded her aunt's mind? Did she sound like a phony, condescending adult when she finally spoke?

"I'd love to have you, but don't you think we better talk it over with your father?"

Nick came storming in. It reminded Nora of the night he'd followed Susannah to Nora's old studio apartment.

"Why didn't you at least leave a note? Brenda called all over the neighborhood. She was worried sick."

Cornelia was still on the couch. She pulled her legs up to her chest and rested her forehead on her knees. "I bet."

Nick started to say something. Nora could tell from the look on his face that it wasn't going to be kind. Then he thought better of it and collapsed on the other end of the couch.

"Nora says I can stay with her," Cornelia said.

Nick glanced at Nora. For the first time they were truly enemies. He turned back to Cornelia. "That's ridiculous."

"Why's it ridiculous? You've been talking about private schools. Nora always says there're better private schools in New York."

"That's not the point. I'm your father. She's your aunt."

"And what's Brenda? Besides a pain in the ass."

"She's trying. Give her a chance. She's never had children."

"Not many pre-pubescents have."

Nick shot another angry glance at Nora. He knew where his daughter picked up her dialogue.

"Anyway, she hates me."

"She doesn't hate you. She's trying to like you."

"Yeah, like it's such a big deal, she has to try so hard."

It really was a replay of that night Susannah had run away to Nora's studio apartment. Cornelia left with Nick. He insisted everything was all right. Nora knew from Cornelia's face that it wasn't.

All that week they talked. Beatrice and Nora talked to each other. They talked to Cornelia. They talked to Nick. They even talked to Brenda. That last wasn't easy for Beatrice.

* * *

"It's not right," Beatrice said to Nora. "For them to be living together that way with Cornelia in the house."

"I don't think that's the part that's bothering Cornelia," Nora answered.

"I have a right to remarry," Nick said.

"Are you and Brenda getting married?" Nora knew it was a cheap shot, but she was getting tired of the discussions.

"You know what I mean. To find someone new. Beatrice remarried after your father died. No one said anything about that."

Nora remembered the night Sam had come for dinner and Susannah had announced she wasn't going to call him Dad. She never had, but she'd brought Cornelia up to call him Grandpa.

"You shouldn't have sent Cornelia off to camp," Nora said.

"What does that have to do with it?"

Nora remembered the morning before Sam had come to dinner. She and Beatrice and Susannah had been sitting around the kitchen table. It was Christmas vacation, and there was an apple pie for breakfast. Beatrice had taken their hands in hers and made another promise.

Men come and go, but there'll always be the three of us.

"She thought you were getting her out of the way so you could bring in Brenda."

"I just thought it would be easier while Cornelia was away."

"That's what I mean."

"If she'll just give it a chance. But she barely even talks to Brenda. And you and Beatrice don't help. You can't make it up to her for Susannah, you know."

But Nora didn't know. "We just want what's best for her."

"Christ, Nora! For a smart woman, you say some dumb things."

"What if she comes to live with Sam and me? There's plenty of room. And there are two of us. It would be almost like a normal family."

"You're too old," Nora said. Beatrice still felt young enough for Nora to say it. "Anyway, she didn't turn up on your doorstep. She turned up on mine."

"You don't know what it entails. It's a big responsibility."

Nora thought of the slip of paper in her safe deposit box. "And you don't think I'm up to it."

"If I didn't, the discussion wouldn't have got this far. You won't have to worry about money. Sam and I will help you with a bigger apartment. Nick will have to pay for Cornelia's living expenses and school, but if he puts up a fight, we'll take care of that too."

Nora noticed the change in tenses. Beatrice had already made up her mind. So had Nora. She wanted to do this for Susannah. She wanted to do it for Cornelia. She supposed she wanted to prove something to Beatrice. And she wanted to do it for herself. Nora had just finished editing an article on the changing patterns of childbearing in America. Though there was usually a man in Nora's life, there wasn't likely to be a child in her future.

But ultimately it was Brenda who made the decision. She pointed out to Nick that she'd done her best, and maybe she had. He hadn't considered when he'd moved her into the house on Woodland Drive what Brenda's best was. Now she, like everyone else, just wanted what was best for Cornelia.

The week before Cornelia moved in with her aunt, Nora told Tony Demarco she wasn't going to see him again. When he'd walked into her apartment that night, she hadn't intended to be so final, but Tony Demarco wasn't a man who invited half measures.

Nora was on the phone with Cornelia when Tony arrived. She opened the door for him, mimed apologies, pointed to the glasses and the ice and the scotch as if he didn't know where any of them was kept in her apartment, and went on talking to Cornelia.

Tony got the message about the alcohol if not the apology. He carried his drink into the bedroom. He was sitting on the bed watching the news through dark glasses when she followed him there ten minutes later.

"I'm sorry," she said. "That was Cornelia. There's a kind of crisis."

Tony didn't take his eyes from the television screen. At least he didn't turn to her. She couldn't be sure about the eyes because of those glasses.

"An airplane hijacking is a crisis, Nora. A famine in Africa is a crisis. Your niece's or your mother's or even your recently sainted sister's latest discontent with the way of the world is not a crisis."

She wouldn't have said it if he hadn't mentioned Susannah. He should have known better than to bring Susannah into it. "Where does a publisher's rejection of the great American novel fit into that list of disasters?"

She stopped. There was no point in sinking to his level. "I'm sorry."

Tony didn't seem to hear her.

"But she's having a hard time." It was the perfect opening. Nora hadn't mentioned the new living arrangements to Tony. There was no point in going through it with him, if Cornelia wasn't going to go through with it. Now she knew Cornelia was. She told Tony about the plan.

Tony finally turned from the screen. "She's a manipulative little bitch."

"She's a twelve-year-old kid."

He took off the dark glasses and stared into her eyes. "Some women learn early."

"Do you have any idea what she's been through?"

"I know what she's been through. I also know how she's learned to milk it."

"For God's sake! What's she milking? The fact that her mother died?"

"Offed herself. Where do you think the kid learned to manipulate?"

Until that moment, Nora had been worrying about logistics. Where could they see each other? When could they see each other? How could she keep Cornelia from knowing that Tony was married? Now she knew she had to protect Cornelia from more than that. There were things you put up with as a woman that you didn't visit on a child.

She told him to get out. He said he'd leave when he

damn pleased. That frightened her a little. She went into the living room to think it over. She heard the evening news team sign off. She heard the door slam. It set up a Force Five wind.

Nora found a two-bedroom apartment. Beatrice and Sam helped with the rent. Guilty, Nick was generous about expenses.

"It would be the same if she were going to boarding school," he told Nora the first time he came to take Cornelia out to dinner. They'd agreed Cornelia would see her father every Wednesday night when he came into town to teach at the hospital, and every other weekend when she went out to New Jersey to spend time with him and Brenda.

"You mean, it would cost the same?" Nora asked.

"I meant if she went away to boarding school, she wouldn't be living home either. That's the way Brenda put it."

It wasn't the first time Nora felt sorry for Nick. This wasn't easy for him.

It wasn't easy for any of them. Though Tony had given Nora training in child care, he hadn't taught her much about discipline. And if Cornelia wasn't a manipulative little bitch, she was a smart kid. Her experience as the product of a broken home and a half-orphan had taught her how to get along, or at least her way.

But if it wasn't always easy, it was frequently wonderful. Nora introduced Cornelia to the joys of old movies. They sat in the worn, springless seats of the Regency and the Thalia and St. Marks Place, high on Jujyfruits and Bette Davis or Katharine Hepburn or Mary Astor. Cornelia taught Nora about the thrill of victory and the agony of defeat. One day Nora picked up the phone in her office to hear her niece announce, "This is your captain speaking," and the entire field hockey team cheering in the background. They wrote a paper on *The Wild Duck*, started out arguing about procrastination, and ended up at one in the morning rolling around on the floor quacking. Nora gave her niece books. Cornelia brought her aunt flowers. Nora

upgraded from an individual to a family membership at
the Metropolitan Museum. On the street Cornelia pointed
out buildings Nora had been passing all her life and rarely
noticed. Nora brought home an article on women in architecture. They spent an entire weekend setting up a highly
unsophisticated stereo system that Nick had bought and
Beatrice had insisted they ought to find a man to install.
They shared sweaters and pizzas and Cornelia's terrifying
adolescent silences. They talked about Susannah. Sometimes they talked about her so much she became the third
inhabitant of that apartment. It didn't keep them from
missing her, but it did keep her alive. Almost.

Cornelia moved from the middle school to the upper.
Nora moved from senior editor to executive editor. As the
years passed and trends changed and Lucy and other
women Nora knew began to talk about their biological
clocks, Nora kept her mouth shut.

21

Nora supposed she ought to be grateful to Max's daughter. If Amy Miller hadn't been at Max's apartment that Friday night, Nora would have been, and the printer never would have found her on Saturday morning. As it was, Max had invited Nora over, but she'd begged off. Her first encounter with Amy was still fresh in her mind. So on Friday afternoon Nora told Max to have a nice evening with his daughter, and on Saturday morning she was still in bed with the *Times* and coffee when the printer called.

He told Nora it was lucky he had her home number. He didn't have to add that he'd already tried Gary Court and half a dozen other people in the advertising department and at the agency. Gary's wife had said he was at a Little League game. On Saturday morning lesser mortals fulfilled their personal obligations and did their errands. The printer told her that if she didn't want to lose one of her biggest advertisers, she better get her ass out there right away.

Nora called the car service first, then Max's number. Amy answered the phone. She said Daddy was out. She added that she'd told Daddy he needed a haircut. "Mom used to cut it for him, but now he goes to this woman around the corner. I went with him once. She looks just like Susannah Hoffs."

"Susannah Hoffs?" Nora asked. The only Susannah in her lexicon was her sister.

"You know. The Bangles."

Nora didn't recognize the reference, but she got the message.

"Tell him I have to go to Pennsylvania. To the printer's. With any luck I'll be back by nine or ten."

"He probably won't want to do anything that late."

Nora decided not to discuss with his daughter what Max might or might not want to do at any given hour. "Tell him I'll call him when I get back."

"I'll try to remember," Amy said and Nora could picture her squaring those thin shoulders to keep the chip from falling off.

"Do me a favor, Amy. Don't try. Just do it."

"They had to go with that hot new agency," the printer said. "Creative geniuses. When it comes to production, they don't know their creative asses from their creative elbows. You're supposed to look at the picture and think if I bought this crap, I'd be romping in the woods with a stud and a couple of cute kids instead of sitting in front of the TV with the slob I'm married to and these juvenile delinquents. You know what this mechanical's going to give you. Blue sunlight and a stud and kids so green they look like they just puked."

Nora studied the mechanical. The printer was right. He was always right.

"You can run a public service thing," he said. "Promote literacy, give blood, and practice safe sex."

"You want to pay for that, Frank? No, we'll run the ad in black-and-white. I'll give the advertiser a break on the rate and tell them their creative new agency screwed up."

She was back in New York before nine. When the car pulled up in front of her building, she saw Max sitting in the lobby. He stood as soon as he saw her get out of the car and came out to meet her.

"Where the hell have you been?"

"Hi, José." Nora smiled at the doorman and tried to haul Max toward the elevators.

"At the printer's."

"I said I'd be over around three. Why the fuck didn't you let me know?"

A woman waiting for the elevator with a Lhasa apso on a leash turned to stare at them. Her expression was more disdainful than the dog's.

"I left a message," Nora said quietly and followed the woman into the elevator.

"Since three o'clock," Max insisted.

"Could we wait?" Nora whispered.

Max stood staring at the lighted numbers above the door. A blue vein throbbed at his temple.

The woman got out. "Since three-fucking-o'clock," he repeated before the elevator door closed.

"You haven't been sitting down there since three o'clock!"

"No. I waited down there for a while. I thought you might have run out for something. Then I went out on the street and called you. After that I called Beatrice. Had to be cagey about that. Didn't want to worry her. I told her I wasn't supposed to see you till tonight, but I was just wondering if you were over there." He walked off the elevator in front of her. "I also called your office. I even went down there. I mean, where else would you be on a Saturday afternoon in June? Then I went home and called you some more. Finally, I came back and banged on your door for a while. I was just getting ready to call the police, or at least the super, and make him open the door."

They went into the apartment. "What if I'd been in here screwing my brains out with someone else?"

"I assume you'd have the sense to call me first and tell me not to come over. Or at least to pick up the phone after a couple of dozen calls."

"You're a Jewish mother."

"I'm a normally cynical New Yorker. When in doubt, I imagine the worst."

She put the papers she'd been carrying on the library table. He sat on the couch.

"Why the hell didn't you let me know?"

"I told you. I did. I left a message with Amy. She said you

were getting your hair cut. By a woman who's a dead ringer for some teenybopper idol."

"Are you sure you left a message with her?"

"Come on, Max. Am I sure?"

She stood staring at him. The vein at his temple was still noticeable. He'd lost the justification for the anger, but he was having trouble giving it up.

"Why didn't you tell her to write it down?"

"Because she's sixteen years old, and I'm not her mother, and, if you don't mind my saying so, I could have told her to chisel it in goddamn stone, and she still wouldn't have given you the message."

His mouth was a thin, unyielding line. Nora wondered how he managed to speak through it. "Why wouldn't she give me the message?"

"Little Electra? I can't imagine."

Max didn't answer. Nora said she was grubby from the printer's. He told her he'd make drinks while she showered. She almost told him if it was so goddamn much trouble not to bother, but she kept her mouth shut and went into the bathroom. By the time she came back to the living room he was on the sofa again. There was a drink in his hand and another on the coffee table. There was also a mean look on his face.

She picked up the second drink. "Listen, I'm sorry. But it was a crisis. And I did leave a message."

"What kind of a crisis this time?"

If she hadn't been so tired, she might have picked up on the "this time." Instead, she made the mistake of telling him, in detail.

Max went into the kitchen, poured himself another drink, and came back to the couch. "Let me get this straight. Some agency gets the tints wrong in an ad, and no one can fix it except the publisher of the magazine?"

She explained it all, how neither she nor the printer could reach anyone else, how the ad was for one of their biggest advertisers, how these days she couldn't afford to lose a single ad, let alone one of her major advertisers.

He leaned back on the couch and stretched his legs out

in front of him. It was supposed to be a relaxed pose, but he didn't look relaxed.

"I find it odd, not to mention downright fucking peculiar, that of the dozens, probably hundreds of people who work for this advertiser, their agency, and the magazine, you were the only one who was answering the telephone."

She told him about the advertising manager and the Little League game.

He asked if the man didn't have an assistant, or if she didn't.

She answered it was faster and safer to do it herself.

He said she was misguided.

She said he didn't understand.

The discussion went on for longer than it should have. They were no longer angry about the afternoon. They were just angry at each other.

Somewhere around eleven they apologized grudgingly. She said she should have called him from Pennsylvania. He said he was going to speak to Amy. They went to bed believing they'd settled something.

They awakened the next morning to the reassuring sound of rain on the air-conditioning unit. It was one of those Sunday mornings that arouse strong emotions. If you were a woman alone, you combed the museum listings and movie pages and prayed that someone else was at loose ends. If you were the mother, or, worse still, the divorced father of small children, you gritted your teeth and counted the number of hours till bedtime. If you were a grown-up waking up next to someone you cared for, you listened to the sound of the rain on the air conditioner and turned over in bed and smiled and made the most of it.

By the time Nora went into the kitchen to make coffee, they were sure they'd settled something.

By the time she came back with a tray, Max was sitting up with the travel section of the paper. It was open to an article on the joys of seeing Scotland by train. He handed Nora the piece. She passed him a mug of coffee.

"I have to let them know at the office when I'm going away."

She handed him a plate with a croissant.

"Well?" he asked.

"Do we have to decide this today?"

He took the travel section back. She picked up the *Book Review.*

Ordinarily she would have made plans by now. Last summer she and Maude had taken a house on the North Fork of Long Island. The summer before, she'd gone to England with a writer who'd just left his wife and started still another biography of one of the Bloomsbury set. And she always spent at least a few days sailing in Maine with Annie and her husband, Mark. But those summers Beatrice hadn't undergone chemotherapy and Nora hadn't been fighting for *AH!*'s life and overseeing a quarterly spin-off.

Nora looked up from the *Book Review.* Max had moved from Scotland to Yugoslavia. What was wrong with him, anyway? Why didn't he read the financial or real estate pages first, like most men? And what about the sports section?

"I've never ridden an Eastern Bloc railroad," he said.

She asked him if he wanted more coffee. He shook his head.

"When does Beatrice finish her therapy?" he asked.

She put down the coffeepot. She turned and sat crosslegged so she was facing him.

"Listen, Max, I can't go away this summer."

"I asked when Beatrice finished her treatments. I know you won't do anything till they're over."

"It's not just Beatrice."

He picked up the travel section again.

"I finally got Wheeler to agree to that rescheduling."

He went on turning the pages.

"The January issue is going to hit the stands on December seventh. Just like Pearl Harbor."

He didn't even smile.

"That's a full week earlier than usual, which means we'll have three Christmas issues this year."

Max tossed aside the travel section and picked up the news. Thank God.

"And you don't really think Lucy can handle the spin-off on her own," said Nora.

Max went on reading the front page.

"Aren't you going to say anything?" Nora asked.

He looked up. His mouth was a thin, unyielding line. She'd seen that expression before, when he was talking to that lawyer who carried peanut butter crackers in his brief-case or Addie for the third time in a row.

"What do you want me to say?"

"That you understand."

"In other words, it's not enough to win. You have to be right, too."

"It's not a question of winning."

He went back to the paper. Later, she knew she should have let it go. Don't give the bastards an opening, David Meadow had taught her. She'd learned the lesson in the office. It just hadn't come home.

"What the hell am I winning?"

He looked up again. "I don't want to fight."

"You think you're not fighting, just because you're not talking?"

He went back to the front page.

"Then that's all you have to say?" she pressed.

He looked up again. Now twin creases of fatigue ran from either side of his nose to the corners of his mouth, indelible as crayon marks.

"What do you want me to say?"

"Whatever you're thinking."

He hesitated, and when he finally answered, he dropped his voice the way people do when they're speaking about a terminal disease. "I'm thinking that we're two people at cross-purposes."

She should have heard it then. When you stop fighting about specific offenses, and start complaining about gen-eral differences, it's all over.

"What the hell does that mean?"

"You like screwing in cars."

"And you don't?"

"I like it. I just don't prefer it. You do. I don't know. Maybe you don't have to take it as seriously that way. Maybe you can pretend you're still a kid screwing around. Maybe—" He stopped. "Hell, I don't know why."

"When you figure it out, I presume I'll be the first to know."

The argument was deteriorating. Max must have realized it, because he picked up the paper again.

"Go on," she said.

He was still holding the paper, but she could tell from his face that he wasn't reading it. He put it down.

"Listen, I know you've had a lousy couple of months. But they're over. Your mother's okay. She has the treatments ahead, but she also has Charlie."

"Florence Nightingale in drag."

"You ought to be grateful for Charlie. I wish to hell he'd married my mother. I wish to hell anyone would marry my mother. Anyway, your mother's okay, and the magazine is under control."

"For the moment."

He sat staring at her. "I take back what I said about your not making many demands."

"What am I demanding? I said I couldn't go away. I didn't even ask you not to."

He went on staring at her. "You really want to know?"

She could tell from his voice that he really wanted to tell her. Things had heated up.

"Sure."

"You've been living on your own and taking care of yourself for some time. You bounced back from a marriage and a long-term affair without too many scars, at least as far as I can see. You just pulled off a pretty impressive coup at the magazine. In other words, you're smart and resilient and not exactly the dependent type. Christ, the first time I hailed a cab for you, you took it as a personal insult."

"I hear a 'but' in your voice."

"But despite all that, despite the fact that you don't need it and probably know it doesn't exist, you still go around looking for safety. Insurance. Airtight promises. I say Beatrice is okay and the magazine's under control, and you say 'for the moment.' I hate to break it to you, Nora, but that's all you're ever going to get. Because there aren't any insurance policies. Not even from the magazine."

"Exactly. That's why I can't go away now."

"And that's exactly why you ought to go away now. Hell, I'm not talking about leaving for a year to make the grand tour. I'm talking about taking off a lousy couple of weeks. You know, like normal people."

"Normal people! What in hell do they have to do with it?"

"You don't get it, do you?"

"I get it that you fought your battles and worked your ass off when you were young, and now that you're in a secure position and can afford to take it easy, you think everyone should."

"Maybe you're right." He picked up the paper again. "In which case it's like I said—"

"*As* I said," she snapped.

"As I said," he agreed. "We're two people at cross-purposes."

Nora had been through it often enough to know the sequence. The first night was always the easiest. When a man slammed the door of your apartment after an argument—even if like Max, he didn't actually slam it—the action set up a breeze of relief. The anger was still fresh. It was easy to summon all the minor bad habits and major character flaws. She thought of the small change Max always left on the night table. She remembered an argument they'd had about affirmative-action hiring. And there was always something nice about having your apartment to yourself again. You could spread out in bed like a butterflied lamb.

Nora knew from her sailing experience with Annie and Mark that breezes were unreliable. They died at sunrise and sunset and unexpected times between. But those were isolated moments. She'd got her first promotion less than a month after she'd left Paul and hadn't had much time or inclination to brood about him. Cornelia had moved in only days after she'd thrown Tony out. She still had the magazine. She still had Cornelia. She couldn't figure out why she felt so abandoned.

"I mean," she said to Beatrice, "it isn't as if I actually was abandoned. It was a mutual agreement. Disagreement. It isn't as if he walked out on me." Nora thought about it for a minute. "As far as I can remember, I never have been abandoned by a man. Unless you count Daddy."

It was the kind of thing you could say only to a mother, and Nora had expected Beatrice, given her world view, to be pleased. After all, you didn't collect four fraternity pins at once by accident. But her mother surprised her.

"Maybe," Beatrice said, "that's because you've never given any of them a chance to."

Anyway, Nora figured she still had the magazine and she still had Cornelia.

Nora knew something was up as soon as she reached the door to her apartment that evening. The top lock was open. She always threw the bolt when she left. The warnings ran through her head. She knew them by heart. They used to run them regularly in the old *American Homemaker*. "Twenty-five Ways to Protect Your Home." "How to Foil an Assailant." "The Smart Woman's Guide to Self-Protection." According to every list, she was supposed to turn around, go downstairs to the lobby, and have the doorman call the police. She was supposed to be alert and think defensively and not give a damn that José might think she was overreacting.

She turned the bottom lock. What kind of a burglar would throw the bottom lock after he was inside the apartment? A Jewish mother burglar? No, she'd never given Max keys.

The foyer was dark, but Nora could see a faint glimmer of light from down the hall. "Cornelia?" she called and wondered if she was asking for trouble.

"I'm in here."

Cornelia was sitting on the bed, her back against the wall, her knees drawn up to her chest. The room was quiet. There was no stereo, no radio. Nora looked carefully. Not even a pair of earphones.

"I thought you were staying at your father's until that summer program started."

Cornelia had planned to spend the summer in New Haven working on a special design project. It didn't hurt that Andy planned to do the same thing.

"I thought I'd come in to see you."

Nora suddenly realized she was sweating, and not just from the expression on her niece's face. "Why didn't you turn on the air conditioner?"

Cornelia didn't answer. Nora walked to the window and switched on the unit. Then she sat in the rocking chair across from the bed and kicked off her sandals. The straps had left streaks of city soot on her feet.

She looked from her feet to her niece and waited. Cornelia's arms were folded across the top of her knees, her forehead resting on her forearms, her hair spilling over to hide her face.

"My father screws around, doesn't he?"

She lifted her head and looked at Nora. "I mean, I'm not trying to make a big thing of it, but he does, doesn't he?"

Nora knew she didn't have time to debate. Silence was an answer. "I don't know what your father does, Cornflake." The baby name slipped out. She hadn't used it in years. "The only time I've seen him since you went away to school was when Grandma was in the hospital. He was worried about you," she added.

"You know what I mean. He did screw around. That's why it happened. That's why Mom killed herself."

Nora's body started out of the chair as if it were propelled by some kind of reverse gravity. The same force lifted her arms to encircle Cornelia. Then she saw how her niece was sitting and sank back into the rocker. Nora knew from the white marks Cornelia's fingers made on her brown arms how tightly she was holding herself. She was a small, compact fortress.

"Your mother didn't kill herself."

"What do you call it?"

"An accident. A cry for help."

"Yeah. That's what you always say. Only he was too busy screwing around to hear it."

"Just where is this coming from?"

"They had a fight. Dad and the lovely Brenda. I wasn't supposed to hear. Hell, how could I help it? She's got a voice like one of those car alarms. Ah-ah. Ah-ah. Ah-ah. It just goes on and on." Cornelia imitated the irritating sound again. Then she began to cry.

Nora moved to the bed. She put one arm tentatively around Cornelia's shoulders. Cornelia stiffened but didn't pull away.

"Okay. Your father wasn't exactly a model of fidelity."

"He was fucking his receptionist."

Nora kept her arm around her niece, but her grip wasn't as strong as the moral certainties of youth. Nick had been fucking his receptionist, just as she had been fucking that artist with the horsy obsession, just as Susannah had been fucking the jewelry king. All for different reasons, but all the same in Cornelia's clear-eyed judgment.

Nora stroked Cornelia's hair. She thought of that morning in the hospital when she'd given Beatrice a shampoo. Beatrice's hair had felt thin and brittle, fragile as a halo. Cornelia's was thick and luxuriant beneath her fingers.

"Your mother didn't mean to kill herself," Nora insisted. "The phone was still in her hand. You don't pick up a phone to say 'I want to die.' You pick it up to say 'Please help me live.' She didn't plan to die. She didn't mean to leave you."

"Maybe she should have thought of that before she took those pills."

Cornelia was right. Intentions were beside the point. Extenuating circumstances didn't figure into it. Nick had betrayed them. Then Susannah had betrayed her. It was that simple. A victim isn't interested in explanations. Nora remembered that.

Cornelia said only two other things that night. She asked Nora if she could stay with her for a while. And she said, when Andy called, that she didn't want to speak to him.

"It's not his fault," Nora said.

"I never said it was," Cornelia snapped. "I just don't feel like talking to him now."

Nora went back to the phone and told Andy that Cornelia was asleep.

22

On radio and television, in offices and stores, on street corners and buses, everyone said it was the worst summer in memory. And it had barely begun. The stench of moldering garbage and rank sewers prowled the streets. Air conditioners coughed and panted and dripped on sweating, unsuspecting pedestrians. Lights flickered and appliances skipped a beat. Con Ed declared a brownout, a drab, dispiriting description to match the mood of the days. That evening Nora had to walk down the stairs from her office and up them to her apartment.

Beatrice was well into her course of treatments. Nora had gone with her the first time, Charlie the second. After that, Beatrice said she preferred to go alone. They both said they wanted to be with her. Beatrice knew that was true. They wanted to be with her, but neither of them wanted to be in that office. Nora didn't have the time. Charlie didn't have the stomach. Beatrice didn't want to be there herself, but she had no choice.

In the waiting room she tried to read. It was better than looking at the other women. For some reason there were few men.

By ten-thirty it was over. She didn't feel good, but she wasn't sick. She hailed a cab and got herself home. Sometimes, during the afternoon and evening, she managed to forget about it for whole minutes at a time. Then it would return as a vague unease, and she'd have to stop thinking about whatever she was thinking about and try to remember what she was worried about. It always came back to her.

But it wasn't a terrible time. It wasn't the worst time. The side effects weren't as bad as she'd feared. There was no nausea, only a little hair loss. The doctors said the prognosis was good. Beatrice told herself things could be worse. Much worse.

Charlie fussed over her, and tried to do things for her, and was there. He wasn't perfect. He wasn't Sam. He certainly wasn't Phil. But he was better than Dan Rather. In the morning, while she waited for it to be late enough to leave for the doctor's office, they sat in the living room of the small sublet and read the paper together. "Listen to this, Bea," he'd say. "Wait till you hear this one, Bea," he'd insist.

And her daughter and granddaughter were there. Sometimes, on the days Beatrice went for treatments, Nora stopped by and shared a cab as far as the doctor's office. Often, she dropped in on her way home from work. Cornelia, who was staying in her old room while she decided whether to go back to New Haven or get a summer job in New York, turned up for breakfast when Beatrice and Charlie were about to make lunch and tied up the phone making plans for the evening with her old school friends. Beatrice worried about Cornelia—Nora had told her about that business with Nick—but at least her granddaughter had come home. Beatrice decided it wasn't the worst of times at all.

Nora never would have bothered to go to the screening if it hadn't been for Cornelia. Of all the perks connected with her aunt's job, Cornelia liked the movie screenings best. All through high school she'd loved being the first to see things, and then going to the same movies a second time with her friends and knowing when to cover her eyes and where the laughs were and how it was going to end. So that night Nora decided to leave work early and meet Cornelia for the seven-o'clock screening.

It was at one of the large theaters on Third Avenue. Nora preferred them to the private screening rooms. For one thing, the smaller rooms were always around Times Square, and if Nora was opposed to violence and gratuitous sex on the screen, she especially didn't like them on the street. For another, at the private screenings you had to pretend to love the movie. At the bigger theaters you could get away without committing yourself or offending anyone else.

When Nora arrived, the usual group was stooging around the lobby, waiting for friends or hoping to be seen. Michael Simon was leaning against one wall doing one or the other or both. Nora hadn't seen him in a year or two. His hairline had inched back, but that was all right. It gave him a lofty brow. Michael had always looked as smart as he was, maybe smarter.

She was debating whether to cut through the crowd to say hello, when he caught sight of her. They met halfway and touched cheeks in a sanitized gesture. They asked each other how they were and reported they were fine. She inquired about his wife and children. He said his kids were okay, and his wife had acquired an adjective. Former. Nora said she was sorry. Maybe it was the news, or maybe it was the way he looked when he reported it, but for the first time since she'd spotted him across the lobby, she remembered all that frenzied groping in the front seat of his car during her senior year at Smith. For a moment she could almost taste the black coffee and smell the acrid aroma of Gauloises.

He suggested they go in and find seats.

"I'm waiting for my niece."

Michael said he'd wait with her. "I kind of miss being around kids since the divorce."

Nora didn't think Cornelia qualified, but she decided to let him find that out for himself.

Cornelia showed up. Michael realized she wasn't a baby, but he still treated her like a kid. "She's really something," he said to Nora as if Cornelia wasn't quite old enough to understand the words.

They went inside.

"If I remember correctly," Michael said, "you're myopic and like to sit close."

"What a memory."

"Nope. I like to sit close too. It was one of your attractions. What about you, Cornelia?"

Cornelia said she'd sit wherever they wanted. They found seats toward the front. Michael asked if anyone wanted popcorn. Nora said she didn't. Cornelia said she'd love some.

Michael stood. "With or without butter?"

"With," Cornelia said, and Michael started back up the aisle.

"Who's he?" she asked Nora as soon as he was gone.

Nora explained.

"He still has the hots for you," Cornelia said.

"Like your grandmother, you have a simplistic world view."

" 'If I remember correctly, you're myopic and like to sit close,' " she mimicked.

"I may look a little long in the tooth to you, sweetie, but I still haven't reached the stage where remembering infirmities qualifies as having the hots."

"Has anything happened since school?"

"Just a halfhearted pass at an awards dinner. His wife wasn't there."

"Why'd you say no?"

"Because his wife wasn't there."

"You wanted a ménage à trois?"

"Very funny."

Michael came back with the largest-size container of popcorn. He'd also brought Cornelia a Coke. If they'd sold stuffed animals in the lobby, Nora had the feeling he would have brought her one of those too. He was trying to be sweet, but he was coming off a little dopey. Nora thought of Max and wondered if her niece thought she was coming down in the world.

"I'm glad we didn't pay for it," Michael said when the movie was over.

"Good production values," Nora said.

"Interesting casting," Michael countered.

"I liked the lighting," Cornelia added.

"Hey," Michael said to Nora. "She's quick."

Cornelia dropped back so that Michael couldn't see her and rolled her eyes at Nora. Nora tried to remember how old Michael's kids were.

They came out of the chilled theater into the steaming night, and stood for a moment, stunned by the heat.

Michael came to first. "How about a bite? If you don't have other plans."

Nora looked at Cornelia. She didn't want to force her niece into anything.

"Sure," Cornelia said.

Michael said he knew a place with a garden just around the corner. He took both their arms and began steering them in that direction.

The maître d' asked if they wanted to eat inside or out.

"Inside," Nora said.

Michael looked at Cornelia. "Unless Cornelia wants to sit in the garden."

Michael hadn't said how long he'd been divorced, but Nora had the feeling he'd spent entirely too many weekends trying to entertain children.

"Inside," Cornelia agreed.

The waiter held Nora's chair. Michael held Cornelia's. Nora told the waiter she'd have a gin and tonic. Michael asked Cornelia what she wanted.

It went on that way through dinner. Michael asked Cornelia where she went to school and what she was studying and how she was going to spend her summer vacation. Cornelia said she'd planned to go back to New Haven, but now she wasn't so sure. Nora had heard her say the same thing to Andy on the phone the night before, but then the tone had been sullen.

"If you're looking for a job," Michael said, "maybe I can help. I know someone at Johnson-Burgee and another guy over at the Municipal Art Society."

Cornelia thanked him and said she'd keep it in mind.

Michael must have figured he'd done his duty. He turned to Nora. It was time for the grown-ups. They traded professional gossip. A staff writer had been fired. An editor was moving. Rupert Murdoch had his eye on something.

"Your name came up at lunch a couple of weeks ago," Michael said. "Someone in the development group was talking about starting up a women's service magazine. To hit an older market."

Nora wondered if Wheeler had heard, and, if he hadn't, how she could make sure he did.

The waiter brought the check. Nora reached for it, but Michael outmaneuvered her. She protested. After all, there were two of them.

Michael took a plastic card from his wallet. "You can do it next time."

They said good-bye outside the restaurant. Nora and Cornelia were going north. Michael was heading west.

"I meant that about a summer job," he said to Cornelia as he put them in the cab.

"You see," Nora insisted, "he's not so bad."

"I never said he was."

"I know your looks. That one in the movie said jerk."

"You know what Grandma always says. 'As long as he makes *you* happy.'"

"He's just a friend. Not even that. A professional acquaintance."

"There's-no-truth-to-the-rumors-we're-just-good-friends is the way the line goes."

Nora didn't answer. She'd had a funny sensation in the restaurant. While Michael had asked Cornelia questions and told Cornelia stories and done everything to entertain Cornelia short of magic tricks, Nora realized how comfortable she'd become with Max. Then she realized, with horror, that it was exactly the kind of thing Beatrice would say. García Márquez said a man knows he's getting old when he looks in the mirror and sees his father looking back at him. Nora supposed the same could be said when a woman opened her mouth and her mother's words came out.

Still, it was odd how easily she and Max had fallen into each other's patterns, at least in certain areas. They had the little things in common—sex and food and the ability to sleep in a bed littered with books and papers and magazines—and the big things—politics and religion, or a lack thereof. Or maybe it was the other way around, as far as big and little. The only problem, as Max had pointed out, was everything between.

It never would have happened if Nora had a state-of-the-art answering machine instead of an aging unreliable model. When she called home from her office to get her messages that afternoon, the tape was acting skittish again, and she missed the beginning of the message. At the time it didn't seem important.

When she thought about it afterward, and she thought about it a lot afterward, she couldn't blame the incident entirely on the answering machine. She should have known something was wrong. She would have, if she hadn't been so eager to think everything was all right. Her skin crawled when she remembered how eager she'd been.

She held the beeper of her machine against the phone in her office, pressed the signal, and listened to the playback. The aging machine had been slow getting started again because Michael came over the wire identifying himself as ". . . ichael Simon." It didn't matter. Nora would have recognized the voice even without the name.

"Remember that friend I mentioned," he went on. "We're having a drink tonight, and he'd like to talk to you." He went on to say that he'd be out of his office and she wouldn't be able to reach him, but if she could make it, it would be great to see her. He gave her the name of a restaurant and told her they'd be there at seven.

"If you can't make it," he went on, "give me a call at my office tomorrow. Maybe we can have dinner. I'd really like to see you again."

Maybe it wasn't eagerness. Maybe it was just habit. Michael Simon had been turning up in Nora's life for a long time. You could almost call Michael Simon a constant in Nora's life.

As she took the makeup case from the bottom drawer of her desk, she thought about the unreliability of it all. A month ago, she'd sat in this office steeling herself to pack the same makeup case under the hostile eyes of two security guards. Now she was hurrying to the women's room to get ready to meet a man who wanted to start a new magazine. Max was wrong about insurance policies, or at least off base. Maybe you couldn't count on anything—men, magazines, anything—but you could cover yourself. That's why she was going to have a drink with Michael's friend from development. And with Michael. Max had also said they were two people at cross-purposes. She thought of dinner with Michael the other night and the fact that he'd bothered to set up this meeting with his contact. She remembered those spring nights during their senior year. She wondered if she and Michael were two people at cross-purposes.

Nora was always clumsy when she hurried. She managed to smudge her mascara. By the time she got it off, there was a patch of angry red skin under her eye. When she tried to cover it with powder, she dropped her compact. Powder spilled onto the tile floor. She had to throw out the puff, but at least the mirror hadn't broken. Nora wasn't superstitious. It was just that she'd had the compact for a long time.

Of course she had trouble getting a cab, and of course the cab got stuck in traffic. She sat listening to the meter clicking off time and money. She forced herself to breathe slowly. It didn't help. She reminded herself that she hadn't gone looking for the man in development or Michael. They'd come looking for her.

The driver had trouble finding the restaurant. It was so fiercely trendy there was no sign. Later that night when Nora sat in her apartment listening to her answering machine, she realized that if the fact that Michael had called her at home rather than at her office on a weekday afternoon hadn't tipped her off, the restaurant should have. It was not a place where grown-ups did business.

Music blared. Patent-leather-haired waiters who looked as if they'd just escaped from a Brassaï photograph bumped and jostled their way through a jungle of miniature tables. Underaged patrons who'd rather be caught dead than speaking English circled each other warily. It was the kind of place Cornelia and her friends haunted. Nora realized she'd got spoiled with Max. He liked adult-rated restaurants that provided elbow room and encouraged conversation.

Michael was sitting alone at a tiny table near the crowded zinc bar. The bar sported wire racks of hard-boiled eggs that looked older than most of the patrons. The development man was nowhere in sight. Nora wondered if the new magazine was a ruse. She wasn't sure whether she was disappointed or flattered.

Michael looked up from the magazine he was reading. She wondered how he could concentrate in that din. Then she noticed the way his eyes narrowed when he saw her, as if he were trying to put her in focus, as if he didn't recognize her, and she knew how he could concentrate because she knew writers. Michael was reading his own words.

He went on staring at her. He looked as if he'd finally realized who she was but not why she was there. Nora thought of Max again. Whenever she walked into a restaurant or met him at a movie, his face creased in a relieved smile, as if he'd been afraid she wasn't going to show. She reminded herself that the smile had usually followed a frown because he'd been waiting for a while. "What I don't understand," he'd said once when she'd arrived only a few minutes late for a movie, "is how you can meet a magazine deadline every month, but can't get yourself crosstown on time." Nora had started to explain that it was because of the former that she had trouble with the latter, but Max had just grabbed her arm and begun dragging her down the dark theater aisle. On second thought, Max's welcoming smile wasn't so sweet after all. It was damn superior.

"Nora!" Michael said. His voice was too hearty, his eyes shifty. He had the manner of a man caught in the act. She was sure he'd been reading his own words.

He stood. She sat. He looked confused for a minute, then sat again.

"It's okay," she said. "I won't tell anyone."

His eyes grew more shifty. "Won't tell anyone what?"

"That you're so mesmerized by your own prose."

His laughter had the tinny ring of guilt. He slipped the magazine into his briefcase.

The waiter came. Nora ordered a drink. Michael went on staring at her after the waiter left. His eyes had turned calculating. He had the look of a sleepy fox. Nora remembered the expression. She'd sat across from it hour after hour, night after night, as the cigarette butts overflowed the ashtrays and they circled each other in a slow dance of expectancy, like the kids around them now. All that talk about how she felt and how he felt and how Paul might feel had been only a prelude, foreplay leading up to the moment when Michael would pay for the coffee or beer and they'd go out into the chill spring Northampton night.

The waiter brought her drink. Michael was still watching her. He wasn't as good at this sort of thing as he used to be. Maybe he'd got out of practice during his marriage, though in view of that pass at the awards dinner she hadn't thought so.

She figured one of them had to say something. "It was really nice of you to set this up."

His face was still wary. "Then you don't mind?"

"Why would I mind?"

"When I saw you, I just assumed you'd come to tell me to bug off."

Nora opened her mouth to reassure him. That was when she saw her. But she still didn't get it. Not yet. For a minute she thought it was a coincidence. Cornelia was meeting a friend. Wasn't this the kind of place where Cornelia's friends met? Then it all fell into place. Or apart. This was no coincidence. Cornelia was meeting a friend. Nora's friend.

She watched her niece make her way down the bar. Several patent-leather heads turned. One of them said something in French. Cornelia ignored him and kept going. She reached the table. She wasn't embarrassed, but then there was no reason for her to be. She didn't know what was up.

Michael's friend arrived. Michael introduced them all. This was Cornelia Demopoulis, the architecture student he'd mentioned. And this was her aunt, Michael shouted above the din. Nora repeated her name, in case Michael had forgotten it. Garrison Henry nodded and turned back to Cornelia.

The air-conditioning was no match for the crowd, or maybe just for Nora. She slipped off her linen jacket. As soon as she did, she was sorry. The skin of her upper arms swung like soft white wattles. How had she failed to notice it before? How had she dared to wear a short-sleeved blouse?

It wasn't even a memory, merely an image winging by. She was in the guest bedroom in the house on Byron Road. Her grandmother lifted her arms to stick hairpins into the thick bun at the back of her neck. Nora watched the soft swaying flesh of her underarms in fascinated revulsion. It gave off an odor, not what the kids in school called B.O., but something thicker and more musty. "Grandma smells," she'd told Beatrice. Her mother had shushed her. It wasn't an odor, Beatrice said, it was old age. You couldn't do anything about that.

Nora tried to pay attention to the conversation. Cornelia said she'd decided to go back to New Haven for the rest of the summer. It wasn't too late to work on the design project. But she'd wanted to meet Garrison Henry anyway. It never hurt to know someone at Johnson-Burgee, she said and smiled at him.

There were hot needles pricking Nora's skin. She knew without looking in her compact mirror that the red blotches were coming out on her face.

The four of them were crowded around a table the size of a checkerboard. Every time Nora moved, her knees bumped Michael's. Finally, she stopped mumbling mortified apologies and pushed her chair back from the table. No one noticed.

Cornelia was still working. She wasn't flirtatious, just friendly and direct. Nora was proud of her, at least she would have been if she weren't so ashamed of herself.

She tried to shrink smaller in her chair. She glanced down at her lap. Her hands lay limp and wrinkled, like old road maps, crisscrossed by too many access routes and detours. Hands were always the giveaway. You could have your face lifted and your tummy tucked and your breasts firmed, but your hands still told the secret. These hands had been editing articles and dialing phones and making love for a long time.

"What do you do?" Garrison Henry shouted over the noise. The words bounced off unforgiving stucco and glazed tiles. Nora's head throbbed. Hadn't whoever designed this damn restaurant ever heard of acoustical materials? Didn't anybody care that they were permanently damaging their hearing?

Nora dragged her eyes up from her lap. "Editor," she mumbled.

Garrison Henry nodded and turned back to Michael and Cornelia. Nora knew he hadn't heard. She also knew he wasn't interested. Maybe she should have said editor-in-chief or publisher, but she knew it wouldn't have made a difference.

She dropped her eyes again. Not to her hands, she wasn't going to stare at her hands, but to her watch. The minute hand dragged through one circle, a second, a third. Fifteen, she promised herself. She'd stick it out for fifteen minutes. For Cornelia. And for her own dignity.

Garrison Henry was talking to Cornelia again, and Nora was glad—she really was—because good architecture jobs didn't grow on trees. Michael was leaning toward Cornelia, his arm stretched along the back of her chair. Nora folded her own arms across her chest. Her fingers probed the flaccid tender wattles of her upper arms. She remembered those nights in Michael's car. He'd had a compact, athletic body. He probably still did.

A waiter bumped Nora's chair. If he noticed, he didn't let on. Garrison Henry was handing Cornelia a card. Michael was leaning closer. His hand was on Cornelia's shoulder now. Blunt fingers splayed over smooth brown skin. Cornelia reached for her drink. Her arm was taut and beautiful. Nora hunched forward in her chair and hugged herself more tightly.

Michael signaled the waiter for another round.

"Not for me!" Nora screamed. No one noticed the hysteria in her voice. Maybe it was the noise of the restaurant.

Or maybe no one was paying attention. "I have another appointment." She managed to sound almost normal.

Cornelia started to stand, but Nora put her hand on her niece's shoulder. It was smooth and strong. No wonder Michael wanted to touch it. You'd have to be a fool not to enjoy the pure tactile pleasure.

"You stay." Nora kissed her niece's cheek. "I'll see you at home."

It wasn't Cornelia's fault. She didn't even know what had happened. And Nora didn't want her to find out. But this time she wasn't trying to protect Cornelia. She was trying to save herself.

She picked up her jacket from the back of the chair, but didn't put it on. In order to put it on she'd have to lift her arms. Then everyone would see her secret. She clutched the jacket to her. She mumbled good-bye-nice-meeting-you-good-to-see-you-good-bye. No matter how many times Nora relived the incident, she never could remember how she got out of that restaurant.

It was still light out. Nora was surprised. She was sure the earth had turned on its axis if not entirely shifted off it while she'd sat at that table.

She started walking. The last rays of the sun scalded the angry red blotches on her cheeks. She didn't know where she was going. She had no plans for the evening. After she'd got Michael's message, she'd given Lucy the invitation to that opening. The ugly rash flamed higher at the memory.

She kept going east to Fifth, then turned north. The steamy air clung to her skin. It was too thick to breathe. When she crossed the street, the surface felt spongy beneath her feet. She might have been sinking into quicksand.

She told herself not to think about it. After all, what had happened? She'd turned up for a drink unexpectedly. Cornelia didn't know there was any more to it than that. Garrison Henry didn't. She wasn't even sure Michael had caught on. For all Nora knew, he thought she'd been there to protect her niece's interests rather than promote her own.

Don't think about it, she insisted, but the rash still itched and burned.

She remembered that night, so many years ago, when she'd gone running down the street to meet a strange boy she'd thought was Paul, and he'd run past her to another girl. She'd never told anyone about that night, not even Beatrice, not even Susannah. The only witness had been a stranger, whose face she'd barely seen and who hadn't been able to see hers in the darkness. Paul had blamed the shameful color of her cheeks on the cold.

She kept walking up Fifth, past the solid limestone buildings with their proper canopies, past the doormen sweating in their somber uniforms. A few looked at her without interest. She didn't live in their buildings. She didn't need a cab. She wasn't a source of Christmas largess or even occasional tips. She was just a middle-aged woman with an angry red face. If she was visible at all.

The sight of those doormen reminded her of that afternoon years ago when she'd followed that mean-spirited woman in her Sergio Valenti jeans up Fifth Avenue and stumbled across the dirty little secret of motherhood. Only Nora knew it wasn't the doormen who'd brought the incident to mind.

She stopped in the lobby of her building to pick up her mail. There was a postcard among the expensive four-color brochures addressed to Occupant. The picture was of an astonishingly green landscape. She wondered if that was what Scotland looked like. She turned the postcard over. Limerick, Ireland. She glanced at the signature. Love, Craig. She looked at the right-hand side of the card. It was addressed to her neighbor. She gave it to the doorman to deliver.

There were two messages on her machine when she got home. One was from Annie, the other from Michael Simon. She played them both back. Sometimes, the machine worked better when she pressed the buttons manually rather than activated them electronically over the phone.

"Hi, Cornelia. It's Michael Simon."

Nora pushed the button and played the beginning of the message again.

"Hi, Cornelia."

She pushed the button.

"Hi, Cornelia."

Again.

"Hi, Cornelia."

Finally she let the message run through. "I'd really like to see you again."

She sat listening to Michael Simon's voice. Michael Simon, the boy from college who'd almost convinced her she couldn't marry anyone else.

"Hi, Cornelia."

Michael Simon, the boy who'd opened his trousers and put her hand inside.

"If you can't make it . . ."

Michael Simon, the man who'd told her on the night she'd become editor-in-chief of *AH!* that she was walking like a woman who'd just climbed out of an illicit bed.

". . . give me a call at my office tomorrow."

Michael Simon, the man who'd made a tepid but sincere —she was sure it had been sincere—pass at that awards dinner.

"Maybe we can have dinner."

Michael Simon, the first penis she'd ever touched.

"I'd really like to see you again."

Michael Simon, her contemporary.

"Hi, Cornelia."

23

Nora had no lunch date that day. She'd planned to order a sandwich in and work straight through, but when she buzzed Jenny a little after one, there was no answer. She walked to the door of her office and stood looking out over the empty desks, the blank computer screens, the silent telephones. It was like a ghost town.

She walked to the elevators and pressed the down button.

Under an oppressive yellow haze, crowds surged back and forth like an army in rout. Cars and taxis blocked intersections. Messengers on bikes careened through, leaving shaken, cursing pedestrians in their wake. Women in various states of summer undress balanced plastic containers of salad as they threaded their way back to air-conditioned offices. Lower-management men in cheap shiny suits or short-sleeved shirts leaned against buildings and handicapped the women. The fumes of hot dogs and sauerkraut and indistinguishable meat assaulted Nora at every corner. A young man told her a Dove Bar would cheer her up. A middle-aged woman in a sleeveless dress bumped into her. Nora jumped back from the collision of sticky skin.

She had no idea where she was going. She had, in fact, no place to go. Then she remembered. She needed a refill for

her compact. The night came back to her. She recoiled
from the memory as she had from the sticky skin of that
strange offensive woman.

The cold air of unreality hit her. Inside Bloomingdale's it
was fall. A man in a short yellow jacket and tight trousers, a
woman in an Edwardian lace dress, a couple in fur con-
verged on her, brandishing atomizers as if they were lethal
weapons. Women hiding behind masks of makeup and men
who couldn't hide their disdain promised to make Nora up,
make her over, make her into what she'd always wanted to
be.

It took her a while to find the right counter. A woman in
a white medical coat frowned when Nora said all she
wanted was a powder refill. She leaned closer and peered
at Nora's skin.

"You really could use a defoliant," she insisted.

Nora wondered when her skin had become a war zone.

That was when she heard the voice booming behind her.
"Nora! Nora!"

Even before she turned, she wondered what Charlie was
doing in the makeup department of Bloomingdale's.

He had to go up on his toes to reach an arm around her
shoulders. His lips were substantial on her cheek. None of
this grazing of skin and kissing of air for Charlie.

"I'm in luck. I was just saying to myself, 'Charlie, you
need a woman's opinion. A lady's touch.' And the next
thing I know, I see you. Come with me. I want to know
what you think."

"I don't have much time, Charlie. I have to get back to
the office."

"Just a minute. I want you to tell me if Bea's going to like
it."

Nora let him lead her to the escalator. His hand cupped
her elbow and propelled her on.

"Bea's been talking about how she can't look at the paper
or a magazine in bed. All we got in there is that one overhead light." He steered her off one escalator and onto another. "You can go blind trying to read by that. I said, 'Bea,
we'll get a lamp for the night table.' She said it's not our

apartment, but I said, 'What's the big deal? We'll take it back to Florida when we go.' So when she went to the beauty parlor today, I decided I'd come here and get something to surprise her." He was steering Nora through the furniture now. "I found something. Chinese. But what do I know? Maybe it's wrong. Maybe Bea won't like it. Then I saw you, I figured I'm saved. Nora'll tell me."

He stopped in front of a display of Chinese lamps and put his hand on the base of one of them.

"So, be honest. You won't hurt my feelings. I can return it. I made sure of that." He stroked the lamp. "So?"

"It's fine."

"You think she'll really like it?"

"I'm sure she will."

Charlie moved the lamp a fraction of an inch, then stepped back to get a better perspective.

"You wouldn't kid me?"

Nora said she wouldn't kid him. She said the lamp was a lot like one they'd had on Byron Road. She was sure Beatrice would like it.

"Of course, you gotta picture it without the plastic on the shade. You're supposed to take the plastic off."

"Of course," Nora repeated. "How else can you use it to cover the furniture?"

Charlie turned from the lamp to Nora and stood staring at her for a minute. Then he began walking.

Nora was shocked. It was as if a tame household pet had turned on her. She hurried after him.

"I was just kidding."

He stepped onto the escalator. She followed him.

"I know you were kidding. That dumb I'm not."

"I'm sorry."

He didn't say anything. Nora had never seen Charlie silent. She didn't know what to do.

"How about some iced tea? Or coffee?" she suggested.

"I thought you had to get back to the office," he said without looking at her.

"I have a minute."

She was a step above him on the escalator. He turned and looked up at her from under hooded eyelids. "Okay."

Lexington Avenue steamed in the hazy sunshine. The crowds were even worse here than around Nora's office. She lost sight of Charlie for a moment, then spotted him again. He didn't take her arm.

They found a coffee shop. Icy wind howled down from an overhead vent. Greeks screamed at each other. Onions sizzled on a grill.

They huddled around a small sticky table. Nora ordered iced tea. Charlie didn't urge her to have anything more. He ordered iced coffee.

The waiter slammed their glasses down. Liquid sloshed over the table. Nora mopped it up with a paper napkin. When she looked up, she saw that Charlie was watching her.

"You're real fast with the words, Nora. A smart girl, Bea says, and she's right."

"Smartass is more like it."

Charlie tore open a package of Sweet 'n Low and dumped it into his coffee. "So the question is, Missy, what're you so afraid of?"

"What do you mean?"

"I mean what scares you so much you gotta hide behind that smart mouth all the time?"

"I said I was sorry."

"You afraid of the boys?"

Nora looked around the coffee shop. How had she let herself in for this? "Do you mean do I like men?"

Charlie laughed. "Don't worry, Nora. I don't think you like girls. I know it's not impossible. Poor Dorothy Gittler. She keeps waiting for her daughter to get married, settle down, have a family. Her daughter got married a long time ago. To that girl she calls her roommate. All you gotta do is watch them around the pool when they come to visit, you know that." He took a sip of his coffee, then smacked his lips. "But I don't think that's your problem."

"I thought we could just have a cold drink, Charlie."

"I wasn't talking about sex, Missy. I think you like men okay that way. I think you're like your mama that way."

"I really don't want to have this conversation, Charlie."

He just went on staring at her. "You wanna know why

you don't like me, Nora? Not cause you think I'm such a schmuck I don't know you're not supposed to put plastic covers on the furniture. Not cause you think I'm not good enough for your mama. Because I took Bea away from you. A little. She needs you, Nora. You'll always come first with her. I hope you got the brains to know that. But now she needs me, too. And you don't like that."

"I'm glad she's happy."

"She's happy. We're talking about you."

"I'm fine."

"Yeah? That's not the way it sounded the other night. That business with your old boyfriend."

Nora shivered. She must be sitting directly in the air conditioner's line of fire. "How did you hear about that?"

"Cornelia. She thought it was funny this old guy, this guy so old he used to be her aunt's boyfriend, went to all this trouble to impress her. She wasn't being mean. She didn't even understand. At that age you don't. Me, I understood. And I didn't think it was so funny. Neither did Bea." He put his hand over hers. "Neither did you, I bet."

Nora pulled her hand away. She didn't need Charlie's sympathy. She didn't want Charlie and her mother talking about her while they lingered over breakfast or read the paper in the living room or sat side by side in bed watching the late news.

"It was nothing," she said.

Charlie went on staring at her. "You wanna know what you remind me of, Nora? The other day your mama and me went for a walk. All of a sudden where do we find ourselves but in front of the Whitney Museum. I said, 'Bea, I never been inside the Whitney Museum. Let's take a look.' So we went inside. You remind me of one of those paintings. You know, the kind with little stick figures. They look like some kid painted them."

"Primitives?"

"Yeah."

"I don't get the connection."

"The people in those paintings, Nora. They don't cast no shadows."

She was as stunned as if he'd made one of his abrupt moves and upset the glasses or overturned the table.

"You're talking about posterity," she said finally. "Children."

"I'm talking about life."

"I have a life. A job. A family."

"Sure, you got a job. Real important. I'm not talking sarcastic. I know a little about the business world, and I'm impressed. So, that's the shadow you cast? A magazine?"

"I said I have a family."

"Take a look at your family, Nora. You got a mama who's being taken care of. You got a niece who's a grown-up. In other words, they both got their own lives."

He took a swallow of his coffee, then chewed an ice cube. "But even before that. Even when Cornelia wasn't grown up. What'd you have? Your sister's daughter. Like a hand-me-down." She started to say something, but he held up his hand.

"I'm gonna tell you something, Nora. I don't care if I hurt your feelings. I don't care if you get angry at me. What do I have to lose? You don't like me already. So, I'm gonna tell you something, and I want you to think about it. For your own good."

For your own good. The phrase had resonance. It always meant something unpleasant was on the way.

"In some ways you're a lot like your mama. You got what they call resiliency. But there's one thing she's got, you don't."

"You?"

He opened his mouth wide to let out the laughter. An innocent bystander might think they were having a good time. "You're not as far off as you think, cause it's connected to me. Your mama's got courage. Guts. Your mama's not afraid to take chances."

"I've taken chances," Nora insisted, though she'd sworn she wasn't going to give him the satisfaction of an argument.

"You're talking about the magazine again. With you it always comes back to the magazine." Charlie leaned back in his chair and narrowed one eye till it was almost closed.

He might have been sighting her through a telescope. "Forget the magazine for a minute. I'm talking about the rest. Where did you take a chance? Not with these affairs you jump out of as fast as you jump in. Not with that husband of yours. From what I hear you played it safe there too. Susannah, she should rest in peace, she was the one who took a chance with husbands."

"And look what happened to her."

"You both ended up divorced."

"I was thinking of more than that."

"I said you got resiliency, Nora." He stopped squinting and opened his eyes wide. "Of course, playing it safe, maybe you didn't need as much as Susannah." He took another swallow of his coffee. She had the feeling he wanted to let that one sink in.

"What I'm trying to tell you is your mama, she's got both. She's got the resiliency and she's got the guts."

"So you think I ought to give up my job, move to Florida, and take a chance on the first man who comes along?"

He opened his mouth to let out another laugh. A woman at the counter turned to stare. "Good, Nora. Very good. No, I'm not telling you you got to live like Bea. I know we're another generation. A couple of old fogies. But that don't mean you can't learn a few things from her."

He stopped smiling and leaned toward her. "So, when're you gonna get smart? When're you gonna stop hiding behind Mama and the magazine? When're you gonna grow up? Before you grow old maybe?"

It had nothing to do with her age. Nora had been reading the obits for years. You could pick up some good story ideas from the obits, like that one about the changing styles in childrearing she'd come up with after the death of Dr. Leon Welch. But this obit didn't give her any ideas, at least not for the magazine.

Kitty Magnelli was a dress designer. Had been a dress designer. A little more than a year ago, *AH!* had done a "Fast Track" feature on her. She was the one who'd taken her computer mountain climbing in Nepal. There'd been a picture of her walking down the Via Veneto talking into a cellular phone, another at the controls of her private plane, a third at a staff meeting, sprawled in a recliner while two women in white worked on her manicure and pedicure and a variety of men and women crowded around with pads and pencils in hand. Nora had hated that photograph the most. It reminded her of Louis XIV on a commode surrounded by his courtiers. Still, she'd run it, because, as the editor had said, the picture screamed power. "It says now," the editor insisted. "It says making every minute count."

"Kitty's computerized schedule," ran the caption, "is entirely booked for the next five months."

Talk about planning. Talk about insurance. Only there'd been a slight hitch. A brain tumor. Kitty Magnelli had plenty of time now. Nora had read somewhere of the inability of the human mind to conceive of infinities. The infinity of space. The infinity of time after your own death.

Nora read to the end of the column as she always did. She liked to learn about the deceased's legacies. Someone was survived by a wife, three children, ten grandchildren. Someone else was survived by a sister, two children, four grandchildren.

There was no mention of survivors in Kitty Magnelli's obituary. The last line simply stated that services would be private. Unlike, Nora thought, Kitty Magnelli's life.

Nora debated for a long time. She knew her mother would want to go along. She also knew it was something she had to do alone. Like getting her divorce.

On the third Sunday in August, she rented a car. When she climbed in, the upholstery burned the back of her legs through her skirt. The air stuck to her skin like glue. She rolled up the windows and turned on the air-conditioning.

On the way out to New Jersey she told herself she'd made the right decision. It was the one place Beatrice couldn't help her. It was the one place you were going to end up alone, so you might as well get used to going there alone.

The streets around the cemetery were lined with cars. It was only two weeks before the High Holidays. Nora should

have thought of that, but of course she hadn't. For twenty
minutes she cruised slowly up one street and down another
looking for a space. They were narrow streets lined with
rickety wooden houses collapsing into sagging front
porches or two-family boxes flaunting their new aluminum
siding. All the streets looked alike. It was like driving
through a maze. Nora took a wrong turn and lost sight of
the cemetery for a while. Finally, she pulled into a supermarket parking lot, locked the car, and left it.

The cemetery was packed. People milled around with a
vague air of festivity. They were there to visit rather than
bury. So was Nora, but she didn't feel festive. As she made
her way along the paths between the graves, gravel
crunched savagely beneath her sandals. The day was growing hotter. The sun pressed down on her head like a tight
helmet. It splintered off the granite and marble tomb-
stones and cracked through her dark glasses.

Nora glanced over the landscape. She'd visited infre-
quently since her mother had moved to Florida. The last
time she'd been here had been for Sam's funeral. The cemetery seemed to go on forever. It was eating up the surrounding neighborhood.

Nora thought of the pictures she'd seen of military grave-
yards. Line after line of plain white crosses marched into
infinity. The similarity stunned comprehension. You
couldn't grasp the lives beneath those crosses any more
than you could translate casualty lists into individual
deaths. Here things were more personal. Old Mr. Shine lay
beneath a massive marble stone, as pretentious in death as
in life. Sadie Mink's children had carved the words "Be-
loved Mother" into her monument. On one footstone there
was a weathered oval photograph of a young man in a stiff
collar and bowler hat. Nora had been passing that photograph for thirty-four years, and she always wondered how
it endured. It was faded and streaked, but it was there.

She went to Sam's grave first. He was buried beside his
first wife, though he'd lived with his second for twice as
long. This was the easy part of the visit.

She tried to think about Sam's life, but ended up think-

ing about her life with Sam. She remembered the books
he'd brought her, how he'd carried on when he found out
she was valedictorian of her high-school class, the way he
used to call every month on the day that *AH!* came in the
mail to discuss the issue. It hadn't been hard to win Sam's
love.

An old man, or a man who, bent under the weight of his
beard and hat and religious responsibility, walked old, approached. He mumbled something to Nora. His accent was
thick, and she couldn't understand the words, but she
knew the intent. His offer was sexual and indecent, but
within the law. As a woman, she could not say a prayer for
Sam. As a man, he was offering to say it for her in exchange
for a small sum.

She shook her head no. He mirrored the movement in
disapproval and shuffled off.

She stood for a while after he left, then bent and picked
up a small rock from the gravel path. It felt warm in her
hand.

She glanced around guiltily, as if she were going to do
something wrong rather than merely superstitious. She
didn't believe in superstition. She didn't believe in religion. She especially didn't believe in a religion that
wouldn't permit a woman to say a prayer for a loved one.
But she did it anyway. She took the smooth, warm rock and
placed it on top of Sam's headstone. It was a superstition,
but it was also a sign that someone had visited, that the
living cared.

The sun was still burning a hot hole overhead in the pale
sky. There were only a few trees around the perimeter of
the cemetery. Their shade was elusive. The monuments
stood baking in the unforgiving light. Nora started back
along the path. The gravel glowed like white-hot coals. It
burned through the thin soles of her sandals. She could see
her father's and sister's tombstone in the distance. The
heat made it shimmer like a mirage.

The stone was a rectangular slab of granite. It ran the
width of four graves, though only two had been dug. Six
letters were cut into its side. H E L L E R. Phil lay under
the E and L, Susannah under the H. They'd bury Beatrice

under the second L and E. The R was for Nora. Men come
and go, Beatrice had said the morning she'd told her
daughters she was going to marry Sam, but there'll always
be the three of us. That was one promise that would be
kept.

Nora stood at the end of her father's grave, her sandals
almost touching his footstone. It was easier to speculate on
his life, because there was so little of her life with him. She
had only a handful of memories, and she wasn't even sure
of those anymore. Could she really remember that time
he'd taken her to his office and she'd sat in the big chair
behind his desk, her Mary Janes swinging high above the
floor, and said someday she was going to have an office just
like it, or had Beatrice merely told the story so often that
Nora thought she remembered it? She knew she no longer
recalled that time he'd lost her or she'd lost him—it depended on your perspective—at the Central Park Zoo, but
she did remember the dozens of times she'd recounted the
incident.

She stood there trying to concentrate on her father, but
she knew she was working up to something else. Finally,
she stepped a few inches to the left so she was standing at
the foot of Susannah's grave. This was what she'd been
working up to.

She never cried anymore, at least not at the cemetery.
She bent and brushed the leaves and grass from the footstone. The marble was smooth, but Susannah's name still
cut sharply against Nora's fingers.

Susannah Heller Demopoulis
June 24, 1941 · · · September 5, 1977

She straightened again. Sometimes it was hard to control
her mind here. It had a habit of running away, like a child
with its hands over its eyes or ears. Sometimes her mind
veered off so completely that the only way she could bring
it back was by forcing herself to think in concrete terms.
Was there anything left of the coffin now, or of Susannah?
She thought of Susannah's beauty.

Susannah had been terrified of turning forty, and Nora

had referred her to *Who's Who of American Women.* The old promises aren't going to be kept, Nora had been saying, but here's the new safety net. Only Susannah had spotted the holes. She'd known you couldn't find new promises to replace the old. But she hadn't known how to live without any at all. She hadn't mastered the only trick that made living possible. And now she lay beside Daddy.

Daddy can't die.

Only he had, and, as beyond comprehension as it still seemed, Susannah had too.

Nora looked at the plot of untouched grass beneath the second L and E and R. Next week Beatrice would finish her course of treatment. Then she and Charlie would relinquish the sublet apartment and return to Florida. In six weeks there'd be a checkup, then, if they were lucky, in three months another. If their luck held, they'd progress to six-month intervals. But their luck couldn't hold indefinitely. Someday there'd be a doctor pronouncing bad news and closing his eyes for a moment to feign pain he didn't feel and telling Nora not to cry, because crying wouldn't help. But not now. Not quite yet.

Another man approached. Nora shook her head before he even made the offer. She wasn't interested in prayers. They were too much like promises. Or, as Max would have put it, like buying an insurance policy. I'll pay my premiums now; you take care of me later. Only it didn't work that way.

Nora bent and picked up a stone from the gravel path. Then she walked around her father's grave and her sister's, placed it on the headstone, and started down the path.

Outside the cemetery there were trees. Nora walked beneath them along the uneven sidewalk. There was a faint breeze. She hadn't noticed it as she'd stood at the graves. Leaves rustled slightly overhead. She could see the movement in the sidewalk shadows.

She watched the motion of the leafy shadows as she walked. It was August, and the foliage was so dense that it blotted out the sun and everything else. Charlie was vindicated. She cast no shadow of her own.

In the supermarket parking lot, the rented car glowed

like a red coal. She unlocked the door on the driver's side.
The handle burned her fingers. She walked around and
opened the door on the passenger side. Then she went
back to the driver's side and started to climb in. The steering wheel was untouchable. The air was so hot she could
barely breathe.

She got out of the car and stood beside it. She'd parked at
the empty end of the lot, but it had filled up while she was
gone. A woman in shorts and a thin maternity top pushed a
cart with half a dozen bags and a boy not much bigger than
a single bag. Every step on the macadam seemed to cost
her. A man sat in the front seat of a station wagon while two
kids wrestled in back. The windows were open and Nora
could hear the shrieks of the kids mingled with the com-
mentary on the Giants game. In another car an elderly
man sat alone behind the wheel. His head rested against
the back of the seat, and his eyes were closed. He was
perfectly still. Nora stood, waiting for her own car to cool,
watching men waiting for women to gather their food.

Suddenly the old man opened his eyes, sat up, and got
out of the car. Just as he did, a woman with a cart reached
it. Nora looked at the cart. There were three bags, but she
could tell from the way the plastic collapsed that each was
only half full. She remembered that morning in Florida
when she'd gone marketing with Beatrice. She could still
see the expression on the face of the woman in the next
aisle as she stared at their cart.

The elderly couple were bent over their wagon. The
closeness of their heads emphasized the blue in her white
hair and the yellow in his. Slowly, with care, or maybe only
pain, they transferred the bags to the back seat of the car.
Then the woman went around to the passenger side, while
the man walked the cart to a scruffy patch of grass beside
the lot.

After they drove off, Nora stood for a while beside the
rented car, though she knew it was as cool as it was going to
get until she turned on the air conditioner. The man had
left the empty cart beside a pay phone.

It probably didn't even work. Half the pay phones in

Manhattan didn't work. What were the odds that a phone on a desert island of seared grass in New Jersey worked?

She started across the lot. The surface felt mushy beneath her sandals. She had to detour around a pothole. It must have been a foot deep at the center.

She picked up the phone. It was so hot she had to hold it gingerly between her thumb and finger, but even without putting it against her ear, she could hear the dial tone. Still, that didn't mean it was working. Sometimes you got a dial tone and nothing else.

She pressed the zero, then dialed a number. So far, so good. When she heard a beep, she didn't even wait for the recorded voice to follow. She pressed in her credit card number. A recorded voice thanked her. A phone began to ring.

Nora looked at her watch. It was almost three. The phone went on ringing. She looked out over the uninspiring countryside. The sun hung lower than when she'd entered the cemetery.

The phone was still ringing. Nora lifted her free hand to push down the lever and sever the connection. That was when she heard Max's voice at the other end of the line. At the same moment she noticed the shadow that stretched out from her feet across the patchy burnt grass.